WAR SONG

BR KINGSOLVER

War Song

Book 2 of The Rift Chronicles

By BR Kingsolver

brkingsolver.com

Cover art by Heather Hamilton-Senter
www.bookcoverartistry.com

Copyright 2020 BR Kingsolver

❦ Created with Vellum

LICENSE NOTES

This ebook is licensed for your personal enjoyment only. All rights reserved. No part of this book may be reproduced or transmitted in any form or by any means now known or hereinafter invented, electronic or mechanical, including but not limited to photocopying, recording, or by an information storage and retrieval system, without the written permission of the Publisher, except where permitted by law.

This ebook may not be re-sold or given away to other people. If you would like to share this book with another person, please purchase an additional copy for each recipient. If you're reading this book and did not purchase it, or it was not purchased for your use only, then please return it and purchase your own copy. Thank you for respecting the hard work of this author.

BOOKS BY BR KINGSOLVER

Get updates on new book releases, promotions, contests and giveaways! Sign up for my newsletter.

The Rift Chronicles

Magitek

War Song

Rosie O'Grady's Paranormal Bar and Grill

Shadow Hunter

Night Stalker

Dark Dancer

Well of Magic

Knights Magica

The Dark Streets Series

Gods and Demons

Dragon's Egg

Witches' Brew

The Chameleon Assassin Series

Chameleon Assassin

Chameleon Uncovered

Chameleon's Challenge

Chameleon's Death Dance

Diamonds and Blood

The Telepathic Clans Saga

The Succubus Gift
Succubus Unleashed
Broken Dolls
Succubus Rising
Succubus Ascendant

Other books
I'll Sing for my Dinner
Trust

Short Stories in Anthologies
Here, Kitty Kitty
Bellator

CHAPTER 1

"Everyone's in place," the voice over my radio said. "We go at sixty."

Sixty seconds before a force of Metropolitan Police and guardians from half a dozen Magi Families stormed the block-long warehouse housing Lucifer's Lair, the most notorious nightclub in the Mid-Atlantic.

I did a last-second mental check of my weapons and armor. Since I knew the inside layout better than almost anyone, I would be in the second wave, following the assault teams who would breach the entrances and secure the building. We had no idea how many demons were in the building. We only knew that the listed owner, the demon lord Ashvial, was dead.

Most of the force were there to capture or kill the demons inside, but my primary mission was to take control of the computer systems, paper files, and the human employees who managed Ashvial's finances. Of course, that was all located in a part of the building I'd never seen.

"Go!"

Aeromancers used battering rams of compressed air to blow the front doors open. Bolts of lightning crashed against the doorframe, shorting out any electronic defenses. And then heavily armored men rushed into the building.

The sound of large-caliber automatic weapons echoed inside, diminishing to occasional shots, the crackle of lightning, and the whoosh of fireballs. From where I was standing outside, the interior of the building looked as though a fireworks show was going on inside.

When things quieted a little, I led my small team in and took an immediate right toward a door in the wall opposite the bar. We crossed the large room without any resistance, although I noted the bodies of three demons. I didn't expect many of them to be downstairs in the middle of the day. Most of them would be on the third floor, where the red light was more welcoming to their eyes.

The door had an electronic keypad, and I sent a spell into it. The door clicked, and I cast another spell into the room beyond to disable any nasty anti-intrusion devices that might be installed there.

Normally, the business offices would have been full of workers on a Wednesday, but our surveillance indicated that only a few employees had entered the building that morning. As a cop, I was paid to have a suspicious mind, and my guess was the humans in charge of the business operation had figured out Ashvial wasn't coming back.

And if it were me, I'd be working overtime to loot the assets and destroy any evidence the authorities might use to connect me to Ashvial's illicit activities. In their own world, demons didn't use money the way humans did, and as far as computers and technology were concerned, they were total idiots. They just couldn't wrap their minds around physics and chemistry performing tasks that demons did with magik.

Sure enough, the reception desk was unmanned, and the cubes in the large room beyond were all empty. That meant any people who were present would be in the offices lining the outside walls of the building.

I sent my team to capture anyone they found, while I headed toward the computer room. The plans on file with the Building Commission showed me where I needed to go.

A spell disabled the keypad on the door, and I slipped inside. One man sat at a console with his back to me.

"Don't even think about touching that keyboard again," I said in my sweetest, gentlest voice, placing the muzzle of my Raider 50 against his skull. "Put your hands in the air, or I'll blow your head off."

It was rather gratifying how quickly he obeyed.

"Now, stand up, and walk toward the wall to your left," I said.

Again, he obeyed. I followed him, handcuffed him, then made him sit down against the wall. A pair of ankle shackles made sure he wouldn't run away. I put a small silver-colored box on the floor a few feet in front of him.

"That's a magitek box," I said. "If you move to either side, or attempt to stand up, it will electrocute you. Do you understand?"

He nodded enthusiastically, but managed to ask in an aggrieved tone, "Who are you?"

"Oh, sorry. I'm Lieutenant Danica James, Metropolitan Police, and this is a raid."

The way his eyes widened told me that he was far more upset that I was a police officer than he would have been if I were a fellow crook.

I sat down at the console, and using my cranial implant, jacked into the computer system. The first thing I checked was what my captive had been doing, then I patted myself on the back. He had been transferring funds from one of Ashvial's bank accounts into a private account in Switzerland, and I was willing to bet it was a personal account that he owned. He wasn't shy, either. The transfer was set up to move ninety million dollars.

I immediately stopped the transfer and changed the passwords to both accounts. Then I accessed the rest of Ashvial's accounts and did the same thing. After changing the passwords to the internal computer system, I locked the console and pulled my consciousness back into the real world. I would give the new access codes to the police's forensic accountants, and let them take care of the detail work.

I dragged my captive out of the soundproofed computer room and into the noise of the raid. Gunshots and the sounds of magikal weapons came from overhead, along with the snarls, roars, and screams of demons. I was still sore from my last fight with a demon, so I gladly turned away from the stairs.

I hauled the computer genius out the door to a waiting paddy wagon and accepted a cup of coffee from a cop standing there. We discussed the weather for a while until all the noise inside stopped, then I went back in to supervise the arrest of the other humans and the cataloging of Ashvial's business records.

When I got the final tally of demons captured and killed, the numbers seemed small compared to how many I'd seen on my previous visits there. I figured some had escaped, and some had probably decided to find other living arrangements after Ashvial died.

I did go up to his office on the second floor. I grabbed a couple of newbie detectives and took them with me. There weren't too many humans who read demon, and most of them worked in research institutions, not for the police.

When I walked in, the first thing I noticed was the statuette. I was a little surprised it was still there. The body of a woman—a human woman—with the head of a dragon. Sharp ridges ran from the top of her head between her horns, down her back to the tip of her tail, which was curled around her feet.

She looked almost alive, as though her skin would be soft and warm. Her eyes were demon red, glowing, and just as when I'd seen her before, I felt as though they followed me.

I pulled out my phone and called Kevin Goodman, head of the Arcane Forensics Branch.

"Kevin, remember that house up by Pimlico? The drug house where the demons were massacred? Can you send the magik detector who was at the house that day over to Lucifer's Lair? I have something I want her to look at."

After I hung up, one of the detectives with me said, "That thing isn't alive, is it? I feel like it's watching me."

"Yeah. I don't know, but don't touch it."

I started going through the papers in Ashvial's desk and filing cabinets, handing them to the detectives with instructions on how to catalog them. We'd been at it for about an hour, when Kevin's magik detector appeared at the door.

"Lieutenant James? You wanted to see me?"

"Yeah. Take a look at that." I pointed to the statue.

She sucked air, then cautiously approached it. I watched the young mage lick her lips, then extend her arm. She stopped with her hand a few inches away from the statue, held it there for a minute, then pulled her hand close to her body, and tucked it between her breast and armpit.

"Well?" I asked.

"That's it," she said. "That's the magik I felt at the demon house that day."

I took a deep breath. "I had a feeling. I think we just closed that case. Thanks."

"What are you going to do with it?"

"Now, that's a question, isn't it? Ward it and transport it out of here."

"Good luck," she said, backing out of the room without taking her eyes off the statue.

"Dani, wake up! It's happened again!"

I felt like I had just fallen asleep, and I was deep in a dream.

"Dani, come on!" Kirsten grabbed my shoulder and shook me.

I cracked an eye, and sure enough, it was still dark. Well, maybe a little light shone through my bedroom window.

"Is the world coming to an end?" I muttered.

"Maybe. Damn it, get the hell up!"

She took hold of my arm and literally dragged me out of bed and into the kitchen where we had a large screen hooked to the datanet. The picture on the screen was of the Palace of Commerce in downtown Baltimore shortly after it was bombed.

"What about it?" I asked, trying to pick up what the commentator was saying.

"That's not Baltimore," Kirsten said. "It's Prague. This morning."

At that point, I woke up and started listening to the announcer.

"...*Human Liberation Army, HLA, called media outlets and claimed responsibility for the bombing. Their website has a manifesto with a list of demands, and it threatens more mayhem to come. At this point, authorities have said nothing about casualties, but the bomb went off at ten o'clock in the morning local time when the building is usually full of people.*"

There were four different Palaces of Commerce, all tied together with a common computer system. The one in Baltimore had been destroyed a couple of weeks before, so only the ones in Buenos Aires and Nanking remained. All except the one in Nanking were built from the same set of plans, the buildings nearly identical.

"I thought you said the Akiyama Family and Ashvial were responsible for the bombing here in Baltimore," Kirsten said.

"That's what all the big Families and their intelligence services seem to think," I answered. "No one has claimed responsibility for that, and the riots stopped when Ashvial died."

Not only had the riots stopped in the Mid-Atlantic but also in Pittsburgh, Atlanta, Charlotte, Detroit, and Kansas City. They continued in Vancouver, Dallas, and Mexico City—all cities under the influence of different demon lords.

"I knew some HLA people at Cambridge," Kirsten said. "Just a bunch of socialist idealists. I can't imagine any of them committing mass murder."

I had never paid much attention to the HLA. I knew they opposed Rifters—especially demons—as well as magik users and the magikal hierarchy that controlled most of the world's wealth and resources. I grabbed a keyboard and tried to check out their website, but got an error.

Kirsten looked over my shoulder. "What does that mean?"

"Either the amount of traffic crashed their server, or the authorities took it down," I said.

CHAPTER 2

I spent the early part of the morning interrogating Ashvial's business manager. Of course, he denied knowing anything about illegal activities, as though I would believe him. The number of demons in Earth's realm who were not involved in something illegal numbered zero. If you worked for a demon, you had to know your paycheck was being generated from some kind of crime.

My previous investigations had revealed that Ashvial was involved with the Akiyama Family, who were based in Japan and China. We found records of extensive phone calls and emails between Ashvial and Akiyama. Since demons didn't use telephones or computers, some human had to be Ashvial's proxy, and I wasn't buying the business manager's denials.

"I swear, I was under the demon's influence," he said for the dozenth time. "I'm not responsible for anything he did."

With a shrug, I said, "Okay. You stick to your story, and I'm sure the judge won't sentence you to more than fifty years. We take a very dim view of human trafficking, and your approval on those invoices is all I need to convict you." I started packing up all the paper I had brought with me to the interrogation room.

"Too bad. If you cooperated, I'm sure I could get that sentence cut in half. But there's no way you're getting off. I've never been to Antarctica, but I hear the prison in the Yukon is a lot nicer, at least in the summer."

We had found evidence that Ashvial was moving huge quantities of Rifter drugs in addition to trafficking thousands of human beings. The boys in the Missing Persons unit in the basement of the police station were going to clear a large portion of their cases due to the business manager's meticulous records.

As I stood, the business manager broke. When he started talking, I sent a summons to my partner, Mychal Novak, to come in and supervise the man's confession. I had a different but related investigation to attend to. I grabbed my motorcycle and rode out to the Findlay estate north of the city.

A few weeks before, my boss, Deputy Police Commissioner Thomas Whittaker, had assigned me to look into the disappearance of a friend's daughter. In doing so, I had uncovered evidence that Martin Johansson, head of one of the Hundred most powerful magikal families, was involved in the human trade, and that one of his partners was the demon lord Ashvial.

At the same time, my Granduncle George Findlay had a heart attack, which brought up the question as to who would succeed him as the Family head if he died. Shortly thereafter, magikal attacks were launched against me and my grandmother, Olivia Findlay-James. Then evidence surfaced that David Moncrieff, the husband of one of my aunts, Courtney Findlay-Moncrieff, was a business partner with both Johansson and Ashvial, as well as the Akiyama Family.

Johansson was murdered, then Sarah Benning, the missing girl, was discovered at the Moncrieff estate. A group of Families raided the estate and found other trafficked humans. We also captured Akiyama Hiroku, the security chief of the Akiyama Family, who was in the process of trying to smuggle underage girls to Japan. The Moncrieff Family members at the estate had been rounded up. My Aunt Courtney and her daughters were being kept in 'protective custody' at the Findlay estate, while David was under house arrest at the Moncrieff estate. Hiroku was being kept at the estate of Deputy Police Commissioner Thomas Whittaker under tight guard.

My objective in going out to Findlay was a personal one—to interview my cousin Karolyn Moncrieff and ask her why she paid someone to kill me.

Osiris Dillon, the Findlay Chief of Security, had outfitted a parlor in the west wing of the mansion for use as an interrogation room. It still looked like an elegant parlor, but magitek devices were implanted in the walls and the ceiling to record visual, audio, and telemetric data. A corner of the room had been partially walled off to hide a truthsayer who watched the proceedings.

I sat in a comfortable chair and waited for Karolyn to arrive. By design, the only place for her to sit was an uncomfortable chair across a coffee table from me.

When Karolyn entered the room, she looked around, sneered at me, then sauntered over and dropped into the chair. Her long chestnut hair fell across her shoulders, framing a face that should have been lovely but had too many hard planes. Her pale brown eyes were habitually narrowed due to her usually frowning expression. Karolyn was tall—not as tall as me, but several inches taller than her mother—and had her mother's curves. She dressed in the latest fashions that showed a lot of skin.

We had known each other our entire lives, gone to school together, and loathed each other with a fierce passion.

"Hello, cousin," she said. "Are you here to give me the third degree?"

"What makes you think that?" I asked. "I'm just here to get your statement for the tribunal."

Mention of a tribunal—a court of the Magi—caused her frown to deepen. The Moncrieff Family was among the Hundred, and my Aunt Courtney was a Findlay—one of the Ten. They were virtually immune from civil authorities, but not from judgement by their peers.

"As I'm sure you know," I began, "twenty-three humans that were being held against their will were discovered at the Moncrieff estate at Elk Neck. Seventeen of them were domestic servants who worked twelve to fourteen hours a day, weren't being paid, and weren't allowed to leave. Since you've lived at the estate all your life, I was hoping you could tell me about that."

Karolyn stared at me, and I was sure she entertained thoughts of murder, but eventually she said, "I don't know anything about the servants. You'd have to speak to my mother about them."

Not her father. Curious that she'd throw her dear old mom under the bus.

"All right, I will. Now, the other six people we found. One of them told us that he was assigned to you, and his duties included activities of a sexual nature." I had seen the guy, and he was gorgeous, not to mention having a body that would cause almost any woman to drool.

She snorted. "In his dreams. He's just a pool boy, and he had some fantasy that he was my personal servant. Follows me around, gets underfoot. You know how the underclasses are. Lying and thieving. You can't trust any of them."

"I see. And what can you tell me about Sarah Benning and the other two girls we found? The empathic projectors? The mage girls?"

Karolyn shrugged. "I didn't pay any attention to them. I assumed they were play things for Hiroku, or maybe some of the other men. I don't play with girls, and I mind my own business."

The direct way she said that while staring straight into my eyes let me know that she thought I should mind my own business, too.

"But you know that men *were* playing with them? Sexual games?" I asked.

Another shrug. "I said I assumed. I don't know for a fact, and didn't care to find out."

"Okay. Now, on the night of cousin Lila's betrothal ball, just before the demon started killing people, you abruptly left the room. It looks on the vids as though you knew what was going to happen. Would you care to explain?"

"No."

"I see. So, it was a complete coincidence that your father and sister left the room, you left the room, and your mother and Karl Rudolf went upstairs to shag, leaving no one in your family in danger of a homicidal demon?"

I finally had her attention. Her eyes popped open, and she sat up straight in her chair.

"What? Who told you Mom is screwing Karl? It's a lie!"

"Oh, well, I guess they could have spent an hour and a half in that bedroom playing chess, but based on entries in your mother's diary and their phone records, my bet is they were having sex. Of course, there aren't any CCTV cameras in the bedrooms, just in the hallways." I was lying through my teeth about part of that. We hadn't been able to crack the ward on Aunt Courtney's diary.

Her face turned an ugly shade of red, rather splotchy, and I fingered the magitek cube in my pocket. If she exploded, I had better be quick to trigger a shield. I knew I couldn't match her magik.

"I thought that was why you were screwing him," I said. "The allure of doing your mom's boyfriend."

She called me several names that weren't very flattering.

"But what I really want to know," I said, "is why you paid Gecid to kill me."

Her demeanor changed completely. "What? Who? Don't flatter yourself, you stupid bitch. I never even think about you. Why would I waste my time and money to kill you?"

I held up the page of floral-scented notepaper with my address written on it.

"Isn't this your handwriting? And your DNA and fingerprints are on the paper."

"Yeah, I wrote it. So what?"

"And why would you be writing my address for someone?"

"Mom asked if I knew your address. I looked it up for her. She said she wanted to send you something. I might have hoped it was something poisonous, but I didn't ask."

I wasn't a truthsayer, but I'd been a cop for twelve years, and I believed her. Shortly afterward, I let her go back to her room. I wondered what she and her mother would talk about over dinner that evening.

"She was telling the truth," the truthsayer said as she came out of her hiding place. She chuckled. "The only lie she told was about the pool boy."

Yeah, that was my impression, also. So, it really was Aunt Courtney Findlay-Moncrieff who wanted me and my grandmother dead. The world made sense again.

I dodged Osiris, going out the kitchen door to collect my bike. I didn't want to talk to him or my grandmother until I had some time to think through the ramifications of Karolyn's admissions.

CHAPTER 3

One of the things that trips a lot of criminals up is falling into habits. Developing conscious or unconscious patterns of behavior. Something works, so they do it again. When it works again, they get comfortable with it.

The outside door from the kitchen led to a short walkway that branched. Turn right, and it took you to the dumpsters, discreetly hidden inside a tall fence. Turn left, and it led to the driveway that delivery trucks used to bring in the groceries. Past that driveway, another walkway took me to a pleasant little grassy area with a gazebo furnished with a small table and four chairs, and surrounded by trees.

Unless the weather was bad, or my expected stay was fairly long, I parked my bike there because it was much closer than the garages.

I turned into that miniature park and discovered my Granduncle George sitting there. It wasn't a coincidence, because he wasn't reading, or having tea, or doing anything else. He was just sitting and staring straight at me.

"Why don't you come talk to me," he said in his soft voice. It wasn't a question. I had never heard him yell, and at family—

and Family—functions, he was always very quiet. But when he spoke, it was with an air of command. He was one of the most powerful mages in the world, one of the richest men in the world. Granduncle George Findlay didn't have to tell anyone that. You felt it when in his presence.

He wasn't physically imposing. His short and slender figure, his hair and closely trimmed beard salted with gray, his sharp cheekbones, Roman nose, and his piercing gray eyes were what you noticed. He was one hundred fifty years old, the second generation of magikers. His parents were the offspring of crippled survivors of a pandemic that killed four out of five people infected.

I walked over and sat in the chair he indicated, and he studied me. The silence stretched, and I tried not to fidget or squirm.

Finally, he said, "Your father would be very proud of you. It's too bad Hunter didn't live to know you. You've grown into a woman who embodies every principle he held dear."

He reached into the pocket of his tweed jacket and pulled out a silver flask. He popped the stopper, took a swig, and passed it to me.

"I'm not supposed to have any fun anymore. No whiskey, no fast women." He chuckled. "Although your Aunt Denise has always been fast enough for me. No cigars, no pot, no strenuous exercise. Take a drink."

I did as he ordered. The whiskey was smooth as silk and burned all the way down. I passed the flask back to him. He stoppered it and put it back in his pocket.

"There," he said. "You're a co-conspirator. Now, tell me the truth, and don't sugar coat it. What in the hell is going on with my family?"

"You mean the Moncrieffs?" I asked.

"That, of course. Someone tried to kill Olivia, and someone tried to kill you. Now, I understand that a policewoman encounters dangerous situations, and probably makes enemies, but an ambush at her home by a pack of rogue mages doesn't sound like an everyday affair. Spill."

"I don't really have any concrete proof—" I started, but he cut me off.

"Don't bullshit me, Dani. You're a terrible liar, and always have been. You're damned good at your job, and that fiasco out at David and Courtney's place proves it. Human trafficking? Dancing with demons? Courting Akiyama? All of it. Now."

So, I told him. It took a while, and I concluded with the interview I had just had with Karolyn. He didn't interrupt or ask any questions. The only response I could see was an occasional twitch and his eyes dilating a little. I understood why his business rivals and partners considered him a fearsome negotiator.

We sat for a few minutes in silence, then he said, "Damn. That girl has always been a problem. She thinks she's a lot smarter than she is. You know she's powerful, right? A strong storm mage."

I assumed he meant his daughter Courtney. I nodded.

"Power without consideration—strength without compassion—has led to many a downfall," he said. "The difference between you and Hunter is that you have some common sense. Your father was the strongest magitek of his generation, but he didn't match either Hunter or you. And unfortunately, he felt the need to carry Hunter's guilt. What your grandfather did is not your fault. Clear all of that kind of crap thinking out of your head, girl. You don't have to atone for his foolishness. Just use your brain and don't invent your own brand of stupidity. Never forget, we're dangerous. The Magi are dangerous—to humanity, to the planet, to ourselves."

He sighed and leaned back in his chair. "Thank you. You've given me a lot to think about. I'm not really sure what to do about my daughter. I'll talk to her mother, but Denise has always been the weaker person in that relationship." He chuckled softly. "Hell, that's probably the pot calling the kettle."

"Is that all, sir?" I asked.

"One more thing. If you get a chance to talk to David, try and find out what in the hell they're all thinking. I can't imagine that his brother Alan was willing to toss everything their Family has built just to save a few dollars on servants' wages."

It was a long drive out to the Moncrieff estate on the Elk Neck Peninsula, but compared to the distance from Police Headquarters, I was already halfway there. I collected my bike and rode out to interview David Moncrieff.

Normally, showing up unannounced at any Magi Family residence and demanding to speak with the head of the house would be considered rude. But since David was under house arrest, I didn't worry about it.

I stopped and had a late lunch at a little crab shack overlooking the Bay. Mychal had taken David's statement when he was first arrested. I called the file up on my laptop and read it while I ate.

The Moncrieff Family was headquartered in Scotland. After the pandemic, the Moncrieff survivors displayed witch magic, but they were wealthy. Marriage to a poor but powerful mage, and subsequent marriages to mages, had mostly produced mages. The current Family head, Alan, was only seventy, which was young for his position.

His younger brother David was a medium-strength aeromancer and a weak pyromancer who was the Family trade representative in North America. David and Courtney had a whirlwind romance when she was still at university. The Moncrieffs were one of the richer Magi Families in the second tier of the Hundred, and he showered her with expensive gifts. During their engagement, he expanded the small manor house at Elk Neck into a fifty-five room Georgian country house patterned on those in Britain.

David was in the library when I arrived, and the Findlay guardian who served as the house's new butler showed me in.

David Moncrieff was tall and lanky, with straight brown hair that he was continually brushing back from his face with his hand. My impression of him had always been that Courtney was the brains in the family, although they seemed to share a lot of ambition. He did work hard, and the Moncrieffs prospered in North America largely due to his efforts and the connection that Courtney supplied to Findlay. Rather a strange relationship, considering the official Moncrieff alliance with Akiyama.

"Thank you for seeing me," I said. "I have a few questions that members of the Council are curious about."

I could tell he wasn't particularly happy to see me, but he was gracious, standing when I entered and offering me a seat. He was in an untenable position, and although his brother had made the requisite protestations to the Council, Alan didn't push with much outrage.

"Who is in charge of hiring and supervising the service staff?" I asked.

"My wife manages the household."

The stiff way he answered told me two things. One, that he understood the import of the question, and two, that he felt the traditional gender roles in an aristocratic house were automatically assumed.

"Including the butler?"

"Yes, of course. I don't have time for such things."

"So, you weren't aware that many of your servants weren't being paid? That they weren't allowed to leave the premises?"

His eyes narrowed and he stared at me. Eventually, he said,

"I don't believe that has been proven. We reject such slanderous allegations."

I nodded. "So, you're saying that you have no knowledge of humans being enslaved to work on your estate. You're also saying that your wife, Courtney Findlay-Moncrieff, is in charge of the service staff, so if such allegations were to be proven true, she is the one responsible. Is that correct?"

The stare turned into a glare. I switched topics.

"You had a house guest, Akiyama Hiroku. Is that correct?"

Moncrieff nodded.

"Mister Akiyama was apprehended on your estate with two underage girls, both projective empaths. Since he had them on a plane trying to take off from your airport, we assume he planned to take them to Asia without their parents' permission. We also have evidence the girls were held here for some time prior to that. Did you have any sexual contact with those girls or with Sarah Benning, or were Hiroku and Karl Rudolf their only abusers?"

He froze, his body going completely stiff. "I believe we're done. Good day, Miss James."

I allowed myself a smirk. "You may dismiss your niece, Mr. Moncrieff, but I'm here in my official capacity. Please address me as Lieutenant James. You can refuse to answer my questions, and attempt to stonewall this investigation, but I assume you understand that any questions you don't answer now will be asked by a tribunal."

He rose and walked out. I logged that into the recording I was making as the end of the interview.

CHAPTER 4

I was on my way back to the city when I got a call.

"James," the familiar voice of my boss said in my ear, "I need you to drop whatever you're doing." He gave me an address in the Chinquapin Park neighborhood. Extremely upscale.

It really wasn't much of a detour from my customary route home, although I usually took the freeway exit into my own middle-class neighborhood rather than ride through areas where the dogs had servants and the nannies had bodyguards.

When I reached the street, I didn't have to guess where to go. Police cars, an ambulance, and a couple of vans from the forensics squad were blocking the street, and the house was cordoned off with yellow police tape. I flashed my badge at a uniformed cop and parked my bike next to my own cop car. My partner had beaten me to the scene.

After donning the mandatory gloves and booties, I entered the mansion and found Sergeant Mychal Novak. His face was grim.

"What have we got?" I asked.

"Aaron Carpenter, oldest son of the Family head. Possible magik, but also knifed and bludgeoned."

He led me to a room that appeared to be a combination office and library. Dark wooden wainscotting and silk wallpaper. To say there were signs of a struggle would be an understatement. A man I took to be Carpenter lay partly on an overstuffed chair and partly on the floor. There was blood everywhere, and several interesting burn marks on the walls and furniture, but none on him.

"Any idea of his affinity?" I asked.

"Electrokinetic," a feminine voice said from behind me.

I turned to see Dr. Ruth Harrison, a psychiatrist and the best magik detector I'd ever met. The Police Department had other detectors on its staff, but with a murder among the Hundred, it made sense that Whittaker would call in someone who was comfortable working with the Magi.

"But not all of the scorch marks are from lightning," Ruth continued, then pointed. "That one, and that one. The rest were caused by pure energy."

"A spirit mage?" I asked. Spirit mages were even more rare than magiteks, my own affinity.

"Either that or a magitek device," Ruth said.

"Or possibly a Fae," I said. "Some of their mages wield the same powers as a spirit mage."

"Possibly," Ruth said.

"Who found him?" I asked.

"His wife," Novak answered. "But I need to talk to you before you see her."

He drew me aside, and Ruth stayed close.

"Doreen Benoit-Carpenter," he said. "She's a spirit mage. The servants heard the fight, although none of them were in this part of the house. It evidently didn't last very long, and then they heard her scream. When they came in, they found her, covered in blood."

Wonderful. My great-grandmother was a Benoit, so Doreen was probably some distant cousin of mine.

He led me around to the other side of the dead man. A bloody fireplace poker lay near the hearth ten feet away, and a bloody kitchen knife lay near the chair.

I turned away. "Ruth? Have you seen her?"

The psychiatrist nodded. "Yes. She's in shock. I'm not sure you're going to get much out of her right now."

"I don't have to get much," I said. "Where is she?"

Mychal and Ruth led me to another room where a young woman with pale freckled skin and long red hair sat on a chair. She wore what looked like a long white nightgown that was drenched in blood. Her face was devoid of emotion, and she stared into space, gently rocking back and forth, her arms crossed over her stomach.

I glanced back at the dead man. Salt and pepper hair. I judged him to be more than double the woman's age, and at least double her body weight.

Crouching down in front of her, I said, "Doreen? Mrs. Benoit-Carpenter? I'm Lieutenant Danica James with the Metropolitan Police. Did you see who did this?"

She blinked a couple of times, then seemed to focus on my face. She gave kind of a jerking nod, then shook her head once. Her face scrunched up, and she burst into tears, burying her face in her hands.

I put my arm around her shoulders and pulled her to me, letting her cry against my chest.

"Did you kill your husband, Doreen?" I asked gently, almost whispering into her ear.

She shook her head violently.

"Okay," I said. "I'm going to find who did, and you're going to help me." I pushed her away enough that she could see my face. "Do you understand?"

She stared at me, tears streaking her face, and then she

nodded. I pulled her back against me and held her while she cried.

After about ten minutes, she wound down, the tension flowed out of her body, and she slumped.

"Ruth," I said, "take care of her, but don't give her anything that will interfere with her memory. I think she saw something."

Harrison nodded, and I turned the new widow over to her care.

After we went back into the library, Novak asked, "You don't think she did it?"

"No, I don't. That doesn't mean she didn't make some of these scorch marks, though. Pass the word, I want everyone in the house interviewed, and ask them all if anything is missing."

Novak looked around at the chaos. "A burglary?"

I shook my head. "I don't think so. How many spirit mages or demons break in to steal something? Who was in the house? What visitors or guests? Not necessarily Carpenters' guests, but look at the staff as well. Delivery men. After that, we need to check his business connections and identify any enemies."

I looked at the body again. In spite of the evidence of a mage battle, he'd been killed by simple physical means. "And why is Mrs. Carpenter wearing a nightgown in the middle of the afternoon? Nothing about this makes any sense."

I chose a small parlor near the kitchen to interview members of the household, and called them in one at a time.

"There were those letters," the housekeeper said. Most of the servants were robots, but there was a human head housekeeper, a butler, a gardener, and three humans and a brownie in the kitchen. "I know they upset him, and the missus tried to get him to call the police."

"Do you know if he kept them?" I asked.

She shook her head. "He might have, or he might have thrown them away. There's a shredder in his study, and lately he's had a fire in the fireplace on colder nights."

It was Indian Summer, with the leaves changing color and the temperatures swinging from almost-summer warm to chilly at night.

I asked the butler about the letters, and he told me, "My impression was they were from some political group. You know, the kind that wants the rich to give all their money away and spend their days working in soup kitchens. But I never saw them."

"Not even the envelopes?"

He seemed to hunch a little, a defensive reaction, like a turtle pulling its head into its shell. "The robots handle the mail. I only see something if it's addressed to me."

One of the servants said something about the mistress "not being well," but refused to elaborate.

But I got the real scoop from the brownie, Cora. She was young, maybe eighty or ninety years old, cute as a button, and said she'd crossed the Rift when she was just a child. She had worked for Carpenter for thirty years, longer than any of the human help.

Cora was absolutely delighted when I spoke to her in Elvish, and she told me everything I wanted to know.

"The mistress is high-strung," she said. "Very nervous, and easily upset." Her face twisted into an expression of distaste. "His children bully her, and he refuses to chastise them."

"She's his second wife?" I asked.

"His third. He divorced the children's mother, and his second wife died in an accident. He married the mistress five years ago. She's actually younger than his children."

"Does she normally wear a nightdress in the middle of the day?"

Cora had been around humans long enough to pick up some of our habits, but I always found it a little amusing when brownies shook their heads in negation. Since she didn't have a neck, she twisted back and forth from the waist.

"His oldest daughter was here yesterday."

"So, his children don't live here?"

Again the body twist. "Five children—two girls and three boys—ranging from twenty-seven to forty of your years. The youngest girl and boy still live here, the oldest boy and girl are married and have their own houses, and the middle one comes and goes. He has an apartment down by the harbor."

I made a note to see if any of the kids had a police record.

After my interview with Cora, I got together with Novak to compare notes.

"Do you know any of Carpenter's kids?" I asked. "I sort of remember a Carpenter from when I was a teenager."

"I went to school with Kel Carpenter," he said, "and I dated his younger sister Dorothy for a while."

"You and your brother seem to have gotten around a lot," I said. Mychal's twin, Marco, had a reputation as a ladies' man.

He blushed. "I like women."

I knew he liked my roommate. Most men did. Mychal was shy, and a bit of a nerd, but intelligent and very good-looking. Kirsten had dated a lot of men, the majority of whom I respected less than Mychal. He was decent, and seemed interested in more than just getting laid.

"The brownie says that Carpenter's kids bullied his wife. Check and see if any of them have a record of any kind. Check their financials. This looks like a crime of passion to me. Maybe one of them has money problems and daddy refused to help."

On my way out of the house, I stopped to talk with Ruth Harrison.

"You don't think she did it, do you?" Ruth asked me.

"No, I don't."

"Is that elven empathy making the call?"

Ruth knew my mother, so she knew about my heritage.

"I don't know. Maybe. Mom says that is among the gifts I inherited."

She winked at me. "I don't think she killed him, either. I could see her killing him with magik but not with a kitchen knife."

CHAPTER 5

It was late when I got home, and I hadn't eaten since breakfast. I was rummaging around in the fridge when Kirsten came into the kitchen.

"Bad day?"

"Long day. I found out that Courtney is the relative trying to kill me." I grabbed an apple, a bar of cheese, and a beer. "And then I got tagged for a murder. Do you know Aaron Carpenter?"

I sat down at the kitchen table, and she took the chair across from me.

"I know his wife, she's a customer of mine."

"Oh? What's she like? I met her today, but it wasn't under the best of circumstances."

Kirsten thought for a moment, then said, "Nice. Sweet, you know, but shy. She's a lot younger than he is, isn't she?"

"Than he was. Yeah, she's twenty-five, and he was sixty-eight. Talked to a brownie that works in their kitchen, and she said Doreen wasn't very happy."

My roommate shrugged. "We never really talked much, but what I sell her are potions used for calming and to help her sleep. I got the impression that she was a heavy cannabis user before I turned her on to some lighter herbs."

"Know anything about his kids? I guess they're all older than her. Closer to our age."

"Oh, yeah. I dated Kel for a while. You remember him, don't you? Tall, with sandy hair, blue eyes? It was about two years ago. He's kind of a playboy, not ready to settle down."

I tried to remember. I had long ago stopped trying to keep track of Kirsten's boyfriends. Some of them only lasted a date or two, and sometimes she had four or five on a string at the same time. Kirsten calling Kel Carpenter a playboy was the pot calling the kettle. But the only man she was currently seeing was Mychal Novak.

"Mychal said he went to school with Kel," I said.

"Yeah, they're the same age."

That would be two years younger than Kirsten and me.

"I met his older sister once," Kirsten said. "She came in with one of my regular customers. I didn't really form an impression of her. How did he die?"

"Bludgeoned, stabbed, hit with magik maybe. The place was a bloody mess. Doreen found him, and she was in a state of shock when I tried to talk to her."

The first place I went when I got to the police station the following morning was the morgue.

"Figured I'd see you today," Kelley Quinn, the medical examiner, said. Quinn was around my age, with short dark-blonde hair, and a perky, pretty, girl-next-door face. I realized that I didn't know what the rest of her looked like, as I'd only seen her wearing a white shapeless coat over her clothes.

"What do you have for me?"

She led me over to an autopsy table and pulled back the

sheet covering the corpse. Aaron Carpenter looked a little better naked with all the blood washed off him, but not much.

"He was hit twice with the poker," Kelly said, "here on the forehead, and here on the left side above the ear. But cause of death was one of the knife wounds. Several could have been fatal."

"How many times was he stabbed?"

"Seven. Six in the front upper torso, and once in the back. At least two of the blows penetrated the heart, and three penetrated the lungs. The pattern, along with the poker blows, leads me to think the killer was right-handed, and the knife wounds indicate a frenzied attack."

"Crime of passion," I said.

She shrugged. "Not for me to say. Anger, fear, who knows? That's your job."

"Any defensive wounds?"

"No. But I think all the wounds except the one in the back came when he was standing. I think the last one was delivered after he fell across that chair."

"Magik?"

"Oh, hell, the room was full of residuals. My guess is that at least three mages cut loose in there."

"Three? Carpenter, his killer, and?" I asked.

"The wife, maybe? Were there any other magik users in the house?"

"Possible. You can't tell what kind of magik?"

"Only from the evidence, and Dr. Harrison is better at that than I am. You saw the various scorch marks."

"But none on him."

She shook her head. "No evidence of magikal damage."

"How about the knife?"

Kelly pointed to a bloody knife lying on a tray. "A chef's knife, eight-inch blade, wide, sharp, and pointed. Forensics says all the blood on it is Carpenter's. They also told me it's a professional knife—expensive—what you'd find in a fine restaurant or a fancy mansion."

"Did it come from the house?"

She shook her head. "Not that we can determine. The knives in the kitchen were a different brand, and the chef's knife was accounted for."

"So, either the cook had her own special knife and she's not admitting it, or the killer brought it with him," I said.

That got me another shrug.

"Helluva knife to be carrying around," I said. "Not easy to conceal."

I headed upstairs to find Mychal and to report to Whittaker. A couple of cops who got on the elevator at the ground floor were animatedly discussing the demon army camped south of Annapolis. Prior to Ashvial's death, the demons had been fighting and looting their way north, but for the past couple of weeks they had been contained by a force of Magi mercenaries and guardians on a peninsula jutting into the Chesapeake Bay.

The argument between the two men had to do with whether we should just let the demons sit there or go in and wipe them out. It didn't sound to me as though either of them had actually fought demons before. I knew that if I got a vote, not fighting them was the way I would go. But considering they were feeding on their human captives, there was a good argument on the other side.

"Anything new?" I asked Mychal when I reached his desk.

"One of the witches in forensics was able to piece together some letters from the shredder," he said.

"You're kidding. How did she do that?"

He chuckled. "She said it had to do with the type of paper and the age of the ink on the paper. She just matched all the pieces."

He held out pictures of the letters she had put together.

"There are three distinct types of letters that might match

what we're looking for," he said. "One set contains threats, or maybe warnings, about what's going to happen to the rich and retribution for Carpenter's sins of exploitation. They're signed with the logo of the HLA. No fingerprints or DNA except for Carpenter's. The second set has warnings or threats from what sounds like a jilted lover. A couple of those letters contain threats against his wife. They aren't signed. The third set are love letters to his wife from some unknown party. The oldest of those have his wife's fingerprints on them, but the later ones don't."

I looked the various letters over.

"Here's the interesting thing," Mychal continued. "DNA and fingerprints of the same unidentified woman are on those last two sets of letters. There's no male DNA on them other than Carpenter's, although the love letters are purportedly from a man named Nigel."

We stared at each other.

"I hate the rich and entitled," I finally said.

"I'm sure the lower classes play the same kind of games," Mychal replied. "What you hate are humans—it's a typical cop thing. Look, do you think you could do whatever it is you do and find out what instructions the mail bot has for delivering Mrs. Carpenter's mail?"

"Sure, I can hack a bot. Let's go talk to Whittaker, and then we can go over to the Carpenters' house. I wonder if any of the other Carpenters, or any other Magi, are getting these kind of letters from the HLA." As we walked down the hall, I asked, "Have you checked out the alibis for Carpenter's kids?"

"The two younger ones who live at home were both at work. They work in the Family business, and they have plenty of witnesses. Kel, the middle son, says he was doing research at the university library. I sent a detective over there but haven't heard from him yet."

"Johns Hopkins?"

Mychal pursed his lips. "No, University of Maryland, down in College Park."

"Is he a student there?"

My partner shook his head. "He went to Hopkins with me. He was vague about the kind of research, and I don't remember him being the studious type. The older daughter was at her home, or shopping, or having lunch with one of her friends. Maybe she went to the gym." He shifted his voice an octave higher with a bitchy cant to it. "What time did you say he died again? My day was just *so* full, and you can't *possibly* expect me to remember *exactly* what time things happened. I don't keep track of *every minute*."

I rolled my eyes. "Like I said, I hate the rich and entitled."

He snorted. "Exactly. She didn't seem too broken up about it. I have a detective trying to chase down all the places she said she was and who she was with and when. The oldest son is in Pittsburgh on business. Noah Carpenter, Aaron's father, *is* upset about his son's death. I spoke to him last night on my way home, and he was spitting mad."

We reported what we knew so far, and Whittaker simply listened. When we finished, he said, "I haven't received any such letters, but I'll ask around. After the bombing in Prague, we have set up a task force to investigate the HLA here in the Mid-Atlantic. Send me copies of those letters."

CHAPTER 6

Novak and I drove out to the Carpenters' house. Forensics was still there gathering evidence, and we still had Aaron's study blocked off, along with the adjoining rooms and hallways.

"Any idea how the attacker got in, or out?" I asked Kevin Goodman, chief of the forensics crew.

He motioned toward the French doors that led to a patio surrounded by a decorative waist-high wall. A small table and four chairs near the wall were shaded by a large umbrella.

"The doors were unlocked. The fingerprints we've found in the room belong to the deceased, his wife, three of his children, and the butler, plus two unknowns."

"The housekeeper said she never came in here," I said. "The cleaning was all done by bots. Which child's fingerprints are missing?"

"The oldest daughter. We don't have hers on file, though. But no prints on the poker, none on the knife. None on the doorknobs, other than those of the deceased and his wife."

"Mrs. Carpenter's hands were covered in blood," I said.

"And she left bloody fingerprints all over the body and the

surrounding area," Kevin said. "But if she killed him, she must have eaten the gloves she was wearing."

"Is there another way into this room?" Mychal asked, motioning toward the hall door and the one to the patio.

"As a matter of fact, there is," Kevin said, leading us to a sideboard that served as a bar. As we walked around the sideboard, we discovered a door in an alcove to our left . It wasn't visible from within the room. Kevin opened the door to reveal a narrow set of stairs leading up.

"Both Mr. and Mrs. Carpenter's fingerprints were on these doorknobs," Kevin said. "The stairs lead to the master bedroom on the second floor."

I glanced at Mychal.

"Most large Family houses have ways to move around privately," he said with a shrug. "I was wondering how she got in here." He moved out of the alcove. "Take a look."

I knew that Findlay House was a maze, but my experience with other Hundreds' homes was limited. I stood next to Mychal, looking out from the alcove, and the scorch marks Ruth had identified as pure energy projections were directly in front of us.

"She was trying to save him," I said. "She must have seen the attacker."

Kevin scratched his chin. "If you came in here, with that great big butcher knife, would she have seen you?"

I thought about it. "Probably not. *I'd* use a magitek cloaking device—"

Both Mychal and Kevin were nodding.

"No one saw any visitors," Mychal said. "No visitors to the staff or the other residents, no deliveries. No one in the house was alone at the time Mrs. Carpenter screamed. Everyone has at least one other person to vouch for them. So, someone snuck in, started a row with Aaron Carpenter, Mrs. Carpenter heard it and came downstairs, and the murderer escaped through the patio."

"So, you're saying that either the killer was an illusionist, a magitek, or is wealthy enough to purchase very expensive equipment but uses a kitchen knife to kill the victim. Or, has another way to hide themselves."

Mychal shrugged. "How much would a cloaking device cost?"

I named a sum that made a fancy robot seem cheap and saw both men's eyebrows rise. "At least that's what I would charge, and I wouldn't sell one to a criminal."

I walked out into the middle of the room. With a wave of my hand, I turned the lights on and then off. I had felt the magitek device the first time I entered the room.

"Look," I said, "it's a little different than using magik to control something mechanical. You're actually creating a device that stores magik—a very specific kind of magik—that can be released on command. Can either of you do an invisibility spell? Maybe not, but an illusionist or a spirit mage can. So, it wouldn't have to be magitek."

"But you could build such a device?" Mychal asked.

"Uh, well, I'm a quarter-elf, and although I can't do any elven magik, I seem to be able to tap into that sort of magik sometimes. But magiteks often use collaborators. If I have an illusionist to help, I can store illusion magik in a device that Mychal can use."

And how did that fit with my mom telling me I didn't have any elven magik? I looked at the scorch marks on the wall. Could I build a box like the one my father had given me only using pure energy instead of electricity?

"Hey, we were going to take a look at the robots, right?" I said, changing the subject.

There were six robots in the house and two more outside. Five of the indoor bots were standard models. But the one that handled the mail and cleaned Aaron Carpenter's study had a customized magitek security system. Accessing the instructions and memory logs of the first five was simple. The last one took some clever manipulation.

All of Aaron Carpenter's mail was delivered directly to him, as was the butler's. That was interesting. Doreen's mail had been delivered to her until about six weeks before the murder. After that, it all went to Aaron. Bills from a number of places were delivered to Aaron, but some were delivered to the housekeeper, and others were forwarded to an accounting firm associated with the Carpenter Family businesses.

Then there were Aaron's children. The older three had their own homes and presumably received mail there. But Aaron was receiving, and presumably filtering, the mail to the youngest daughter, although not the son living at home.

"Mychal, run a background check on the butler and his accounts. Carpenter didn't trust him. Also check the youngest girl," I said. "Try and figure out what she does in her spare time, how she spends her money, who she hangs out with."

"Got it."

"And check with that witch in forensics. See what else he was shredding. This guy either didn't trust the people around him, or he was a major control freak."

That taken care of, I sought out the family doctor, who was supposedly monitoring Doreen Carpenter's health and state of mind. I found him in the kitchen, sampling the cook's berry pie.

"Is Mrs. Carpenter available so I can ask her some questions?" I asked.

"Oh, no. Her health is very fragile. She shouldn't be subjected to any additional strain."

I sat down across the table from him. "I see. Well," I turned to Mychal, "Sergeant Novak, perhaps we should consider bringing in our own doctor for a second opinion. And please, contact Noah Carpenter and let him know that we're having difficulty getting any cooperation in finding his son's killer."

"Sure thing, Lieutenant Findlay-James," Mychal said, whipping his phone out of his pocket.

"Oh, I'm sure you don't need to go to all that trouble," the doctor said. "I currently have Mrs. Carpenter sedated, but I can let you know when she's able to meet with you."

I had to fight the urge to kill the man. I held my breath and counted to ten. "That won't be necessary, Doctor," I said. "I'll be posting a policewoman in her room with instructions to let me know when Mrs. Carpenter is ready to talk. I will also instruct her to break the arms of anyone who attempts to give the lady of the house any more drugs."

I turned back to Mychal. "Call Dr. Harrison and ask her to come over and do an assessment of Mrs. Carpenter's condition. And escort Dr. Quack out of the building and make sure the uniforms know he's *persona non grata*."

The doctor started to protest, but I gave him 'the look' and he shut up. I leaned forward and stared him directly in the face. "When I left yesterday, I gave explicit orders that she was not to be given anything that would interfere with her memory. I am seriously considering charging you with interference with a police investigation."

Nothing in our background check of Doreen Carpenter revealed why there would be a physician monitoring her around the clock, or why she would still need sedation twenty-four hours after her husband's death. The potions and herbs Kirsten was supplying her were fairly mild and didn't indicate a condition as fragile as the doctor suggested.

I pulled Cora, the brownie, aside and asked her in Elvish, "Is that doctor here to attend Mrs. Carpenter regularly?"

"Oh, no. He was the first Mrs. Carpenter's doctor, and the children's."

"Who is the current Mrs. Carpenter's doctor?"

"I don't know, Lieutenant. A doctor has never come to the house to see her."

That begged the question of which one of the kids was suddenly concerned about their stepmother's health.

There were some other questions that were above my and Novak's pay grade. Even our connections inside the Ten were likely to get us stonewalled. But our boss was the head of a Hundreds Family. So, I called him.

"Boss, can you find out what's in Aaron Carpenter's will? Dispositions to his children, current wife, ex-wife, etcetera? Someone in the family called in a doctor for Mrs. Carpenter. He isn't her normal doctor, and he's keeping her sedated."

"Yeah, I'll see what I can dig up. What's the doctor's name?"

I told him and he hung up.

Of course, I could have asked Noah Carpenter, but I didn't know his relationship with his daughter-in-law. The inner workings of the ruling Families—like mine—often resembled the machinations, intrigues, and conspiracies of a medieval court.

CHAPTER 7

"Your grandmother called," Kirsten said when I walked in our house that evening.

"Yeah, she called me, too, but I was busy." I knew what Olivia wanted and was dreading the conversation.

I pulled out my phone, but called someone else.

"Hi, it's Danica James. Yeah, long time. I've got a business proposition for you. Got some time? Sure, tonight is fine. Do you know where the Kitchen Witch Café is in Hampden? In an hour, then."

I hung up and saw Kirsten was standing there.

"Want to go out to dinner at Jenny's? I'll introduce you to an old friend of mine. A cousin, actually."

Kirsten shrugged. "Sure, why not?"

We rode our bikes over to the restaurant, and as we pulled into their parking lot, I saw that our dinner partner arrived before us.

"Wow," Kirsten said. "I never saw one of those in bright pink before."

The 'one of those' was a very high-end German sports car.

"You ain't seen nothin' yet," I told her.

We pushed through the door, and I headed for the splash of pink and blonde sitting in a booth along the wall.

"Hey, Cuz," Mary Sue stood and drew me into a hug. She smelled of roses.

"Mary Sue Dressler, I'd like you to meet my roommate, Kirsten Starr."

I was used to being around Kirsten, but standing between her and Mary Sue really made me feel like the ugly duckling. You could stick a picture of either one of them on a poster, label it 'Blonde Bombshell,' and no one would argue.

We gave our orders to the brownie waitress, and Mary Sue asked, "So, what's up? Saw you on the media vids a few weeks ago. The Metro's most famous and beautiful police detective. You should cash in on all the fame."

I felt my face flame. "I'm not really into the publicity."

She shrugged.

I turned to Kirsten, "Mary Sue and I are distant cousins, and we went to university together. She's also a magitek, and a damned good one."

Kirsten's eyes widened a bit. "I thought all magiteks dressed in black leather and rode motorcycles."

Mary Sue laughed. "There always has to be an exception, and I'm allergic to biker testosterone. Besides, I have an interior design business. You know, customizing mansions for the rich and useless. So, pink and cream make Mrs. Trophy Wife feel a bit more comfortable. Say, is that why you wanted to talk to me? Thinking of turning your house into a magikal fantasyland?"

It was my turn to laugh. "Kirsten is a witch, so most of your whiz-bang would be lost on her."

Our drinks appeared—my beer, Kirsten's Cosmopolitan, and Mary Sue's pink Mojito.

"How would you like to get rich?" I asked.

"As long as it's legal. I've got a cousin who's a cop." Mary Sue winked at Kirsten.

"Findlay wants to build a magitek factory. Weapons, transportation, defensive systems."

She didn't look excited. "That sort of thing is more your expertise than mine."

"I don't need a designer, I need a businesswoman to run the place. Make sure the manufacturing operation is efficient, high quality, and cost-effective. It doesn't have to produce only that sort of goods, but they'll pay the rent. You could manufacture your own designs, also. Chief executive officer, chief operations officer, chief aesthetics officer, grand high poo-bah—I don't care, you can have whatever title you want."

A bit more interest showed on her face. "How does that fit in with Findlay owning the place? They're usually pretty hands on."

"I have no intention of becoming a Findlay employee. We'll set it up as a separate corporation and give Olivia a piece of the pie in exchange for her money."

"It's illegal for a magitek to own a factory."

"That's why we make Olivia the chairman of the board," I said with a wink. "We give her thirty-four percent, and we each take thirty-three. We can still out-vote her."

"And your role?"

"Chief designer. Mary Sue, my grandmother wants me to go to work for them full-time, and I don't want to. I figure if I can give them the same results, they'll leave me alone. But I need one of the top magiteks in the world to do it. You know you'll make money if you go into business with Findlay."

She nodded. "Lady Olivia is a force of nature, but I can deal with her."

We hammered out a lot of details while we ate and more over after-dinner drinks. By the time we walked out of the restaurant, I felt like I had a viable alternative to offer my grandmother in exchange for most of my freedom.

"Is she really that good?" Kirsten asked as we walked to where our bikes were parked.

"Yeah. She graduated number one in our class, while I was second. She's a lot more ambitious than I am, and she's a lot more girly than I am, so that should make my grandmother happy. They've always gotten along."

"She looks a lot like you."

I laughed. "Don't ever say that around any of the Magi. Her mother and father were married at least a dozen years before she was born, but she doesn't look at all like any of her sisters."

"You mean, your father…"

"I have no idea. Mary Sue is two months older than I am, so I wasn't around to see what kind of relationships my father had back then. My parents never married, and they didn't start living together until I was born. But elves aren't monogamous, so my mother wouldn't have gotten bent out of shape if he screwed someone else. She has at least six half-sisters and half-brothers that I know of, all from different mothers." I chuckled. "That's another way you'd make a good elf."

***

My phone rang at three o'clock in the morning. I fumbled for it, cracked an eye to look at the screen, and groaned.

"James," I answered.

"Sorry to do this to you, Lieutenant," the voice of a dispatcher said, "but we've got a homicide in Roland Park."

I told her to text me the address and rolled out of bed. Roland Park was another neighborhood full of Magi mansions. I pulled on some clothes, dragged a brush through my hair, braided it so no one would notice it hadn't been washed in a couple of days, and headed out.

The address was only about half a mile from my place but in a whole different stratosphere. I rode through neighborhoods with fences and walls lining the streets. The mansions inside the guarded perimeters made no pretense of understatement.

When I reached my destination, the servants' quarters, which were the size of Aaron Carpenter's home, looked luxurious compared to mine and Kirsten's house. A uniformed cop checked my ID at the gate, and I rode up the drive to the house. Small and rustic compared to Findlay House, which could rightly be called a palace, but still large enough to get lost in.

"Lieutenant James?" A uniformed police sergeant approached me.

"Yes. What's going on, Sergeant?"

"This way, ma'am."

He led me through the foyer, up a curved grand staircase, and then through a series of hallways to a large set of carved double doors. I judged we were at the rear of the house, and other than three cops and a couple of forensics techs, I didn't see anyone.

"My partner and I were first on the scene," he said. "You got here pretty fast."

"I live up in Lauraville," I said. "It's not too far."

He pushed open the door, and we entered a suite of rooms. A spacious sitting room, with a bar on one side, led to a set of French doors open to a balcony. The furniture was opulent, Louis XIV, maybe? If not, excellent copies. Doors off to the left side that I assumed led to closets, dressing rooms, or bathrooms. Another set of double doors were open to our right.

A man and a woman lay on the bloody bed. The murder weapon—an axe—was buried in the woman's forehead. She wore a flimsy nightgown, he wore pajamas. From their gray hair, I estimated their ages to be well over a hundred.

"Who reported it?" I asked.

"The butler found them, and their security called it in," the sergeant said. "That was at two-oh-seven. We arrived at two-twenty. Butler said he heard noises that woke him up. Looks like entry was through the balcony. He said that the doors out there are rarely locked when the family is in residence."

"Identification?"

"Joseph and Elaine Greer."

Solidly in the Hundred, maybe top twenty-five or thirty. I had known a couple of their grandkids, or maybe great-grandkids. The Greer Family was big in chemicals.

I wheeled about and crossed the sitting room to the outside door. No evidence it had been forced. Stepping out on the balcony, I looked around and saw a table with four chairs, one of which lay on its side. A three-pronged grappling hook still hung on the balcony railing, its rope dangling down to the garden below.

"Secure all of the security videos," I said. "Send their security chief to me. All of the security personnel are to be considered suspects. I want them all disarmed and detained. I want as few people as possible in that garden and on the lawn until the sun comes up and forensics can properly search the area."

"Yes, ma'am." He scuttled off, leaving me to scan the area.

I pulled a set of night goggles out of my pocket and put them on. Magikally enhanced, and with magnification, the goggles gave me the ability to scan the area between the balcony and the outside wall thirty yards away.

Unless the Greers' guardians were in on the plot, someone had managed to scale a ten-foot wrought-iron fence with spikes on top—probably with embedded sensors—make their way across an open expanse of lawn, climb over a four-foot-high stone wall surrounding a garden, skirt a bunch of rose bushes, and climb a rope up to the balcony. Then he or she entered the house—all of that without being seen—walked through the master suite, and beat the Greers to death with an axe. After that, he or she made their escape out the balcony again.

Assuming they escaped.

I pulled out my phone. "Dispatch, I want the area around the Greer mansion in Roland Park completely closed off to non-official traffic, foot and vehicle. In and out. I want every available man out here as soon as possible. We may have a killer on the loose in the area. I also want at least two magik detectors here on the double. And ask Deputy Commissioner Whittaker to call me at his earliest convenience."

When I hung up, I found a man in Greer colors with stars on the epaulets of his uniform waiting for me. His face reminded me a little of a bulldog, and I could see the muscles in his jaw clenching.

"I'm General Gustav Braun, Director of Security."

"Thank you for coming so quickly. I'm Lieutenant Danica James, Metropolitan Police." I showed him my badge. In a case like that, every little detail had to be perfect.

He shot a glance through the open door to the bedroom. We hadn't moved the bodies yet, but seven people dressed in white forensics uniforms were busy in the room. Braun seemed to pale a little, and I didn't blame him.

I led him out to the balcony and ran through my reasoning. "General, I find it extremely strange that someone could do all that without detection. Or don't you have the normal security precautions in place?"

"I understand the question, but I don't like the implications," he responded. "I'll order an immediate investigation."

"No, you won't. You'll tell your men—all your men, all the servants, no matter what their duties—to stand down and turn in their arms. Security will be provided by the Metro Police and the Magi Council. I will spare you dealing with the family.

Sergeant Novak and I will take care of that. I have given orders that no one leaves the premises, and anyone trying to get in will be detained. As a matter of courtesy, after you've handed me your sidearm, you will remain free to assist with my investigation."

He took a deep breath, straightened, and puffed his chest out, but he still wasn't tall enough to look me straight in the eye. We had a staring contest for a minute or so, then he deflated. We both knew that I was following protocol, and it was in his interest to cooperate. Using two fingers, he drew his pistol from its holster and handed it to me.

"Thank you, General. I appreciate the indignity of your situation, and I promise I'll try not to add to it. I'm going to need your help, and if you have any ideas or suggestions, I'll be glad to hear them. I don't like anything I'm seeing any better than you do."

He nodded.

"If you could, please assist my sergeant in rounding up your men, collecting their arms, and provide a secure place for them to wait until we can interview them."

After he left, I started my own search through the house and cancelled every magitek device I came across. A couple of times, that left me in the dark, but I had the night goggles to help me find the nearest light switch.

That's what I was doing when Novak found me, about forty minutes after I showed up. He had a lot longer drive in from his Family estate in the country.

"What's up?" he asked. "I saw the crime scene. What are you doing?"

I told him, then said, "I've been thinking about it, and I don't see any way this was a family member. Disgruntled employee? Maybe. Find out from the staff where Greer's private office is, and check to see if there are any letters like those HLA manifestos Carpenter received. I'll have Whittaker send a detail to their office building as soon as it turns light."

"Yeah, makes sense. I'll get on it."

"And have someone start calling around to find out who sold that axe. I can't imagine there are that many stores in the city selling axes. Hell, I'm not even sure where to start looking."

"You're not a gardener," he said. "I'll ask the Greers' gardener."

"So, maybe the killer didn't bring it with him?"

Novak shrugged and went away, while I continued my search for magitek devices.

Kirsten probably would have known about gardens and axes, but growing up with my mom, I'd never seen one in real life, only in vids. Elves didn't use tools to work with wood, and they certainly didn't cut down trees.

Whittaker called twenty minutes later, and I told him what had happened and what I had done so far. He promised that a force of mercenaries would arrive within an hour, and told me that more cops were already on the way.

"You're doing fine," he said. "Stick to protocol, and try not to offend anyone."

"I'm trying. Their security head was a little put out, but he's a professional, and I promised I would keep him inside the investigation."

"A good idea. I've known Gustav for more than thirty years, and I would be shocked if he was involved in killing Joseph and Elaine."

CHAPTER 8

Deputy Commissioner Whittaker showed up at the scene around eight o'clock in the morning. He was always an early bird who gave me grief because I wasn't a morning person. I almost said something to him about being late, but he handed me a cup of hot coffee that smelled of caramel, and I shut up and took a sip.

Tom Whittaker was the head of his Family, which specialized in security services, including police, security guards, and military units, along with manufacturing arms and munitions. My paycheck actually came from one of the Whittaker companies, and the Metropolitan Police Force was a private enterprise contracted to the Council.

He brought a company of mercenaries wearing his Family colors with him, and they quickly assumed responsibility for the security of the Greer estate. That freed up a lot of cops for other duties.

He stood at the Greers' bedroom door and surveyed the scene.

"A little bit of overkill, wouldn't you say?"

"I think it was intended to send a message," I replied. "Not sure who the message is for, though."

"No notes, messages, claims of responsibility?"

"We haven't found anything, although I have Novak looking through Mr. Greer's office. I wondered if it could be connected to the Carpenter murder."

I led him through my reasoning concerning the killer's entrance and exit, then told him I had disabled all the magitek devices I could find.

"I haven't found one that could provide invisibility, though. So, I'm thinking that illusion magik is a lot more common than magitek. It could be a mage, a witch, or a Fae."

"Someone covered by an illusion should still show up on CCTV and trip lasers or motion detectors," Whittaker said.

"That's where I'm headed now, to go through their video and electronic logs."

"Keep me informed. I have a meeting with the Greers' children in half an hour, and we'll see what comes of that."

The security monitoring room was in an annex on the north side of the main house. Two burly cops guarded the door, and another cop sat on a bench in the hallway with a woman in Greer colors.

"This is the computer operator," the cop on the bench told me. "Didn't know if you'd need her for anything."

"Good thinking," I said. I smiled at the Greer computer specialist. "All I need is the administrator's password."

"I can't give you that without authorization."

I nodded to the cop. "Go find General Braun and either get a written order for me, or ask him to join us."

The cop trotted off, and I took his place on the bench.

"You were on duty last night?"

"Yes, ma'am. I came on at eleven."

"And everything was normal with the systems? Everything working correctly?"

She nodded, then took a deep, shaky breath. "I didn't check

the logs. I relieved Jurgen, and he said everything was nominal, and I took his word for it." She twisted in her seat to face me, her manner earnest. "We have state of the art systems. The servers were replaced last year, the software updated and patched last summer. We haven't had any problems in over a year."

"You checked all the cameras, though? The alarms?"

"Of course. We have a checklist, and we have to log the status of all the cameras and sensors. It would be my job if I didn't take that seriously."

"Are you a mage?"

"Yes, ma'am. An electrokinetic." She shrugged and glanced down. "Not very strong. I'm not a James or anything like that."

"You know who I am?"

"I've seen you on the media vids. The Carpenter murders. Believe me, after that happened, General Braun made it clear nothing like that was going to happen here. We went through a complete security check over the past two days."

I wondered who—outside the Greer Family and employees—knew about that security check. And whether anyone from outside was involved. It would be so easy to open up a system, test it, and flip a couple of switches before you logged out.

"How much magitek do you use in the security systems?" I asked.

"The controller for the peripheral sensors on the fence and the gates. Other than that, none."

"You upgraded the servers and the central software. Did you replace any of the TV cameras or peripherals or alarms?"

She shook her head and I sighed. If anyone knew about that single point of failure, a magitek would have no problem disabling the sensors on the fence. I would have to determine if that would send an alert.

It took me two hours working through the system before I was able to test the magitek controller. It looked like it was working. It gave me all the proper feedback and passed all the standard tests. The only problem was that I could have driven an armored personnel carrier through the fence, and the sensors wouldn't have transmitted anything to the central monitoring station. The controller sent its alerts to another magitek device hidden in a tree across the street from the Greer estate. Forensics didn't find any prints on the device.

"Could a non-magitek set all that up?" Whittaker asked me.

"Not a chance. A magitek had to re-program that controller. Not only a magitek, but someone with computer training."

"Would he have to physically access it?" Novak asked.

I shook my head and held out the box I found in the tree. "I don't even have to physically touch this. I could sit at that bus stop down at the corner and do it all. But the test logs show that the intrusion system was working properly yesterday morning. Someone tampered with it sometime after three o'clock yesterday afternoon. We need to find that guy Jurgen."

❦

It was well past noon by the time Novak and I managed to get out of the Greers' house and hit Jenny's for something to eat.

"We know how, but we don't know who," Novak said as we waited for our meals.

"That's why we're going to visit Jurgen as soon as I finish rebalancing my blood sugar and caffeine levels. Six cups of coffee and no food has me so jittery my eyeballs rattle. What have you found out about Carpenter's younger kids?"

Novak opened his mouth, then closed it, and gave me a quizzical expression. When he spoke, he said, "Your mind takes as many sudden turns as your driving. What has you thinking about Carpenter's kids?"

"That young lady working the monitors at Greer's. She's

about the same age as Carpenter's youngest daughter, and she screwed up because she's got the hots for that Jurgen fellow. She trusted him instead of doing her job."

"And the connection?"

"The HLA. Idealistic radicals are romantic. Look at how many romance novels have good girls falling for bad boys."

"I never read any romance novels."

I rolled my eyes and leaned back to allow the brownie waitress to set my fish and chips down on the table. "And you consider yourself educated."

Novak chuckled. "I thought the HLA were anti-magik. How does that fit with using magitek?"

"Fight fire with fire. Everyone agrees the bombings of the Palaces of Commerce here and in Prague were magitek-enhanced. And I haven't found anything that says the HLA is anti-magik. They're anti-Magi, anti-magiocracy. There are a lot of mages who aren't from the ruling Families who don't like the current system. Besides, magiteks are mainly blue-collar mages. We work in the factories, we don't own them. Name a single Family in the Hundred that is known for magitek."

"James used to be."

"Yeah, and the Magi have made damned sure we know our place. There are more laws and regulations with my name on them than I can count. I'm barred from owning a magitek factory. I can sell the devices I make, but I can't employ more than two people to help me make them. And there's a list—as long as my arm—of devices that I'm not allowed to make except under special license granted to Families in the Hundred."

He stared at me, blushing a little, then looked down at his plate. "I didn't know that."

I took a bite of my fish and burned my mouth. Deciding to let it cool down a little, I leaned forward and said, "My grandmother said that Findlay's intelligence operatives are hearing of discontent among the smaller Families about the rule of the Magi. It's not just the ungifted who think the wealth should be shared."

"And who do they think is going to hold the demons in check?" Mychal asked.

With a shrug, I said, "We fought the demons in our own self-interest. I'm not sure that entitles us to shit in golden toilets while people starve."

CHAPTER 9

Jenny let me park my bike inside her back fence, and we took the cop car down to the harbor to look for Jurgen Schwartz. The address we had was in Highlandtown, an area with three hundred-year-old rowhouses that had been renovated so many times that the original owners wouldn't recognize them. In the early twentieth century, the homes had been cheap houses built for dock workers, but I figured Jurgen's place would sell for two or three times the price of my house in Lauraville.

We parked on the street around the corner from Jurgen's house. It was one of the larger ones, three stories from the street with a walk-out basement in back.

I sent Mychal down the alley to cover the back door while I approached the house from the front. A glance down at the sidewalk brought me to a halt. There was a blood trail leading to Jurgen's front door. Looking back, I saw that it abruptly ended at a vacant parking place on the street.

I rang the bell and waited. When I didn't get a response, I spelled the locks on the door and cautiously pushed it open.

Jurgen wasn't the most fastidious housekeeper, but I didn't

know many young men who were. The place wasn't half-bad, the décor about thirty years out of date. As with most of the old rowhouses, it was twelve feet wide, and there weren't any dividing walls on the ground floor. The blood trail continued across the living room and up the stairs in front of me. But there was another blood trail that split from the one I'd been following and led in the other direction, to the rear of the dwelling.

I walked through the living room, dining room and into the kitchen to open the backdoor for Mychal.

"He's not home?" Mychal asked in a low voice when he entered.

I motioned to the stairs leading from the kitchen to the basement and the evident blood splatters. "You check that out, and I'm going upstairs."

I found a lot more blood in the hall upstairs. A bloody knife lay on the floor where one blood trail originated. Five feet farther was a splash of blood against the wall and the door frame with a bullet hole in the middle. Whoever had been shot had slid down the wall to the floor. He or she hadn't stayed there and left the second blood trail when they crawled down the hall, made it to their feet, or were picked up by someone else, and descended the stairs.

When Mychal joined me, he said, "Bled all the way to the back door in the basement, outside, then the blood disappears on the parking pad. No car."

We called dispatch and asked for a murder team, then we searched the rest of the house. One of the three bedrooms on the second floor served as an office. The walls were decorated with HLA posters, and we found pamphlets and other HLA literature.

"Well, your instincts were right," Mychal said. "He definitely was HLA."

"Yeah, and they're proving to be a ruthless bunch. Axemurdering old ladies and eliminating witnesses. Maybe Jurgen was considered a weak link."

Mychal nodded. "An identifiable link. You forgot to mention using bombs for mass murder."

"Yeah, that, too. Search this place. Any names, phone numbers, addresses, no matter what they're written on."

I looked around. There was a printer, but no computer. Strange for someone whose job was computers.

"Check for a phone, and see if he owned a car."

"There's a parking pad in the back, but like I said, no car," Mychal said. "The top three floors are built out over the pad."

"Yeah, the blood trail out the front door ends at an empty parking space on the street. I'll put out word to the hospitals."

※

"Two different blood samples," Kevin Goodman, head of the forensics lab told me. "What it looks like is, one person pulled the knife and slashed or stabbed the other. Then your knife wielder got shot as a reward. The shooter ran, then the one with the knife dragged himself down the stairs to the basement, where he vanished."

"He?"

Kevin nodded. "I feel fairly confident. I haven't run across too many women who wear a size thirteen men's shoe. He left footprints in the blood."

"Lieutenant," someone called. I turned and saw a uniform trying to stop a young woman, who simply ducked under the cop's arm and continued toward me.

"May I help you?" I asked, my hand on my pistol.

"I'm Jurgen's girlfriend," she said, pulling her jacket aside just enough to flash a badge at me. "Is there somewhere we can talk?"

I signaled Novak to join us, then took her out the kitchen door to the back of the house.

"I'm Detective Sergeant Carmelita Domingo," she said when the three of us were alone, "although my cover name as Jurgen's girlfriend is Dolores Hernandez. I'm with the HLA task force. DC Whittaker sent me."

Carmelita looked more like a high school girl than a cop. Wearing tight leggings, trainers, and a baggie sweatshirt, she barely topped five feet, with straight black hair hanging to her waist. The Domingo Family was one of the Ten and allied with Findlay, but that didn't mean she was related to them. Still, I minded my manners.

"It looks as though he's got himself in a mess," I said.

She sighed. "Lots of book smarts, very little common sense. DC Whittaker said you folks think he's tied into the murders up at the Greer mansion."

"What's his talent?" I asked.

"Electrokinetic, but not very strong. You know, a lot of those end up in computers and communication."

That described me, to a certain extent. I considered my electrokinetic abilities as an enhancement to my magitek talents, not a talent in itself.

"We think he allowed a magitek to sabotage the Greers' security system and covered it up," I said. "We found a device. When we came here to talk to him, we found evidence of a fight with someone else. There's a lot of blood upstairs, but no bodies."

"He always carried a big folding knife, five-inch locking blade," she said.

"That sounds like the knife we found. How about a gun?"

Carmelita-Dolores shook her head. "I never saw one, and he never mentioned having one." She gave me a faint smile. "He left me alone here several times, and I've searched the place rather thoroughly."

"We didn't find a computer," Novak said. "Did he have one?"

"Of course. Two. One of those fancy expensive ones. You know, the kind that fold up into a pocket? He carried it everywhere with him. And a more conventional one that stayed in his office upstairs."

"He must have taken them," Novak said, "because we haven't found either one."

My phone rang, and when I answered, it was one of Whittaker's assistants.

"They've found him," I said when I hung up. "He showed up at UM's emergency room with a bullet hole in him. Said he was shot by a mugger."

Novak chuckled. "Well, let's go get him."

I saw the look of alarm on Carmelita's face.

"There's no hurry," I said. "He's still in surgery. Sergeant Domingo, what do you think?"

"He's the best link we have into the HLA. I don't want to lose that, and if a bunch of cops show up and arrest him, his usefulness will be over."

"But they tried to kill him," my partner said.

"Someone did," I replied. "Let's go get a cup of coffee somewhere private and talk this over."

We found an upscale pizza place about a block away that was almost deserted in the middle of the afternoon. Domingo ordered a personal crab pizza and a latte, while Novak and I stuck with coffee. The off-hand way she ordered reminded me of Novak and made me think our young detective sergeant had grown up with money.

For the next couple of hours, we received a quick and dirty briefing on the Human Liberation Army, its ideology and beliefs, its organization, and its internal conflicts. As with any movement with members all over the world, it wasn't homogeneous, and the factions didn't always play well with each other.

Domingo was brief but thorough, and displayed her intelligence in an understated way.

"So," Domingo said, "you have the violent wing, whose members think a repeat of the French Revolution is the only answer, you have the dilettantes and college students who are there for the parties, the drugs and the sex, and you have the serious, public political face. The radicals can hardly stand to be in the same room with the moderates, and both find the hangers-on contemptible."

"I always thought the HLA was anti-magik, but Danica says they're anti-Magi."

"Anti-establishment," Carmelita said. "There are a lot of mages and witches involved, but very few from the Families. It attracts magikers from the lower classes. But from what I've seen, the movement has managed to recruit an unusual number of magiteks."

Mychal raised an eyebrow.

"Told you," I said. "We're the under-appreciated group. You won't find any rich aeromancers from the Ten wanting to change their status, but people like Schwartz with a little bit of electrokinetic talent are going to feel slighted. Why aren't they invited to the fancy parties with the beautiful people?" Both of my companions blushed slightly and dropped their eyes.

"Dead on," Carmelita said, looking up. "Most people don't have any concept of the difference in power between someone like Jurgen Schwartz and Olivia Findlay. They're both electrokinetics, right?" She laughed.

Novak gave me a quizzical look.

I chuckled. "Mychal, you know how you're always looking down your nose at me because I don't keep up with Family politics? Now you know how it feels. Ms. Domingo is obviously a student of history."

Our companion finished off the last bite of her pizza and nodded. "I've always been fascinated by the emergence of the

Magi and the Rift War. Even the demon lords feared the Findlay Family. Still do, probably."

"So," I asked, "what are we going to do about our Mr. Schwartz?"

On our way back to Jurgen's house, I got a call. Novak and Domingo waited for me, and when I finished, I said, "It appears that Jurgen Schwartz got the better of the deal. That was Whittaker. A man named Robert Earling was involved in a car crash about half a mile from here. ME says the cause of death was a stab wound."

Carmelita nodded. "Bob. That was the leader of Jurgen's HLA cell."

CHAPTER 10

After a conference with Deputy Commissioner Thomas Whittaker, I found myself on detached duty—assigned to the HLA task force, but still nominally in charge of the Carpenter and Greer homicides through Novak. I wondered when I was going to find time to sleep.

Before we left Whittaker's office, he handed me a small, square package.

"Schwartz's computer," he said. "It was in his pocket. We also recovered another computer from Earling's car that appears to belong to Schwartz. We've already started working on that one, but this has a magitek security device incorporated into it."

I unfolded the package and saw that it was one of the most expensive portable computers on the market.

"I'll take a look at it tonight," I told my boss, and he nodded.

I also found myself with another new partner, Carmelita Domingo, also known as Dolores Hernandez. University Hospital wasn't very far from Police Headquarters, so she and I walked over there to visit our suspect. It would have taken us twice as long to drive, even using police parking privileges.

I rarely walked around downtown during the day. It was brisk—a breezy but clear autumn day. The tall buildings of the corporations blocked out the sun for the most part, and there was a lot of traffic. The people on the street varied from business people to teenagers hanging out in groups, to beggars and druggies looking for a handout.

On the way, I pumped Carmelita-Dolores for more information about the HLA.

"Jurgen is just a foot soldier, mostly a hanger-on," she said. "Like most underground groups, they're compartmentalized, with most members unaware of anyone above them or outside their cell. But because of his position with Greer, they took a lot of interest in him. I just didn't know that was what they planned to do. I know Bob Earling was his contact with people above him, but I hadn't gotten the chance to follow up."

"That's probably who shot him," I said.

"Looks that way."

"Do you think they're behind the Palace of Commerce bombings?" I asked.

She was silent for at least half a block, then she turned her face up to me. "I didn't want to believe it at first, but after the Greer killings, I think there are HLA fanatics who would do almost anything."

There was a cop on the door of Jurgen's hospital room because he was a gunshot victim. We had to break our cover before the cop would let us in, but I gave him a stern warning not to disclose our secret.

I had seen pictures of Jurgen, but he turned out to be bigger than I imagined. I figured him for late twenties, well over six feet, broad shouldered, and handsome. The bullet had taken him high in the left chest, missing any vital organs or major blood vessels. It had fractured his scapula, though, so it would be a couple of months before he could use his left arm. Magikal healing was expensive.

He was groggy but attempted a smile when he saw his girlfriend.

"What did you get yourself into?" she asked, taking his free hand and bending down to kiss him on the forehead.

"Got mugged."

"In the upstairs hallway of your house? That's a little hard to believe. Who shot you? Bob?"

His smile faltered.

"Are you aware that the police have an all-points bulletin issued for your arrest?" I interjected. "They want you for the murder of Joseph and Elaine Greer."

Jurgen might have been groggy from the drugs, but he was cognizant enough to be alarmed. He tried to sit up, winced, and settled back on the bed.

"That wasn't me."

"Oh? That's going to be hard to prove. We know you tampered with the security system."

"One of Bob's friends."

"Bob's dead," I said. "They're probably going to charge you with that murder, too."

"Bastard shot me."

"Before or after you stabbed him?"

He stared at us, his eyes shifting back and forth between me and Carmelita. Finally, he said, "Who are you?"

"The woman who is going to decide where you spend the rest of your life. Stonewall me, and you'll be a permanent resident of Antarctica. Cooperate, and depending on how much you help, you could end up in the Yukon or in Gettysburg. Your choice." I leaned over him. "But understand me. You won't be judged by a regular court of law. You're going to be facing a Magi tribunal."

He was already pretty pale from blood loss, but his complexion managed to turn even whiter.

About that time a nurse came in and told us Jurgen needed to sleep and that we should come back later.

"In a minute," I said. "Please, just one more minute alone with him."

The nurse reluctantly nodded and slipped back out the door.

"Tell us who Bob's contact is," I said.

"You'd better tell her," Carmelita chimed in. "She's dead serious, and you're in a lot of trouble."

"Susan Reed. In College Park. I don't have her number, but she's head of the HLA on campus."

On our way out of the hospital, Carmelita said, "Susan Reed is his ex-girlfriend. I'll bet she's the one who recruited him." She snorted. "And I'll bet my trust fund that he lied when he said he doesn't have her number. He only said that because I was there. He thinks I don't know that he's seeing three other women besides me."

※

I made arrangements for Carmelita to pick me up the following morning for a visit with Susan Reed. Then I walked over to Kirsten's shop.

"You look tired," she said when I walked in. "What time did you leave this morning?"

"About three thirty. My bike is up at Jenny's. Do you suppose we can take your van out to Findlay?"

"Definitely, and you're not driving."

I called my grandmother. "Can I talk you into feeding Kirsten and me this evening? We have a business proposition we'd like to discuss with you."

A long silence at the other end, then, "Business proposition? Am I going to like this?"

I chuckled. "Your blood pressure will appreciate it if you put yourself in a positive, receptive mood."

"That's what I'm afraid of. Come on out. I think the cook plans fish for this evening."

Even though we left before most businesses closed, we were still headed in the wrong direction for end-of-day traffic. Unfortunately, the aerodynamics of the van precluded me from enhancing it as an aircar. It took us an hour to get out to Findlay.

After parking the van, I dropped by Osiris's office to give him a heads-up about the HLA and the Greer and Carpenter murders.

"You're sure the HLA has a magitek working with them?" he asked.

"Positive. I found proof. Any of your systems that are magically enhanced need to have a non-magikal backup. Osiris, these people are crazy."

"We've deployed magitek systems you or your father designed all over the world."

I grinned at him. "Backing them up should keep you busy, then."

Kirsten and I slipped into the main house through the servants' entrance, and I led her up the back stairs, through a maintenance corridor, and out into the hallway with my grandmother's suite of rooms.

"Is it really necessary to come in that way?" Kirsten asked. "I never get to see all the fancy furniture and art."

"And you miss all my snotty relatives. Believe me, I'm doing you a favor."

I knocked, and a maid answered almost immediately. She looked me up and down, obviously less than happy with the way we were dressed. Especially me. Kirsten usually wore a long, old-fashioned dress at the store, as befitting the stereotype of a witch.

"Good evening, Mistress, Miss Starr. Her Ladyship is in the sitting room."

"Thank you, Hilda." She didn't move out of my way until I handed her my coat. When I was in high school, I tried to refuse letting the servants wait on me. Then I discovered that such behavior seriously offended them. The head housekeeper finally confronted me and asked why I wanted to turn all the servants out on the street to starve. She came about as close as she could, within propriety, of accusing me of being selfish and self-centered, not to mention a socialist.

In the sitting room, Olivia sat in one of three chairs surrounding a small, round table by a bay window that faced east toward the Bay, although one really couldn't see that far. We took our seats, and Hilda poured us each a glass of sherry. My grandmother had spent years attempting to culture my appreciation of fine sherry, an effort that still hadn't succeeded. But I had learned to fake it and to recognize the various varieties.

"So, a business proposition?" Olivia asked after Kirsten and I had taken a polite sip. "I checked my inventory, and I really don't need another bridge or any swamp land this month."

"How about a magitek factory? One that produces not only weapons and security systems but also home appliances and decorations. One that pays for itself."

With that last part, I had her attention.

"Why do I feel as though I should hide my credit card?" she asked.

"I've decided that I don't want to come to work for Findlay," I said, "but I am interested in setting up a design business with an attached factory. I have someone who is business savvy and a great marketer to run it, and we'll let you in for one-third ownership."

She threw back her head and laughed, a deep, genuine burst of appreciative mirth. When she sobered to a chuckle, she said, "And I assume that I get to finance this venture as my one-third contribution."

I grinned at Kirsten. "See? I told you she was sharp."

Kirsten blushed scarlet, but Olivia chuckled.

"You also get to control two-thirds of the factory's output," I said. "Cost-plus pricing. You will also share one-third of the profits from the other third of the production."

She sat back in her chair, sipped her sherry, and studied me, with occasional glances at Kirsten. I could almost hear the wheels turning in her head.

"And who is this business and marketing genius who is going to make us all rich?" she asked.

"Mary Sue Dressler."

I could tell I surprised her, and her brow knitted in thought. Presently, she said, "She just finished a total renovation of Gloria Flanagan's house in Dublin. Very impressive, and ungodly expensive. Took two years. Not just the magitek, but the entire interior design."

"Think about bringing the price down with factory output and the mass marketing of such devices and services," I said.

"She's good?"

"As good as I am at what she does, and she enjoys the business side of things. She's a perfectionist, obsessive about the little things. When we were at university together, I just cared if a project worked. She wanted to saw off the sharp edges and make it pretty as well."

"And what are you going to do?"

"Design the weapons, security systems, and transportation enhancement devices. All the stuff I'm good at. I design them, turn the designs over to the factory employees, who engineer and produce them. Mary Sue makes them pretty enough to sell, or discreet enough that people don't realize what they are. You won't have to wait a month to get a single device, you can have a hundred produced in the same amount of time. She says that we might even be able to work a deal with Dressler Robotics to sell them control systems if we can undercut their present supplier."

"Let me think about it," she said. "Are you hungry?"

※

After dinner, when Kirsten and I were getting ready to leave, I asked, "What are you going to do about Courtney and her family?"

Olivia frowned. "I'm not sure. George is dithering. Akiyama Benjiro has offered a ransom to buy his uncle back, and the Magi Council is arguing as to whether to hold a tribunal or simply to levy a substantial fine and some kind of sanctions to try and hold Akiyama accountable for engaging in human trafficking."

"You didn't answer my question."

She took a deep breath. "I suppose I didn't. Courtney and the Moncrieffs would probably be included in such a settlement."

"What about Courtney trying to kill me? And you?"

Olivia looked incredibly unhappy. "It's probably better that you don't bring that up in public. Especially with your Uncle George."

"You're kidding."

She shook her head.

There was a time, when I was younger and more self-righteous, when I would have blown up. But I had become somewhat immune to the ruling class's immorality. What I did instead was simply turn and walk out.

"So, people die and it just gets shrugged off?" Kirsten asked as we climbed in her van.

"Welcome to the fun and games of the rich and powerful. Besides, no one of any importance died, right?"

Just a bunch of idiot assassins Courtney paid. I didn't feel sorry for them, but some of them probably had families who would miss them.

Kirsten shot me a look. "So, we need to continue to watch our backs."

I nodded. "Yeah. And without the extra security Uncle George was providing but now seems to have forgotten about."

CHAPTER 11

It didn't take me long to crack Jurgen's computer. In addition to the information he stored there, he had a secure lockbox set up online. That took a little more effort to open, but I managed it.

The online storage was where the good stuff was hidden. As Carmelita had said, the boy was intelligent, and he had sniffed out a lot more information about the HLA than they thought he knew. Names, online IDs, secure lockbox locations, and connections to insurgent networks in other countries. I copied it all off and asked Kirsten to hide the chip in her greenhouse.

The following morning, Carmelita picked me up at my home around nine o'clock. Her sporty two-seater wasn't as expensive as Mary Sue's car, but it was close to the range that might raise eyebrows if purchased on a cop's salary. With the last name of Domingo, though, she probably felt she was slumming by driving it.

"Nice ride," I said.

She laughed. "Cop issue, believe it or not. Contributes to my cover. I think they busted a drug dealer and confiscated it."

We drove down toward Washington, and she parked in a

neighborhood that was just a touch shabby, south of Beltsville and north of the university.

"Student ghetto," Carmelita said. "This is where the aboveground headquarters of the local HLA group is located. The house is owned by a guy named Elesio Gomez. I've met him a couple of times, and he has the hots for me. I'm pretty sure we can find Susan Reed through him."

Gomez turned out to be short and stocky, with curly red hair and a mustache. I figured him to be very early twenties in age. He welcomed us into his house, where we found around a dozen more college-age people in various rooms, some working on designing posters, a couple organizing a march on campus, and several in the kitchen debating the ethics of slaughtering all the demons versus simply enslaving them. I silently wished them luck with either endeavor.

Our host led us to a back bedroom and closed the door.

"Have you heard?" Carmelita, playing the role of Dolores asked. "The strike against the Magi in Baltimore?"

"Yeah," Elesio said. "I wondered if that might be an HLA cell." He seemed excited and happy about the murders.

"There's a problem, though," Dolores said. "Bob Earling is dead, and Jurgen is in the hospital. The doctors don't expect him to survive. But the mages have ways of extracting information even if he never wakes up. Bob told me that if something went wrong, I was to contact Susan Reed."

Elesio's jubilation melted away. "What do you mean?"

"I mean the cops may soon know everything Jurgen knows. About me, you, Susan, the whole operation. That was pretty stupid, you know. Blowing up buildings is one thing, but sneaking into a Magi's residence and killing him? Why did we do that?"

"To strike directly against the mages," Elesio said, a hard tone in his voice. "We have to hurt the oppressors, make them fear us."

He suddenly seemed to notice that a complete stranger was listening to their conversation.

"Who is this?"

"She's on our side."

"Who is she?"

Dolores gave him a smirk. "That's a secret. Bob and Jurgen's secret. They said she needs to meet Susan, and only Susan."

He shook his head. "I can try and get in touch with her, but I'll let her decide what she wants to do."

Dolores smiled and sidled up to Elesio, pressing her breasts against him and looking up into his face. "Jurgen's out of the picture now. Nothing to keep us from getting together." Her expression changed to a frown. "But if you don't trust me, then I'm not going to play. Jurgen was a real man, one who could make decisions, take action. I thought you were important, but if all you are is a messenger boy, then I guess I need to find someone else. I don't do common."

She whirled away from him. "Come on, let's go," she said to me. Then, over her shoulder, "You know how to get hold of me. Tell Susan to call me. And tell her I won't be coming down here again. I'm staying the hell away from places Jurgen might be telling the cops about."

Elesio had it bad, and he panicked. "Wait! Look, I can't just tell you how to find Susan, but let me get in touch with her. You can wait around until tonight, can't you?"

"Let's go," I said. "He's useless. I can't believe you were interested in him."

Five minutes later, we had an address and a telephone number for Susan Reed, and Elesio thought he had a date lined up with Dolores for the following Saturday night.

On our way back to the car, I said, "I'm not sure we should tell them Jurgen is still alive."

"I'm hoping that the HLA will make a play on Jurgen in the hospital," Carmelita said, stopping by the car to make a call on her phone. When she finished talking to someone, she told me, "They're boosting Jurgen's protection with a couple of mages and a magitek. If the HLA wants to shut him up and sends an assassin, we'll try and capture him."

As we drove over to Berwyn Heights, an upscale suburb east of the university, I said, "Elesio is obviously an idiot, but we can't depend on people not recognizing me. I've been in the news a lot over the years, and especially in the last month."

Carmelita nodded. "Yeah, I thought about that and discussed it with DC Whittaker when he assigned you to this investigation. We're not going to even try and hide who you are. Danica James, one of the most notorious magiteks in the world, bastard step-child of a Ten Family, cut off from her inheritance, bitter and rebellious. Bleeding heart who thinks the Magi are arrogant and corrupt and need to be taken down a few notches so the rest of humanity can breathe and reach their full potential."

"Yeah, that's all true, but I don't agree with mass murder as a method of protest."

She shot me a look.

"Whittaker knows me pretty well," I said, grinning at her. "The only part of that story that isn't true is about being cut off from my inheritance and being bitter about it. I don't want the damned inheritance. But do you think we can get the HLA to buy it?"

"I met Susan Reed a couple of times," Carmelita said. "She's past protesting. As far as she and people like her are concerned, they're at war. The Magi, the demons, the vampires. And as you've already guessed, they aren't against recruiting magik users to use as weapons. Susan is a witch, and there are a lot of witches in the HLA."

"Have you thought about things such as truth spells?" I asked.

"She's not that good a witch. But if it makes you feel better, we can get you a charm." She pulled on a chain around her neck and showed me a small pendant.

I laughed. "I already have one. My roommate is a witch, and a damned good one."

Kirsten supplied me with charms and potions, while I supplied her with magitek to protect and run her business. It was a good arrangement. And since her mom taught in the Witchcraft Department at the University of Maryland, we had access to experts in the field.

We knocked on the door of a nice, two-story brick neo-colonial home with a manicured lawn and well-kept flowerbeds. The woman who answered the door looked completely out of place.

"What the hell are you doing here?" she demanded. "And who the hell is this?"

"Bob is dead," Carmelita-Dolores said. "Jurgen got shot and may not make it. He said if anything happened to him, I should go to you."

I assumed the woman was Susan Reed. She appeared to be in her mid-twenties, medium height, overweight, with a splotchy complexion and dishwater-blonde hair twisted and held up with a barrette. Her clothes that morning consisted of a University of Maryland sweatshirt and sweatpants. A sneer, that I assumed was habitual, completed her outfit.

Her attention shifted to me, and I saw her eyes widen. "I don't know what you're talking about. I haven't done anything wrong, and if your cop friend thinks she's coming in, she'd better have a warrant."

I gave her an indulgent smile. "Don't worry. Dolores said she could introduce me to someone of influence within the HLA, someone who might be able to use my talents. But if she was wrong, no problem. I can hook up with someone else. Come on, Dolores. Let's not waste any more time here."

"You're Danica James," Reed said.

"Yes, I am." I turned to walk away. "We can try and contact one of those other names we found on Jurgen's computer," I said to Dolores.

I made it about two steps when Reed called, "Wait!"

Looking back over my shoulder, I saw that Dolores was still standing on the porch with Reed in the doorway. The HLA member looked as though she was unsure of what to do.

"You have Jurgen's computer?" Reed asked.

"Yes. A lot of interesting information," I said. "Combined with the magitek device I found at the Greer mansion, I think I understand enough as to what's going on. I could turn it all over to my superiors, but I haven't figured out how that would do me any good. So, I called Dolores. It turns out that we seem to think a lot alike."

Reed shook her head. "I don't understand. What are you doing here?"

"Looking for like-minded people. Until I cracked Jurgen's computer, I had no idea the HLA was potentially an effective organization. I always thought it was just a bunch of idealogues playing games and making fancy speeches."

"Your Family is in the Ten," she said.

I barked out a laugh, not having to fake much to put some bitterness into it. Members of my family had tried to kill me repeatedly in recent weeks.

"James is definitely not one of the Ten," I said. "Findlay would be happy if I just went away and they could pretend I never existed. Do you know how many laws and restrictions I have to put up with because I'm a magitek?" I snorted. "I have no love for the Magi."

Turning away again, I walked down to where Dolores's car was parked on the street. Dolores stayed, and after talking to

Susan for another ten minutes, she joined me. We got in the car and she drove off. As soon as we were away from the house, her face split into a grin.

"Nice job. I think she bought it. She said she had to confer with other people on some mysterious 'council,' but that she'll call me in a day or two."

"Sounds good, and in the meantime, I think we should get hold of Novak. I'm pretty sure I know who our axe murderer is."

CHAPTER 12

We met Novak at a café in Columbia, southeast of Baltimore. The area had been an upscale bedroom community for Baltimore and Washington before the wars, and nothing had really changed in that respect.

In spite of the rain, we sat outside on a covered patio warmed with a magitek grid. Novak had suggested the place, and just the presence of the magitek warned me about the prices. My suspicions were confirmed when I opened the menu. Carmelita didn't seem surprised.

After we submitted our orders through the compu-menu, I said, "When I cracked Jurgen's computer, I found some files he had stored online. He might have made a good cop, but instead he's going to spend the rest of his life in Antarctica. Essentially, he kept dossiers on members of the HLA and of some other underground organizations he was in contact with. One of the HLA radicals is identified as a magitek who lives here in Columbia."

"There might be a lot of magiteks affiliated with the HLA," Carmelita said. "You also can't assume all of their contacts are sympathetic with the radicals' goals or methods."

"Yeah, but this guy is cross-referenced with Bob Earling," I said. "He has a police record, including arrests at anti-Magi protests, and he was enrolled at the university at the same time as Susan Reed. He's at least worth checking out."

My companions both nodded.

"And if we take him down?" Novak asked.

"We do it quietly and turn him over to Whittaker. I don't want Susan Reed or any of his other contacts to know about it."

"Makes sense to me," Carmelita said. She called Whittaker, and using the information I gave her, got a secret search warrant authorization for our suspect's home.

"Do we want backup for this?" Carmelita asked.

I shook my head. "Not if we want to keep it quiet. If a SWAT team cruises into the neighborhood, someone will call the media, and it will be on the newscasts before he's even been booked."

"You said he knows Susan?" she asked.

"Yeah."

"Then I guess I should go in first." She cast a spell, and Susan Reed sat in front of us instead of Carmelita.

I jumped, my heart in my throat. The transformation had been so sudden and taken me by surprise. "You're an illusionist."

"Aeromancer, but yeah, I'm pretty good with illusions, too."

※

We ate our lunch and then drove over to the suspect's home—or more accurately, his parents' home. I had done my research the evening before and found out that Justin Beaver worked for a company owned by one of the Hundred. He was a mage of little power and married to a witch. Their older son—Carl—was a magitek who flunked out of the University of Maryland, and his roommate at the university was Bob

Earling. Carl, age twenty-five, lived with his parents and had no record of employment.

Carmelita, wearing the illusion of Susan Reed, drove her sports car, while I rode with Novak. I had him park around the corner, and we watched Carmelita park on the street in front of the Beavers' residence.

By previous arrangement, she fussed with her purse, checked her makeup, and took her time getting out of the car. I walked past, staying on the sidewalk, and used my magik to disable all of the active magitek devices in the house. There were seven active and quite a few more that were inactive. When I finished, I stopped and peered at the house next door, as if trying to read the address, then proceeded down the street.

I stopped at the corner and turned to watch. Novak took up his position at the other end of the block.

Carmelita rang the bell, and a short while later, the door opened. Since she was wearing a listening device, both Novak and I could hear the conversation.

"Susan! What are you doing here?"

"Bob and Jurgen are dead. The cops also know that magitek was used in the Carpenter and Greer murders. You need to get out of here."

"Shit! How do they know about me? How did they die?"

"Are we going to discuss this out here on the porch?" the fake Susan asked.

"Oh, no. Come in."

Carl ushered her into the house and shut the door. That was our cue to move. Novak's assignment was to watch the back door while I hung out by the garage on the side of the house and watched the front.

Then I heard a third voice through the device Carmelita carried—male, older, deeper, rougher. "What the hell's going on?" I thought I detected a slight Eastern European accent.

"The cops know about my devices that were used in the Baltimore attacks," Carl said.

"Jurgen and Bob are dead," Carmelita said. "The cops killed them."

A string of curses erupted from the third voice. What followed were sounds of confusion. People rushing around, cryptic comments, not much in the way of understandable conversation.

"Where do you plan to go?" fake Susan asked.

"None of your damned business, you slut," the rough voice responded. Then, much closer, "How do I know you weren't followed? How did you find out about the cops killing them? It wasn't on the news."

"I have sources." Susan's voice was shaky. "Let go, you're hurting me."

That was my cue. An illusion usually wouldn't hold up with direct contact. I headed for the front door, drawing my weapon. I magiked the lock on the door, turned the knob, and pushed it open.

Beyond the foyer, a tall, burley man with a three-day growth of beard held onto the Susan illusion by the arm, shaking her. To my eyes, Carmelita still held the illusion, but I had no idea what the big man saw. Noises came from upstairs through a stairway to my right, and I assumed that was where Carl had gone.

"Hold it! Hands in the air!" I called, pointing my gun at the man. "Let go of the girl!"

Carmelita then showed her police training. She stomped hard on the man's foot, twisted away from him, and threw herself to the floor, giving me a clear line of fire.

The big man turned and ran into the next room.

"Go!" Carmelita said. Out of the corner of my eye, I saw her draw her pistol. "I'll take Carl."

I launched myself after the man and at the same time heard a door at the back of the house crash open.

"Halt!" Novak shouted, followed by the sound of his pistol firing.

I raced through the house into the kitchen to find Novak standing over the man, who was lying on the floor. One of his legs was ruined, almost blown off at the knee.

I skidded to a stop, holstered my pistol, and reached into a belt pouch for a first aid kit. Pulling a tourniquet out, I knelt down and placed it on the man's leg, then tightened it until the flow of blood slowed.

As soon as I finished, I said, "Call Whittaker. Tell him we need an ambulance, and tell them to keep things quiet. I'm going to go help Carmelita."

Drawing my sidearm, I went back through the house and up the stairs. I found Carmelita in a bedroom putting handcuffs on Carl Beaver.

Whittaker showed up with what I always called a 'stealth ambulance,' not that it wouldn't attract attention. I'd tried to tell him before that his 'not officially an ambulance' looked like a hearse, but he hadn't listened.

We didn't find any identification we could trust on the wounded guy. None of the three IDs he carried were legitimate, so we didn't even know his name. I sent his fingerprints to the station, but he didn't turn up in the worldwide database. Very curious.

They hauled him off to the hospital, and while Novak and Carmelita interrogated Carl Beaver, I took a look around his bedroom and his basement workshop. I had been correct that he had a magitek security system installed. I wondered if his parents, who were obviously supporting him, knew how much their security system was worth.

When I had hacked his academic record at the university, I found that he was an average student, and none of his professors seemed impressed with his magikal ability. The contents of his workshop belied that assessment. He had three cloaking devices, each of which would sell on the black market for my yearly salary. Not an easy device to create, and the spells required not only power but also finesse.

There were at least a dozen electromagikal devices that performed different functions, and a couple of listening devices. Stick the listening device on the outside of a window, and the mage controlling it could hear anything inside the house from a couple of blocks away.

Then there was the experimental rocket launcher. That one alone was enough to win him a sentence to the arcane prison in Gettysburg for five to ten years. Magiteks weren't supposed to play with explosives. For Mary Sue and me to manufacture such things for Findlay, we needed to get a special license, courtesy of Olivia, and put strict security procedures in place.

But the crowning glory was a box about the size of a soccer ball. I knew what it was as soon as I touched it. An enhancer such as that was probably used for the explosions that brought down the Palace of Commerce buildings in Baltimore and Prague. If the Magi suspected that Carl was in any way connected to those two bombings, his future home would be in Antarctica, not Gettysburg.

I pocketed several of the devices, including a cloaking device, and bagged the rest for evidence. All the explosive stuff went to the police station. Even a magitek who was a cop was barred from touching those.

CHAPTER 13

"What are we going to do with Susan Reed and the rest of this HLA cell?" I asked Whittaker. Novak, Domingo, and I were debriefing in his office along with Lieutenant Luis Cappellino, leader of the HLA task force, who I knew was related to both the Whittaker and the Novak Families.

Whittaker nodded to Carmelita, indicating she should answer.

"We're going to let them stew for a while. I think we have figured out who is responsible for the Carpenter and Greer murders. So, we'll let the rest of Reed's revolutionaries run around in a paranoid tizzy and hope they lead us to people higher up."

Cappellino spoke up. "Carl Beaver might have been responsible for the device used in Prague, but it doesn't look as though he was the one who actually triggered the explosion. As best we can determine, he hasn't been out of the Mid-Atlantic for at least three years, let alone to Europe recently. DNA tells us that the man Mychal shot is of Southern European descent, and it links him to some minor Families in Italy and the Balkans, but we can't identify him. We did match his fingerprints to unknowns found at the Carpenter residence, so he was there."

"And that means I can clear the murders?" I asked.

Whittaker nodded. "Go home. Write up your reports tomorrow. You two have been working your butts off this week."

He didn't have to twist my arm.

As we headed out the door, Mychal asked, "Do you know if Kirsten has any plans this evening?"

I shrugged. "Not that I'm aware of. I've barely seen her this week. Why?"

"I was thinking of calling her and asking her out to dinner."

I gave him a smile. "I'm willing to bet that she'll say yes."

And sure enough, when I got home I found Kirsten freshly showered and putting on makeup.

"Hot date?" I asked.

"Mychal's taking me out to dinner at the Belvedere." The Belvedere Hotel was an ancient Baltimore landmark, and the restaurant in the penthouse was the priciest in town.

"I guess I'll have to find my own dinner, then."

Kirsten laughed. "Oh, that reminds me. Remember the guy you were dancing with at Lila's ball?" She jumped up and grabbed her purse, rummaged around in it, and handed me a business card. "Aleksandr, right? I was at lunch with a vendor at Florio's and ran into him. He wants you to call him." She winked. "He said he neglected to get your number, what with the demon killing people and all that."

I read the card.

Aleksandr Janik
Senior Trade Representative
Janik Enterprises
North American Operations

Aleksandr Janik. His Family was a member of the Hundred, from somewhere in Europe, and allied with the Novak Family. Yeah, I remembered him. Tall, dark, and definitely handsome. Wonderful dancer with intelligent banter. He had some sort of business dealings with my grandmother.

"Okay," I said. "I'll call him, but not tonight. It's been a rough week, and all I want is some peace and quiet."

After Mychal picked up Kirsten, I called a Chinese place and ordered takeout, then rode over and picked it up. When I got home, I kicked back, opened a bottle of wine, and watched an old vid while I ate. Then I took a long hot bath and went to bed. I had no idea whether Kirsten made it home or not.

***

The following day, there weren't any Magi murders, demons slaughtering tourists down at the Inner Harbor, or teenage magikers doing stupid things in public. So, Kirsten and I joined Mary Sue out at the Findlay estate to talk business with my grandmother. We went over the contracts Olivia presented, and they seemed fair.

The corporation she set up was outside of the Findlay Family. Cerberus Corp. was an entity with one hundred shares of stock. Each of the principles got thirty-three shares, and Kirsten got one, a seat on the board of directors, and she was named chairman of the board. I was sure having the business named after the three-headed dog that guarded the gates of Hell contained a secret joke, but Olivia didn't offer an explanation.

Then we drove up to the port of Wilmington in Olivia's limo, and she showed us the three buildings she had bought from Findlay and then sold to the new corporation for almost nothing. A small office building and two warehouses.

"Findlay leased them to Akiyama and Moncrieff," Olivia

said. "Since they were involved in illegal activities, which violated their leases, we severed the leases, and the Magi Council confiscated the contents. The buildings are far enough away from other buildings and the port that we shouldn't have to worry too much if there's an occasional accident."

I felt my face warm. I had only blown up one small shed when I was learning to control my magik, but my grandmother had never forgotten it.

I gave Mary Sue all my files containing the documentation and spells for the magitek devices I had invented or built from my father's designs, and then we retired to a delightful little café overlooking the Bay for drinks and seafood.

On our way back to Baltimore, I was feeling pretty good when my phone rang. One glance at the screen killed my good mood as surely as a bullet.

"James," I answered. I listened to the dispatcher, and when I hung up, I said, "Justus Benning was just assassinated. His wife is in the hospital. The dispatcher said we aren't sure if the bomb was planted on their car, or if they drove over a mine set in the road."

Olivia gave the driver orders to speed up, and I spent the rest of the ride trying to access the police databases through my phone.

I knew Justus Benning as the case I had just closed involved their missing daughter. Diana Benning—his second wife—was much younger than her husband, and they had two daughters.

The search for Sarah Benning had uncovered a human trafficking ring involving vampires, demons, and at least two Hundred-level Families, plus the Akiyama Family—one of the Ten. Benning had made enemies, so I needed to consider the Akiyama and Moncrieff Families, including my Aunt Courtney, as well as the HLA, in any list of possible suspects.

The Bennings had been riding in an armored limo with lead and trail armored vehicles. The detonation had lifted the limo off the road and flipped it over. Both the driver and the guardian riding in the front seat had been torn apart by the blast.

"The bomb went off under the front of the car," Novak told me as we walked around the destroyed limo. "The Bennings were in the back, at least partially sheltered from the force of the blast. They were traveling at a fairly high rate of speed, the car did a back flip, and the APC—the armored personnel carrier—behind them hit the limo. Killed the driver of that vehicle, too. The other guardians inside have all been transported to the hospital, and so has Diana Benning."

"So, Justus was killed, and Diana survived?" I asked.

Kelley Quinn, the medical examiner, walked over and said, "It looks like the man died of a broken neck. I'll have to do the autopsy to give you a definitive opinion, but take a look."

She led us over to the wreck. The bodies had yet to be moved, and Justus lay crumpled, head down, on the underside of the limo's roof. His head was at a very unnatural angle.

"You can see the blood on his clothes," Kelley said. "None of the wounds bled very much, which leads me to believe he died very quickly. The woman landed on top of him, and her wounds were much bloodier. It didn't look as though any of them were very severe. She may need some reconstruction, though. Her face was a mess. Neither of them was wearing a seat belt."

Diana Benning was a stunningly beautiful woman, but magikal healing meant that she probably wouldn't have much in the way of scars.

I turned back to Novak. "What does forensics have to say about the bomb? Magikally enhanced?"

He shook his head and walked beyond the wreck to a crater

in the road. "No magik detected, and from the crater, they think the bomb was planted in the road. The blast that made this hole was directed upward, not downward."

"Someone mined the road," I said, and he nodded.

I wasn't a bomb expert, but considering that both front tires were still intact and attached to the limo, it appeared the bomb had gone off directly under the engine. The rear of the car was remarkably undamaged.

"The car didn't hit the mine," I said. "So, either there was a trip plate on the road that the tires ran over, or it was set off by someone watching from the side of the road."

"Pretty tricky timing it exactly right," Novak observed.

"Not really," Kevin Goodman, head of the forensics team, said as he joined us. "Set up a radio signal from a hand-held laser aimed across the road. When the car breaks the laser beam, it sets off the bomb. Taking into account the speed limit on this road, it's a pretty simple calculation."

"Was traffic that light?" I asked. "How many cars—including the lead APC—might have broken the laser beam?"

"That's why I said hand-held," Kevin replied. "Switch it on as soon as the APC passed."

"I'm assuming they were targeted," I said to Novak. "Who knew they were driving this way today?"

"I already started checking that," he said. "They were going to an art gallery soirée, followed by dinner reservations at the Belvedere. This is on a direct route from their home to the gallery." He shrugged. "I called the gallery, and they had two hundred confirmations in answer to their invitations. At least twenty employees of the gallery, the five artists and their entourages, the press, and the caterers knew who was coming."

"Well, let's check whether any of those people have any connection whatsoever to the HLA."

Novak nodded. "Akiyama and Moncrieff weren't too happy with Justus Benning," he reminded me. The Novak and Benning

Families were allied, so Mychal was clued into Family politics, grudges, and feuds.

"Yeah, I know, but if this was a Family hit, it will be a miracle if we ever nail who was responsible. Let's focus on the HLA for now."

Later, when I talked on the phone to my boss, I was a little more truthful about how I felt.

"The HLA?" Whittaker asked. "Don't you think that's a strange coincidence?"

"To be honest? Can you convince my Granduncle George to cut off Courtney's access to a telephone? Limit her visitors? Do I think the vengeful bitch killed Justus Benning? Of course I do. Can we execute her without proving it? If so, I volunteer. She's tried to kill me at least twice, so we could call it self-defense."

Silence on the line, then a deep sigh. "Yes, I guess going after the HLA is our best bet. Carry on, Lieutenant James."

CHAPTER 14

The following morning, Carmelita and I showed up at Susan Reed's home.

"You're an aeromancer, so you can shield yourself, right?" I asked Carmelita.

"Yeah, sure. Stay close to me and I can shield you, too."

I shook my head. "If something goes down, shield yourself and don't worry about me. Just cover my back and I'll cover yours."

Susan answered the door looking a lot better than the first time I met her. In fact, she looked a lot like Carmelita did when she wore a Susan illusion.

"We heard about the hit on the Bennings," Carmelita-Dolores said. "We also heard that the cops busted some more HLA members."

"Where did you hear that?" Susan asked.

I chuckled. "It's not exactly a secret. Do you know a guy named Carl Beaver? Between him and Jurgen Schwartz, the Magi are getting a lot of information about the HLA. Do you mind if we come in?"

She acted like she wanted to say no, but Carmelita started

forward, and Susan backed up. The house was very nice inside, reflecting the way it looked from the outside. I had done some more research on Susan and discovered her parents had died in a car wreck a couple of years before. As an only child, she inherited the house and a large insurance payment. Since she didn't have to work, that left her free to spend her time scheming with the HLA.

It quickly became apparent that Susan wasn't the only one in the house. From the foyer, I could see through the living room to a room beyond where several people sat around a large table. There were also noises of people moving around upstairs.

"Freaking cop," a man's voice said from behind me as I moved farther into the house. "Freeze. Stay right where you are."

I did as he said, standing still and holding my hands away from my body.

"I'm not here as a cop," I said.

"Right," the man said, "and I'm the Easter bunny. Frankie, search her."

A young man to my right started forward. I cast a spell, disabling every firearm within ten feet of me by locking their triggers. It made my own pistol inoperable as well, but I had my father's lightning box in my pocket.

"Frankie," I said, batting my eyes at him and smiling, "touch me and I'll break both your arms."

I heard a pistol cock behind me. Dropping into a crouch and whirling about, I swung my leg out and caught someone in the side of the knee. He lost his balance and fell, dropping his pistol, which clattered against the floor. I was on him before he finished falling, grabbing him by the hair, holding him up, and dragging him in front of me as a shield.

I threw an arm bar across his throat, then drew my knife—a demon-hunter's special with a brass knuckle grip and a foot-long Bowie-type blade.

"We can be civilized, or not," I said. "Your choice. We walk in here offering to help, and you pull a gun on me. Now, let's make no mistake. I can take all of you out if I wanted to, or I could arrest all of you, if that's what I intended. You couldn't stop me. Yes, I'm a cop. Danica James, Hunter James's granddaughter. And if you think I have any love of the Magi, you're very mistaken." I looked over at Susan. "Dolores said you folks are serious. Who's in charge? I'm not in the mood to play games with a bunch of stupid kids."

The guy I was holding couldn't have been much older than twenty-one, and he was having trouble growing his first beard. None of the people I saw were any older than Susan.

Carmelita-Dolores laughed. "I told you she wasn't someone to screw around with. Carl's out of circulation. You need a magitek? I brought you the best. If you're not interested, there are other resistance fighters we can talk to."

"Let him go," Susan said.

"Gladly—he stinks. But with the understanding that I'm going to kill the next person who pulls a gun on me," I said, triggering the lightning box to send its lowest voltage charge at a lamp sitting on a table in the corner. It exploded, and everyone in the room jumped.

I let go of the guy I held, and he slid to the floor. A wet stain spread on the front of his jeans.

"Now," I said, "can we go to meet the people you said are the action guys?"

Susan turned and led us through the house and out onto the deck in the backyard. When the three of us were alone, she said, "That wasn't very smart. You could have been shot."

I shook my head. "Check it out. None of those guns work anymore. I'm a magitek, remember? Now, are you the person I need to talk to, or are you just a little girl playing revolution?"

Susan leaned on the rail and stared off into the distance. After a couple of minutes, she said, "Carl and Slobodan were two of the key operatives in this area. The HLA is really just a public front for the real revolutionaries, you know." She held her hand in front of her and let a flame play back and forth across her fingertips. "You're right. Those kids in there are playing revolution. But the people who are really serious are mostly magik users."

"Witches and mages from the lower social tiers," I guessed.

She gave me a lopsided grin. "And younger sons and daughters of the Hundred and the Families below that. Just like medieval Europe, you start slicing the pie too many times, and there isn't enough to go around. When one small group has ninety percent of the world's total wealth, they shouldn't be surprised when the masses want a taste. That's what happened to trigger the first atomic wars. The elites were too damned stupid to understand that people who are starving have nothing to lose."

Susan chuckled. "If the Magi weren't so self-absorbed and greedy, they would understand that the revolution could be bought off with ten percent of their wealth, and living standards for the whole world could be upgraded if they'd just manage to hoard twenty-five percent less."

"And what do you want?" Carmelita-Dolores asked.

With a shrug, Susan said, "A slice of the pie, just like everybody else."

She seemed to make a decision. Pushing herself away from the railing, she said, "I'm still not sure I trust you, but if you're a plant by the Magi, I'm screwed anyway. Meet me tomorrow night at Luigi's in Columbia. You know where it is?"

I nodded. An upscale Italian wine bar and restaurant run by a witch.

"They're closed tomorrow for a private function," Susan continued. "Tell the guards at the door that you're there for the cannelloni special. They'll ask if you're meeting someone. Tell them that Assunta is expecting you."

Carmelita gave her a strange look. "If we are working for the Magi, you're going to let us in, and you don't care? You aren't going to protect your comrades until your dying breath?"

Susan barked out a laugh. "You can probably find some people like that in the Movement, but I've found that most people care only about themselves. Like I said, you could buy off everyone in the world for a fraction of the money that the Magi wipe their asses with. People who have nothing aren't greedy. Me? Yeah, I'm greedy. Give me a couple of million, though, and I'll be happy."

※

Back in Baltimore, I stopped by Enchantments. I filed my report with Whittaker online from there, then waited around for Kirsten to close the store.

We wandered down to the harbor and hit a rowhouse pub called Jack's for beer and fresh oysters. On the way, I told her about Susan Reed's take on the world economy and revolution.

"She has a point," Kirsten said, "and witches do resent the mages. Let's face it, the top mage Families are bullies. I also understand Olivia's point of view. If it wasn't for the mages, we'd probably be dinner in a world ruled by demons, and no one wants that."

"Yeah," I said. "The way the Families live has always bothered me, though. You've seen how Findlay and Novak and the other powerful Magi live. Are gold-plated bathroom fixtures really necessary? Luxury foods flown in from all over the world? I mean, Mychal couldn't afford his suits on his cop salary, and we get paid three times as much as non-magikal cops of the same rank."

Kirsten shrugged. "If they didn't pay you that much, they wouldn't have any mages on the police force. You'd go to work for Whittaker's business, or for Osiris. A low-rank Findlay guardian makes as much as you do. The Families have money to burn."

Once we found a table at the restaurant and took receipt of the oysters and beer we ordered, I asked, "Are there any small business organizations that you belong to? I mean, some way to pool political power?"

She laughed. "Political power? Outside of the Hundred, that's a joke. The Magi control everything. Yeah, I'm a member of a couple of associations. That's how I get health insurance and property insurance for the shop and our house. There are associations that pool purchasing power, but I have very few competitors, and I try to sell unique goods. Not the sort of thing you buy in bulk quantities."

"Good evening," a deep male voice said. I looked up and discovered Aleksandr Janik standing over us. Tall, with dark-chocolate eyes, dark hair, tanned skin, and a wonderful smile that lit up his face. "I hope I'm not interrupting anything."

"Oh, no," Kirsten said. "I think we've pretty much solved all the world's problems. Join us?"

Janik hesitated and looked from her to me.

"Yeah," I said. "Do you like oysters?"

He pulled up a chair. "As a matter of fact, I do. That's why I dropped in, but the menu isn't usually as attractive as it is today." That was accompanied by a grin and a wink.

Kirsten laughed, and I blushed.

"Is that one of those lines you practice in the mirror?" I asked.

"It is," he said, his smile growing larger, "and I've been waiting ever since Marco's betrothal for a chance to use it."

I felt my face warm up even more. "You're terrible."

"I am, but only around you. I gave Kirsten my number so you could call me. Did she tell you?"

"Yes, but I've been busy."

"Oh. I'm sorry." He looked crestfallen.

"With work," Kirsten said. "Have you heard about the mage murders?"

"Ah. Of course. Yes, I have. So terrible."

"Dani isn't dating anyone," Kirsten said. "She just works all the time. She really needs a diversion."

I felt my eyes pop wide. I stared at her and tried to kick her under the table. She expected it and moved her leg so I kicked the table leg instead. She batted her eyes at me.

"Surely you don't work every night," Aleks said.

"She doesn't."

I wanted to kill Kirsten.

"No, I don't, but my schedule is rather erratic," I told him. "It makes it difficult to plan things."

"When is your next scheduled day off?" he asked. "Perhaps you could join me for dinner some evening."

I took a deep breath and tried to think. "It's supposed to be Friday, but I don't know, what with everything that's going on."

"Friday it is," he said. "You have my number, right? If you can't make it, call me. Now, where should I pick you up?"

CHAPTER 15

One of Courtney's attempts to murder me had resulted in the destruction of my motorcycle. Insurance companies don't make money by paying claims, so it practically took an act of God to convince them that I didn't burn up my bike on purpose. But they finally came through, and I ordered a new bike.

The motorcycle shop had called several days before to tell me it had arrived, but with various members of the Magi inconveniently getting murdered, I hadn't found time to pick it up. Since I was going to be working in the evening, attending Susan Reed's revolutionary happy hour, I took the morning off to claim my new bike.

I rode into town with Kirsten, then walked from her store over to the motorcycle shop.

Basically, the new bike was exactly like the one that was flambéed, just two years newer. But it didn't have the magitek customizations—gyroscopic stabilizers, turbocharger, electrical anti-theft system—not to mention the recoilless rifle for demon and monster hunting. The magitek enhancements were legal—although expensive if you weren't a magitek—and the recoilless rifle was legal only because I was a cop. Even so, the paperwork I had to fill out just to buy the damned weapon was insane.

I took the long way home, enjoying the fresh air as I rode over the Key Bridge across the Chesapeake Bay. The bike performed well, and although it wasn't quite comfortable yet, I was excited.

After wheeling the bike out to my shop in back, I was able to quickly attach the magitek devices. The magitek-powered recoilless rifle took a little longer to install, but I finished all the work in plenty of time to down a beer, take a shower, and ride back downtown to meet Carmelita.

We drove southwest from Baltimore to Columbia, which wasn't a city in the conventional sense, but rather a collection of villages and commercial areas surrounded by residences scattered through the forest. My understanding was that it was planned that way at the end of the twentieth century, and it really hadn't changed much. I knew the area fairly well because that's where Kirsten's parents lived.

Most of the area west and southwest of Baltimore, all the way to the Potomac River, had a lot of small towns and estates owned by mages, witches, and humans who comprised the upper echelon of the merchant and professional classes. If, as Susan Reed said, the Magi controlled ninety percent of the wealth, the next tier down probably controlled another five percent, and the remainder was split up among the ninety-nine percent of humanity below them.

To an extent, Susan was correct that the majority of humans were barely scraping by, but she, as did Kirsten and I, fell into the tier that controlled five percent of the wealth—those who weren't considered rich but never worried about missing a meal. I would have been surprised if Susan and her fellow revolutionaries truly planned to distribute the Magi's wealth among the masses. History's lessons were that revolutions simply changed who sat at the top of the social hierarchy, replacing the old lords and ladies with new ones.

I didn't really blame the revolutionaries, but I didn't have any sympathy for them, either. I completely rejected their methods. Mass murder, such as bombing the Palace of Commerce, offended my sense of right and wrong. A lot of salaried bureaucrats, not to mention maintenance and janitorial staff and people who just picked the wrong day to do business there, had died in those bombings, leaving their families to starve. And no one deserved to die the way Joseph and Elaine Greer did.

"You're awfully quiet," Carmelita said as we wound our way along the road leading to Luigi's in the village of Owen Brown.

"Thinking about revolution," I said, "and how it's usually just trading one master for another."

"You're right about that," she said. "Even the revolutions of the proletariat in the twentieth century left the proletariat still grubbing in the dirt and building their new masters' castles. But, hell, trying to claw our way to the top is what makes us human. If it wasn't for that stubborn refusal to accept our lot, we'd be demon food now."

"That's kind of what my roommate said, and she's not even a mage."

"Doesn't matter," Carmelita said. "I believe that humans would have fought the demons off even without magik users. We're just that damned stubborn. Of course, without magik users, we wouldn't have the Rift or the demons."

Without my grandfather we wouldn't have the Rift or the demons. I shot her a look, but she didn't seem to notice. Maybe I was just oversensitive and she didn't mean that as a dig at me.

She pulled into the parking lot for an apartment complex.

"You don't mind walking, do you?" she asked. "I prefer to leave the car here in case we have to leave in a hurry. If I die in there, you don't need keys, do you?"

I shook my head. "No, but I won't leave you in there. You have a premonition or something?"

"Naw, just trying to cover all the bases, that's all. I've felt like I'm walking on eggs ever since I started working on this case."

Luigi's was about a city-block's distance away. We walked over there and knocked on the door. The parking lot held half-a-dozen cars, most nondescript middle-class vehicles. We waited a couple of minutes, then a man pushed the door open and stuck his head out.

"We're closed tonight."

"We were hoping to get some of the cannelloni special," I said.

He cocked his head to the side and looked us over. "You meeting someone here?"

"Assunta."

Nodding, he pushed the door farther open and held it for us to walk past him. "Wait here."

"Turn off your phone," I murmured to Carmelita.

"Why?"

"So it still works after we leave."

She gave me a puzzled look, then her face cleared as she understood. I spent the next five minutes studying a menu while Carmelita-Dolores looked at the pictures hanging on the wall. Susan came from the back and motioned us to follow her.

"We're still waiting on a couple of people," she said. "It'll give me a chance to introduce you."

She led us to a back room where a dozen men and women milled around, drinking either beer or white wine and snacking on cheese and little meatballs. It was an eclectic group, ranging in age from Susan up to a white-haired woman with a million wrinkles who was riding in a powered wheelchair. I recognized a few people. A Baltimore businessman who was a vocal democracy advocate, a prominent doctor who was on the board of

Johns Hopkins Hospital, and a media newscaster with blonde hair as perfect in real life as it was on the screen in my kitchen.

No one even blinked as Susan introduced Carmelita as Dolores Hernandez, an emissary from the Mexico City HLA. But everyone knew who Danica James was, and few of them seemed happy to see me.

"I'm surprised," said Professor Alvin Blair, a tall man with dark, tousled hair, "that you expect to leave here alive. You must have a SWAT team waiting outside for your signal."

I batted my eyes and smiled at him. "I'm surprised you let me in at all. Most members of polite society prefer not to be seen with a James. You know how it is, your grandfather commits one *faux pas*, and your family is ostracized for all eternity." I leaned close and whispered conspiratorially, "If my intentions were nefarious, I wouldn't need a SWAT team."

Eventually, everyone who was expected arrived, and we sat around a large table. It quickly became apparent that the purpose of the meeting was to determine whether I should leave alive. Cute people, but I had to admire their honesty and forthrightness. None of that stab-you-in-the-back stuff.

I turned to the woman in the wheelchair. "Mrs. Donnelly," I said, "I assume you are the truthsayer?"

She gave me a toothless smile and nodded.

I returned her smile. "Well, ask your questions, but first I would like to say that I came here in good faith, under the assumption no one would try to murder me. But if that assumption is erroneous, I hope you all have your affairs in order. I haven't survived this long completely due to luck."

The smiles vanished. An hour later, they seemed satisfied that I really was unhappy with the world's rulers and ready to join their revolution. Obviously none of them, including their truthsayer, had ever dealt with the Fae. As I was only one quarter elf, I could lie, but my mother had raised me to believe that doing so was a terrible thing to do. Besides, avoiding the truth and telling a lie were two entirely different things, as any self-respecting Fae could have told them.

As Carmelita-Dolores and I walked out, I cast the spell that killed all the phones in the place. We hiked from the restaurant over to the apartment complex where we left her car.

"You said that's a department loaner?" I asked when we got about fifty feet away.

"Yeah, why?"

"So, you're not particularly attached to it?"

She shook her head.

"Well, let's leave the car and walk over to that bar we passed and I'll buy you a drink."

"Okay, sure."

We turned toward a footpath through the apartment complex that would lead to the bar. When I judged we were a safe distance away, I sent a surge of magik toward the car, setting off the bomb someone had placed under it. The explosion was very loud. Obviously, the charade we had just played was a formality. Someone at that meeting had decided ahead of time that we deserved to die.

"Holy shit!" Carmelita said, throwing up an air shield between us and the car. A fountain of flame shot about twenty feet into the air.

"I guess parking way over here wasn't as unobtrusive as we hoped it would be," I said. "Sweet folks, them revolutionaries. Axe murderers and car bombers. C'mon, let's go get that drink."

While we walked, I pulled out my phone and called Novak. "Hi. Carmelita's car just blew up. Big fireball." I gave him the address. "If you can make sure everyone knows there were two women inside, I'd appreciate it."

"Where are you now?" he asked.

"Walking over to the bar where you are. I could use a beer and a shot." I turned to my companion. "Carmelita?"

"Margarita. Make it a double."

I could hear sirens. The residents of the apartment complex had called the police and the fire department. Anyone who was parked close to Carmelita's sports car would be very unhappy since it was a very powerful bomb. Magikally enhanced. It seemed that Susan and her friends didn't need my magitek expertise. Either that, or Carl Beaver had made some devices I hadn't found at his house.

CHAPTER 16

The drag about being dead was that it left me without a place to sleep. Danica James getting blown up was news, so we knew the media would stake out my house as well as the road outside the Findlay estate. Carmelita had the same problem, but she said a friend of hers was low-key enough that no one would know about him.

"That's what happens when you work all the time and don't have any friends," Kirsten said when I called her. "What are you going to do? Sneak into the greenhouse at my shop?"

Both of us had done that a couple of times when we drank a little too much. It wasn't bad, warm with a comfy old chair.

I laughed. "The news media will probably have your shop staked out, too. No, I'll ride up to Mom's. No one will think to look for me up there, and the media are oblivious to us being related." Hell, the media probably didn't know my mother existed, in spite of her responsibility for supplying most of the electricity to the city of Baltimore.

"And what are you going to do about your date with Aleks Janik?" Kirsten asked.

I mentally checked a calendar and discovered it was Wednesday night. My date with Aleks was Friday.

"I don't know. I can't call him if I'm dead. Which reminds me, can you call Olivia? I certainly don't want her waking up to news that I've kicked the bucket. Whittaker should have the sense to call her and Osiris, but I'm not going to depend on it."

"Yeah, I can do that. I can call Aleks, too, if you want me to."

I thought about it. "I'll have Mychal tell him. They're buddies, right?"

Novak smuggled us into the police station, where Carmelita's boss gave her a new car and I retrieved my new bike. I called Mom, told her I was planning to spend the night, and took off, heading south. Once I got on the freeway, I turned north and let the motorcycle go. There was a slight possibility that someone in a helicopter might have been able to track me, but no one in a car was going to match my hundred miles per hour behind a magitek-enabled wind screen. And without the magitek device that made me invisible to the traffic monitors, any non-cop trying to follow me would be stopped before they went a mile.

By the time I reached Mom's house, I was close to being frozen solid and wondering if I could talk Mychal or Carmelita into helping me craft a magitek shielding device for the motorcycle. It was late fall, and winter was never any fun on a bike. The previous winter, I had driven my cop car most of the time, but using it when I wasn't working was a violation of department policy. No one would say anything unless I really abused the privilege, but as a lieutenant, I was supposed to be a good example.

"Hot tea?" Mom called out as I pushed through the front door.

"Please," I answered.

I shed my coat, gloves and helmet in the alcove and went

into the sitting room with the magikal 'fireplace.' Of course, no elven home would actually burn wood, but it looked and felt like a fire was roaring in the hearth. Two comfortable chairs sat in front of it with a low table between them.

I knew I was prejudiced, but I had always thought my mom was the most beautiful woman I had ever seen. She seemed to have the most attractive features of both human and elf. For either race, she came across as exotic, with her white-blonde hair, slanted green slit-pupiled eyes, high cheekbones, and curvy figure. Her body and face were rounded and softer than a pure-blood elf but harder, sharper, and slimmer than a human. At six-feet-four, she moved with a grace that human dancers could only envy.

From her, I had inherited my height, my boobs, the shape of my face, and the silver streaks in my brown hair, along with strength, speed, and reaction time beyond that of normal humans. According to her, I had also inherited elven empathy and a feeling for the world around me. And I inherited my magik from my father.

My chair was always the one on the left. Since I was only a quarter-elf, I was pretty much ambidextrous, whereas Mom was left-handed, like almost all elves. As I sat down, she pushed a steaming mug toward me, along with a double shot of pale-green *agavirna* in a small crystal glass. I took a sip of the powerful elven liquor, then a sip of tea.

"So, rough night?" she asked.

"Not too bad. Someone tried to kill me with a magitek bomb. Amateurs." I took another sip of *agavirna* and another sip of tea. Between the warmth within and the warmth without, I felt myself relax.

"Another one of your relatives, or the same one?"

"No, not Aunt Courtney or another Findlay this time. Revolutionaries. Anti-Magi, anti-Rifters. You know, overthrow the oppressors while lining their own pockets. They're probably all under arrest by now. But I'm supposed to be dead, at least for a little while. So, I'm on paid leave. Need any help with anything around here?"

I knew that all the participants in that meeting at Luigi's were followed when they left. The plan was to arrest them at their destinations, along with everyone else found there. At least forty people had been arrested by the time I left the police station. Luigi had also been arrested, his restaurant closed, and he was out of business. That was regrettable because he was a great chef.

"Feel like doing maintenance on the generators?" she asked.

"Sure. Room and board?"

"I'll take that deal," she said with a grin, holding up her shot glass. I clinked mine against hers, and tossed the liquor back, then took another sip of tea.

We talked for a little while, she fed me a chicken pie when she discovered I hadn't had dinner, then we went to bed. It had been a few years since I slept in my own bed, my own room. It seemed smaller than I remembered it.

Before the Rift opened, the dam at Loch Raven Reservoir was just that—a dam. It held the water from two rivers in a flooded valley and provided drinking water for Baltimore City.

As the polar and Greenland ice caps melted and it became evident that the oceans were rising, governments began paying serious attention to global climate change. Then many major coastal cities were turned into thermonuclear infernos during the Dislocation Wars. For some reason, Baltimore was spared from being bombed, as was Wilmington on the Atlantic side of the Delmarva Peninsula, and they became the major seaports on the east coast.

With coal and nuclear-generated power becoming untenable, turbines were installed at both the north and south ends of Loch Raven Reservoir—where the Gunpowder River flowed in and where it flowed out. Those turbines powered electric generators to supply the Baltimore-Washington Metropolitan electrical grid. Other sources included wind and wave generators on Chesapeake Bay and in the Atlantic, and turbines installed on the Potomac.

My father, Lucas James, engineered the Loch Raven turbines. While they were being installed, he met the Gunpowder Falls Park ecologist, a half-elf named Amelie Jorensdottir, and they became friendly enough to produce me. And now that he was gone, I unofficially maintained the magitek enhancers on the generators that increased their electrical output by a hundred times. Mom could maintain everything except the magitek devices, and if I wasn't around, she would call my grandmother and ask to borrow another magitek to do the work.

I doubted that more than a couple of dozen people in the entire metro area knew that Findlay and James actually controlled a large portion of the electricity that fueled the city. Mom could really care less if the whole Metroplex went dark—she didn't use any electricity herself, except for her truck—but she took the money the Families paid her to keep it running. Elves didn't have much use for human technology, but they understood human economies and finance just fine.

So, after breakfast, I wandered over to the dam and took an elevator down to where the turbines were located. I checked everything out and didn't find anything that needed repair or maintenance, which I expected. Mom was a competent engineer, and there was nothing magikal about the turbines, but it was always a good idea to check the entire system from end to end.

I took the elevator up to the generators. Water turned the

turbines, which powered the generators, which produced electricity. Then a pair of magitek enhancers on each generator multiplied the electricity. Dad once told me that we could hook up a laser to one of the generators and probably barbeque a chicken in West Virginia.

There were eight turbines housed within the dam, so sixteen magitek enhancers to service. Mostly it was checking to ensure they were working properly, not leaking magik or deteriorating due to age. Magikal spells didn't last forever unless they were extremely strong. I finished half of them in the morning, stopped for lunch, then verified the other half before dinner.

When I got back to her house, Mom had a stringer of yellow perch she had caught.

"I wondered if you might like to grill these," she said.

There was a hopeful look on her face that almost caused me to laugh. Elves didn't burn wood—not even dead, dried-out wood that had naturally died or limbs that fell from a tree. But my father had turned her on to fresh fish grilled over an open fire, and she loved it. After he left us, she would have me start a fire and cook the fish.

"Sure, let me get washed up," I said. "By the way, we need to replace an enhancer on generator six, and it probably wouldn't hurt to do a full replacement on that entire turbine assembly. It's out of balance and kind of wonky."

She nodded. "I have the funds in the budget. Will the enhancer hold out until the new turbine arrives? Probably take six to eight weeks."

"Yeah. It will take me that long to get the new enhancers built. Did I tell you we started a business, a factory? Mary Sue and I? Olivia's financing it for a third of the profits."

Mom laughed. "Does that mean all my new enhancers will be pink?"

"I'm sure that can be arranged."

I set up the grill on a rocky beach on the river downstream

from the dam, gathered dead wood, and started a fire. Mom came down with the fish, some fresh vegetables, a jug of her homebrewed beer, and a couple of wooden folding chairs she had made. I grilled the fish and veggies, she poured the beer, and we sat by the fire and ate as we watched the sunset.

"It's good to have you home, sometimes," she said, a satisfied smile on her face. "We haven't done this very much since you started on the police force."

"Kirsten and I were out here twice last summer," I said.

"I meant just you and me. Like when you were little."

I laughed. "I don't remember you letting me drink beer when I was little."

She shrugged. We watched the stars come out, and when the fire died down and the night got cold, we gathered up all our things, and our trash, and hiked back to the house.

CHAPTER 17

The following day, I hauled my kayak out of the garage and paddled up to where the Gunpowder River flowed into the reservoir. Two run-of-the-river turbines were installed there. The output from them didn't feed into the main power grid, and the funds to operate and maintain them came from different sources. One generated electricity for the Findlay estate, and the other sent electricity to the Findlay shipyard in Wilmington. The excess electricity was routed to the Novak estate at a below-market price.

As I inspected the eastern generator, I thought about all the work I had done on that system since I was fourteen years old, and that until recently I had never met anyone from the Novak Family. Mychal and his twin were only two years younger than I was, and I found it curious that my grandmother never tried to marry me off to either of them. She'd certainly tried to set me up with every other eligible bachelor in the Mid-Atlantic.

By the time I got back to Mom's house, I was regretting my decision to travel by kayak. Muscles I hadn't used in more than a year were signaling their profound displeasure.

To my surprise, she had company. When I carried the kayak

up from the river, I saw a fancy European car parked in the driveway. I put the kayak away and circled around the back of the house. I didn't recognize the car, and I was officially dead.

The back stairs led to the bedroom level, where I knew there wouldn't be any visitors. For one thing, anyone the house didn't know wouldn't find any of the bedrooms, only a long hallway that spiraled up to the cupola, which my engineering training actually labeled as a belvedere. I doubted that the elves really cared about human labels, though, and the structure was usually translated as a cupola.

Quietly advancing to the top of the inside stairs, I heard voices downstairs—my mom, Kirsten, Mychal, and then Aleks. I listened for another minute and didn't hear anyone else.

"Dani," Mom called, "you can come down. Everyone here knows you're alive."

Thanks, Mom. Aleks might know I was alive, but after a day of working on turbines and generators, not to mention paddling twenty-five miles, I doubted I was very attractive.

"I'm a mess," I called back. "Let me take a shower."

After the shower, which included washing my hair, I was presented with another problem. I didn't have much of a selection in the way of clean clothing. The only clothes I brought with me from Baltimore was what I was wearing. I stood in front of my closet and perused the outfits in it. It was an interesting gestalt moment comparing my current tastes to those from my university days. Then I discovered the clothes proved to be a bit snug. Especially the tops. Nothing like an in-your-face reminder that I was maturing.

Nothing to be done about it. I used a magitek device to dry my hair, applied minimal makeup, checked my image in a mirror, and went downstairs.

The kitchen had a new table that wasn't there that morning —or maybe I should say that the table in the breakfast nook had grown, as had the nook. The house reconfigured itself as needed. The four of them sat around the table with an empty chair between Aleks and Kirsten. A bottle of wine, five glasses, and a platter of bread and cheese adorned the table.

Aleks practically knocked his chair over jumping to his feet. He pulled out the vacant chair for me. I remembered the lessons in manners and etiquette I had suffered through at Findlay House when I was younger. Although a lot of the mannerisms the Magi affected were somewhat over the top, and I absolutely didn't need a man to take care of me, the demonstration of respect did feel good.

"Thank you," I said as I sat down. "Is that grape?" Referring to the wine. Mom's hobby paid her more than her salary. Winery, brewery, and distillery. She was a wizard at turning healthy food into booze, and the Magi fell all over themselves bidding on what she produced.

"Sour Cherry," Mom said.

I felt my face warm when I realized that I'd licked my lips. Aleks filled my glass, and I took a sip of some of the gods' own nectar.

"I am amazed at your mother's wine," Aleks said.

I chuckled. "Most people are." I leaned close to him. "She cheats. Magik."

Everyone laughed.

"Not just wine," Kirsten said. "There's nothing like a hot toddy made with her chestnut liqueur."

Mom shrugged. "Everyone should have a hobby, and living alone out here, I have plenty of time to play with various ideas."

I loaded a slice of bread with several different cheese samples. The wine and bread were Mom's, the cheese came from various elven and human craftsmen. She usually traded her wine, beer, and spirits for those things she didn't make, grow, or hunt herself.

"So, what's the news?" I asked between bites.

"One hundred nineteen arrests as of the last count I heard,"

Mychal said. "The one major name still at large is Susan Reed. She slipped the roundup and disappeared." His face grew somber. "Someone discovered where Carmelita hid on Wednesday night. They broke into her friend's apartment. She killed two men and escaped, but her friend was killed. She's out at Domingo House now."

"So, is there any point in me continuing to play dead?"

Mychal shrugged. "If I were you, I'd hang out and relax until Whittaker calls you in. When was the last time you actually had a few days in a row off from work?"

Kirsten laughed. "She doesn't know what to do with herself if she isn't dodging bullets or wrestling with monsters. What's she going to do out here?"

"Grill the fish we're having for dinner tonight," Mom said. "I have a couple of walleye that should feed this group quite well."

The fish turned out to be about five pounds each, enough to feed twice as many people as we had. We set up the grill and repeated the dinner Mom and I had the previous evening. It was a little louder and more boisterous. Mom seemed to enjoy it, and I couldn't remember having that kind of party out there since Kirsten and I were at university.

When our visitors got ready to go back into town, I suddenly ended up alone with Aleks outside.

"Not exactly the date you had in mind," I said.

"I loved it. Your mother is quite incredible."

I smiled. "Yeah, she is."

He reached for me and pulled me into his arms. We were the same height, standing nose to nose, looking into each other's eyes.

"You are also quite incredible," he said. And then he kissed me. It was a very nice kiss, and when he drew back, studying my face to gauge my reaction, I leaned in and tried it again. Nice the second time, too.

"Maybe we can still do that dinner sometime," I said.

"I would like that. Let me know when you're resurrected."

I laughed and kissed him a couple of more times before Mychal and Kirsten reappeared and they all drove off.

The following day, I helped Mom cure meat and can fish for winter. We didn't work very hard, though. Aleks called around noon, asking me out to dinner. I still hadn't been officially told I could go out in public, so I suggested that he drive up to Mom's and from there we could go to one of the bayside seafood shacks where I was unlikely to be recognized. It was nice to have a man offer to take me to a fancy restaurant, but I knew a dozen places with great food at half the price and a tenth the pretention.

Again, I had a problem with something to wear. I could borrow something from Mom that fit me up top, but I was a little too hippy for her pants, and her taste in dresses was decidedly elven. I didn't want to stand out that much in a backwater bar and grill.

In the end, I wore a wrap dress that had hung in the closet for the past ten years. As I studied myself in the mirror, I noted that I had been a lot more extroverted back then. The dress left no doubt that I had legs.

I had warned Aleks not to dress up too much, but his Magi concept of 'dress casual' was definitely a lot fancier than I expected. It was Saturday night, though, a lot of the locals were out on date night, and older couples tended to get dolled up for such things.

I think he was a little surprised at the quality of the food, but he shouldn't have been. People who had lived by the water for generations had a pretty good idea what to do with food that came out of the water.

After dinner, he took me home, and after about five minutes of kissing and pawing each other, it seemed a little silly to stand outside in the cold, so I invited him in.

He was slow and gentle when I wanted him to be, hard and strong when I wanted that, and delightfully funny.

"You know that I'm not making or looking for any kind of commitment," I said at one point. "Just fun, right?"

He smiled. His voice dropped into a deep purr that sent shivers down my spine. "Right. I always had you figured for a good-time girl. Love 'em and leave 'em Dani." He licked me and the shivers ran wild. "That's okay. I'm used to rejection. Just be gentle when you throw me out in the street."

I found it difficult to believe that he got rejected very often. We didn't get a lot of sleep, and I didn't mind. Mom winked at me when we went downstairs around noon and fixed us breakfast without a word. Aleks stuck around all day, and we took a hike around the reservoir, then ate dinner with Mom. He stayed the night again, but took off very early on Monday morning.

"I have a meeting with Lady Olivia Findlay-James this morning," he said as he kissed me goodbye, "and I really don't want to have to explain why I'm late."

"Coward."

"I admit it. I'm booked up tonight, but I'll call you tomorrow when I'm finished with work."

"You don't have to."

He gave me a wicked grin. "Well, in that case, I'll call you only if I want to."

CHAPTER 18

Whittaker called me about ten o'clock. "Where are you?"
"Hiding out, like you told me to. Remember? I'm supposed to be dead."

Silence, then, "Well, not any more. Someone knew that Domingo was still alive and tracked her to her friend's house."

"A leak?" I asked.

"Possibly. Anyway, I need you in here. We have a rash of murders that look like demons killing mages."

Wonderful. "Okay, I can be there in about an hour."

As I rode into the city, I thought about what Whittaker had said. Demon killings weren't rare, but it was unusual for them to attack mages. Of course, with Ashvial gone, there wasn't a central authority among the demons in the Mid-Atlantic.

No one really understood power relationships among demons, only that they were hierarchical. On the human side of the Rift, demon lords were the top level, but considering that the dozen of them we knew about on Earth weren't at war with each other for supremacy raised the question of what was above them. Some type of demon we had never seen on our side of the Rift? Or a demon that we didn't know about? If I were the demon king of Earth, I might prefer to stay anonymous rather than chance the combined power of the Hundred showing up on my doorstep.

And then there was that statuette Ashvial had in his office. A possibly living sculpture that looked exactly like a being I had seen in my dreams several times before ever seeing the statue. We knew that demons communicated across the Rift, and there was evidence from the traffic in cross-Rift drugs that they could travel both ways. Could that statue be a means of communication?

The second I set foot in the police station, people I ran into told me, "Whittaker is looking for you." After the tenth person said that, I decided I should probably go see him before I did anything else.

"About time you showed up," he greeted me.

"I usually do when I know I'm expected to." I dropped into a chair in front of his desk. "Demons killing mages?"

His frown deepened. "Killing Magi. A rash of demon attacks all over the Metroplex, and it appears members of the Hundred are being targeted. They are too similar to brush off as random assaults." He took a sip of his coffee. "That's what I need you to concentrate on this morning, but you should also be aware that there has been another assassination similar to that of Justus Benning. Mavis Dressler was ambushed last night on her way home from the opera."

Mary Sue's grandmother. Not the head of the Dressler Family, but like my grandmother, the sister of the Family head. Benning was a Novak ally, and Dressler was a Findlay ally. I couldn't remember an obvious assassination like that since I had joined the police force. If I counted the failed attempt on my grandmother, that would make three in a few weeks.

"Have there been any other such assassinations lately?" I asked, "Or assassination attempts?"

Whittaker stared at me, his mouth pursed in displeasure.

Finally, he said, "A couple of attempts. One on my son, but we assumed that was because he's a cop. An attempt on Liam Flanagan in Ireland last month. The murders at your cousin's betrothal ball. Gunther Janik died in the POC bombing in Prague, but I wouldn't put that in the same category. A lot of Magi died in the bombings here and in Prague."

"Any deaths among the Akiyama or Moncrieff allies?"

He shook his head. "Not that I know of, nor among any of the Zhow alliance."

There were ten member Families of the Magi Council. Akiyama and Zhow were headquartered in the Far East, Antonov and Morozov in Russia. The others were mainly of Western European descent. The virus that caused the magik mutations had not spread widely in Africa or Southern Asia. The Carvalho and Domingo Families controlled Central and South America.

"And the demon murders?" I asked.

Again he shook his head. "Mostly younger Family members. People who aren't closely guarded, but again, allies of Novak, Carvalho, Findlay, Domingo, Gelner, or Kennedy."

Those were the Families among the Ten known as the Western Alliance.

"If I had a suspicious nature, I might think someone was trying to shift the balance of power on the Council," I said.

"If you didn't have a suspicious nature, you wouldn't be a very good cop. Now, get out of here and find the demons doing these killings and who is behind them. There is easier prey than mages."

Whittaker gave me an address on the south side of the harbor where a demon-mage battle occurred earlier that morning. I took the bike and rode over there. The day had taken on a decided chill, and I made a mental note to ask my partner about building a magitek air shield.

The Federal Hill area had gentrified before the wars, and

before the water in the harbor rose, and again afterward. The area had originally been row houses, and all of the restorations had attempted to keep the look of the old neighborhood. Lots of young professionals and younger Magi lived there, among the bars, restaurants, and trendy shops they attracted.

I had no trouble finding the murder scene. A two-block area was cordoned off, with crowds of curious people, news media, and so many drones flying around overhead that they were running into each other. I drove inside the police cordon and parked my bike.

"Sergeant," I waved a uniformed cop over. "Tell the media types that they have five minutes to pull their drones out of the area, or I'm going to order you and your men to start shooting them down."

He grinned. "Yes, ma'am."

I stood there, in full view of several reporters, pulled a cube out of my pocket, and aimed a lightning bolt at a drone that was obviously in violation of several laws. It crashed to the ground about ten feet in front of me, and I kicked it aside as I walked past it.

It was obvious pretty quickly that I was late to the scene. The bodies had all been gathered up and transported to the morgue, but the blood and gore remained. I went looking for my partner.

"When?" I asked Novak when I found him.

"Last night, sometime after they left the bars, but before sunrise. We had the first report at about four o'clock, and the fighting was over by the time our people got here at four twenty-two."

There were multiple outlines drawn in chalk that I could see, on both sidewalks and on the street.

"How many?"

Novak shook his head. "We found seventeen human bodies out here on the street. We've cordoned off a four-block area.

There were also casualties inside several of the houses. Another three dead and five injured. Witnesses say some of the residents tried to help the people being attacked on the street."

"And we're sure the attackers were demons?"

"The five dead demons we found tend to support that assumption."

I sucked in a deep breath. Novak took me around the area so I could see the aftermath of the carnage. We also examined the three houses the demons had attacked. I thought about those cops I overheard at the station who were gung-ho about fighting demons.

I let Novak deal with the crime scene and rode over to the morgue. The place was a madhouse, as the staff there tried to sort out the bodies and match body parts to their owners. I found Kelley Quinn, who looked like a woman who needed a stiff drink.

"I realize it's a little early," I said to her, "but what do you have so far?"

She stopped, looked around, and said, "What do you need?"

"Identifications if you have them. COD is pretty evident. But I need to try and piece together what happened. Preliminary information from the scene indicates the demons ambushed them as they left a bar."

Kelley closed her eyes for a long moment. When she opened them, there was something haunted in her face. "Young mages. Some we're going to identify only by DNA. The bodies are too mangled. The demons we recovered are all standard demons, and they were all killed with magik."

She picked up a tablet and tapped on it, then turned it so I could see the screen. All five demons were registered as employees of Lucifer's Lair, with Ashvial's bar listed as their place of residence. Ashvial was dead and the bar was closed down. At least two hundred demons had lived there, and at least half of them had escaped his demise and the subsequent raid by the police that took possession of the premises.

"Do you have anything on the mages?" I asked.

She tapped on the tablet some more and showed me the screen.

"Thanks, Kelley," I said. "Let me know when you have final results."

"I do have some results on the other murders," Quinn said.

"Other murders?"

"Yeah, that bar the demons took apart out in Columbia, the vampire rampage in Canton, and the three demons who busted up the bar in Annapolis. Fourteen dead, more than thirty in the hospital, and that's not counting minor injuries."

"When did all this happen?"

"Last night. Where have you been? It's the only thing that's been on the news."

"In a different world. Send me everything you have."

She nodded, then turned away to answer a question from one of her staff.

I headed back to the Federal Hill slaughter site and found Novak. He appeared as tired as I was beginning to feel.

"It looks as though we have five different groups who left a bar called the Devil's Den when it closed." He pointed to the bar at the end of the street. "That was about four o'clock this morning. As soon as they got out on the street, the demons attacked. A brawl ensued, and the humans got the worst of the deal."

"All drunk and probably didn't understand what was going on," I said.

Mychal nodded. "Probably. Some of them fought back. There are scorch marks from fireballs and lightning on the walls of the houses and on the street."

"How many survived?"

"We have five people in hospital, and seven who came out of the fight unharmed or with minor injuries."

"You've talked to all of them?"

"Yeah. I sent you the interviews."

"Any common denominators?"

He nodded. "Fairly predictable. The bar is a hangout for younger members of Novak and its allies. David Moncrieff and Joseph Johansson are the owners of the bar."

"Have you talked to whoever runs the bar?"

"I was waiting for you."

I gave him a raised eyebrow.

"Remember your experience at the Devil's Reef?" he asked. "The Devil's Den has the same ownership and a demon manager. I try to learn from my more experienced colleagues and not repeat their mistakes. Backup, ya know?"

My face flamed. I was lucky the manager at the Devil's Reef was a bad shot.

"I'm glad to see you're following procedure," I said. "I'll note it on your next performance evaluation."

His smirk didn't help my mood.

It turned out that the bar manager was a little more intimidating than the ifrit I had encountered at the Devil's Reef. Silthraxith was a major demon. Seven-and-a-half feet tall, wide as a door, green, with curving horns, and hair covering her head and shanks. Fire demons were usually red, or at least a shade of pink. Frost demons were some shade of blue. I wasn't sure what power a green demon wielded, but I wasn't in a hurry to find out.

A female demon wasn't something I expected. And since she wasn't wearing any clothing, her sex was readily apparent. She had a sidekick who was a demon of the same race who she didn't bother to introduce. He was about six inches shorter than she was, had less hair on his head and back, and was likewise green and naked.

To my knowledge, no one had ever determined if demons were mammalian and used their breasts to nurse. And if not, did they have breasts in their own world, or only in ours?

"Lieutenant Danica James, Metro Arcane Division," I said, showing my badge. "This is Detective Sergeant Novak. We're investigating the excitement outside this morning."

Silthraxith smiled, displaying a remarkable set of dentition, complete with three-inch canines. "As you say, Lieutenant, it happened outside. I run a peaceful establishment. It is up to your human police to keep order on the street." Her voice was remarkable, sibilant and rather melodious. Not at all what I normally associated with a demon.

"Well, in that case, I'm going to have to close all the bars in this area to assist our efforts to keep order. We can't have any more incidents such as the one we had this morning."

The grin slid off her face, and steam began rising from her. Literally steam. I had heard of water demons but never seen one. They were pretty rare in eastern North America.

"I don't think my employers will be very happy about that."

"Tell them to take their complaint to Deputy Police Commissioner Whittaker," I said, handing her my business card along with Whittaker's. "But until further notice, I'm declaring this place and every other drinking establishment in a four-block radius as part of a crime scene."

She licked her lips with a foot-long forked tongue, and her eyes narrowed.

"I doubt you have the authority to do that," she said.

I shrugged. "Ashvial had some doubts about my authority, too. In the end, his opinion didn't matter very much. And as for David Moncrieff and Joseph Johansson, they aren't in a position to say anything. Moncrieff is in protective custody, and Johansson is busy trying to distance himself from his father's business dealings." The third owner of record, Ashvial, wouldn't be lodging any protests in Earth's realm.

Novak and I walked out, and the demons didn't try to stop us. When we got outside, Novak took a couple of the little magitek boxes that all cops were issued, set them on either side of the door, and activated them. They didn't require a mage to make them work, but they created a yellow barrier over the doorway. No entrance.

Of course, the demons could let customers in through the back door, and the city would pull their business license. Since they were demons, they would also be barred from ever working anywhere on Earth again. That would mean having to live in the Waste. It was part of the truce agreement that allowed demons to stay in our dimension.

CHAPTER 19

No sooner had Mychal and I finished dealing with the demon than we ran into Garland Novak, Mayor of the Baltimore-Washington Metroplex. Like me, Garland was a bastard, the son of Franklin Novak and an untalented human woman. For the first time, I realized that he was Mychal's half-brother, although twenty or thirty years older.

"Mr. Mayor," I said, stopping in my tracks. The alternative would have been to knock him down and walk on his body, and I doubted my boss would approve of that.

"What's going on down here? Someone called my office and said you were shutting down all the businesses in the area."

Bad news traveled faster than light, evidently. I had spoken to the demon only two minutes before, and hadn't mentioned a shutdown to anyone else.

"This area is a crime scene," I said, "and begging your pardon, but you shouldn't be here either. You could be contaminating evidence."

I heard Mychal snort behind me, followed by a coughing fit.

"You can't just shut down all these businesses!"

"Excuse, me," I said, and pointed down. "We might need

that spleen to help identify a victim, and I'm sure his or her family would want to bury as much of the body as we can recover."

The Mayor looked down and realized his foot was partially on a bloody body part. He stared at it and turned pale.

"Mychal! Can you get him out of here before he pukes?"

My partner brushed past me, grabbed his half-brother by the arms, and steered him toward an alley that seemed to be blood-free.

If the scene in front of me wasn't so dire, I might have laughed, but there was no humor in the carnage around me. I was impressed with Mychal and how much he had progressed in a few weeks. He was handling things much better than the first slaughter scene he and I had worked together.

It was pretty obvious what had happened. When the bar closed, a couple of dozen young, drunken mages spilled out into the street, heading for their cars or walking home. It wasn't a main street, but rather a mostly residential street paralleling the main north-south street through the Federal Hill area, connecting the Inner Harbor with the Patapsco River bridge. Shortly afterward, a group of demons attacked them. Those who survived, and witnesses from the houses along the street, agreed there were between twenty-five and thirty demons.

For the most part, demons hunted alone or in pairs. They only staged such coordinated attacks at the direction of higher demons. With Ashvial dead, there were no demon lords in the area that we knew about, but the Arcane Division estimated there might be as many as a thousand major demons in the Metroplex. I could accuse Silthraxith of ordering the attack, but I had no proof. And for all I knew, there could be a dozen other major demons within a few blocks of where I stood.

But why?

It seemed too much of a coincidence that two bars owned by my Aunt Courtney's husband, David Moncrieff, should be involved in major violent incidences within a few of weeks of each other. And then there were the other attacks to take into account.

As I pondered that, my phone rang.

"James."

"What's going on down there?" my boss asked. "The Mayor is upset that you're closing down all the businesses."

"Only the bars in the vicinity of the crime scene," I answered. "And the Mayor is an idiot."

"I won't dispute that," Whittaker said.

"Is there any way you and Olivia can talk my Uncle George into locking down Courtney Findlay-Moncrieff?"

A long silence followed. Before he could respond, I asked, "How many bars does David Moncrieff own? And how many of them are run by demons? How many coincidences can dance on the head of a pin?"

I heard a barked laugh on the other end of the phone.

"I'm having a difficult time figuring out why this attack happened, or any of the other Rifter brawls we had last night," I said. "Remember the Rifter riots downtown that ended with Ashvial's death? Wouldn't you agree that the amount of civil unrest we're seeing lately is unusual? HLA. Rifter riots. Rifters attacking young mages. Akiyama's, Johansson's, and Moncrieff's criminal activities. A demon army south of Annapolis. The bombings of two Palaces of Commerce. Either the world has suddenly gone crazier than usual, or some of this ties together."

Whittaker tapped his fingers on his desk so loudly that it was audible across the phone. "It's not just here. Similar problems have occurred in the British Isles and Europe. Maybe we should discuss this with the Magi Council. I'll get back to you."

That evening, I found myself in a circular room that I'd never seen before in Police Headquarters. It looked exactly like the Magi Council room in the bombed Palace of Commerce—a room that no longer existed in a building that was in the process of demolition.

A semi-circular bench along one side was raised higher than the rest of the room. Sitting in high-backed chairs were the ten Family heads of the ten richest and most powerful mage Families in the world. Franklin Novak chaired the meeting, with my Granduncle George Findlay on his right. The others were Akiyama Benjiro, Hugh Kennedy, Zhow Dong Fun, Antonio Carvalho, Santiago Domingo, Jakob Gelner, Ivan Morozov, and Roman Antonov.

None of the Family heads were really in the room with me, although Thomas Whittaker, Mychal Novak, Carmelita Domingo, Luis Capellino, Osiris Dillon, and a dozen other people involved with Arcane security in the Mid-Atlantic region were. The Council members were illusions, projected magikally, as were a couple of hundred other people in the audience from around the world.

There were live representatives and a truthsayer from each Family of the Ten, and such people would be physically present in all the other rooms around the world where people gathered for the meeting. To say that the Magi weren't very trusting would be an understatement. It was quite a production.

I had sat in tribunals in the old Council Chambers, usually as a witness to the proceedings, but sometimes to give testimony. For a tribunal, there were usually three Councilors present, sometimes five, and sometimes only one. The one I had attended with five Councilors was the trial of a sixteen-year-old boy who was subsequently sentenced to spend the rest of his life at the penal colony in Antarctica. Since the Councilors were all Family heads, they tended to take a dim view of patricide.

My boss, Deputy Commissioner Thomas Whittaker, made a presentation detailing the chaos going on around the world, specifically focusing on demon attacks and incursions. He also provided an update on the investigation of the Palace of Commerce bombing in Baltimore.

Then a man named Piotr Janik gave a report on the POC bombing in Prague, including a clamp down on the HLA throughout Europe. Luis Capellino reported on our investigation of the HLA in the Mid-Atlantic.

Osiris followed by telling the Council about the discovery of a human trafficking conspiracy involving Akiyama, Moncrieff, Johansson, and Ashvial, and the raid on the Moncrieff estate on the Elk Neck Peninsula outside of Baltimore. He mentioned Ashvial's death without naming the person who killed him.

Whittaker concluded by outlining the results of my investigation into the deaths of the head of the Rosenblum Family at Lila's betrothal ball, the attempts on my life, that of my grandmother, and of Liam Flanagan, and the new murders of Justus Benning, Joseph and Elaine Greer, and Aaron Carpenter.

When Whittaker finished, Franklin Novak said, "This is all very disturbing. What is it that you think this Council can do?"

Akiyama Benjiro spoke using a translation spell. "It doesn't appear as though there is much for the Council to do. The Rifters, especially demons, have always been a problem. If Deputy Commissioner Whittaker and his counterparts in other places are not up to the job of keeping the demons in line, we should replace them with people who can. We are having no such problems in China."

"And what about the involvement of David Moncrieff and Akiyama Hiroku in human trafficking?" my Uncle George asked.

"I have seen no proof," Benjiro said, "only wild accusations and pointless speculation. Uncorroborated tales about my honorable uncle from the granddaughter of Hunter James. Everyone knows she has a grudge against my Family, even though there has never been any proof we were involved with the demons who killed her father. Her Family is the reason for these problems. They are disgraced, and she attempts to pull others down with her."

"Her Family is Findlay," Uncle George said. "We do have proof of the trafficking allegations, which was provided to all members of the Council. What I'm concerned about is the coordination of all these various demon attacks. And do we really think a bunch of rag-tag hippies such as the HLA have the resources to blow up two of the most secure facilities in the world?"

"I have listened to enough of this slander," Benjiro said.

"I see no case to concern this Council," said Zhow Dong Fun, head of the Family headquartered in Canton, China. Although they weren't formally allied with the Akiyama Family, they were close business partners, their domains overlapped, and they often saw their interests as being aligned against what they considered western attempts at dominating the Council.

"I'm afraid I disagree," Franklin Novak said. "I am ordering a tribunal to assess the human trafficking accusations against David Moncrieff, Martin and Joseph Johansson, Courtney Findlay-Moncrieff, Akiyama Hiroku..." He named a couple of dozen more people, including two Akiyama ship captains, several lower-level functionaries, and even Aunt Courtney's butler.

"This is outrageous!" Benjiro erupted. "Either you set my uncle free in the next twenty-four hours, or I shall consider all orders of this Council as without authority. I see what is happening here. The Western Alliance is trying to take over the Council, subjugate the East, take our trade, and enslave our populace. You shall pay for such disrespect!"

His image vanished, followed almost immediately by that of Zhow.

"What the hell?" I asked Whittaker after the meeting ended.

"I think that's a declaration of war," he said, "but I'm not sure. We haven't had a war since we reached a truce with the Rifters."

Osiris heaved a deep sigh. "This isn't about human trafficking. Our intelligence has been warning us that Benjiro is deeply immersed in a philosophy of Shinto Nationalism, which led to Japan's imperialistic invasions that started the second world war. His father was far more reasonable, but Benjiro was born after the Rift War. He seems to think he can ally with the demons and not get his tail burned."

CHAPTER 20

As I was getting ready to go to bed, I answered the phone and heard my mother speaking Elvish.

"There's been a coup at Findlay. Do you remember your favorite place to go fishing when you were twelve?"

"Yes."

"Be there in the morning at seven. Make sure you're not followed."

She hung up. I stood there, stunned and staring at the phone. The number she had called from wasn't one I recognized.

"What's going on?" Kirsten asked.

"That was Mom. She said there was a coup at Findlay."

The Ten had been stable during my lifetime. Changes in power—internecine struggles—happened on a regular basis in different Families, but not at the very top of the hierarchy. Granduncle George had been in power since my father was a boy. The only other incident I could remember shaking up the top levels at Findlay was when my father and Granduncle Richard were killed when I was thirteen.

"Is your grandmother okay?"

"I don't know. Mom didn't say. She wants me to go out to Harper's Ferry. Seven o'clock in the morning."

"Well, we'd better get going then. I'll get food and water, you get clothes and your weapons."

I let what Mom told me sink in. A coup. If the attack had come from outside the Family, she would have used a different word. That had to mean Aunt Courtney, who was the most powerful mage of her generation in the family. And that meant I was in danger, which meant Kirsten was in danger, too.

"We should take your van," I said.

"Okay, but we need to go to my shop to get it. Move!"

I grabbed as much weaponry and protective gear as I could carry on my motorcycle, along with clothing for the mountains in late fall. I had some stuff at Kirsten's shop, and luckily all our camping gear was there.

We sealed up the house—both mechanical and electronic locks, as well as magikal wards—and rode downtown to Enchantments.

Once we got there, we loaded everything we might need in her van and repeated the procedures for sealing the shop and the property behind it. I attached a couple of magitek devices to the van in case of trouble, checked it for magikal and electronic tracking devices, then we took off. It was just after one o'clock in the morning, and the route I planned would take about three hours to drive. But I wanted to make sure no one followed us, and that we arrived early enough to scout out what we might be walking into.

I headed southwest out of Baltimore toward Washington.

"This isn't the way to Harper's Ferry," Kirsten said.

"It's one of the ways," I replied. "We're going by way of White's Ferry."

"Oh, okay," she said, settling into her seat and closing her eyes. We had gone that way to go camping a couple of times. In days long gone there had been a cable ferry that crossed the

Potomac, but it had been replaced by a bridge before we were born.

Somewhere between Gaithersburg and Poolsville, on a stretch of back road where I couldn't see a single set of head or tail lights, I stopped and engaged Carl Beaver's cloaking device that I had attached to the van. The device's illusion wasn't perfect, and Kirsten reported that the van's lights were still visible, even though the van wasn't. Deciding that might attract the wrong kind of attention, I turned the device off and we continued on our way.

By that time, I was sure we weren't being followed, not even by a drone. Still, I switched our route several times. As far as I was aware, only four people knew of the place we were going, but my mother's message indicated we were in a life-or-death situation. Best to be overly paranoid and safe.

Our destination was where the old states of Maryland, Virginia, and West Virginia met, just east of the confluence of the Shenandoah and Potomac Rivers. My father had built a cabin in the area, far away from the city, and we used to go there on the weekends. I remembered when I was twelve, he and Mom and I spent the whole summer at the cabin, fishing, kayaking, swimming, and cooking on a charcoal grill every night.

After Dad disappeared, Mom told me that I owned it. Kirsten and I tried to go out there every year to do any needed maintenance and to make sure everything was okay. Kirsten loved the place, but it always reminded me of my father and made me sad, so I didn't go there very often. And other than the three of us, the only other person who knew of the cabin was my Grandmother Olivia. At least, I hoped so.

We turned off the main roads and made our way to the unmarked private road leading to the cabin. One hundred feet after the turnoff, I stopped, got out, and attached a magitek alarm onto a tree, aiming the beam across the road. If anyone drove past that point, I would receive an alert.

A short time later, the road ran between two large rocks. I got out again and placed a device on either side of the road, then keyed them to a third box, which I dropped in my pocket. The devices were similar to the electrical anti-intrusion boxes I had on the front door of Kirsten's shop, only stronger. No vehicle that relied on electricity would make it past those rocks.

I drove another couple of miles, then pulled off to the side of the road.

"Stay here and wait for me," I told Kirsten. "If anyone comes along without me calling you, shoot first and ask questions afterward."

"Right." She reached over and pulled a Raider like mine out of a clip under the dash. "Be careful."

Trying not to make too much noise, I slipped out of the van and started up the road in the dark. I took a pair of magitek night goggles from my pocket and put them on, then pulled up the hood of my jacket. In the mountains, the fall nights were definitely a lot colder than down by the coast.

I left the road when I was about half a mile from the cabin. A game trail that deer followed to go down to the river was still where I remembered it, even after twenty-plus years. It ran around the side of a low hill within about fifty yards of the cabin. I left the trail and climbed up to the top.

The cabin below me was completely dark. It didn't look as though anyone had been there since Kirsten and I visited it four months before. The double garage and the workshop occupied a separate building.

I watched for about five minutes, and then the front door opened. My mom stepped out onto the porch, turned, and looked up at me.

"It's all right," she called. "It's safe to come in."

I left my hiding place and walked down the hill toward her. When I reached her, we drew each other into a hug.

"Is Kirsten with you?" she asked.

"Yeah. She's waiting with the van."

"Tell her to come in. My truck is on the left side."

I used my phone to call. "Bring the van in," I said. "Park it in the right-hand bay of the garage."

Mom led me into the cabin. "Have you eaten?"

"Not since dinner."

Lights were on inside. Mom had blacked out the windows with a combination of curtains and a spell. The ground floor had no internal walls, except those closing off the bathroom and the laundry room.

Olivia was sitting in a large chair near the fireplace in the sitting room section, and I felt a surge of relief when I saw her. I crossed the room in three big steps and leaned down to hug her.

"When Mom said there was a coup, I was so worried about you."

She stood and gathered me in her arms. I hugged her tight, and when I looked down, I saw tears running down her cheeks.

"I was worried about you, too," she said. "George refused to admit that Courtney is an immoral traitorous bitch, and she killed him. She killed her own father."

I thought about a conversation I'd once had with Kirsten. I said the Families were like a medieval feudal aristocracy. Obviously complete with patricide.

We stood there, hugging each other for another minute, then I let go of her and let her sit down.

I realized someone else was there. Turning, I saw Osiris Dillon sitting on a couch in the far corner of the room.

"Thank you," I said.

He shrugged. "We've been covering each other's backs for a long time."

Kirsten walked in and Mom shut the door. Kirsten came to sit by me, and Mom went into the kitchen.

"What happened?" I asked.

"There have been a rash of deaths at the estate and at our offices all over the world the past three weeks," Osiris said. "Top managers, two of my commanders, other security personnel. Accidents, health issues, a couple of obvious assassinations. It seems that your aunt subverted a number of upper and midlevel Findlay employees with payments and promises of promotions."

He shifted uncomfortably in his seat. "Last night, Courtney attacked her father, and her insurgents took charge of the security systems. An assault force, primarily Akiyama soldiers, but also some Moncrieff and Johansson guardians, along with a couple of hundred demons, attacked Findlay House. They took control of our facilities at the harbors in Baltimore and Wilmington. Lady Findlay-James and I, as well as some of our guardians, escaped before Courtney's traitors came for us. I dispersed the people loyal to us and told them to lay low. It was your grandmother's idea to go to Ms. Jorensdottir."

"She's family," my grandmother said. "I knew she wouldn't turn us away."

Osiris took a sip of his coffee. "At the same time, an operation freed Akiyama Hiroku at Whittaker's estate. Hiroku is now commanding the Akiyama forces here in North America."

"Demons?" Kirsten's voice came out almost as a squeak.

"Yes," Osiris said. "I don't think we need to guess about Akiyama's intentions anymore. It's obvious they think the Magi Council has too many members."

"So, what now?" I asked.

"We have a plane waiting to smuggle us to Ireland," Olivia said.

Findlay had extensive holdings in Ireland, as did their Flanagan and Kennedy allies.

Mom set two bowls of stew and fresh bread on the coffee table in front of Kirsten and me. "We needed to make sure you girls are safe as well."

"I don't understand how all this works," Kirsten said. "I thought you said Courtney has gained control of the Findlay Family."

"Not exactly," Olivia said. "She may have physical control of some of our most valuable holdings, but she doesn't have the bank accounts, the ships at sea, the overseas holdings, or our allies. And since we do most of our banking through Novak, Domingo, and Martineau—none of whom are friendly with Akiyama—I don't expect she'll have much luck getting at the money. I also think she'll fail at getting recognition of her for George's seat on the Magi Council." She chuckled, an ugly sound. "It all would have been easier if she'd managed to kill or capture me, but she's not as smart as she thinks she is."

"She'll fold what she can into Moncrieff," Osiris said, "and increase their wealth and prestige. She'll have greater leverage in her dealings with Akiyama. And over the coming weeks, I'm sure some of Findlay's captains, pilots, managers, as well as some of my guardian commanders, will be persuaded to support her. But her bold move failed when Lady Findlay-James escaped."

Kirsten and I were dead tired, so as soon as we finished our dinner, we wished everyone good night, and we all went to bed.

CHAPTER 21

I woke up to the rattle of dishes and the smell of cooking sausages, and when I made my way downstairs, I found Mom in the kitchen making pancakes.

"Need some help in here?" I asked.

"You can set the table and then roust everyone," Mom replied.

It was full daylight outside. "What time is it?"

"One o'clock in the afternoon."

Over breakfast, I asked, "So, what's the next step?"

"You'll need to drive them to Pittsburgh," Mom said. "I need to get back to Baltimore. My father is coming in with a company of warriors the day after tomorrow."

"From Iceland?"

She nodded.

"I didn't think the elves cared about what the Magi did," I said.

"They care about Akiyama allying with the demons," Mom answered. "The old thing about the enemy of your enemy and all that. The Fae think that having an intelligence outpost in the Mid-Atlantic is a good idea."

I didn't even ask where they planned to stay. They could establish a city in Loch Raven Park, and no one would even know they were there.

I thought about what was going on all day, and when we sat down to dinner that evening, I said, "We'll drive you to Pittsburgh, but I'm not going to Ireland. Kirsten can go, but you're going to need someone you trust here."

Kirsten snorted. "And who's going to watch your back? No, I'm not part of the Findlay Family, so I doubt anyone is going to mess with me. I'm only a witch, so I'm beneath their notice. I'll be staying even if you don't. Besides, if this thing truly turns into a war and not just political jockeying amongst the Magi Council, you're going to need someone to liaise with the witches. We may not be enamored with the Magi, but we damned sure aren't going to lie down for the demons."

Mom chuckled. "The Magi have always underestimated the witches."

"Well, I guess there's more urgency for this than ever," Olivia said, producing a tiny computer chip from her pocket. "Amelie, can you insert this under Danica's skin? It doesn't matter where, she just has to touch it for it to work."

"Can I see it?" I took the chip between my thumb and one finger. "What is it?" I sent my consciousness into it and was surprised. It was the most technologically advanced piece of electronic equipment I'd ever touched.

Osiris answered, "It interfaces with your implant. It has the locations, identifications, and pass signs for all the intelligence operatives in our network. Worldwide. It's also a communications device."

Olivia chuckled. "You'll never again be able to ignore my calls."

"And a tracking device?" I guessed.

"Yes, but not a listening device," Osiris said. "You have to answer a call on your phone or place a call. And you'll note that you're not in the database, although there's a proxy where someone can leave you a message."

"You can also tap into a database or data stream and route it through that chip to a remote location," Olivia continued. "Either to me, to one of our computer systems, or to a computer of your own."

"You'll be tied into our network here in North America automatically," Osiris said.

I stared at the chip and let what they said sink in. "And if some of your assets turn? You said that was a probability."

The corners of Olivia's mouth twitched slightly. "I can track you. Osiris can track you. No one else can. You're the blind spot in the network, but you can see everyone. Dani, I told you once, you are my heir. No matter what that bitch Courtney thinks, I am Findlay now. All of my passcodes, my accesses, my pathways are encoded in that chip. If something happens to me, it's all yours."

"But I don't want it."

She shrugged. "I didn't ask you if you want it. You can give it away, if you wish. Pick someone such as Mary Sue who would appreciate it. Hell, give it to Courtney to buy your safety if you're stupid enough to trust her, but it will be your responsibility until you do." Her smile widened. "Don't worry. I'm planning on sticking around long enough to dance on Courtney's and Benjiro's graves."

I turned to Kristen. "See, I told you she wasn't really nice. She just puts on a good front."

Olivia simply smiled and batted her eyes.

Mom and I discussed where to insert the chip. I didn't want it just under the skin, because if might be detected. Kirsten suggested that it could be damaged, considering my proclivity for injury. Mom finally made a tiny cut under my right breast and slid it in there, then applied her healing touch to close the incision.

That evening, I spent four hours in my father's workshop at the cabin preparing a magitek shielding device and a couple of more precautionary surprises. I labeled them and included brief instructions, then stuck them all in a canvas bag I found on a shelf.

The following day, all the way to Pittsburgh, my grandmother and Osiris tried to talk me out of my decision to stay behind. The trip took a long time—driving on back roads—but I wasn't taking any risks. Kirsten had cast a spell to change the van's color, and we traded license plates with my mom's truck. We left the house with the cloaking device engaged and didn't turn it off until we hit a major freeway.

Even so, I was nervous as we approached the airport.

"How many other choices did you consider for airports?" I asked.

"We have planes that are capable of a non-stop to Ireland waiting for us at six different airports," Osiris said. "If things look dicey, keep going to Cleveland."

Olivia chuckled. "Dani, we've been playing this kind of game since before you were born. In Cleveland we have the choice of a plane or a boat that can take us to Buffalo, where we can sneak across the lake to Toronto. Courtney and Hiroku can't cover all our options. They just don't have the manpower."

"I would suggest going back through Gettysburg or Harrisburg," Osiris said.

"Maybe," I replied. "I was thinking about going through Morgantown and back by Harper's Ferry. I want to confirm that the cabin is still a safe hideout. If Courtney had a witch scry you, I don't want any unpleasant surprises in the future."

Kirsten shrugged. "It's probably safe. I doubt anyone is able to scry through the combination of my wards and your mother's, but it doesn't hurt to check."

The Pittsburgh airport was west of the city, and it was the largest airport outside of Baltimore-Washington in the Mid-Atlantic. It was almost four hundred miles from the coast, but every large coastal city other than Baltimore had been nuked at least once.

Osiris directed me to take the cargo plane exit off the freeway. Once I was out of traffic, I engaged the cloaking device again, left the road, and turned onto the tarmac. Dodging cargo trucks and airplanes was fairly easy, and none of them moved very fast. Osiris spent the entire time muttering into a secure microphone and listening to his earpiece, giving me directions occasionally.

I drove past the various company offices and hangers, including those of Findlay, until I reached a giant long-haul cargo plane sitting near the entrance to one of the runways. Its engines were idling, but as we approached, the pilot began feeding more power to them in preparation for takeoff. Since I knew we were invisible, the only way they could know of our approach was from Osiris.

Bringing the van to a stop next to a passenger stair, I called, "Last stop on the Pittsburgh line. All ashore that's going ashore."

Olivia leaned over the back of my seat and hugged me. "Take care of yourself."

"You, too," I said. "Don't take any chances, okay?"

They opened the door and Osiris jumped out. Olivia followed him, I knew that at that moment, they were suddenly visible, and if anyone was watching the place, things would get very exciting very quickly.

"Osiris!" I called. He turned back, and Kirsten passed him a tote bag.

"Once you're on board, activate that device," I said. "It should block any weapon, missile or magikal."

His craggy face split in a grin. "Thanks. Take care of yourself, Dani."

They took off running the few steps to the stairs, then up them into the plane. I turned the van around and headed for the exit. No sooner had I pulled away than something exploded on the runway where the van had been parked.

"Woohoo!" Kirsten shouted. "I think a little bit of evasive driving might be advisable!"

I swerved hard to my right, then after about twenty yards, back left toward our destination, and stepped hard on the accelerator. In my rearview mirror, I saw the large airplane start to lumber forward. I also triggered the magitek shielding device.

Another explosion to my left put a hole in the tarmac. Then a huge fireball, obviously magitek enhanced, launched from the Findlay control tower. It flew over us and splashed down outside the airport fence in a small copse.

"I think someone up there loves us," Kirsten said with a grin.

"Maybe so, but once we're through the gate, we'll be on our own."

She hefted the Raider in her lap. "Just don't wreck us."

As we neared the gate, I saw a couple of men come out of a small guardhouse and stand there. They couldn't see us, but it made me suspicious.

"Fire a couple of rounds at those guys," I said.

Kirsten leaned out her window and pulled the trigger twice. The men didn't seem concerned, and as far as I could tell, the bullets bounced off something at the gate.

"Roll up your window!" I shouted.

I swerved, taking the van to the right of the guardhouse and through the chain-link fence. Terrible noises of rending metal, but the shielding device protected the van. We bounced across a shallow ditch, into an open field, and about fifty yards later, back onto the road. I couldn't see much in my mirrors, but I was more concerned with what was in front of me.

"Yeah! That did it," Kirsten said. "They're all mixed up. Let's hear it for invisible delivery vans!"

CHAPTER 22

We stopped and grabbed some burgers near the university in Morgantown. A potion from Kirsten kept me awake, and we made it to Harper's Ferry after midnight. The magitek alarm I had set on the road into the cabin told me that no one had crossed its path since Mom and my party left the previous day.

Not wanting to get cocky, we left the van—invisible again—and hiked in to the cabin. Kirsten confirmed that the wards were undisturbed, and we spent the night there.

We opened some of the canned goods in the pantry for breakfast, and while we were eating, Kirsten asked, "Where are we going?"

"Mom's first, I guess. At some point, we have to get you back to your shop and to our house. The plants in the greenhouses won't take care of themselves forever."

She nodded. I knew the greenhouses were a concern. She always fretted about them when we went away.

"And what about you?"

I chuckled. "I'm a cop, remember? My name isn't Findlay,

and I'm fairly certain that Whittaker and Novak will shield me. Maybe Domingo as well."

"What are you getting through that implant your grandmother gave you? Any news?"

I shook my head. "I haven't accessed it. I've had more important things on my mind, such as getting here in one piece. Let's worry about us, and then we'll worry about the rest of the world, okay?"

Kirsten's face relaxed. "Yeah, that sounds good."

I reached out and put my hand on hers. "You and me, right? We take care of each other, and the rest of the world better stay out of our way. Never doubt it, Kirsten, I'll let Findlay fall into the Rift if the choice is between them or you."

Her eyes misted over, then she gave a forced kind of chuckle. "Don't get all mushy on me," she said. "Yeah, I think we'll be all right. They say war is hell, but for two girls who are veterans of Baltimore's dating scene, it should be a walk in the park."

We took a roundabout route to my mom's place—from West Virginia up into Pennsylvania, and then south. Kirsten drove while I cautiously accessed my new implant. I didn't try to contact anyone, just explored the cyber realm it opened for me. There was a message drop where Olivia let me know they had safely escaped. There were areas where messages were left for other Findlay operatives. Each operative had access only to their own direct mail, but I evidently could see everything except Olivia's business. I even had access to Osiris's private folders, but as far as I could determine, he was blocked from mine.

There were still people loyal to Olivia in Findlay House and other parts of the estate, as well as most of the staff working at the ports in both Baltimore and Wilmington. A database listing those who were untrustworthy or openly supporting Courtney was being built by some anonymous IT operator with the username of 'Dexter.' That was my father's middle name.

We stopped by the prison in Gettysburg because it was run by the Whittaker Family. We pulled into the facility, and I showed the guards my credentials. They allowed us into the administration building, where I placed a call to my boss.

"Thank God you're safe," Tom Whittaker said when he answered the phone. "I haven't been able to get any information on what's going on at Findlay."

I told him that Olivia and Osiris were probably in Ireland by that time. I also filled him in on what Osiris had said about Courtney's coup.

"Akiyama is working with demons?" he asked.

"According to Osiris, there were a couple of hundred demons involved in the takeover at Findlay House. He said Akiyama used them as shock troops. He also said that Hiroku is in Wilmington and commanding the Akiyama and allied forces in North America. How did that happen?"

"Yeah, some of my people were paid off, and he escaped. I've dealt with it. But I really can't believe Courtney pulled it off," Whittaker said.

"Money and death," I replied. "Boss, I have the body counts, and at least two hundred of the top people at Findlay in the Mid-Atlantic—family and employees—are dead. Many of them were killed by their own subordinates. If you don't flinch at killing your own father, then you probably don't have many scruples on who else you murder."

"Very true. What about Denise?" He meant my Grandaunt Denise Butler-Findlay, Granduncle George's wife and Courtney's mother.

"As far as I can tell, she's being held at the estate. One report says she knows Uncle George is dead, but not who killed him. I'm wondering whether that is going to get pinned on me, Osiris, or Olivia."

A moment of silence followed. "Hmmm," Whittaker said. "I hadn't thought of that."

"The Council rather frowns on patricide," I said. "With two rival claimants to Uncle George's seat on the Council, it would follow that they would blame each other for his death."

"Unless Courtney passes it off as natural causes," Whittaker said. "That would be the smartest thing to do, and she isn't stupid."

"Well," I said, "in any case, Kirsten and I are trying to keep our heads on our shoulders. At some point, we'll show up in public again, and hopefully, I'll still have a job and some protection."

"Count on it."

The other call I made was to Mary Sue. "Drop by the funhouse for dinner tomorrow," I said when she answered, then I hung up. She would recognize my voice, and although I doubted anyone might be bugging her phone—Mary Sue was a magitek and far from stupid—no one would know her private name for my mom's house. The Dressler Family were one of Findlay's closest allies, and since we were the same age and went to the same schools, we had known each other since pre-school. I figured she knew about the events at Findlay House. I wondered how various Findlay allies—many connected by marriage for decades—were dealing with the sudden Family civil war.

※

We came at the reservoir from back roads that most people didn't even know about. Shortly after we entered Loch Raven Park, Kirsten said, "Whoa! Did you feel that?"

"We crossed some kind of veil," I said. "I'll engage the

shield, but keep going. If no one's shooting at us, we're probably okay."

The road took us across a bridge over a narrow part of the lake. On the other side, we encountered a 'Road Closed' sign, a small turn-around area, and a detour sign pointing us back the way we came. I looked past the barricade, and the road looked fine to me.

"Park the van," I said. "Gather your weapons and clothes. I think we're backpacking from here."

"What's going on?" Kirsten asked. "Things feel a little strange."

"Things feel a little elven. If they aren't showing themselves, then we're going to have to push the issue. But I'm not going to expose the van. Elves have no appreciation for technology, or how much things cost."

Kirsten snorted. "After watching you trying to get the insurance company to pay for your cycle, I can just see myself saying, 'Honest, this root grew into the engine.'"

I laughed. "Something like that."

We shouldered our backpacks and headed down the road. We'd gone about a hundred yards when Kirsten started singing an Irish ballad. Normally, I would have joined her, but I didn't want to scare the wildlife. Her voice was sweet enough that even the Fae couldn't bitch about it.

Four hundred yards along, well out of sight of the van, an arrow flew across our path. It suddenly stopped and hung in the air. We walked up to it, and Kirsten reached out and grabbed it.

"You know, Dani," she said, loudly enough for anyone in the forest to hear, "I've heard all my life about what great people the elves are, but this is just plain rude. First they make us walk, then they try to play games with our heads, then they try to intimidate us. Absolutely not cool."

I also raised my voice to make sure I could be heard. "Instead of being assholes, you could simply check with my mother, or my grandfather, to verify whether we should be here. But this game isn't very mature."

To emphasize my displeasure, I sent a lightning bolt from my magitek box at the tree where the archer hid. The small crack of lightning made Kirsten jump, and I was sure it did the same to the elves hiding in the forest.

"C'mon, let's go," I said, urging my companion forward. We walked another few steps when an elf stepped out of the trees into the road in front of us.

"Danica James and Kirsten Starr?" she asked.

"Yes. You could have asked that half a mile ago. You know, it's six miles to my mother's house from here. You don't suppose we could get our van and drive, do you?"

The elf didn't react, except a slight twitch of one eyebrow. We all stood there for a couple of minutes, then she said, "You may drive your vehicle to the house."

I took off my backpack and put out my hand. Kirsten gave me the keys, then dropped her pack and sat down on it. I turned and raced back to the van.

Another elf came out of the trees and ran with me, easily keeping pace. Kirsten or any other full-human would never have been able to do that. I wasn't out of breath when I reached the van, but he hadn't even worked up a sweat.

"Would you like a ride," I asked, "or is it some kind of elven macho thing to prove you can keep pace with a machine?"

I got a hint of a reaction, one corner of his mouth turning up for a second. "I'll take a ride."

He was a very stereotypical elf. Exotically handsome with long silver hair past his shoulders, silver eyes, brown skin, slender build, and over seven feet tall. He carried a bow with a quiver of arrows across his back. He also had a short sword, a long knife, and a revolver hanging from his belt.

I wondered how Kirsten was going to react to the elves. To my knowledge, she had never spent much time around them, but she had gone to school in England for two years, and elves were more common there.

No one really knew where the Rift would move next. It was permanently open in our world, but in the other worlds it connected us to, it evidently opened and closed. When it moved into the North Atlantic islands, Scandinavia, and Northern Europe, elves came through into our world. Along the Chesapeake Bay and along the Atlantic coast of North America, we got monsters, which were also common in South America when the Rift moved there. Other parts of North America, India, and China got demons. Southern Europe, the Middle East and Central Asia got vampires and shifters. A different kind of demons came through in Africa. Basically, the whole world was screwed up.

We drove back to where I left Kirsten, then she and I loaded our packs into the van and proceeded to Mom's house. Evidently the word had gone out that we were acceptable, because we saw a number of elves, and several elven structures, along our way. It appeared that the illusions were no longer affecting us, because we certainly weren't doing anything to disperse or penetrate them.

When we pulled into the driveway to Mom's house, we saw at least twenty trucks of different sizes parked off the road in the trees along the way. Some were armored assault vehicles. All had Findlay markings, but I doubted any of Courtney's minions knew where they had disappeared to. I expected the elves cast an illusion on the vehicles when they left Loch Raven and drove out into the world. A few humans wandered around, and I assumed they were Findlay guardians.

Elves love children. Possibly because they have so few, they consider them precious. And since elves didn't mature until they were close to a hundred years old, to them I was barely more than a baby. I parked the van, got out, and was halfway across the yard when a tall elf emerged from the house and was on me in two steps. Grabbing me up, he swung me about like a child, a grin on his face.

"So beautiful!" my grandfather said in Elvish. "Every time I see you, you're taller and more lovely!"

Which was a lie. I hadn't grown an inch in twenty years, but an elf girl would continue growing until she was over eighty, so he still considered me a little girl. He hadn't changed at all from when I first remembered him. Taller than almost any human, with golden hair and eyes, he was the personification of what humans envisioned an elf lord to be.

We hugged each other, and then I introduced him to Kirsten.

"*Grapa*, this is my *brefonia*, Kirsten Starr of the Starr coven in Baltimore. Kirsten, this is my *Grapa*, my grandfather, Joren Dilensson of Iceland," I said, mostly in English.

"My, she is very young," he said, still in Elvish.

"No, *Grapa*, she's a human witch. All human. She's a fully grown woman."

Kirsten was five-foot-eight, but my grandfather was seven-foot-six, and the last time I was Kirsten's height was before I reached puberty.

Mom came out and leaned on the door jamb with her arms folded across her chest. "Glad you made it. Any troubles?"

"Minor problem in Pittsburgh," Kirsten said. "But Olivia and Osiris got away, and we got away. Stopped by the cabin last night, and things are okay there."

"Sounds good," Mom said. "Have you eaten?"

"Canned stuff at the cabin and hamburgers along the way," Kirsten said.

She had my mother's number. The mention of hamburgers, which Mom was convinced came through the Rift with the demons, set her off.

"Oh, shit. Come in and eat some decent food," Mom said,

and ushered us all into the house so she could feed us and catch up on the news.

As we walked toward the house, me leaning against my grandfather, his arm around my shoulders, Kirsten leaned close and asked, "*Brefonia?*"

I had taught her a little Elvish, but relationship concepts weren't something we had explored.

"It means bond mate," I said. "Nothing sexual. Like a sister—related, but not by blood. By claiming you, it places an obligation on my clan to protect you."

"I can live with that," she said, wrapping her arm around my waist.

CHAPTER 23

"You seem to have settled in," I said to my grandfather. "How many people did you bring with you?"

"Two hundred," he said, "thirty of whom are what you call intelligence operatives. People who have special training to fit in with human society. With a glamour, they can go anywhere amongst your Families. Depending on how we deploy them, they can pass as either mages or witches. The rest of my people are warriors. We are very concerned about this alliance with the demons that your enemies have embraced."

He chuckled. "We've already managed to insert three operatives—two men and a woman—into Findlay House. Your Aunt Courtney hired them to take the place of people she either killed or fired."

My mom said, "Dani, the demon army south of Annapolis broke out of their containment. They launched an assault to the west and overwhelmed the Magi troops. Demons from the Waste joined them. The Magi troops are fighting a rearguard action as they retreat toward the airport. The last word we had was that Whittaker was flying in reinforcements."

"And Wilmington?" I asked. "I heard that Akiyama Hiroku set up his headquarters there."

"The Akiyama-Moncrieff forces hold the Findlay estate, Elk Neck, and Wilmington, while demons control the area west of Annapolis between the Waste and Baltimore," Mom said. "The good news is that Whittaker, Novak, and Domingo have a major manpower advantage around Baltimore."

I thought about it, imagining a map in my mind. "Did I tell you about the deal Olivia, Mary Sue, and I worked out?"

"The magitek factory in Wilmington? Yes, you told me. What about it?"

"Mary Sue will be here for dinner tomorrow night. Courtney and Akiyama may think they have the upper hand, but we have a hole card they don't know about." I shook my head. "I can't believe that the Akiyama and Moncrieff Families are gullible enough to ally with demons."

Joren gave an elven shrug, tilting his head to the side and lifting that shoulder. "People believe what they want to. Even elves do stupid things at times. I understand that this territory lacks a demon overlord."

He was among the people I trusted most in the world. "I have something I need to show you. In the van."

We put on our coats, and Kirsten and I led my mother and grandfather out to where the van was parked next to Mom's garage. I opened the sliding door, and Kirsten muttered a spell. A box appeared behind the driver's seat. Kirsten crawled in and lifted the wooden box, revealing the statuette I had taken from Ashvial's office. Its red glowing eyes watched us.

Joren sucked air through his teeth.

"Ashvial, the demon lord, had this," I said, "Kirsten and I warded it, and I've had it in my workshop since we cleared his nest of his demon followers."

Joren and Mom studied it.

I told them about the drug house where the demons were slaughtered. "I couldn't figure out what was so valuable that a powerful demon would give its life to protect it. The magik detector from our forensics unit says this statuette left the residue she felt at that house."

"I think we should move it to your father's workshop," Mom said. Even more than twenty years after Dad disappeared, she still called it Dad's workshop and not mine.

I slid the wooden box over the statuette and latched the box to the base the object sat on, then lifted it up. It was only two feet tall, but it weighed about eighty pounds. I carried it into the shop behind the garage, and cast a spell to unlock the door. I put the box in a secure closet, Kirsten and I reset all the spells, and then we trooped back into the house.

"Have you ever seen or heard of such a thing?" I asked as Mom poured tea. "It almost feels as though it's alive."

"It's obviously an object of power," Joren said. "Demons are a different kind of lifeform than humans and elves, or even vampires. Whether that thing is alive or not, I cannot say."

"It hasn't done anything," I said. "I haven't touched it, and we always warded it before any attempts to move it."

"I wonder if it's a way to communicate across the Rift," Joren said.

I told him of my speculation that there was a higher power to which the demon lords owed fealty.

"We have discussed that as well," he said. "Your reasoning is sound. Without a king or a queen, one would think the demon lords would vie for supremacy, but we've seen none of that. I would hate to meet the being that statue was modeled after."

I didn't tell them about my dreams. I couldn't even imagine telling my mother about the ones that included the demon and my father. But how could I dream about such a creature before I knew the statue existed?

Mom never paid much attention to the news, although she did have a small comm terminal in her office. I, on the other hand, needed full access to the datanet when I was a student, so I had a connection and a screen in my bedroom. After we ate, Kirsten and I settled into my room, and I turned all the technology on. We sat and watched for a couple of hours, switching through to various newscasts.

We had taken pictures of the statue, so I set a search on the datanet for a match. Joren said that in their own world, the Fae had no mythology that included demons, although dragons had crossed a rift into their world about one hundred thousand years before. I was thankful we didn't have them to deal with.

The news was primarily about the demons advancing on Annapolis and the suburbs south of Baltimore, but there were a few stories about murders, mage battles, and demons in the city. I connected with a newscast out of Vancouver, and it reported a major battle between two different mage forces there. The vids showed fighters in Akiyama and Findlay colors battling near the harbor.

Kirsten and I had been driving for the most part of the previous three days, so we went to bed not long after dark. The world was crazy, but I had no problems falling asleep.

The being the statuette was modeled after came to me in my dreams. Eight feet tall with a fertility goddess body, she was imposing. Her human body was pale pink, and her dragon face, head, and the sharp ridges running from the top of her head between her horns, and down her back to the tip of her tail were blood red. Her tail tip twitched back and forth like a cat's. A snake-like tongue flicked in and out of her mouth. She didn't speak, just stared at me with those red, glowing eyes. Then she reached for me, and I jumped away from her. I landed on something hard and woke up on the floor beside my bed in a cold sweat.

We had alerted the elves and the guardians to watch for Mary Sue. She showed up at five o'clock, driving a baby blue sedan instead of her hot pink sports car, which threw people off a little.

"Oh, my," she said, when she crawled out of the car. "Are any of these guys single?"

I laughed. "No idea, but elves aren't particularly monogamous, so if you can entice any of them, have fun."

An elven woman walked past, six-and-a-half feet of exotic bronze beauty. Someone guaranteed to give human women a definite inferiority complex.

"The competition is a little stiff, but there are more men than women here," I said with a chuckle.

Mary Sue watched the woman and licked her lips. "Well, maybe a couple of them want to try a taste of the exotic." Turning back to me, she said, "Glad to see you're in one piece. Things in Wilmington have been rather exciting. You know, I've lived a sheltered life. Never seen a full-blown mage battle before."

Mom welcomed her into the house and poured her a cup of tea and a shot of *agavirna*. Joren cruised through shortly thereafter, and I introduced them.

After he left, Mary Sue turned to me, eyes wide, and asked, "How tall was your grandmother?"

I knew she meant Mom's mother. "About like Mom, I think. Six-four or thereabouts. She died before I was born. Mom says I'm built like her." I had not inherited the slender, willowy elven body type. I had heard people describe me as 'athletic'—not as curvy as Kirsten or Mary Sue—but I was at least thirty or forty pounds heavier than Mom.

Mary Sue tossed off the shot, shuddered, then took a sip of her tea.

"So, what's going on with our business?" she asked. "I half-expected to see Akiyama guardians knocking down the door and taking over, but everyone seems to be ignoring our buildings in Wilmington."

I told her that Olivia was alive, well, and relocated to Ireland. "Remember that one share of the company stock that Olivia allocated to Kirsten? She also transferred the Wilmington properties into Kirsten's name as well. Those buildings aren't associated with anyone named Findlay, Dressler, or James." I shook my head. "I hope I'm half as smart as that old lady is when I get to be a hundred."

I had spoken with Olivia and Tom Whittaker earlier in the day.

"We have several potential orders," I said. "Sounds like a few million bucks worth of magitek devices. Did you talk to your uncle about robots?"

Her perfectly-manicured eyebrows shot up. "Yeah, I did, but we haven't nailed down a contract yet," she said.

"Between Findlay and Whittaker, they want an initial order of a thousand weaponized magitek drones," I said. "Tom Whittaker said more of their allies might be interested once they see what the drones can do."

"And you have plans for these things."

I grinned. "Originally designed by Hunter James, and refined by Lucas James. Nasty little things that did a lot of damage during the Rift War. We can take a look at the plans and current drone technology, and figure out what we can improve."

And that's what we did after dinner. I also ordered the new magitek enhancer for the generator for Mom's turbine.

"I don't even have a factory yet," Mary Sue complained. "I've hired exactly two employees."

"Better get a move on, Cuz. Gotta make money while the making is good. Wars don't last forever, ya know."

Kirsten snorted. "The Rift War lasted twenty-five years, and nobody really won. Let's hope we don't have to deal with this garbage that long. I want to sell pretty-smelling soaps and feel-good potions, not weapons of mass destruction."

CHAPTER 24

A late-season hurricane hit the Carolinas that night and barreled up the Eastern Seaboard, shutting down the ports of Baltimore and Wilmington. Sea traffic from Europe was shuttled toward the port in Montreal. Findlay took advantage of it and launched a major offensive against the Akiyama facilities in Montreal and gained control of the ports both in Montreal and Quebec City.

For a while, forecasts showed the storm might track up the Chesapeake, but it veered more to the east, and we had to endure seventy mile an hour winds and torrential rainfall only for a couple of days. Wilmington was hit harder, but Mary Sue reported that our buildings didn't sustain any damage. In the wake of the storm, she transported most of the equipment she had ordered to Wilmington. With all of the other traffic going into the area—as Akiyama and Moncrieff dealt with cleanup and construction—our shipments weren't noticed.

Two weeks after our meeting at my mom's house, Mary Sue reported that she was ready to start production. She had hired thirty magitek engineers and another thirty engineers, draftsmen, and warehouse personnel. She had transferred the office personnel from her own business to Cerberus Corporation.

The storm slowed down military activity in the area, and intelligence reports from Findlay said that Courtney had finished her purges. After talking to Olivia and Whittaker, I decided to venture out and go back to work. Kirsten reopened her shop and moved back to our house in Baltimore, with two elven roommates taking over our guest bedroom.

Mychal Novak picked me up and drove me into the police station for my first day back at work. He was driving a shiny new unmarked car.

"The Council fired the police commissioner last week," Mychal said as we drove. "They didn't frame it as a firing, of course. He's been moved to a position in the Mayor's office. The joke going around is they wanted all the idiots together in one place. Whittaker is now the commissioner."

As soon as I entered the building, the desk sergeant pointed me toward Whittaker's new office. Being at Mom's and simply watching the news hadn't prepared me for the true situation I would be facing.

"You're coming up in the world," I said as I walked into Whittaker's big new office.

"So are you. It's good to have you back," my boss said, as he slid a captain's badge across his desk toward me. "Help yourself to some coffee. Novak's a lieutenant now, still reporting to you. You're in charge of the Arcane Major Crimes desk. Congratulations and good luck."

I filled a cup from a carafe on the credenza.

He gave me a dry chuckle. "Things have changed a lot since you were here last. In addition to the normal monster-eats-human murders, we have more assassinations—such as the Carpenter and Greer cases—gangland-style hits of Akiyama, Moncrieff, and Findlay personnel, and demons running around wild without a demon lord to control them. I've given Novak his own vehicle and a new partner, so that Toyota you souped up is yours full time. Can't have you catching pneumonia riding around on that damned motorcycle in the winter. And pick yourself a new partner. You are not—repeat not—to go out investigating cases without backup. Under any circumstances. Understood?"

I sighed and nodded. He sighed.

"All of the Families want things to be as normal as possible. Mage wars are bad for business. My budget's increased, and we're hiring additional cops into the Arcane Division. Just between you and me, I'm hiding a lot of Osiris's people that way."

He went on to tell me that Courtney had challenged Olivia taking George Findlay's seat on the Council. She accused Olivia of using magitek to kill George, and claimed that she, as his daughter, was the legitimate heir anyway.

I had to hand it to the bitch—she managed to accuse both my grandmother and me without even naming me.

"Gee, you really know how to welcome someone back after a vacation. Do you have a case for me, or am I just supposed to wander around and generally clean everything up?"

He projected a map on the wall. The Metroplex was carved up into different colors, and few of the lines were straight.

"The light blue is the territory we hold," he said. "Red is demon, purple is Akiyama-Moncrieff-Findlay, dark blue is controlled by other members of the Five."

"Who is 'we'?" I asked.

"The Metropolitan Police under authority of the Council. The lines on this map change—sometimes hourly. Our job is to make sure the light blue area doesn't get any smaller. If it gets larger, that's a bonus. And to answer your question, I want to clean everything up. By tomorrow, preferably, but I can give you until next week."

Kirsten's shop and the Inner Harbor were inside the light

blue, as was my house, Loch Raven, and the Novak and Domingo estates north of town. Most of the Port of Baltimore, the Port of Wilmington, Findlay House, and most of the coast from Wilmington down to Virginia—with the exception of Annapolis—were shown in purple. West of the coast and south of Baltimore were Red.

The Findlay estate was a small purple area inside light blue, and anyone traveling from the Novak or Domingo estates to the city would have to cross a purple area.

"If those colors denote territory," I said, "some people may be a little uncomfortable."

Whittaker nodded. "Anywhere Akiyama personnel go, they go in an armed convoy. I don't think anyone from Findlay-Moncrieff goes anywhere at all. We had a rash of assassinations, and Courtney is now a widow."

"I heard. I assume that's not a case you want me to handle. How extensive is this little disagreement?" I asked.

"I'll let your aunt find her husband's killer, if he wasn't hiding under her bed. Other than North America, South America, and Europe? Not much going on at all. My intelligence sources tell me that in Japan, China, and Southern Asia, no one really knows about the war. I mean, they know about it, but it doesn't impact anyone's life or business. Akiyama definitely has the upper hand and the momentum. If we struck a cease-fire right now, they would be the clear winners. But we're launching an offensive to take back the Port of Baltimore at midnight tonight."

Confused, I shook my head. "You and my grandmother keep saying there's a war going on. Where are the armies, the navies? How can you have a war without governments?"

Whittaker sighed. "It's more like battles between medieval feudal states. No one has true armies anymore, except a few places in Africa and South America. The combatants have private security forces, mercenaries, and police forces. The Magi Council has hired mercenaries from me for decades."

He got up from his chair and took his cup to the credenza where he poured more coffee. "Here in Baltimore, it's urban guerilla warfare—gang warfare. We're pretty sure the Palace of Commerce bombing here in Baltimore was carried out by Akiyama operatives. The HLA attack in Prague was a copycat. All sides are disseminating a lot of propaganda. The HLA is against all the Magi. The Grand Coven has come out in favor of democratic elections and inclusion of witches on the Council. The Rifters are being opportunistic, as you would expect. And God help us if the masses of humanity decide they're sick of it all and revolt."

"What you're describing is chaos," I said. "How can there be any order if everyone is fighting everyone else, and there are too many sides to keep straight?"

"I'm glad you grasp the fundamental problem."

CHAPTER 25

That evening, I went to meet Kirsten at Enchantments. Downtown and the harbor had seen rioting, looting, and general mayhem over the previous few months. At first, people picked up the pieces, hauled off the debris, fixed their buildings, and got on with their lives.

That was no longer the case. Windows boarded up, stores smashed and burned, piles of debris littered the street, burned-out wrecks of cars. There were more cops and soldiers on the street than civilians. Most of the larger office and apartment buildings had contingents of security guards. The area looked more like the fringes of the Waste than the Metroplex's foremost tourist attraction.

"Let's go to Jenny's," Kirsten said as she got in the car.

After a day of reading incident reports, intelligence assessments, case notes, and statistics on the violence engulfing the Metroplex, I was horrified.

"Are you crazy? We're living in the middle of a war zone."

Kirsten chuckled. "You're letting your job get to you. Were you outside at all today? I did about triple a normal day's business. Pent-up demand. I've been closed and all my customers just flooded the place. Mychal and Aleks are going to meet us for dinner, and I'm starved."

As I drove, I noticed that there were a lot of uniformed cops on the street, both on foot and in patrolling cars. Reaching out with my magik, I also encountered an unusual amount of drones overhead. At least downtown, Whittaker was controlling the streets.

I relaxed a little bit. "So, what kind of gossip did you pick up from all those customers?" I asked.

"The mages are anxious, concerned. But a lot of my customers are trophy wives and the Magi's children. As long as the supply of cosmetics isn't affected, they don't get too worked up. The witches are either oblivious, or the politically aware among them are excited that the magiocracy is undergoing a shakeup. The norms are concerned about the demons and the escalating violence." Kirsten shrugged. "About what you'd expect."

Not what I would expect, but I lived in a different world than her customers. On the way up the north-south freeway, I saw a lot of little red and blue blinking lights in the sky over the freeway. More drones.

The neighborhood around the Kitchen Witch Café was lit up, decorated, and there were a lot of people out on the streets. It was a completely different scene from the part of the city we had just left.

"Christmas?" I said.

"Yeah, Christmas. Only a month of shopping time left. Do you realize what all this craziness with Findlay has cost me? I lost three weeks of time between Samhain and Thanksgiving. Do try to keep the lid on things for another month, okay?"

Walking along the sidewalk, I couldn't see anything in the faces or demeanors of the shoppers that indicated fear or concern. People sounded happy, laughing and chatting. The shop windows were filled with goods.

Aleks had arrived at the restaurant before us and dropped Kirsten and my names. Jenny had seated him in a private booth. When we approached the booth, he jumped up and came toward me, taking me in his arms, and kissing me. Right there in the middle of the restaurant. Some of the other customers cheered and clapped while my face felt as red as the Santa hanging above the kitchen door.

"I was so worried about you. You're all right, aren't you?"

"Yeah, I'm fine. Let's sit down."

"Mychal had an errand to run, but said he'd be right back," Aleks said as he took my hand and led me back to the booth. We ordered drinks and an appetizer.

Mychal showed up about fifteen minutes later carrying a shopping bag, slid into the booth beside Kirsten, and gave her a kiss. Looking at my roommate's smiling face, I realized that her relationship with Mychal might be more than a passing fling. He made her happy.

The brownie waitress took our orders and almost immediately brought our drinks.

"To the new captain of the Arcane Division's Major Crimes Unit," Mychal said, raising his glass.

I thought Kirsten's eyes would pop out of her head. "You're joking!"

Shaking my head, I said, "Just goes to show you really can sleep your way to the top. I go on an enforced vacation, catch up on my sleep, and get promoted. The only downside is that I have to find a new partner."

Kirsten turned a puzzled face toward Mychal.

"They promoted me to Lieutenant. I have to choose a new partner also." He looked at me. "Any ideas?"

"For you? Davis. He's an electrokinetic, good shot, smart, but a little bit reckless. You're more cautious and methodical. I think you'd make a good team."

"Just what I need, another reckless partner. And you?" he asked.

"I have to speak to her, but I'm thinking Carmelita Domingo. I've learned the advantages of having an aeromancer for a partner. Of course, my reputation precedes me, but my last partner didn't die, so that's a mark in my favor."

Mychal and Kirsten laughed, Aleks looked a little confused, but I didn't attempt to explain.

After dinner, the four of us stood out on the sidewalk in a cold, blustery wind trying to decide what to do.

"I came with Mychal," Aleks said.

"I came with Dani," Kirsten answered.

"Need a ride home?" I asked Aleks, and so I ended up driving back downtown.

His place turned out to be an apartment in a fancy high-rise about six blocks north of Enchantments. I knew the area but didn't hang out there much. Expensive boutiques, expensive bistros, expensive galleries, and expensive apartments. Most of the inhabitants of the area were young, midlevel mages and witches working in the corporate offices of Magi businesses located downtown. The fringes of the area included centuries-old brownstones to the north and west, the traditional arts district to the north, office buildings to the west and south, and the harbor district farther south where Kirsten had her shop.

I went up with him, curious to see his flat. The lobby downstairs had marble floors and crystal chandeliers, with paintings and sculptures I was willing to bet weren't copies. His apartment was a little more subdued. Heavy brown-leather furniture in the living room with a dining nook, a wet bar, an open-galley kitchen, and two bedrooms, each with its own bath.

"Very nice," I said. "Although I admit, I expected fancier. No hand-carved marble toilets?"

Aleks laughed. "I saw some apartments like that, but I grew

up with pretention, and I don't need it. One would think European history would warn the Magi about extravagance, but they haven't seemed to get the message. Would you like a drink?"

He moved behind the wet bar. I took a look at the bottles arrayed there.

"A cognac, if you please. Where did you grow up?"

"The Janik Family is based in Munich, and I spent my childhood there and in Prague, mostly. I went to university at the New Sorbonne, in Lyon."

"I heard Janik suffered some casualties when the Palace of Commerce was bombed in Prague."

He nodded. "My Granduncle Gunther and five of my cousins. I also lost a lot of friends. Before I took this job, my office was in the POC." Walking out from behind the bar, he presented me with a snifter, clinked his glass against mine, and kissed me. "If I had stayed in Prague, I'd probably be dead, too, and I never would have met you. I think you are spectacular, Captain Danica James."

I stepped back, took a sip, and half-turned away. "We barely know each other. I prefer to take things slowly."

Aleks grinned. "As you wish. Will you spend the night?"

I wanted to, but... "I didn't bring a change of clothes. I think, especially with my new position, I should be a little discreet."

He closed the distance between us and nuzzled my hair. "Too bad."

Turning my face to his, I said, "I didn't say I wouldn't go to bed with you, I just said I can't stay the night."

※

A couple of hours later, I kissed him goodbye and started out the door. He held up a two-inch gold tube on a gold chain—a key to his apartment.

"No, I can't." I said.

"Yes, you can." He slipped the chain over my head. "The closet in the other bedroom is empty."

I suddenly felt a little light-headed. "What about your other girlfriends?"

"If you become a bother, I'll let you know." The man had a way of dropping his voice into a purr that lit parts of me on fire. "Anytime you decide you don't want to use it anymore, just leave it on the table next to the door. For now, if you find another woman in here, arrest her, she's a burglar."

He backed me up against the wall and kissed me. For a few moments, I almost decided to get undressed again, but managed to put my palms against his chest.

"I'll call you." I opened the door and fled. With his key. I was flustered, a bit apprehensive, uncomfortable, and embarrassed, but there was no way I was leaving that key behind. If the man wanted to put that much effort into making me feel special, I'd let him. On the way down the elevator, I wondered if there was someone still alive in Findlay House I could pay to smuggle all those fancy dresses in my closet out to me. For the first time in my life, I had someone I wanted to wear them for.

CHAPTER 26

I had a cop uniform, but I almost never wore it, except for funerals and the yearly ceremony when they handed out medals. I always got one. I had a scrapbook where I paired the citations for bravery and outstanding service with the reprimands for breaking protocol, procedures, and rules.

But I figured a captain should dress up a little more than a street detective. I chose a pair of black slacks, a white shirt, and a red jacket, along with a newer pair of boots that I brushed a dab of polish on. Then I put some lipstick on. I even used a couple of barrettes to hold my hair back from my face instead of my standard braid.

I drove into the office through the city, avoiding freeways and major streets. When I was first on the police force as a beat cop, I spent every day driving around residential streets, watching kids play soccer in the road, the old men hanging out in front of the liquor stores and carry-outs, the women gossiping on their front steps. I had seen pictures from before all the wars, and some things hadn't changed very much. I knew some cops looked at the humans in the poor neighborhoods only as potential criminals. But the majority of them were the people we were sworn to protect against the criminals.

My route took me past the rubble of the Palace of Commerce. It would probably be spring before it was all cleared away and the new building started. I also drove by Aleks's apartment building and realized it was only a three-block walk from my office.

Then I turned a corner, and my reflective mood hit a brick wall. Minor demons, vampires, and a few shifters were blocking traffic with a demonstration. It didn't appear to have gotten violent. Yet.

I flipped on my radio. "Dispatch, this is Captain James. Any idea what the demonstration in front of Police Headquarters is about?"

A female voice answered. "Police brutality, Rifter rights, Rifters are getting a raw deal—pretty much the same old deal. The poor babies are treated abominably because they can't munch on whomever they please."

I choked on a laugh. "What's your name, officer?"

"Luanne Armstrong."

"Who's overseeing security on the demonstration?"

"Lieutenant Cargill."

I thanked her and disconnected. It took me some time to slowly make my way toward the building without running over anyone. At one point, a couple of vampires decided to beat on my car, but a shot of electricity from one of the magitek devices put a quick end to that.

Once I was in the office, I looked up Luanne Armstrong. Witch, twenty-three years old, been on the force a year. Exemplary record, although one note in her file from a supervisor said she had a 'smart mouth.' My kinda girl. In my new position, I needed an assistant. I checked out the rest of her qualifications, then put in a requisition.

Next, I sent out a message to Lieutenant Luis Cappellino to

have Detective Sergeant Carmelita Domingo report to my office at her earliest convenience.

And then I opened my messages and wished I hadn't. There was a reason they paid captains twice what they paid lieutenants—they had to put up with twice as much crap. I started sifting through the cases and assigning them.

By mid-afternoon, I had whittled my backlog down to a manageable pile. One of the biggest chunks of work still to deal with were the cases assigned to a Lieutenant James. I dealt with them all at once, dumping them on Lieutenant Mychal Novak.

Picking up the phone, I called Human Resources. "This is Captain James in Arcane. I put in a requisition for an assistant this morning. Where is she?"

The snotty little girl on the other end of the line started telling me about how they were processing requisitions from two months ago, and that I would just have to wait my turn. I didn't hang up, I just set the phone down on my desk and walked two flights of stairs down to HR.

"May I help you?" the receptionist asked.

"Yes. Where is Dorothy Ridgeway?"

"Uh, Ms. Ridgeway is busy—"

"That isn't what I asked. Where is she?" I pushed my jacket back and put my hand on my hip, revealing the Raider and my captain's badge pinned to the holster.

The receptionist had an epiphany and pointed to a cube about thirty yards away. I walked over there.

"Ms. Ridgeway?" I said to a pretty young thing who was busy painting her nails.

"Yes?"

"I'm Captain Danica James." I sat on the corner of her desk, letting my jacket fall open to reveal the Raider. "I don't know who you are used to dealing with, but you're dealing with me now. And when the Major Crimes Unit of Arcane Division puts in a request for personnel, I expect you to pay attention to it. Do I make myself clear?"

She stared at me, her eyes like saucers.

I reached over, picked up her nail polish and put the cap on it. "Now, pull up all personnel requisitions for my unit," I said.

"Personnel files are confidential," she stammered.

I didn't touch her computer, but the information I asked for appeared on her screen.

"We aren't going to get along very well if you argue with me and give me excuses every time I ask you to do something."

About that time, a man showed up. "I'm Joseph Moskowitz, recruitment supervisor. Can I help you?"

I smiled at him. "Yes, you can tell Commissioner Whittaker that I'm not happy with the way you and your staff are doing your jobs. Now, I understand the red tape required to hire new personnel. But simple transfers within our division should be pretty easy, don't you agree? Now, if all of those requisitions," I gestured to her screen, "aren't resolved by the end of the week, I'm going to talk to the commissioner myself. Do you understand?"

"You can't come in here and intimidate me and my staff! You don't understand how things are done around here."

I snatched Ridgeway's nail file from her desk and buried it in a wall thirty feet away.

"Unfortunately, I understand all too well how things are not being done around here. I guess the end of the week is too long to wait. I'll have to go speak with him now."

Half an hour later, a woman in a police uniform, almost as tall as me, with dark skin and black curly hair, stuck her head through my door. "Captain James? I'm Luanne Armstrong. I understand you wanted to see me?"

"Yes, come on in. Have a seat. We spoke on the radio this morning, didn't we?"

"Yes, ma'am."

"Do you like dispatch, Officer Armstrong?"

She reacted with alarm, and I immediately wanted to kick myself.

"Yes, ma'am. I'm sorry, ma'am. Did I say something inappropriate?"

"No, you didn't. I'm sorry, I guess I came at this the wrong way," I said. "You aren't in any trouble." I pulled up her file on the computer and turned the screen so she could see it. "I'm looking for an assistant. A uniform who can keep my schedule, keep the brass off my back, take care of paperwork and crap work my partner and I don't have time for. You may be used as a driver. Part time in the office, part time in the field. Fast track to detective in four years. Are you interested?"

Fifteen minutes later, I had a new assistant. I was on my way out of the building when Carmelita called me. "Hey, congratulations on your promotion."

"Are you downtown?" I asked.

"Yeah. Downtown. Just got off shift."

"Meet me at Whodunit," I said. The bar next to the cop station was owned by a former detective.

Sergeant Domingo must not have been very far away, because I met her at the door of the bar.

As soon as we walked into the bar, I regretted my choice of place to talk to her, as I was besieged with congratulations and offers of free drinks. But Ed, the owner-bartender, put an end to that.

"Buy her drinks another night," he announced to the crowd. "Her drinks tonight are on me." Ed Donatello had been my second partner when I got my detective's badge. We had made a good team until a demon chewed off the lower half of his left leg, and he took an early retirement.

"And her drinks are on me," I said, motioning to Carmelita.

"Nope," she said. "I'll buy her first one. This woman saved my life."

Ed chuckled. "A lot of cops can tell that story."

He filled our orders, and I led Carmelita to a booth in the corner.

I wasn't going to make the same mistake as I did with Luanne, so I said, "I need a new partner, interested?"

Her brow furrowed. "I didn't know captains had partners."

"This one does. The Commissioner considers me too valuable to sit in the office." That wasn't exactly what he said, but I figured he didn't want my head to get too large.

She smiled. "Sure!"

We clinked our glasses together, and then the bomb went off outside, blowing in the front door of the bar. I ducked under the table and met Carmelita there. When the debris stopped pattering down and the only sounds I could hear were people screaming, we emerged and looked around.

"Oh, hell," Carmelita said. "We've been dealing with this kind of crap ever since the Council fell apart." She took a long pull on her beer, jumped up, and headed for the entrance, pulling her pistol as she went. Another girl I figured I could work with.

Outside, we discovered the explosion was due to a car bomb. The car it was in was destroyed, and a couple of dozen pedestrians on the street were blown to kingdom come. The bomb didn't carry out its intended purpose, however. No one inside the bar was killed, and there were only a few minor injuries to people sitting near the door.

Ed had wards set on the front of the building, except for the door, of course. Whoever set the bomb should have known an ex-cop would have bought protection.

CHAPTER 27

When I fell out of bed the following morning and looked at the clothes I'd worn the day before, I wondered why I should try to look nice. Soot, blood, and other things I didn't want to think about soiled the pretty red jacket. I mumbled something to that effect to Kirsten.

"That's why they pay you more," she said. "When you were a beat cop, they gave you a uniform allowance and barely enough to eat. When you made sergeant, they paid you enough to eat and let you wear what you wanted. Carve some time out during the day, and we'll go shopping for clothes you can wear to work. Black leather and jeans aren't going to cut it anymore. As to those," she waved at my ruined clothes, "I'll take care of them tonight after work, and they'll be good as new in the morning."

Having a hearth witch as a roommate was a wonderful thing.

By the time I got to work, the HLA had announced they were responsible for the bombing at Whodunit. "A strike against the oppressive Magi secret police," was the way they put it. Propaganda. If we were such a secret, they wouldn't have found us drinking in a bar across the street from the very public Police Headquarters.

Carmelita and Luanne were waiting for me outside my office. I opened the door, and using my magik, entered my access code into the security database.

"Put your hand on the sensor," I said. Luanne complied, then I had Carmelita do the same. "Okay, both of you now have access to the office. Luanne, that's your desk. Carmelita, that one is yours."

One of the perquisites of being a captain. There was an outer office with three desks, and an inner office.

I put Carmelita to screening the cases that had come in overnight, then I spent some time orienting Luanne to her new job and what I wanted her to do. By the time I finished, Carmelita had the case reports sorted out, and in another twenty minutes, I had them all assigned.

"Armstrong, you have the office. Domingo, you're with me."

We walked down the hall to the elevator, and Carmelita asked, "What's up?"

"We're going to try and find Susan Reed."

I led her down to the parking garage and claimed my car. As soon as we were out of downtown, I took the car airborne. We flew down to College Park, then I set the car back on the ground to drive to Susan's house in Berwyn Heights. We had put cameras on the house to alert us if Susan ever came home, but none of them had given an alarm. I didn't necessarily trust that.

As I expected, the house was warded. Also as I expected, so were the cameras. Susan was a witch, and had proven to be a smart one. A full-scale parade could have marched into the house, and the cameras wouldn't have seen a thing. The ward on the house prevented us from gaining entrance, but it didn't stop my magik from shutting down the electricity at the circuit box outside the garage or the water at the meter. Since it was the end of November, anyone staying in the house would be very uncomfortable.

I set up two magitek cameras—one in a tree across the street, and the other on a light pole on the next street, aimed at the back of the house. Carmelita used her aeromancy to float up to where I wanted the cameras placed.

"Okay," she said when she landed after setting up the second camera, "what's next?"

"We pull in your boyfriend Elesio Gomez for questioning."

"My boyfriend! Not hardly."

I laughed. "But he has the hots for you."

"He'll be suspicious."

"Maybe, but my bet is that you can spin a story that will bring him out to meet you. Give him a call."

Elesio wasn't one of the HLA members arrested after Carmelita-Dolores's car blew up. We had considered him too low level to be involved in planning the murders and bombings. As it was, the two hundred or so radicals we did pull in filled the jails and took weeks to interrogate.

Sure enough, Elesio had it bad. Carmelita-Dolores was cute as a new kitten, and he never suspected that she was six or seven years older than she appeared, a condition not uncommon among magikers. She set up a meeting with him at a pizza place in College Park.

We parked behind the restaurant, and she went in first. I followed a couple of minutes later and took a table across the room from them. It turned out that Elesio wasn't quite as gullible as I had hoped, and he brought two friends with him. My elven heritage gave me better hearing than a human's, and I could hear their conversation.

Carmelita pouted, pushing out her bottom lip. "I wanted to see you, not your friends."

After a couple of minutes, the friends got up and went

outside. I made a call and asked for a couple of uniforms to come help me with a bust, then I followed Elesio's friends. They had retreated to a car and were sitting in it smoking a joint while they waited on him.

When the cop car showed up, I approached it and showed the cops my badge. "See that car over there with the smoke? I think those are HLA radicals we want to question. Can you please take them down to your station?"

After the bombing at Whodunit, the HLA wasn't the police's favorite group. The two cops bracketed the car, tapped on the windows, and arrested the occupants. After they drove away, I went back into the restaurant, ate the sandwich I had ordered, and waited.

Carmelita soon left with Elesio, and I followed. He seemed confused that his friends weren't waiting for him, but their car was still there.

I walked up to where Carmelita and Elesio were standing and flashed my badge. "Elesio Gomez, Dolores Hernandez," I said, "you're wanted for questioning about the Human Liberation Army's bombing of a bar in Baltimore."

He looked like he was going to faint, but before he could try to run, I grabbed him and slapped a pair of cuffs on him. I also cuffed Carmelita for show. Taking both of them by the shoulders, I steered them around the building and shoved them into the back of my car.

I got in the driver's seat, then swiveled around so I could see him.

"I don't know nothing about no bombing," Elesio said.

"Where's Susan Reed?" I responded.

"I dunno."

"That is not what I call cooperative. Who does know?"

After fifteen minutes of bullying him, I had a list of places to check and a couple of names. I was also convinced that he wasn't deep enough into the HLA that anyone would trust him with information concerning their terrorist activities.

Carmelita-Dolores was far less cooperative, refusing to answer any questions at all. I turned Elesio loose, warning him to find a better set of friends to hang out with.

"And as for you, young lady, you're going down to the station. I don't appreciate your attitude."

We left Elesio standing in the parking lot. We already knew the car he came in wasn't his, but I didn't care how he got home. A block away from the restaurant, I pulled over and took the cuffs off Carmelita. She crawled into the front of the car.

"You can be a major bitch when you want to be," she said.

I laughed. "I guess we know who takes which role in a good-cop-bad-cop interrogation."

We drove down to the local cop shop, where they had put Elesio's friends in separate interrogation rooms. I checked in with the lieutenant in charge, and then we spent about forty-five minutes with one suspect and half an hour with the other. In the end, we charged both of them with suspicion of terrorist activities just so we could hold them.

"Okay, now what?" Carmelita said as we left the station.

"Three suspects, one name in common," I said.

"The lawyer."

"Gold star for the little lady. Let's go see him."

Gordon Montoya was a criminal defense lawyer Elesio had met a couple of times, and he suspected Montoya was sleeping with Susan. Our other two suspects had named him when they asked to call a lawyer. They had been watching too many crime videos. The concept of civil rights for criminals was a relic of a time long gone, but it made good drama. Arcane Division operated by a different set of rules, and in terrorism cases, especially against the Magi, we really didn't have any rules as long as we restored order and the ruling class's peace of mind.

Carmelita pulled out her laptop and checked on Montoya.

He had a history of representing human radicals as well as personal injury cases against corporations. His office was in the better part of downtown Silver Spring, and his house was north of there, in an area of large homes on large lots carved out of the forest. She also checked his banking records.

"I'm Captain Danica James," I told the receptionist, "and this is Detective Sergeant Carmelita Domingo. We'd like to speak with Mr. Montoya."

She buzzed him, then said, "There are two policewomen to see you."

"I'm on a call," the box on her desk squawked, the quality terrible. "Give me five minutes."

She looked up at me and I nodded. "We'll wait."

We sat and admired the pictures on the wall for seven minutes, then the box squawked again. "Send them in."

His office was intended to convey money and success. Montoya was medium height, with dusky skin, slicked-back black hair, and a pencil mustache. His affluence was signaled by a five-thousand-dollar suit and forty extra pounds.

I identified ourselves and took a chair in front of his desk. Carmelita wandered around, studying the pictures on the walls, a couple of small statuettes, the flower arrangement on a sideboard, his coffee service, and the liquor bottles. Her moving around seemed to distract and annoy him, and I silently applauded her.

"What can I do to help the Metropolitan Police?" Montoya asked.

"We're looking for a woman named Susan Reed," I said, showing him a picture I had taken of her at the HLA meeting in Columbia.

He peered at the picture, then shook his head. "I may have met her once or twice, but I wouldn't know where to find her."

"Our information is that she paid you twice in cases involving the defense of HLA radicals," I said. "We've also been told that the two of you have a personal relationship. Maybe we can start over?"

Montoya squirmed a bit. "I'm not at liberty to discuss my clients."

"I didn't say she was your client. I said she paid you to defend HLA radicals. We're investigating the source of those funds. We think they might have come from a bank robbery."

While the upper classes—both magikal and human—conducted most of their transactions using bank transfers, the lower classes still mostly used cash issued by the Families through their bank holdings. Novak and Domingo were the two major banking Families, but worldwide, at least a dozen banks printed paper money that was generally accepted for goods and services. Radical groups such as the HLA often robbed banks in poor neighborhoods to finance their operations.

"I wouldn't know anything about that. I'm an honest businessman."

"Since you started out by lying to me, I would take issue with that statement. When was the last time you saw Susan?"

"Look, you can't barge in here and accuse me of criminal activities."

"Ah. That's the third time this morning I've run into people who've been watching too many vids," I said. "Mr. Montoya, I represent the Magi Council, and I can do pretty much what I damned well please in investigating crimes against the Hundred. I'm also investigating the bombing of a bar in Baltimore, for which the HLA has claimed responsibility. One policeman was killed, and three were wounded."

I leaned forward, putting my hands on his desk, and gave him a tight smile. "Now, unless you want to continue this discussion down at Police Headquarters, where the hell is Susan Reed?"

He broke out in a sweat. Carmelita ceased her appraisal of

his nick-nacks and plopped her butt down on the back corner of his desk, leaning toward him.

"Did you catch my last name?" she asked. "You do business with my grandfather's bank. We know where you get your money, and where you spend it. One phone call, and I'll have all your records. I'm sure our forensic accountants have the time to sift through them."

The sweat poured off him. He was breathing so hard I was afraid he might hyperventilate.

"She's staying with me."

"That would be your house on Emmet Road?" I asked.

"Yes."

"And is she there now?"

"I don't know. She goes out."

"And what does she drive when she goes out?"

She was using one of his cars, and we quickly looked up the description and the license plate.

"Well," I said, "I'm afraid I'm going to have to take you and your employees into protective custody, confiscate your phones, and shut down your office." I nodded at Carmelita, who left the office to take care of the receptionist and any other employees on the premises. "It's really for your own good. These radicals can be somewhat murderous if they feel threatened."

I pulled out my phone and called Novak. "Are you doing anything important, or just sitting around drinking coffee and flirting with the waitress?" I asked.

"Shutting down a bar run by a demon who got pissed at a customer and ate her."

"Lovely. Let the uniforms take care of it. I need you in Silver Spring with a couple of more detectives, and put out a stealth APB for this car." I gave him the license number. "I don't want it stopped, just identified and followed. Also send four uniforms to the office of a lawyer named Gordon Montoya in Silver

Spring. And send a couple more detectives to watch an address I'll text you. I think we've found Susan Reed."

"Is that all?"

"One of those fancy coffees you like would be nice." I hung up. "Mr. Montoya, thank you for your cooperation. I'm sure your HLA contacts will appreciate all you're about to do for them."

CHAPTER 28

I called Whittaker and got search warrants for Montoya's office and residence just to be on the safe side, then we waited until the uniforms and two detectives from the Silver Spring station showed up. The uniforms took Montoya, his receptionist, and a paralegal down to the station, and I told the detectives what to search for. Then Carmelita and I headed over to Montoya's house.

"You know, I like this captain gig," I told her as we drove. "Snap my fingers and get all the help I need. I used to have to do everything myself."

She chuckled. "Letting power go to your head?"

"Hey, life is good."

We parked down the street from Montoya's address and walked up to his driveway. He wasn't the type who enjoyed manicured lawns. The house was hidden in trees. I placed a magitek warning device on the driveway to let me know about any cars going in or out, then we snuck through the forest to the house. No signs of anyone about, but there were three garages, so the car Reed was using could be in one of them.

I stuck another magitek device on the back door, then we retreated to the street to wait for Novak.

"So, you think Susan is that high in the HLA?" Carmelita asked.

"We managed to pick up every one of the people at that meeting in Columbia except her. Since then, we've had two bank robberies and the bombing at Whodunit. The robberies followed the HLA pattern. If we captured all the top people in the HLA, someone is still directing things. If not her, then I'm betting she knows who is."

I opened my laptop, plugged into the datanet, and triggered my implant, sending my consciousness into the data stream. Susan Reed's accounts hadn't been touched since the last time I'd checked, which was shortly after she eluded our dragnet. She might be living off Montoya, but Susan was a high-maintenance girl, and I was betting that some of the money from those bank robberies was finding its way into her pockets.

While I was hacking the banks, I checked on the major Findlay accounts and renewed the blocks I'd set to keep Courtney from accessing any Findlay funds. It was the least I could do for my grandmother.

Then I checked my police files, reading reports from the detectives under me, assigning two new cases, and retrieving the search warrants Whittaker had ordered.

Someone tapping on my car window pulled me out of the net, and I looked up to see Novak standing there. I shut down the computer and got out of the car. He handed me a large takeout coffee.

"Thanks," I said and took a sip. "This is good. What is it?"

"Caramel mocha. So, what are we doing?"

I took another sip. "I could grow to like this. When's your next performance appraisal?"

He rolled his eyes.

"We're waiting for Susan Reed to either leave the house, or

come home." I said. "Gordon Montoya says she's been staying with him and driving one of his cars."

"We're going to bust her?"

"I'm thinking more about tailing her and finding the rest of the HLA radicals who are pulling off their operations. Once we're sure she's not in the house, we'll search it and plant bugs, but I don't want to tip her off. Where are you parked?"

He pointed up the street. "On the other side of the house. This street's a dead end at the school up there."

"Settle in. I have no idea when she might appear."

We waited until well past sunset. A car came up the street about eight o'clock and pulled into the driveway, tripping my alert.

"That's our cue," I said to Carmelita, then I called Novak. "We're going up to the house. Hang tight, and if a car comes out, follow it."

"Let's go," I told Carmelita. Reaching in the glove compartment, I pulled out two pairs of magitek night goggles. "Put these on. They have a simple on-off magitek control."

Lights went on in the house. A car matching the description of the one Susan was driving was parked in front of the garage. Windows in another part of the house lit up.

"Should we test the wards?" Carmelita asked.

"No. If she's any good, then she's set a selective ward that will let her in without lowering the ward. Touching it might alert her that someone's here."

The first thing I did was plant a tracker under the bumper of Susan's car, and a microphone under the driver's seat. Then we walked around to see what we could see. We got within five feet of the building, and I peered as best I could through the lit windows. Carmelita was too short to see anything, but I felt better with her there to cover my back.

Susan was in a room in the back of the house, changing

clothes. I figured she was getting ready to go out, so we retreated to my car and called Novak.

"Mychal, I think she's getting ready to go out somewhere. We're going to go out to the main street and wait for her. You follow her when she leaves. We'll switch off every so often so she doesn't get suspicious of a tail."

"Sounds good."

We waited forty-five minutes, but then her car came down the driveway and out onto the street. At the end of the street she turned right, and I followed her. Novak made the turn in behind me.

Susan took the freeway north toward Baltimore, but when she got to the city, she merged onto the beltway around the city. My tracker made it easy to keep her in sight, but all I was getting on the microphone was music, and her taste was terrible. Carmelita seemed to like it, though, and I made a vow not to let her choose music if we ever had a long drive together. She and Susan were about the same age, so maybe I was too old for what they liked.

Susan's destination turned out to be in the north part of Owings Mills, a Baltimore suburb uncomfortably close to the Findlay estate. I knew Findlay guardians liked to hang out at a couple of bars there, and another one was frequented by some of the servants. I didn't want to see any guardians who had switched allegiance to Courtney.

Susan passed the bars and drove to a house in a semi-ritzy neighborhood. She parked in the driveway and went to the front door. It opened and she went inside.

"Quick, who lives there?" I asked Carmelita.

My partner tapped on the keys of her laptop as I drove farther up the street and turned around.

"Someone named Carleton Farringdon. Mean anything to you?"

"Yeah. Damn." I called Novak. "We need some heavy backup. Park and shield. I'll call Whittaker."

"Why? Who lives there?" he asked, and when I told him, he cursed.

"Let me in on the secret," Carmelita said.

"Shield us first." I took a nervous glance at the house. "Carleton Farringdon is a spirit mage. Got busted and sent up to Gettysburg when he was about sixteen. Has a real bad attitude toward the Magi."

"Busted for what?"

"He put together a gang—some mages, some vampires. They were running Rifter drugs, trafficking girls. I was still a uniform then, and Novak was new on the force. When a couple of detectives from Arcane went to arrest him, there was a full-scale battle. A lot of people died, and the whole neighborhood was devastated."

"And they only sent him to Gettysburg?"

"Farringdon used to be just below the Hundred. His father paupered himself to keep his son out of a stiffer sentence. The Family was ruined, but Carleton got only ten years. Needless to say, he's not fond of the Magi."

I called Whittaker and explained the situation. He cursed. Very creatively.

"What do you want me to do?" I asked. "Wait until she comes out and keep following her? It was an hour-and-a-half drive up here. My bet is that when she leaves, she goes back to Montoya's, and she'll figure out he's disappeared." I glanced at the house. "There are five other cars parked in the driveway or on the street, so it looks like a meeting. We can try and pick up everyone who leaves, but I'll need more manpower. If we do that, we can tail Farringdon when he leaves next. Easier to take him out in the open."

Silence, then, "I'm thinking."

I was glad he was, and that it wasn't my decision. I turned to

Carmelita. "Take those night goggles and record all the license plates in the driveway and on the street. Maybe we can figure out who else is in there. And for God's sake, be quiet and careful."

"Damn straight." She pulled the goggles over her eyes and slid out of the car.

"Do you have any magitek tricks up your sleeve for an assault that would minimize collateral damage?" Whittaker asked.

"Given enough time to collect the equipment. I have an enhancer, but I'd have to retrieve it from my mom's house, and then I'd need a portable laser cannon and the strongest portable generator you can find."

I heard him snort. "Your mom's house? No one can get within five miles of Loch Raven. There's some kind of ward in place around the lake. What's she doing out there?"

"It's a veil, not a ward," I said. "My grandfather's in town."

"Your grandfather?" His voice rose, almost to a squeak.

"Yeah, the elves are concerned about mages working with demons."

More silence, then, "The last time we took Farringdon down, we had three spirit mages, and that wasn't enough. I have three on the force now."

"I know a spirit mage, but he's a civilian," I said.

"Who?"

"Aleksandr Janik. Look, can we just wait until their little party is over, tail them when they leave, and pick them off one at a time?"

He didn't answer me directly. "The Germans have a militaristic tradition. Most Janiks serve in their version of guardians between university and their careers. What would your souped-up laser do?"

"Obliterate the house from this reality. I'm not saying there wouldn't be any collateral damage, you'd probably want to evacuate the houses behind it for, oh, half a mile, maybe a mile."

Carmelita opened the car door, slipped inside, and quietly closed it. She picked up her laptop and began typing.

"Give me a couple of minutes and I can probably tell you who else is in that house," I told Whittaker.

It took my partner about five minutes, then she turned the screen so I could see it. I read the names and the magikal talents of the owners aloud. Whittaker started cursing again.

"If I was this Carleton Farringdon," Carmelita said, "I would know that another trip to Gettysburg was off the menu."

I nodded, waiting for Whittaker to come up with a genius plan that would take down the bad guys while leaving all the good guys still alive and walking. I was sure Farringdon was well aware of the difference between the magikal prison in Gettysburg and the one in Antarctica.

CHAPTER 29

"I'm sending in as many men as I can gather," Whittaker said. "Either you or Novak needs to set up a staging area. We'll need to evacuate the houses in the neighborhood."

"I'll have Mychal do it," I said, and Whittaker hung up.

Great. It was ten-thirty at night, and half the houses in the area were dark, and their occupants had probably gone to bed. I got on the phone and told Mychal what he needed to do. He wasn't happy. Both of us knew there wasn't a good place nearby to gather a couple of hundred personnel and equipment. After looking at a map, we decided on a cul-de-sac two blocks away. I watched his car turn around and drive away.

Fifteen minutes later, a dozen or so vehicles showed up and blocked the street. I got out and walked down to meet them.

"Captain James?" a man in tactical gear with a Whittaker patch on his shoulder asked as I approached. Whittaker mercenaries, and the symbol on the patch indicated the troopers were mages.

"Yeah." I read the nameplate on his chest. "Captain Conway? We need a very, very quiet evacuation of every house on this street, and the next streets over, except for number thirty-six nineteen. That one's our objective."

He shook his head, looking at the mostly dark houses along the street. "Just exactly what do we have in that house?"

"We aren't sure how many people are inside, but there's at least one psychopathic spirit mage, two pyromancers, an electrokinetic, a witch, and a general mage with unknown capabilities. That's assuming they drove here alone. We know that from the license plates of the cars parked outside the house. It's an HLA meeting."

A helicopter flew high overhead, and to me, it sounded incredibly loud.

"Can you tell that fool to fly higher?" I asked. "I'd rather we use quiet little drones if you need aerial surveillance."

Conway nodded. "Will do. When do you need those houses cleared?"

"Yesterday."

He chuckled. "Of course."

And of course the evacuation didn't go quietly. Dogs barking, babies crying, people talking loudly. We tried to take as many residents as possible out their back doors to minimize the chaos on the street, but fairly shortly someone in our target house peeked through a curtain to see what was going on.

I got on the phone. "Mychal, I think our chance at stealth has flown. Move people in. You've got men on the street behind Farringdon's house, right?"

"Yeah. I'll set things in motion. Dani? You tie yourself to Carmelita, and tell her that maintaining her shield is her only job. No heroics, you hear me? Kirsten will tear me a new one if you get yourself killed."

"Will do. Take your own advice, okay?"

I grabbed Carmelita and passed along Novak's orders. She grinned nervously.

"Aye, aye, Captain."

Two men and a woman walked up to me and identified themselves as Whittaker's spirit mages. I placed the two men about a hundred feet on either side of Farringdon's house and kept the woman with me and Carmelita across the street two houses away.

When everyone was in place, I sent a robot up to the door of Farringdon's house and had it ring the doorbell. Nothing happened for several minutes, but I had it continue to ring the bell. Pretty soon, the door opened.

"What do you want?" a woman's voice yelled. Susan Reed.

I used a loudspeaker to answer. "Everyone in the house needs to come out, one at a time, with your hands empty and held away from your body."

The door closed. We waited. After five minutes, I had the robot start ringing the doorbell again.

When the door opened again, a bolt of lightning fried the robot, then the door closed.

I picked up the microphone for the loudspeaker. "You're completely surrounded and completely outnumbered. You have the option to surrender or die, but we aren't going away. Don't be stupid."

"You have such a soft, gentle way of inducing compliance," Carmelita said.

"Hell, what am I supposed to do? Send in a keg of beer and hope they drink themselves into a stupor?"

She shrugged. "Works for me."

The door opened and Susan Reed stepped out. She stood on the porch for a moment, then raised her hands and started walking toward us. The door closed behind her.

"She is an illusionist, among other things," Carmelita said.

"Susan, stop." I said as she reached the middle of the street. "Stop, turn right, and walk down the middle of the street."

Susan kept coming. I pulled out my Raider and fired at the street in front of her. The explosive incendiary bullet blew a hole in the pavement, but the woman didn't flinch or slow down.

"Shields up!" Carmelita shouted. "That's not Susan!"

"Fire!" I shouted. Heavy weapons cut loose all along the street. The thing that looked like Susan exploded, very loudly and spectacularly, sending a fireball thirty feet in the air. When the debris stopped raining down and the smoke cleared, the hole in the pavement was five feet wide and two or three feet deep.

"Nice call," I said. I suspected the thing we destroyed was probably a household robot with a little extra explosive attached, but I'd let the forensics team figure it out later. The presence of the explosive was disturbing. I got on the radio Conway had given me.

"Captain Conway, assume there are explosives in the house."

"Roger that, Captain James. I'm going to move people a little farther away."

One of the second-story windows broke, followed by a fireball arcing out of it toward the troops on my left. It splashed against an invisible shield twenty feet from anyone.

"Wow." Carmelita breathed.

"Magitek shield," I said absently. "A magitek works with an aeromancer to store magik in an enhancing device. Any mage can trigger it. The larger the device, the stronger the magitek engineer, the more power can be stored, the larger the shield can be generated, and the more times it can be used."

"But it runs down?"

"Yeah, like a battery. It has to be recharged."

"And that's the kind of thing you can do?"

I glanced down at her. "We build that kind of thing in factories. Magitek engineers design them, usually a technician builds them. What I can do is this."

I sent my magik into Farringdon's house, killing all the electricity. The lights went out, along with the heat. A second spell caused all the locks to pop open. My third spell was designed to disable any firearms inside. I picked up the microphone again.

"If you're tired of your parlor games, we're waiting for you to come out, one at a time, with your hands in the air."

A bolt of pure energy blew the front door off its hinges and lanced toward us. It hit Carmelita's shield, and I found myself flying backward through the air with her. Thankfully we landed on a grassy lawn, and she managed to hold onto her shield, but it still felt as though I'd been dropped on my back from ten feet in the air. Which I had.

Gasping for breath, my mind a blackness filled with pain, I saw three bolts of energy blast from our three spirit mages toward the house, through the open space where the front door had been. Silence followed.

The woman spirit mage leaned over me. "Are you all right?"

"It probably depends on your definition of all right." My vision was still sprinkled with incredibly bright white lights.

"I think you can probably send your people into the house," she said.

"Farringdon survived a battle with other spirit mages before."

Her grin held no humor. "Not with me, he didn't. Besides, Captain James, we cheat."

She held out a magitek enhancer on her palm. "I believe you made this, or at least that's what Commissioner Whittaker told me."

"I do a little side work for spare change occasionally," I said, taking the hand she offered. She pulled me to my feet, and every rib I owned protested. I picked up my radio. "Captain Conway, send a shielded team in. Tell them to be careful."

The inside of the house's first floor was a shambles. Farringdon was dead, but to my amazement, the others were all alive, although unconscious. I had no doubt Farringdon's bolt would have killed me if not for Carmelita's shield.

There were seven people besides Farringdon in the house. Rather than take any chances with them, Whittaker had them all taken to Gettysburg instead of the jail downtown.

As I was supervising all that, my phone rang.

"James."

"Where the hell are you?" Kirsten asked. "Are you all right? I think I just saw someone who looks like you on the news."

I glanced at my chrono and discovered it was almost two o'clock in the morning. "Just getting ready to go home. It's been a long day. Why are you still up?"

"Watching a newscast. Really exciting. There's some kind of mage battle going on up in Owings Mills, and they evacuated an entire neighborhood. You're not involved in that, are you?"

CHAPTER 30

"Do I get overtime for days like this?" Carmelita asked when I dropped her off at the gates of the Domingo estate at four o'clock in the morning.

"Dream on. You would if you were simply a detective, but as a sergeant, you're considered supervisory personnel."

"Who do I supervise?"

"You can boss Luanne around when I'm not in the office."

"Fat chance. The woman is twice my size, and she's got an attitude."

"That's why I hired her. Quit whining, you make twice what she does."

"You really are a bitch."

"Yup. See you Wednesday."

"Today's Tuesday."

"And that's why I hired you. Keen sense of the obvious. Sleep in. Turn off your phone. I'm going to, and Whittaker can screw himself. We just busted the HLA leadership in the Metroplex. You'll be a hero next time you show up at Whodunit."

Carmelita grinned. "Drive safe."

If it wasn't for one of Kirsten's potions, I wouldn't have trusted myself to drive the forty minutes home. I parked the car, stumbled into the house, and poured myself a hot bath with a large dollop of healing oils. A healthy portion of aged whiskey comforted me as I soaked for an hour, then I crawled into bed.

The phone rang, and as I struggled to find it, I saw there was light outside my window. In spite of my best intentions, I had forgotten to turn the damned thing off before I went to bed.

"James."

"Where are you?" Whittaker asked.

"In bed. What the hell do you want?"

"Did anyone ever tell you that you're insubordinate?"

"Every boss I ever had."

I heard him chuckle. "When do you plan on coming into the office?"

"Tomorrow. I don't even know what day today is, but whatever tomorrow is." I hung up, turned off the phone, and went back to sleep.

When I next awoke, the sun had shifted. I got up, took a shower, and felt a lot more human than I had earlier. Kirsten had left a note on the kitchen table, *Come down to the shop and we'll go shopping.*

One of our elven bodyguards, Llerywin, was lying on the couch watching an old vid on the screen in the living room.

"Where's your buddy?" I asked.

"Siarin went into town with Kirsten."

"So, Siarin is Kirsten's bodyguard and you're mine?"

She sat up, "Oh, no. We take turns guarding the house and the shop. We were told that you didn't need a bodyguard, but Kirsten does."

"Who told you that?"

"Your mother."

I laughed. "I'm not going to ask exactly what she said."

"Kirsten left some apple tarts. They're tasty."

They were, and that's what I had for breakfast with a cup of coffee. I stuck my head out the door and discovered that the temperature was frigid in spite of the bright sunshine, so I dismissed the idea of riding my bike. On the drive in, I reflected that having a car was nice sometimes.

It was midafternoon when I arrived at Enchantments. Kirsten immediately turned things over to her assistant and hauled me back out the door.

"I have a friend who sells clothes that are exactly what you need for work," she said. "They're a little pricey but worth it."

"I was thinking more about a bargain store chain," I said. "I mean, if I'm going to be destroying my clothes on a regular basis, why pay more?" The jeans and leather I normally wore took a lot of abuse.

The shop she took me to was owned by a witch, and the high prices were due to the spells she set into the fabric. The owner showed me a lovely blue satin blouse, very girly with ruffles. I about swooned when she slashed it with a knife—or tried to slash it with a knife. The fabric didn't cut.

"Oooh, I like that," I breathed.

"Wash and wear, also," she said. "Blood, dirt, soot, fecal matter—all comes out with grocery-store detergent, or in a sonic cleaner if you have one of them."

"You don't happen to sell jeans and casual clothes like this, do you?"

"Sure." She led me to a back room. "A lot of my customers are bikers. They're very hard on their clothes."

Even the eye-popping bill didn't stop me from hauling an armload of clothes out of the place. I had even ordered a new spelled-leather biker jacket. What good is money if you can't spend it occasionally? Besides, my salary had just doubled.

We hauled it all over to Kirsten's shop, and I stashed it in her back room. Since I still had a few dollars in my bank account, I offered to take her out to dinner to thank her. To my surprise, Aleks walked into her shop just as we were about to leave.

I felt myself light up at the sight of him.

"We're on our way to Jack's," Kirsten said. "Care to join us?"

We asked Siarin if she wanted to go with us, but she declined. "I'm going back up to your house, and Llerywin and I are going to that Kitchen Witch place. Great food."

Jack's Oyster House was down the hill from Kirsten's shop, right on the street that ran around the harbor. As we walked, I noted the lack of people out on the street. It was a part of town that catered to pedestrians and tourists, and though the evening was brisk, it seemed rather deserted.

I mentioned it, and Kirsten said, "It's been this way since the riots and then the bombing of the Palace of Commerce. It's gotten even worse since Lucifer's Lair closed. There have been a number of muggings and demons snatching humans right off the street, even in the middle of the day."

A single woman was walking about a block in front of us, and suddenly three demons appeared, two in front of her and one behind. She screamed. I took off running, drawing my Raider. Aleks pounded along just behind me.

When I drew close enough that I could be sure of my shot, I stopped, aimed, and fired at the demon with its back to me. It arched its back and staggered. I fired again and resumed running.

One of the demons grabbed the woman. Aleks extended his arm, and a ball of white energy left his hand. It hit the third demon, and it disappeared. That caught the attention of the demon holding the woman, and it turned toward us. I stopped again, aimed, and fired. The demon was a couple of feet taller than the woman, so I wasn't worried about hitting her. My bullet hit it in the face and exploded.

Aleks let loose with another energy ball, and the demon I had shot in the back disappeared, just as its companion had done.

We reached the woman just as the now-headless demon dropped her. I caught her in my arms and pulled her away.

Other people on the street were screaming and shouting, and a uniformed cop ran up to us. I identified myself, then turned the woman over to him and his partner. I gave them a brief synopsis of what we'd witnessed, and made sure she was all right and the cops had everything under control.

As my companions and I continued down the street, Kirsten said, "See what I mean? It's bad for business."

The upside was that we didn't have any trouble finding a table overlooking the harbor at Jack's. We entered our order and sat back to watch the sunset.

"What happened to those demons?" Kirsten asked Aleks.

"They were converted into energy," he said. "Broken down into their atomic particles."

Her brows knitted.

"Aleks is a spirit mage," I said. "Even rarer than a magitek."

He nodded. "I pull energy from the world around me. What I did with those demons was concentrate the energy, then redirect it."

"Spirit magik is very similar to that of elven mages," I said. "I had three spirit mages on that job last night. One of the HLA radicals we captured was a spirit mage. I was very thankful that we came out of that without destroying the neighborhood and losing a lot of lives."

Our drinks came along with three dozen oysters, and we dug in.

"Have you ever used a magitek enhancer?" I asked Aleks.

He shook his head. "Not entirely sure what that is or how I'd use it. Isn't that what your grandfather used to create the Rift?"

"Yeah, but that wasn't his intention. He wanted to scare humans into dismantling their nuclear weapons and end the wars."

"It worked," Kirsten said.

"Not in the way he intended," I said.

Humans had destroyed all their nukes in the aftermath of his demonstration. No one wanted a repeat of seeing a ravenous hoard of demons boiling out of another Rift. One was bad enough. That was before they discovered the Rift moved around, and that different beings came through in different locations.

I continued, "Anyway, the woman I spoke with last night said that a small enhancer could be used by a spirit mage to focus the energy she wielded and control it better."

"I'd like to talk with her," Aleks said.

After dinner, we walked Kirsten back to her shop. I gathered a few of the clothes I had bought to take to Aleks's apartment, and she put the rest in her van to take to our house. Then Aleks and I walked to his place to spend the night.

CHAPTER 31

The unfortunate part of the exciting night with Farringdon and his HLA buddies was the news organizations showing me at the scene. It was almost impossible to block all the drones they had constantly flying over the city. That evidently alerted my Aunt Courtney to the fact that I was still living in the Metroplex.

A week after the Farringdon affair, I left the office about six o'clock to meet Aleks for dinner at a fancy steakhouse. I walked because the restaurant was only about six blocks from my office, and parking in downtown Baltimore had been a mess ever since the invention of the automobile.

The harbor in Baltimore was surrounded by hills to the north, so everything going north was uphill. It was cold and gray, but the lights and decorations for Christmas seemed to make the weather feel appropriate. There were people out on the street, and the surviving stores were staying open to catch as much business as they could.

The attack came as I crossed a small, sort of sunken, park surrounded by skyscraper office buildings. I entered the park at street level and proceeded to the three sets of wide stone steps on the other side, leading up in three different directions between the tall buildings. I often used it as a shortcut.

I heard the distinctive sound of a fireball and automatically triggered the magitek device I carried at all times. It set up an electrical field around me—a poor substitute for a true shield, but that was something my magikal talents couldn't produce.

The fireball hit the field, causing a flash of electrical energy mixed with fire. Hot and uncomfortable, but at least I didn't get charbroiled. I dove for cover behind a fountain with a sculpture and drew my pistol. Before I could look around to try and see where the fireball had come from, a bolt of lightning hit me. The electrical field surrounding me dealt with that a lot better.

Two more fireballs flew in from different directions, and the heat level turned up significantly. Looking around wildly, I tried to see where the attacks were coming from. A man stood at the top of one of the staircases, and I snapped off a shot in his direction.

Another lightning bolt lit up my magitek shield. I spun around and saw another man standing at the open side of the park. I fired at him, and he went down. At the whoosh sound of more fireballs coming at me, I leaped up and ran toward the steps to my left. The fireballs splashed behind me.

The little lightning box that my father built for me when I was a child had four settings. The personal shield was step one. The second setting loosed an electrical charge thirty feet in the direction I pointed it. The charge was enough to knock out a man or stun a demon. The third setting would launch a lethal hundred thousand volt, one hundred fifty milliamp lightning bolt at my target. And phase four would blanket a twenty-foot radius around me with a sustained hundred thousand volts. When my daddy made that box, he wasn't worried about collateral damage, only about keeping his little girl safe.

I triggered step four.

A man appeared on the top of the stairs ahead of me, levelling his pistol at me. I fired and he flinched. I took the steps three at a time, firing again. Then I got close enough, and the lightning hit him. He did a shaking, stumbling dance and collapsed. I ran past him as a fireball splashed down behind me.

At the top of the steps, the walkway widened, creating a corner I could hide behind. I skidded to a stop and peered back around to see if anyone followed me. Two men were starting up the steps. Taking a deep breath to steady myself, I stepped out, aimed, and shot one and then the other, then ducked back behind the corner.

I waited, expecting more attackers. It took a couple of minutes, but three more men made their appearance at the foot of the stairs. Two fireballs roared up toward me, and I ducked back until they passed by, then I popped back around the corner and fired three shots. They all ricocheted off a shield. Evidently, the third man was an aeromancer.

Pulling back out of their sight, I ejected the magazine from my pistol and loaded more ammunition. By that time, I was sweating. If I ran, they had a clear shot at me in what amounted to a tunnel between two buildings. If I stayed where I was, they could advance on me behind the aeromancer's shield.

Looking around for another way out, I couldn't see one. There weren't any doors in the buildings to either side. I took inventory of the magitek devices I carried and realized I didn't have any that might help me.

In desperation, I activated another box—an enhancer—and linked it to my father's lightning box. I hadn't ever tried that before, so I didn't know if it would do anything. Taking a deep breath, I dove forward into the archway, activating the third setting on the lightning box and pulling the trigger on my Raider as fast as I could.

The thunder was deafening in the closed space as a massive lightning bolt exploded down the stairway. When my sight returned, I saw three bodies sprawled on the stairs. The walls of the two buildings and the stairs were scorched black. Beyond, the park was on fire, and the fountain I'd hidden behind was destroyed.

I rose and stumbled away, half-blind and totally deaf. I made it to the next street, emerging into a very quiet evening. People on the street stared at me. I broke into a run, putting as much distance between me and my attackers as I could.

Half a block away, I turned and looked back. Every person on the street was still frozen, some looking at the space between the buildings where I had been, some watching me. No one came out of the walkway.

A uniformed cop came toward me, pistol in his hand and fear evident on his face. He shouted something, but I couldn't hear him. I held my pistol out to my side. He shouted again, and this time I read his lips and dropped my gun, wincing slightly as it hit the ground, and hoping it didn't discharge.

"I'm a cop," I said, but I couldn't hear me either. "Captain Danica James, Arcane Division. My badge is on my belt, right side, under my jacket."

He didn't look convinced. He said something else, and I figured out that he wanted me to turn and face the wall. I spread my arms, my hands held wide away from my body. Shrugging my jacket off my shoulders, I said, "I'm going to drop my jacket."

I managed to wriggle out of the jacket and let it slip to the ground. With one foot, I kicked it away from me.

"My ID is in the inside left-breast pocket," I said, then cursed myself for my wording as his eyes flickered toward my chest.

Another cop approached, bent down, and picked up my jacket. He fished inside it and pulled out my ID on its lanyard. After looking at it, then at me, and assuring himself the picture matched my face, he nodded to his partner.

"Sorry, Captain," he said. I faintly heard that as my hearing began to return. The second cop stepped forward to hand me my jacket.

"Not a problem, officer," I said. "Following proper procedure will keep you alive long enough to draw your pension."

I saw him relax a little and felt tension flowing out of my body. I slowly bent down, picked up my Raider, and holstered it.

"What's going on?" the first cop asked.

"I was ambushed in the park." I gestured toward the walkway between the two buildings. "Mages."

The second cop moved as though to go check it out.

"No! Don't go in there. Call for Arcane."

The cop pulled out his radio and made a call. My hearing was returning, and I could hear all the bystanders talking and calling out. A drone with the markings of a media company circled overhead.

※

Aleks glanced at his watch as I approached. "I was beginning to think you'd stood me up," he said as the maître d' showed me to his table. I knew I was forty-five minutes late, and wasn't sure he would still be there.

"Small problem. Thanks for waiting."

I looked up at the waiter, who had evidently been waiting for me along with Aleks and appeared immediately.

"A double Irish whiskey. On second thought, make it a double."

"A double double Irish whiskey?"

"Yeah. It's been a rough day."

CHAPTER 32

"Okay," Whittaker said, "I've read Novak's official report. Why don't you tell me what really happened."

We were sitting in the Commissioner's office the morning after I'd been ambushed.

"I was on my way to Lonsby's to meet a friend for dinner," I said. "I cut through that little park across from the Hedrik Hotel, and the next thing I know, someone's tossing fireballs at me. There was also an electrokinetic. I defended myself."

Whittaker nodded. "Quite ably. We recovered nine bodies, and three more men were admitted to the hospital with severe electrical burns."

"I only saw seven."

"Whatever you unleashed into that park would have done your grandmother proud. Our experts estimate the power of the lightning bolt that hit the park at about a billion volts—as strong as a natural lightning bolt. A large cloud-to-ground natural lightning bolt. With the energy contained by the buildings around it, all that force was amplified." He leaned back in his chair. "Now, how in the hell did you generate that much power? I thought your electrokinetic talents were very weak."

I licked my lips as I pondered what he said. My grandfather's experiment with magikally enhancing a nuclear bomb flashed through my mind.

"You know that little lightning box I carry? The one my father made for me?"

He nodded.

"I linked an enhancer to it."

His mouth fell open, and he stared at me. He acted like he was about to say something a couple of times, but the wrinkles in his forehead and his frown deepened each time. Finally, he shook his head.

"Holy Mother of Jesus," is what finally came out.

The discovery I had made excited me. "That box has several settings, and although I never thought about it before, I think I now understand how he built it. I think it must contain a stepped-phase enhancer coupled to an electrokinetic storage unit that draws on my natural electrokinetic magik. Add a more powerful enhancer to it, and if the effects multiplied at a logarithmic rate, that means that..."

Whittaker waved his hands. "Stop. You've just sailed way past my technical understanding of magitek. I'll take your word for it. I don't even understand how my magik works, just how to apply it. My degree is actually in geology."

My boss was an earth mage, a geomancer. Not a lot of call for causing earthquakes in an urban environment, so I'd never seen him actually use his magik. Geomancers usually found jobs in mining and construction. Need a tunnel through a mountain to build a road? Hire a geomancer. Need a hundred-foot-deep hole for the foundation of a skyscraper with underground parking? A geomancer could do that in a day, whereas mechanical equipment would take a month. As long as you had a place for him or her to put the dirt and rocks, of course.

"I didn't know you could do something like that," he said.

With a shrug, I said, "I told you I've never tried it before. I was in a tough place. Two pyromancers were coming after me, protected by an aeromancer. No place to run. I've linked multiple enhancers together when I didn't have one large enough to do the job, but that was a temporary solution. So, I gave it a shot."

"Well, we have the identities of the men who attacked you. Three of them are, or were, Findlay guardians. Two were Moncrieff guardians. I think it's pretty obvious who ordered the attack, but the way things stand, there's not much we can do about it."

"Take it to the Magi Council and impose sanctions?" I suggested.

He shook his head. "About the only leverage we have is to cut off their access to the Port of Baltimore, and we've already done that. The only Findlay ships allowed into the harbor are those your grandmother authorizes. Moncrieff, Akiyama, and Findlay ships sailing under Courtney's orders are blocked, and they're blocked from Montreal as well. They're using Wilmington for all their shipping to the east coast."

He offered to assign extra men to me as bodyguards, but I turned that down. I already had two elves following me around after Siarin and Llerywin reported the ambush to my mother and grandfather.

Gildor and Elbereth had introduced themselves to me, but as far as I could tell, they changed the glamours they wore on a random basis. They would have stood out otherwise. Gildor was as tall as my grandfather, with bronze hair and bronze eyes. Elbereth was around six feet eight inches tall, with silver hair down to her butt and silver eyes. They also glamoured their car. I was fairly sure they were the two cops who followed me to work that morning. I assumed there were two more who would work the night shift.

I went down to my office, checked in with the detectives who reported to me, stole a cup of fancy coffee from Novak, then entered my private domain, where Carmelita and Luanne were busy dealing with paperwork.

Pulling up our caseload on my computer, I took care of my bureaucratic obligations, assigning new cases and reading reports. With the additional manpower Whittaker was hiring, I had enough detectives to cover all the crimes on the list, and I rather wistfully wished I had something to do that was more exciting.

It was close to noon when Kirsten called. "Are you really busy? There are a couple of women here looking for you."

"Who are they?"

"Beatrice and Karolyn Moncrieff."

"Don't let them out of your sight. They're probably there to plant a bomb. I'll be right there."

I practically flew out of the office, grabbing my coat and telling Luanne and Carmelita, "Both of you, with me."

Novak and his partner were out on a case, but I had faith the disguised elves wouldn't let me escape their protection. As I trotted down the street, I reviewed what I knew about my two cousins. Their grandfather George and their mother—my Aunt Courtney—were weather mages. Karolyn had a number of the talents that went into that, but the talents didn't all fit together properly. Still, she was far stronger magically than anyone I wanted to tangle with.

Beatrice was younger than Karolyn and me by about ten years, and I didn't know her at all. She had always struck me as shy and mousey, and I couldn't remember a thing about her magik. Her father, David Moncrieff, had been a medium-strength aeromancer and a weak pyromancer. From the research I did at the time of the demon murders at Findlay House, I gathered that his ambition was his strongest attribute—probably a major reason his older brother Alan sent him to North America rather than keep him home in Scotland.

Luanne was doing a good job of keeping up with me, but

Carmelita was practically running and falling behind. I stopped and let her catch up.

"Look," I said, "a friend of mine runs a witchy apothecary shop. Two women—mages—who are definitely not friends of mine just walked into her shop asking for me. Carmelita, I want you to go around the back through the alley and set up an air shield to prevent anyone from leaving through the back gate. Luanne, I want you to come inside with me."

Luanne was a medium-strength aeromancer—not in the same class as Carmelita or Mychal—but I figured she could handle an air shield of sufficient strength to blunt an attack from my cousins.

When we reached the block with Kirsten's shop, I sent Carmelita down the alley. "It's the third gate on the right."

Then I grabbed Luanne's sleeve and pulled her close. "Stay right next to me. If I reach out and grab you, shield both of us, okay? If things go south and I'm too far away, shield yourself."

She nodded. Her face showed excitement, but not fear. I thought that was a good sign.

We entered the shop and saw Kirsten standing behind the counter. Her eyes met mine, and she gestured with her head toward a small alcove where she served tea to special customers. I walked over there and found Karolyn and Beatrice sitting at the small table, a teapot in the middle of it. Each of the sisters had a dainty teacup in front of them.

"What can I do for you ladies?" I asked.

Their eyes looked beyond me, taking in Luanne and a petite young woman—I assumed it was Elbereth—who had followed us into the shop.

"It's a private matter," Karolyn said. "Family business."

"You'll have to forgive me, but I dealt with a bit of family business last night, and it wasn't pleasant."

Karolyn shook her head. "No tricks, Dani. We're not here to kill or kidnap you."

Beatrice anxiously played with her teacup, picked up one of the little cookies from a plate, then put it down. She turned her face up to me, and I could see she was in some distress.

"It's about Dad," she said.

Karolyn didn't look very happy either, nor did her face display her normal disdain for me.

"Luanne, can you throw a soundproof shield around this little room?"

"Yes, ma'am."

"Do it, please." I stepped into the alcove and took one of the remaining chairs. Sound from the outer room ceased.

"Okay, what's going on?"

Karolyn braced herself, acting like she wanted to say something, but hesitated. She tried again but couldn't manage to speak.

"Our mother killed our father," Beatrice blurted out. "She and Karl drowned him in the bathtub."

"I see. Did anyone witness this murder?"

Beatrice nodded. "I did."

Well, that put a different light on things. My mind raced. I probably couldn't arrest Courtney, let alone prosecute her, but one of the first things that flashed through my head was what Alan Moncrieff, the Family head, would think about his brother's demise.

"Tell me what happened."

I knew that Beatrice and her father were close, but I had been told he and Karolyn didn't get along at all. No one had mentioned the relationship between Karolyn and Beatrice. Karolyn reached out, took Beatrice's hand, and squeezed it. The two sisters looked at each other, and Karolyn nodded. She didn't let go of the younger woman's hand.

Haltingly at first, Beatrice began to tell her story. She had gone to her father's suite of rooms at the Moncrieff estate at Elk Neck to talk to him. The door off the hallway was unlocked, so she entered. The lights were on, and the bedroom door was open. She heard noises, and she followed the sounds to find her mother and Karl Rudolf drowning her father in the bathtub. Horrified, she ran to Karolyn. When the two of them returned to their father's room, they found him dead.

I listened to the whole story without interrupting. Beatrice was in tears by the time she finished. Karolyn's face showed rage.

"I'm not sure I can do anything," I said. "Commissioner Whittaker and I discussed your father's death, and we don't see any way that we can investigate it. The situation with Moncrieff and the Council isn't exactly cordial. What I would suggest is to contact your Uncle Alan and tell him what you told me."

Karolyn shook her head. "Moncrieff has sold its soul to Akiyama. I'm sure Alan would be outraged, but he's kind of stuck. He backed Mom's play to ally with Benjiro, and defied the Council."

"Does your mother know, or suspect, that you saw what they did?" I asked.

Beatrice shook her head. "I don't think so."

"We didn't tell anyone that he was dead," Karolyn said. "We let his valet find him. I didn't want Mom suspecting anything. I don't trust her."

"I can understand why," I said. "What about taking a trip to Scotland? Do you think your uncle will protect you?"

The women looked at each other, then Karolyn shook her head. "No idea."

"Do you trust Olivia? What if I could smuggle you to Ireland?"

Blank looks. Beatrice turned to Karolyn, whose eyes took on a distant look as she stared past me. After a minute or so, Karolyn said, "At least she wouldn't try to murder us. Is that where she is?"

"She and Osiris. That's why your mother hasn't been able to

consolidate her hold on Findlay. They have Kennedy protection there."

Karolyn gave a jerky nod. "That might work. How?"

"Whittaker can get you on a plane. We still hold the airport here. We'll need to get your statements for evidence if we ever bring your mother up on charges before the Council. Where are you staying?"

"At Elk Neck. Mom and Karl are living at Findlay House," Karolyn said.

We agreed that they would come into town Saturday evening, as though they planned to go clubbing, and spend the night.

As I walked them out of the shop, Karolyn hung back.

"I know you and I have never gotten along," she said. "I was really nasty to you when we were girls. And it's not like the enemy of my enemy is my friend, or anything like that, but you're a straight shooter. You've got that morality thing, and I know you won't stab me in the back."

She took a deep, shaking breath. "What Beatrice didn't tell you was that Dad's bed was all messed up and there was a bottle of wine with two glasses on the bedside table. When she saw them, Mom was naked but Karl was clothed. She got Dad drunk, took him to bed, then afterward I guess they went to take a bath. Candles and everything. Karl came in, and they killed him, then they went back to her room and spent the night together. I've been such a damned fool."

She shifted her gaze toward Beatrice, standing on the sidewalk, waiting for her.

"I love that girl. She's really sweet, kind, vulnerable. Everything I'm not. She used to follow me around like a puppy when she was young. Mom never had time for her. For either of us. If they hurt her, I'll kill them, and that's a promise, not a threat."

I nodded. "I'll talk to Olivia and Whittaker. We'll get it arranged."

CHAPTER 33

I went back to the office and spoke to Commissioner Whittaker. He agreed to my plan. Next, I sent a message to Olivia through my implant. Her response came within five minutes. "Of course, they can come here. I'll have a plane waiting for them."

Kirsten and I went home with our elven bodyguards, stopping for food at a couple of shops on the way. Having a house full of hearty appetites put her in a good mood, and I figured they might save me from eating leftovers the rest of the week.

Two more elven warriors were waiting for us at our house—the night shift I was expecting. Folodin and Fasparin were brothers, and although they told me they weren't twins, I had a hard time telling them apart. Kirsten was so deep into her relationship with Mychal that she wasn't looking at other men, but in years past, she would have been all over them.

So, we had six elves plus Mychal joining us for dinner. I put the extra leaf in the dining room table and set it with the good china I had given Kirsten years before. She sent me and my new shadows to the liquor store, and we brought back a case of wine. The smell when we walked into the house was divine.

By the time we finished dessert, I surveyed the wreckage and confirmed that leftovers weren't going to be a problem. Cleaning up wasn't either. The elven women waved their hands, and within fifteen minutes, I was putting the china away.

"Can you do that?" I asked one of the F brothers.

"Of course."

The way he said that irritated me. "But that's women's work, right?" I asked.

Siarin laughed. "If you want the job done right, you call a woman. Men are much better at making messes than cleaning them up."

Kirsten looked puzzled. "I thought elven society was a matriarchy. Aren't the women in charge?"

All of the elven women laughed. "And that's why," Siarin said.

I had never seen an elf blush, but the tips of all the males' ears turned pink, and the women laughed harder.

Llerywin said, "Men are too controlled by their emotions. They get excited and start chopping off heads without thinking. That makes them good warriors, but good decision making requires a calmer personality."

Considering that all the elves—male and female—carried swords that were almost as long as Kirsten was tall, I didn't think that was a metaphor.

Soon after, Gildor and Elbereth took their leave, and the rest of us retired to our rooms. The F brothers said they planned to stay awake all night, and Kirsten set them up with a bunch of vids they could watch. To my surprise, they seemed to favor romantic comedies.

It didn't seem as though I had been asleep very long when a flash of light and a sound like a gong signaled that something was attempting Kirsten's wards. I leaped out of bed, grabbed my Raider, and also picked up my laser rifle where it sat next to my bedroom door. Cautiously pulling open the curtains, I flinched back as a fireball splashed against the wards.

Obviously, Courtney was persistent. I found my phone and called dispatch, then pulled on a pair of pants and strapped on the holster belt for the Raider. Picking up the electrical box and the rifle, I headed for the stairs. Mychal and Kirsten, both nude, met me on the landing. Mychal had his Raider, and Kirsten had a glowing witch stick in one hand and an athame in the other.

"Demons," Kirsten said.

I barreled down the stairs to the tune of the gong going off twice more to find the four elves, their swords drawn, guarding the doors and the windows in the dining room.

"Demons!" I shouted.

"Yes, we know," Llerywin said, as calmly as if she were commenting on the weather. "The question is, do we go out to meet them, or hope the wards hold and they can't get in?"

Something crashed against the front door, and the house shook.

"We've never had a demon attack us before," Kirsten said.

"Mychal, stay with her," I said. I nodded to Llerywin. "I have help on the way, but I worry about our neighbors."

"Then let's go out and see if we can bring some order to the situation," Siarin said.

The door flew open. "I'm closing it behind you," Kirsten said, then started to chant.

The F brothers lunged toward the door. A demon appeared, and one of the brothers spitted it with his sword. The demon melted, just as Ashvial did when he was shot by my mother's elven arrow.

I followed the brothers out with the elven women behind me. I saw a blue demon—a frost demon—across the street. I triggered the guidelight on my rifle and saw a red dot appear on his chest. I triggered the laser, and his chest disappeared.

The elves each engaged a demon, using magik as well as their spelled swords. I shot two more attackers with the laser rifle. Lights started going on in the houses around us.

A demon fell out of the sky, landing right in front of me and reaching for me. I shot him at point-blank range, severing his arm from his body. But he was too close and bowled me over before I could shoot him again. I rolled, trying to get away from him, but he grabbed my leg with his remaining arm. Drawing the raider, I pressed the muzzle against his head and pulled the trigger. He didn't let go.

A sword flashed, and his head spun away from his body. He still didn't let go. The sword fell again, and I was free, but the demon's hand still clutched my calf.

The world lit up, as though a miniature sun had sprung to life twenty feet above the street. I could see two demons heading toward me, and I shot both of them with the laser.

Quiet. No sounds at all. No demons, except for the bodies of those I had shot. Two elves were still standing in front of me. In the distance I could hear sirens gradually growing louder.

"Where are the others?" I asked the woman nearest to me.

"Around back," was the answer.

"And up here." I looked up and saw Siarin standing on the roof. "I think we got them all," she said.

A car skidded around the corner and screeched to a stop forty feet away. Two men jumped out with their pistols drawn. I recognized them as detectives I commanded in the Arcane division—both mages.

They cautiously approached, surveying the damage and inspecting the bodies of the demons. For some reason, the one who had grabbed me hadn't melted either.

One of the cops walked up to me. "Captain James? What's going on?"

He appeared to have trouble keeping his eyes on my face,

and then I realized I was naked above the waist. And cold. Damn, it was cold, with tiny flakes of snow falling.

"Demon attack," I said. "Luckily we had some elven friends spending the night with us."

Both of the elven women were completely naked, so that attracted the detectives' attention even more than my chest.

More cars showed up, mostly marked cars carrying uniformed officers.

"What's that?" one of the cops asked, pointing to the little sun lighting the scene.

"I thought we needed a little more light," Kirsten's voice came from the doorway behind me. "Demons don't like sunlight."

Proving they were all heterosexual, every cops' attention turned to her, the elves and I forgotten.

A drone buzzed overhead. I swung the laser toward it and vaporized it.

"Last damn thing I need are topless pictures of me on the morning news," I said to the nearest cop, who gaped at me.

A fire truck pulled around the corner, attempting to navigate its way between cop cars and cars that had been parked on the street before our little battle. Our house looked fine, although one bush was burned and another one had icicles hanging off it.

The garage of the house to our left was burned, along with the car inside it, but the rest of the house looked okay except for a little char. The house on our right had caught fire, but it was out. The firemen rushed around, then their captain showed up.

"We had a call about the fires, but they seem to have gone out."

Kirsten walked up, wearing an old, baggy dress she wore for cleaning house. She handed me a sweatshirt and said, "Our neighbors are going to be upset with us. I figured if I put the fires out, they might cut us a little slack."

The fireman shook his head. "Put them out? How?"

She waggled her fingers. "I'm a witch."

He stared at her, paled a little, then said, "Do you need a job?"

The sweatshirt helped with two things—the men quit staring at my chest, and the night got a lot warmer. I couldn't feel my bare feet, though, and wished I had a little of Kirsten's magik.

I called the detective over and asked, "Where's Lieutenant Berger? Who's coordinating tonight?" Sam Berger was an old partner of mine, and not my favorite cop. One of the first things I did when I was promoted to captain was move Berger to the night shift so I didn't have to interact with him.

"Uh, I guess you were kinda busy," the cop said. "The damned demons have gone crazy all over town. Attacks at Novak, Domingo, and Whittaker. Attacks downtown. An attack on the airport. Lieutenant Berger responded to the attack at the Whittaker estate, and the last I heard, he was down."

"So, who's coordinating?"

"Sergeant Johansson. He's out at the Novak estate."

I rolled my eyes, pulled my phone out of my pocket, and called dispatch. That was all we needed—Martin Johansson's younger son involved. Who knew what side he was on.

"This is Captain James, Arcane Division. I'll be online in five. Do you have communications with Commissioner Whittaker?"

"Yes, ma'am. Voice only."

"Tell him to call me, and route coordination through me. Tell Sergeant Johansson to worry about Novak, and leave the rest to me."

"Thank God," the dispatcher said. "It's been chaos the past hour."

I found Mychal talking to a couple of uniforms. "I need you to get online and coordinate the police out at Novak and Domingo, and try to keep that fool Johansson from doing any more damage."

"What's going on?" he asked as he followed me into the house.

"We weren't the only ones attacked. This kind of crap is going on all over the Metroplex."

I opened my laptop and logged in. The last thing I wanted Whittaker to find out was that I didn't need a computer to access the secure police systems. A flood of reports hit my screen, and it took me ten or fifteen minutes to sort them out.

The fighting at Novak was over, but the assault at Domingo was ongoing. An earthquake was reported west of Baltimore. That was where the Whittaker estate overlooked the Patapsco River. Whittaker mercenaries had repulsed the assault on the airport. Downtown Baltimore looked like there was a demon riot going on, with widespread fires and destruction.

Kirsten set a cup of coffee down beside me, and I gave her a smile of thanks as I picked up my ringing phone. It was Whittaker. I took a large swallow, burned my tongue, and answered, "James. How are things in your neck of the woods? We're having a lot of fun here."

CHAPTER 34

Thankfully, I was working from home, and Kirsten fed me. It was late afternoon before I looked up from the computer, and my eyes were tired and burning. I had to spell my phone to renew its charge.

The demons had disappeared, the fires had all been put out, and the body counts tabulated.

There were no reports of trouble from Findlay House, the Moncrieff estate at Elk Neck, or anywhere near Wilmington, but several of the Novak-Findlay-Domingo allies among the Hundred had been attacked. I was beginning to understand what the Rift War had looked like.

I joined Kirsten and Mychal in the kitchen. He looked as worn out as I felt. Kirsten handed me a small potion bottle, and I drank the contents without asking what it was. I immediately felt better. Then she put a bowl of soup on the table, along with a large glass of fruit juice.

"Are we really in a war against the demons?" Kirsten asked softly.

Mychal and I looked at each other. "They're becoming much more aggressive," I said, "but I'm not sure if that's happening only here in the Mid-Atlantic, or if it's happening worldwide."

Mychal shook his head. "I talked with my uncle, and he said some of our allies in Europe reported demon incursions yesterday, but nothing on the scale we are seeing here. He thinks what we have here is Akiyama testing us. They're sending their demon allies against us to test our strength." Mychal's uncle was Henri Novak, the Family's head of security.

"Do you know anything about Akiyama's military strength?" I asked.

"Our intelligence says they have an armed force of at least forty thousand magik users and two hundred thousand human troops. Most of those are in Asia. But they could arm at least that many more within a couple of months. That's a far greater army than we could field, even if we could hire all of Whittaker's mercenaries."

"Their magitek facilities are larger than ours also," I said, "and more directed at designs the military could use. I did a paper on their factories when I was at university. Of course, I had only public sources of information, but those indicated that most of their magiteks were what I would call technician level. They seem to have put a lot more funding into such uses, whereas we go where the money is—catering to wealthy Magi."

The magitek-powered Akiyama cargo plane I had disabled at Elk Neck showed how far our Far-Eastern competitors had come. The design was clumsy, but the execution was solid. Before I went to bed, I called Mary Sue. She reported that she had produced the first prototypes for the drones Findlay and Whittaker had ordered and promised to deliver them to me the coming weekend.

The following morning, after an uninterrupted night's sleep, I took care of the most pressing business I had, then took my car, and flew out to the Whittaker estate overlooking the Patapsco River west of Baltimore. It wasn't necessary, but I was curious. I did call ahead, because being shot out of the sky wasn't on my to-do list.

The Patapsco wasn't a large river until it widened where it emptied into the Chesapeake, but it ran through a deep, narrow ravine it had carved for itself over the millennia. The Whittaker estate was comprised of a series of walled compounds arrayed across a ridgeline on the east bank. The main residential compound, surrounded by fifteen-foot stone walls, had the best view. Flanking it on three sides were three more compounds used for housing and training the mercenaries who provided the Family with most of its wealth. Most of the arms factories were located in West Virginia.

I circled above the area, and the damage from the earthquake was immediately apparent, but as far as I could tell, none of the walls or the buildings had sustained any damage. The river had changed its course in several places, and the road leading to the estate was cracked and jumbled. I wondered when they dug the wide, deep ditches outside the walls. I'd never seen them on previous visits.

I set the car down on the driveway inside the main compound, and rolled to a stop near the garages. As I started my trek up the sidewalk leading through expansive lawns toward the front door, two very large shaggy gray dogs raced down the hill.

My first instinct was to draw my weapon, but instead, I stood very still and extended my hands. They slowed, approached me cautiously, stretched to sniff my hands, and began wagging their tales. I had met my boss's Irish

Wolfhounds before, and in spite of being the size of ponies, they were quite gentle and friendly.

Following the dogs, Tom Whittaker came down the steps, wearing khaki pants and a white, open-collared shirt with the sleeves rolled up.

"Good to see you," he called. "Come on in and have a drink."

"I'm on duty," I replied. "My boss frowns on that sort of thing."

He grinned. "We won't tell him."

"I was curious to see the damage from the earthquake," I said as we walked up to the house.

Whittaker chuckled. "No earthquake, just some minor changes to the local topography. The demons weren't expecting the ground to open up and swallow them, or for the river to change course and wash them away."

"I noticed some ditches outside the walls that looked like they had been burned. I thought fire didn't affect most demons."

"It doesn't. Those were tunnels filled with a magikal compound comprised of thermite, white phosphorus, and hydrogen peroxide. We triggered a magitek device that collapsed the tunnels, and contact with air ignited the mixture. Rather explosively. We discovered during the Rift War that demons don't like it very much. I also instructed our magiteks to try your little trick and link an extra enhancer to each of our lightning generators. The effect was quite astonishing."

I imagined it would be. The enhancers on the lightning generators installed on the compound's walls were huge—three-cubic-foot boxes.

Inside the house, he ushered me into his office, poured us each a drink, and offered me a soft leather chair. We discussed the events of the previous night and preparations for any new incursions. I also gave him an update on production of the drones he had ordered.

"I'm a little short-handed," I said. "Sam Berger was the night-shift supervisor, and he's out of commission."

"Sam died this morning," Whittaker said. "His injuries were too severe." He suggested a couple of other senior lieutenants to take Berger's place, and we agreed on one.

"Are we still on for Saturday?" I asked.

"The Moncrieff girls? Not a lot of nightclubs going to be open in Baltimore after the rampage downtown," he answered. "Are you sure their mother is going to believe they're going out clubbing?"

"The clubs that can be open, will be," I said. "Depending on whether they think we can provide security. They don't make any money when they're closed."

"Yeah, even during the Rift War, bars managed to serve customers."

"I need that security on Friday night as well. The media will report it, and people will feel safer coming out on Saturday. The more people out and about, the easier it will be to make those women disappear."

He regarded me for a long moment. "Done."

CHAPTER 35

Kirsten, the elves, and I went downtown on Friday night. Kirsten looked at me like I was crazy when I first told her what I planned to do.

"Are you shooting for the trifecta? You've been attacked by mages, then demons, and now you're trying for vampires tonight?"

But the enthusiasm she exhibited in deciding on an outfit for the evening was a little unsettling.

"I didn't say you have to go with me," I said. "It's liable to be dangerous."

She shrugged. "Probably, but you need someone to watch your back, and I haven't been out dancing in forever."

The elves seemed to have no qualms at all about going out, and I guessed it was because they were bored. The F brothers adopted glamours that were only slightly less intimidating than their natural forms, while the women took their cues from Kirsten, conjuring outfits that appeared to invite hypothermia but covering up with long, heavy coats. Of course, their actual clothing, hidden by the glamours, was magikally hardened leather and brass over wool. But that didn't keep me from shivering at the sight of them wearing only mid-thigh skirts and translucent tops with nothing underneath.

Not having the shielding abilities of my companions, I took one look at the temperature outside and pulled on thermal tights, thick socks and jeans, a turtleneck and a sweater, topped by an insulated thigh-length leather jacket. The same way I would dress if I planned to ride my motorcycle. It didn't matter how sexy I dressed, I didn't feel sexy when I was shivering and my teeth were chattering.

I also loaded up with magitek devices, including a couple of extra enhancers. And I reminded myself—again—to talk to Mychal about helping me create a personal shielding device.

We drove downtown in three cars—Kirsten and I in my police car, bracketed by the elves in their glamoured armored assault vehicles. I used my access credentials, and we parked in the garage under Police Headquarters.

"Our normal routine?" Kirsten asked.

"Might as well see what's open," I replied.

A lot of wreckage from the demon riot was still apparent—burned out buildings and cars, wreckage strewn about. There were about half as many people on the street as what I would normally expect on a Friday night with winter closing in. A closer inspection revealed that while there were demons about, they were of the minor breeds—succubae and incubi, liliths, a few devils, and the omnipresent imps. I saw no standard demons anywhere. Vampires were the dominant race other than humans.

Uniformed cops and Whittaker's mercenaries were out in force. A cop or a soldier on every corner. Combined with the evidence of the riot, it wasn't very inviting, but it did feel somewhat safe.

Our favorite kick-off point for a night out, the Gaslight Grill, was closed, its windows boarded up. Jack's was also closed. The Faraway Inn was open and only about half full, so we went in and ordered drinks with several pounds of boiled shrimp, a platter of crab fluffs, and the kitchen-sink nachos. Just because the elves had glamoured themselves a foot shorter than their actual size, it didn't mean their appetites had shrunk. I hoped the war ended before I went broke feeding them.

From what I could overhear of the conversations around us, I guessed that none of the other patrons had been downtown for the riot the night before. I could understand why those who had, and weren't either in the morgue or the hospital, would be shy about sticking their necks out.

After that light snack, we headed up the hill to what usually was the liveliest vampire club in town. Bran's Castle was run by vampires for humans, and part of its allure was an unhealthy number of vampires hanging out to thrill the human patrons. I knew they had been cited a couple of times for discriminatory labor practices, but I couldn't figure out why a human would want to work there.

True to their reputation, the bartenders, bouncers, and waitstaff were all vamps. About a third of the clientele was as well. I didn't see a single demon of any type.

The band was playing an eerie sort of gothic music, but I found that more to my taste than the heavy metal some vamps preferred. After our drinks were delivered, it didn't take long for a number of men—human and vampire—to ask the three ladies I was with to dance. One vamp did approach me, but he took the hint when I snarled at him.

"That was rather anti-social," one of the F brothers—Folodin possibly—said with a grin. Their glamours were quite different, making them a little easier to tell apart.

"Was it? I was hoping I came across strong enough. It saves the trouble of breaking his arm later."

"Not a fan of vampires, I take it," Fasparin said.

"I had a bad experience in high school. First person I ever killed. I caught flak for weeks at school."

He chuckled. "So, you do consider them persons."

"Sure. They're sentient. They have some rather disgusting dietary habits, but so do some humans. Don't you consider them persons?"

"Vermin."

"Ah. That's a very enlightened attitude."

He grinned and winked at me. "Some of our people hunt them for sport. Personally, I prefer deer. It tastes a lot better."

"There aren't any deer in Iceland."

He sighed. "That is true. We sometimes go to Scandinavia or Canada to hunt. There were deer in Alfheim, though."

"You came across the Rift?"

He sighed again. "Yes, but not by choice. I came over with Joren. Wrong place at the wrong time. The Rift opened and just swallowed us up." He took a sip of his drink. "I miss the trees. That's what's nice about Loch Raven. Iceland doesn't have any trees."

Two bars run by demons were still operating. We hit both of them, and they were practically deserted. Another vampire bar was about half full, and then we went to a human bar. The bouncers at the door were turning away demons and vampires.

I danced a couple of dances with men who asked me, and one each with the F brothers.

Siarin and I were on our way back from the ladies' room when I came face to face with Karl Rudolf, my Aunt Courtney's lover and conspirator.

"Why, hello, Danica. You're looking well." Although he had lived mostly in North America for the past fifty years, he still had a trace of German accent.

"Hello, Karl. I'm surprised to see you here. It doesn't seem like your kind of place." I was on the older side of the people in the bar, but Rudolf was fifty years older than me. He was a stocky man, several inches shorter than I was, with a short beard and rust-colored hair cut in a long flat-top. Wearing a tweed jacket, he looked like the university professor he'd been before inheriting control of his Family.

"I was in the mood for some music, and I do like to dance," he said. "Would you share a dance with me?"

That surprised me, but I figured he wanted to talk, and I was curious.

"Sure." I followed him out onto the dance floor. He danced like a middle-aged university professor, too. When the song was over, he offered to buy me a drink, so I went back to his table with him. His bodyguards responded to some sort of unspoken signal and vacated their seats, leaving us alone. Siarin managed to be unintrusive but hovered just behind one of Rudolf's guardians.

"I heard a rumor you were staying out at Findlay House," I ventured, picking up my drink when it slid out of the compumenu on the table.

He gave me a ghost of a smile. "Yes. Your Aunt Courtney has suffered so many losses in such a short time. She needs a friend to lean on."

"And is Aunt Veronica staying there, too?"

"Ah, no. My wife is in Vienna. She and the girls don't feel safe here after what happened at Lila's betrothal. But I have business interests in the Metroplex that I need to attend to. Have you seen your grandmother recently?"

"No, I believe she's traveling. Granduncle George's death hit her hard, and then there was all that unpleasantness with the Council." I couldn't figure out what he wanted. Surely he knew Olivia was in Ireland.

"Yes, the Council is being difficult," he said. "Speaking of rumors, I heard that Olivia wanted to bring you into the Family business. Of course, you should speak to Courtney if you are still interested in that."

I batted my eyes at him. "I don't believe Oliva and I ever

discussed that. I've just been promoted to captain, and I'm very happy working for the police."

I finished my drink, thanked him, and excused myself, going back to the table where Kirsten and the elves awaited me. Shortly thereafter, Rudolf left with a girl young enough to be his granddaughter. I wondered what Aunt Courtney was doing that left her lover at loose ends. I couldn't believe she would send him out to spy. His ham-handed attempts to extract information from me were laughable.

We called it a night and trekked back to the police station. On the way, we passed the little park where I had been ambushed by the mages.

"Holy crap," Kirsten said. "This place looks worse than the riot areas."

"It looks like a full-scale mage battle happened here," Folodin said.

The walls of all the buildings around the park were blackened, and the windows facing the park shattered. The nice little fountain was a pile of rubble. The trees were all either burned or looked as though they had exploded. My legs felt a little weak with the realization of how close I'd come to dying the way my attackers did.

A couple of blocks along, a gang of young vampires came down the street toward us. They were rowdy—laughing and shouting back and forth to each other. Acting a lot like a bunch of drunken human teenagers. When they saw us, they quieted down, whispering between themselves.

The elves all dissolved their glamours and drew their swords. The vampires turned and ran.

CHAPTER 36

I got up early the following day and drove out to Loch Raven. Mom had called and said the generator and the turbine had been delivered, and Mary Sue planned to meet me there with the magitek enhancer for the assembly.

Kirsten had to work, and the elves did something similar to a coin flip to determine who got to go with me and who had to stay in the city.

I arrived shortly after Mary Sue did, and Mom fed us breakfast. Then Mary Sue went out to her car and came in with the new enhancer. It was pink. Mom turned a baleful eye on me, and Mary Sue burst out laughing.

"And here's the invoice," Mary Sue said, handing Mom a piece of paper.

Mom studied the invoice, then she burst out laughing. I looked over her shoulder. The charges for the enhancer were detailed, then down at the bottom was a line that read, 'Discount: color pink −25%.'

"Did you bring the drone prototypes?" I asked.

"Yeah. We can play with them after we install the turbines."

"You're going to help me?"

"Gotta make sure you do it right. After all, you only finished second in your class at uni." She winked at Mom.

We also had the help of six huge elves, whose strength I greatly appreciated. A task I thought would take all day was done by lunchtime.

We were just finishing up when Aleks called. He had been in Pittsburg negotiating warehouse space for a Midwest distribution center.

"Hey, do you want to go out to dinner and a play in Columbia tonight?" he asked.

"I can't. Have to work. We had a little demon trouble while you were gone."

"Yeah. I saw the damage downtown. Soon, though, okay?"

"Soon. I promise."

"Do you know Karl Rudolf?" he asked, changing subjects. "He called me, said that since Olivia Findlay wasn't with the Findlay organization any longer, Courtney Findlay-Moncrieff wanted to meet with me to talk about the distribution deal I was negotiating with Olivia."

"That's not entirely true," I said. "I think you should probably check with Frank Novak before you do any business with Courtney. She controls only a small part of the Findlay empire."

After lunch, Mary Sue brought out the drones. All three were leaf green on top. The bottoms of each were painted in a different color—sky blue, cloud white, and cloud gray.

"Camouflage," she said. "The only variations on the assembly line are color and what kind of magik you want to use for the weapons. So, get that from the customers, okay?"

We took the drones down to the lake, and she demonstrated their capabilities one at a time. The first drone shot impressive bolts of lightning, the second had a flame thrower, and the third fired a small missile, about six inches long with stabilizer fins. The explosion was obviously magikally enhanced and impressive.

"Using the plans you gave us, we enhanced the motors, so they're basically self-charging. We've had one drone flying for a week now without landing or refueling. And that electrical trigger you devised is amazing. Even a non-mage can control and fire the things," Mary Sue told us.

"I had to figure out how Kirsten could use all the magitek devices I've built into her greenhouses," I said.

We put the drones into the trunk of my car so I could take them to Whittaker. I was packing up to leave when my mom and Joren came out of the house.

"Do you have an operation scheduled tonight?" Mom asked.

"Yeah, why?"

"Concerning Courtney Moncrieff's daughters?"

That stopped me. "Where did you hear about that?"

Joren spoke up. "One of the assets we have inside Findlay House overheard a conversation between Courtney Moncrieff and a man named Karl Rudolf. Your name was mentioned, and they talked about laying an ambush for you when you met the women—her daughters."

"That's lovely," I said. "We have a leak."

"If we have assets inside their operations, we'd be foolish to think they don't know what we're doing as well," Joren said.

From what elven history I'd studied, the elves had been experts on intrigue a couple of hundred thousand years before humans created their first farm.

"Thanks for the warning. Unfortunately, I don't have any way of calling things off or changing the plan. We'll just have to ambush the ambushers."

"Do you need any help?" Joren asked.

"I'll take all the help I can get," I said. "I don't know what we're facing. Courtney's tried to kill me three times using mages, once using demons. Maybe this time she'll just post snipers."

Joren beamed. "Right answer. Where should my warriors and I meet you?"

On my way back to town, I called Whittaker and told him what Joren's people had heard. Our phones were secure magitek devices, so I didn't worry about eavesdroppers. We made some changes to our plan, and I hoped they would be enough.

<hr />

My team was comprised of Mychal Novak, Carmelita, Luanne, and four elves—the F brothers, Gildor, and Elbereth. Altogether, Whittaker had committed two hundred men to the operation, and Joren was bringing thirty-five warrior mages.

Mychal and I entered the club two hours before the scheduled rendezvous and took a booth in the back corner near the washrooms. Carmelita and Luann showed up an hour later and took a table by the front door. The elves, wearing their glamours, came in shortly after and sat at a table in the center of the room near the dance floor.

The band started playing, and they weren't half bad. The club we had chosen was the one where I saw Karl the night before. I told myself it was pure coincidence, but how had Courtney and Karl found out about our scheme? It had to be a leak at Police Headquarters, and Whittaker had discreetly assigned a small team to investigate it.

Unless Karolyn and Beatrice had sold me out. I refused to believe I was that gullible.

"Don't you think we should attempt to talk to each other on a first date?" Mychal suddenly said. "So, I like long walks on the beach, pina coladas, and blonde witches with curvy figures."

I laughed. "And here you are, stuck with me. Yeah, you're right. We shouldn't act like we're a couple of cops waiting for something to happen. Okay, I'll go first. I was mostly raised by my mom, with a lot of time spent at Findlay House. Attended school at Roland Prep, then they shipped me off to the Huntingdon School in western Pennsylvania—either because I was a bad influence, or to protect me, or to protect the girls at Roland, depending on who you talk to. Then Johns Hopkins for a magitek degree with a minor in computer science. And you?"

"What made you decide to become a cop?"

"A mental condition. Sheer stupidity."

Mychal laughed. "I can relate to that. Where did you meet Kirsten?"

"At Huntingdon. She was there voluntarily—scholarship student. You might have noticed, she's the kind of woman the Magi want for their trophy wives. She's not a mage, but she's a strong witch. Good breeding stock."

Mychal blushed so deeply I thought he might combust. "That's not how I see her. That's not who I am."

"No, I don't think so, either. She's not the trophy wife type. I saw her set a man's crotch on fire once."

He barked out a laugh. "Yeah, I can see her doing that. She doesn't suffer fools."

"Our sisters just walked in," I said.

To my immense gratitude, he didn't turn around. "Anyone with them?"

I waited to see who came in behind them. "Doesn't look like it, but people at three different tables took a visible interest."

Using my implant, I sent a message to my team, including Mychal, identifying the suspect tables.

What constraints are we under? A message came back from Gildor.

Since you aren't a cop, just be discreet and don't get caught. Avoid harming any innocents, I sent back.

His table was in my line of sight, and I saw him nod.

Karolyn and Beatrice were dressed to impress—and to catch someone impressive. What Kirsten called fishing clothes. They took the booth right behind Mychal. It was available because the shield he had cast in front of it prevented anyone else from sitting down there.

They ordered drinks and some munchies. Sure enough, the tables I had identified continued to take an extraordinary interest in our sisters.

A tall man at one of the tables I identified stood and went to the washroom. One of the glamoured elves followed him. The elf came back a few minutes later, but the tall man did not.

Carmelita jumped up and came over to the sisters' booth. "Beatrice! Long time no see," she said and sat down. "How's it going? What are you up to?"

It turned out that Carmelita and Beatrice went to high school together, unsurprising as the children of the Hundred tended all to go to one of three or four schools.

All sound from their booth suddenly ceased, and I knew Carmelita had cast a sound shield over them. She stayed there for about five minutes, then went back to her table with Luanne. Next, one of the glamoured elves came over to the sisters' booth and asked Beatrice to dance. After he returned her to their table, the other two elves came and asked both women to dance.

I kept my eyes on the watchers. Some of them were starting to get bored. All of them were watching other women, at least a little bit. I sent a signal out for my main distraction.

Loud, boisterous, and flaunting it—obviously half drunk—Kirsten and Mary Sue blew into the place like a hurricane, drawing every eye in the place.

I sent a signal to the elves dancing with the two sisters. They immediately changed their own glamours and cast glamours on the sisters. The elf with Beatrice led her back to the washrooms, then out the back door. The elf with Karolyn took a roundabout route toward the front door on the side of the room away from my blonde friends.

I followed Beatrice, and Mychal, Carmelita, and Luanne followed Karolyn. The women cops paused in the doorway to discuss which bar they should hit next. The remaining elves followed me, stopping in the hallway and blocking the exit.

Mary Sue and Kirsten made their way to my booth and took our seats. With any luck, Courtney's men had lost us in the confusion.

Outside the club, each of the women was immediately surrounded by a phalanx of glamoured elves and ushered into a waiting armored limo. I crawled in beside Beatrice, and the driver took off for the loop around the harbor to the freeway.

"Did Karolyn get away?" Beatrice asked. I held up my hand as I accessed my implant, then smiled.

"Yes. They're taking the eastern route to the airport and we'll meet them there." I pulled a recorder out of my pocket. "Now, I need a statement from you—an official statement—of what you saw at your house the night your father died."

CHAPTER 37

We fell in behind an armored personnel carrier with Whittaker markings, and another one fell in behind us. I knew the vehicles were mage shielded, as was the limo we rode in. Our driver was a human mage, but the other three people in the car with us were elves. It would be the same in the car that carried Karolyn and Novak.

Everything went smoothly until we slowed down on the exit ramp to the airport. That's when a volley of fireballs splashed down on the road ahead of us and on our vehicles.

"Well, that settles the question of whether your mother wants you back, or whether she wants you dead," I said. Beatrice's eyes were large in her face, her shock evident.

Lightning lashed out toward the cars, and more fire rained down on the road. The cars slowed. We might have been shielded, but the road was melting in front of us. With a loud crack, the road buckled, and the ground shook with a mini-earthquake. The car we were riding in lurched as the ground heaved beneath us, and then we were rolling over into the ditch. Luckily, by that time, we had slowed quite a bit, and we were all wearing seat belts.

The car came to a stop on its side. The door next to me was up, so I reached for the handle.

"Everyone stay in the car!" one of the elves said. "We have to maintain the shield."

The ground continued to move under us, bouncing the car around. Lightning and fire fell on us, the thunder rattling my nerves. I wondered what our attackers would try next.

Whittaker and his commanders had spent a considerable amount of time identifying the best spots for an ambush. Their prime candidate was that exit ramp. So, although the pounding we were taking seemed to go on forever, it actually lasted about ninety seconds. That's when Whittaker's troops and ten of Joren's elves cut loose on our attackers.

Just as a couple of demons bounced off the elves' shield around our car, the night lit up like a fireworks display. Balls of energy hit the two demons, and they vanished. The mages attacking us turned their attention to the mages who were attacking them. Things got a lot more chaotic, but after a couple of minutes, the ground stopped moving, and we stopped being bounced around.

I looked out the windows and saw shadowy figures moving around, but the trees hid most of them, and it was impossible to tell which side anyone was on. I pulled my magically enhanced night goggles from my bag and put them on. The scene gained clarity.

It appeared that human mages were primarily engaged with other human mages, while the elves were hunting demons, and the demons were hunting us. Very convenient when the demons funnel into an area the elves could easily defend with their swords. I saw a lot of headless demon bodies lying around.

The demons broke first. Being essentially selfish beings, and with the promise of a human meal growing less likely by the second, the ones remaining decided to go elsewhere for dinner.

The elves let them go, turning their attention to the mages attacking us.

Humans and elves had basically left each other alone during the Rift War while both fought the demons. I quickly understood why. Humans greatly outnumbered the elves in our world, while the average elf wielded magik as strong as the second tier of human mages. Their strongest mages, such as my grandfather, Joren, were in a league all their own. Lightning bolts that put Olivia's best efforts to shame pounded down on Courtney's mages. Blasts of wind blew them off their feet and hurled them into the trees. The trees themselves attacked them. And when the combatants came within physical proximity, the elves' spelled swords often beat down the human mages' shields.

I felt for my phone and called Mychal.

"Novak," he answered.

"Are you okay?" I asked. "Where are you?"

"Yeah. At the airport. I'm watching one hell of a lightshow west of here. Is that you?"

"We were ambushed."

"I had a feeling. I changed our route, and we came through Glen Burnie. Wow. That lightning is spectacular."

"Are you outside? Get the hell into the hanger! Get her on that plane!"

"I was waiting for Whittaker's boys to get here. We're still in the—" The call abruptly ceased. I tried to call him back, but no answer. I called Whittaker.

"Mychal is at the airport, but I'm not sure where. His phone went dead."

"I have people there and more on the way," he said.

I hung up, and said, "Let me out. I need to see what's going on."

One of the elves pushed open the front door of the car and crawled out. Once he was on solid ground, he opened my door.

I scrambled out and looked down into the car at Beatrice trying to follow me.

"Stay in there," I said. "The elves will keep you safe."

I turned and looked in the direction of the airport and saw flashes of light.

"That's Karolyn," Beatrice's voice said beside me.

"How can you tell?"

"Her lightning always has a weird tinge of green. Dunno why."

Crap. I turned to the elves who were all out of the vehicles and had formed a protective ring around Beatrice and me.

"We still need to get this young lady to her plane, and we also need to help the other young lady at the airport. Got anything quicker than walking to get us there?"

We were still at least a mile from the cargo hangers where the plane waited to take the sisters to Ireland.

"We can have cars here in five minutes," one of them said.

I pointed to the lightning at the airport. "As soon as possible."

He barked out orders in Elvish, and the elves split into two different groups—one running toward the airport, the other into the woods to our east.

"It will take our warriors only a couple of minutes to reach the airport," he told me. "The others went to get the vehicles Joren and his warriors came in."

I knew there was no way I could keep up with the elves going to the airport, so I stood around and fidgeted while I waited. Most of the fighting around us was winding down. Two helicopters with Whittaker markings passed low overhead on their way toward the airport.

Four minutes and thirty seconds after the elves departed, the first truck showed up, with three more following it. The flashes of green lightning in the direction of the airport had ceased, replaced by flashes of red and white. I grabbed Beatrice and jumped into the lead truck along with four elves, and the driver took off.

We bypassed the passenger terminal and sped toward the cargo warehouses. When we reached the area, we almost drove into the middle of a mage battle. Whittaker had stationed a group of mages and a company of human soldiers to guard the plane, and if Novak had just taken Karolyn inside, they would have been all right.

The armored limo they came in lay on its side next to a large hole in the tarmac. The undercarriage of the limo was warped and twisted, and it was pretty obvious that a bomb of some type had gone off under the car. Magikal shields weren't perfect, and they couldn't protect against everything. The concussive force of a bomb going off under a shielded limo had to go someplace. Magik bent the laws of physics, but it was still subject to them.

Three other vehicles in the area were damaged, two of them on fire. The Whittaker men were fighting from inside the hanger, and when the elves showed up, they attacked the assaulting force from the rear.

We hustled Beatrice out of the car and into the hanger. A large cargo jet sat there, its engines idling. I turned the girl over to three women in Whittaker uniforms that I recognized as former Findlay guardians—people who had served under Osiris. They urged her up the steps and into the plane.

Looking around, I saw Mychal sitting on the floor with his back against a stack of boxes. His head was bandaged, and one of his arms was wrapped tightly to his torso. I walked over and squatted down in front of him.

"You don't look so good," I said.

He lifted his head and opened his eyes. "I screwed up."

"Where's Karolyn?"

"I don't know. When I woke up, I was here with a medic working on me."

I sprang up and whirled around. Locating a Whittaker man with officer's insignia on his shoulders and a mage patch on his sleeve, I strode over to him.

"Where's the woman who was in the limo?"

He shook his head. "They captured her. She put up a helluva fight, but we couldn't get to her. I lost three men trying." He pointed in the direction away from where I'd come. "Drove off that way."

I made a command decision. "Tell the pilot to take off. Getting one of them out of here is better than worrying about both of them."

He nodded and pulled out a radio. A minute or so later, the jet revved up its engines, and Whittaker's troops lay down a barrage of fire, clearing the area outside the hanger. The jet started moving, and I felt its magitek shields engage. It carefully steered around the crippled limousine, then turned and headed along the taxiway toward the runway. A fireball splashed harmlessly against its shield.

When it reached the runway, it didn't slow down, but gained speed and was soon airborne. I figured Whittaker had precleared it for takeoff.

I turned back to the officer. "Do we have any tracking on the vehicle that took her?"

"Yes. It's on the freeway headed north. We're tracking it with drones, helicopters, and we have vehicles following it. Commissioner Whittaker wants you to call him."

I did so.

"Dani, we can stop that car," Whittaker said, "but I have no idea what will happen. They haven't acted like they care if she dies."

"They're probably taking her up to either Findlay House or Elk Neck," I said.

"Elk Neck," he replied. "They don't use the road from Findlay to the freeway. They would have to drive past the

Novak and Domingo estates, and that hasn't worked very well recently."

"So, we can either risk her life by stopping the car, or hope that they don't kill her once they take her out of the car."

"They had a chance to kill her when they captured her. She was unconscious."

I ground my teeth together so hard my jaw ached. "Yeah, let them go. We'll see if we can figure another way to get her away from her family."

CHAPTER 38

We took Mychal to the hospital where he was treated for a three-inch cut on his head, a concussion, and a broken arm. His father sent guardians, and they took Mychal to the Novak estate. He hadn't had his seat belt on when the bomb went off and got tossed around the inside of the limo. An elf who was standing outside the limo was killed.

From what I could gather, Karolyn fought like a mama bear, and tried to make it to the hanger, but was overwhelmed by the sheer number of attackers. When all the smoke and lightning cleared, we counted twenty-four human and elven corpses, along with a dozen demons. The two trauma hospitals where we sent the wounded had a busy night.

"Tell me some good news," I told Whittaker when he called me after midnight.

"Susan Reed escaped from Gettysburg."

No one ever escaped from the prison in Gettysburg.

"I said good news. How in the hell did she do that?"

"Want to hear the bad news?"

I took a deep breath. "You really are a sadist, you know?"

"Brian Crozier escaped with her."

Crozier was the pre-eminent non-demon crime boss on the east coast until I put him behind bars six years before. That had earned me a promotion to sergeant.

"She's been there a couple of weeks, and she managed to escape? No one escapes from Gettysburg," I said.

"We had an escape thirty or thirty-five years ago," Whittaker said. "We're investigating, but it had to be an inside job. I'm sending a couple of truthsayers up there first thing in the morning."

I thought that Susan teaming up with Farringdon was bad, but Farringdon was simply a psychopath. Crozier was a criminal genius in addition to being a psychopath.

"Any other kernels of joy you'd like to drop on me before I go home and go to bed?"

"Helen Dressler-Findlay formally endorsed Courtney's claim to Findlay this evening."

Helen was my Granduncle Richard's widow. Her three daughters had a potential claim to Findlay after Courtney, her sister, Karen, and a few others, including me, if you went down that rat hole far enough.

"Goodbye," I said, and hung up.

※

When I straggled into the office mid-morning the following day, I told Carmelita about Susan.

"Watch your back," I said. "I doubt that woman has a forgiving heart."

She laughed. "The problem is, all of the information we have on her is useless now. She can't go back to her home, or access her bank accounts, and she's not going near her HLA contacts."

I nodded. "She's starting a new life. Crozier has been out of commission for the past six years and totally cut off from communicating with his old organization. It splintered after his arrest, and after a short internal war, three different gangs formed with three of his old lieutenants in charge. I don't think any of them will be glad to see him."

"Is he a mage, a witch, or what?" Carmelita asked.

"A mage, and a fairly strong one. He has both aeromancy and hydromancy. One of his favorite ways of killing people who displeased him was to draw all the water out of their bodies. I understand that it's fairly painful."

She shuddered. "So, if he can't count on his old followers, what will he do?"

"Oh, I didn't say that. I don't think any of the current top crooks want to step aside for him, but a lot of those underneath them will take their chance."

"Where do we start?" she asked.

"With Miss Tina Stewart, Crozier's old flame. He's going to want to screw her or kill her. Maybe both."

When I arrested Brian Crozier, and he realized he was going in front of a Magi tribunal instead of a regular court of law, he ordered his mistress to sell his mansion and certain other assets to raise money for bribes. To do that, he gave her a power of attorney. Tina double-crossed him. She sold the mansion to herself for a pittance, appropriated the rest of his assets, took his right-hand man into her bed, and set herself up over the Crozier organization.

That sparked a war with several of the other criminals in the organization, not because of loyalty to Crozier, but because they didn't like taking orders from a woman. Tina was a powerful witch, with a talent for blood magik and an affinity for controlling demons. The war didn't work out well for her rivals, but she did lose control of Crozier's drug markets to Ashvial, and some of her human trafficking, firearms trafficking, and extortion businesses to other of Crozier's minions.

She maintained her hold on illegal gambling, money laundering, and counterfeit goods, as well as the prostitution and human trafficking that she had personally run for Crozier. One of her specialties was supplying vampires and sex demons—succubae, incubi, and liliths—to upscale human and vampire customers. It wasn't strictly illegal, as long as the minor demons were willing. Drugging or spelling or coercing them was frowned upon, however. Supplying humans to demons was definitely illegal.

We drove out to Tina's place north of Columbia. Crozier's family had been a successful third-tier Magi family after the Rift War, but after Brian's parents died in suspicious circumstances, he was the only heir. His record showed run-ins with the cops starting in high school. By the time he reached university and started pimping out his fellow students, loan-sharking, and dealing drugs, he was well on his way to a successful career. His mistake was trafficking underage humans and drugs that came across the Rift.

But in spite of Tina's treachery, he had enough funds to disperse among the Magi that he got only ten years in Gettysburg instead of life in Antarctica. It had pissed me off and given me my first lesson in how corrupt the magiocracy actually was.

A vampire guard came out of the gatehouse. "What do you want?"

I showed him my badge. "Please tell Miss Stewart that Captain Danica James is here to see her."

He looked skeptical, but went back into the gatehouse and made a call. His expression was replaced by one of baffled curiosity when he buzzed the gate open.

"That was pretty easy," Carmelita said.

"Tina likes me. Likes pulling my chain. Likes sparring with me. Thinks I'm funny," I said.

A robot butler showed us in to what once might have been a parlor or a salon. Tina had redecorated it into a harem, complete with couches and beautiful young men and women without any clothes. Tina wasn't wearing any, either, but I didn't worry about being over-dressed.

Tina Stewart was a little under six-feet tall, and as curvy and voluptuous as they came. Thick, wavy black hair spilled down her back, a perfect counterpoint to her pale skin and startlingly blue eyes.

"Danica!" Tina cried, rising from her couch and tumbling the young man who shared it with her to the floor. "It's so good to see you! It's been much too long. Come in, come in."

She noticed Carmelita.

"Ooo, isn't she sweet? How delicious." Turning her face back to me, she said, "But I'm sure you didn't bring her as a present. Too bad. Captain, now, I hear? Congratulations."

I didn't waste time on false pleasantries. "Brian escaped from Gettysburg last night."

Tina froze, her smile sliding away. Her mouth pursed, and she took a ragged breath. "Well, I assure you he isn't here."

"I didn't think he was. Not enough blood on the floor."

That earned me a nasty look.

"I just thought I'd drop by and deliver the news personally," I said. "Also, he escaped with a woman named Susan Reed. I would appreciate you letting me know if either of them contacts you."

"Oh, of course I will."

I chuckled. "Tina, you'd be a fool to try and take on Brian. And Susan's his new witch. Just call me, okay?"

She invited us to have some tea, and I accepted, which surprised my partner. We chatted for half an hour, and I inspected some of Tina's new art. As I expected, it all had an erotic flavor.

As we were driving away, Carmelita asked, "Do you think she'll call you?"

"Oh, hell, no. But I left half-a-dozen bugs in her house and on her property. I also got the number and internal ID code for her phone. Simple for a magitek."

I was rewarded before we even reached the end of Tina's driveway. Her phone call came in through my implant.

"Tony, Brian's escaped from Gettysburg!" As opposed to the languid, devil-may-care attitude she tried to project in person, she was practically shrieking in panic. I assumed Tony was Anthony 'Big Tony' Pelosi, one of Crozier's lieutenants who took over most of his drug trade that Ashvial didn't snag.

"No one escapes Gettysburg," Tony replied.

"Bullshit. James was just here looking for him."

"James. The cop?" Deep sigh. "Hell."

"I'm pretty sure he'll go to the cabin," Tina said. "We need to do something."

"Hell, he could go a lot of places. Why there?"

"That's where he is, Tony," she practically screamed. "I know it. I know him!"

"Okay. Round up all the muscle you can and send them over to my place. I'll get my boys together, and we'll all take a ride up to the cabin."

Tina's voice scaled down a few decibels, but it was still shaky. "Thanks, Tony. I owe you one."

I called Whittaker and told him what I'd learned. "Do you know where this cabin she's talking about is?" I asked.

"Crozier's family owned a lodge on Triadelphia Lake. His parents are deceased, so I guess the ownership would fall to him."

His parents were deceased because he killed them for the insurance money, something I uncovered but was never allowed to prove. His plea deal with the Magi tribunal had shut down the investigation into his truly serious crimes.

"I'll put together a team and send them out there," Whittaker said. He gave me a set of map coordinates to meet them.

The location turned out to be a church parking lot.

"Captain James?" A mercenary commander I had met before came forward to meet us when we arrived. "We have four helicopters loaded with men ready to drop into the woods around that house."

He led me over to a truck and showed me a screen. "We have a drone up. We haven't seen any activity as yet. The commissioner said to wait for you to give us the go."

"We're waiting for a gang of criminals to show up and assault the place," I said. "They should drive right by here sometime this afternoon. We encircle them and nail the people inside the house, as well as the thugs who want to kill them."

CHAPTER 39

The sandwiches the mercenaries offered us were pretty good, and we sat around, watched the video from the drone, and played cards. By the time Big Tony's men showed up, I had won two hundred bucks.

"I think you cheat," said one sergeant about twice my age after a streak where I'd won five out of seven hands.

"Of course I cheat, but until you catch me at it, stop whining and deal the cards." Even the rough old sergeant laughed.

We allowed Tony and his men to park along the road and fan out into the forest. The drone overhead tracked their movements as they surrounded the cabin, which was about twice the size of my house. Cute little vacation spot, similar to the one I owned out by Harper's Ferry.

The plan was to let them go in after Crozier and Susan, then we would close in and take them all. And as per usual, the plan went sideways almost immediately. As soon as Tony's men were in place, they let loose a barrage of lightning, fireballs, machinegun fire, and explosives.

The house wasn't warded, and no one fought back. When the noise stopped, what little was left of the cabin was on fire.

"I guess they were really happy to see their old boss again," I said to the mercenaries' commander.

"Well, at least we know how they're armed," he replied.

The overhead drone broadcast an order to lay down their arms and come out of the woods to the road with their hands up. Two minutes later, the magikally shielded helicopters set down in the area around the cabin and troops poured out of them. As soon as all the soldiers had disembarked, the ones I was with launched an attack into the woods at the gang members' backs.

"What do we do?" Carmelita asked.

"Watch the drone screen," I said. "They're all mages and trained soldiers. I'm not going to get in their way. If you think your shield is strong enough, you can go watch the fun."

She gave me a really funny look, but didn't make any effort to go see the fighting up close. We stood there and monitored the fighting through the drone's cameras.

Shortly after the mercenaries moved in, a voice behind me said, "You bitch. You'll pay for this."

Whirling around, I saw Big Tony about ten feet away with a gun pointed at me. He fired, and I dropped to the ground, at the same time attempting to draw my pistol. It wasn't necessary. Tony's bullet ricocheted off Carmelita's shield.

"Drop the weapon," I said, pointing my Raider at him. He shot at me again, with the same effect.

"Drop the shield," I said, much quieter. I felt air move around my face and fired the Raider. The explosive incendiary blew Tony's arm off at the elbow.

"How's your first aid?" I asked Carmelita.

"Adequate," was her response.

"Good. Do you want to do the tourniquet, or the bandage?"

The battle took a little over twenty minutes, and thirty

thugs were arrested. Five were killed, and two of the mercenaries were wounded. The mercenaries' medics patched up the wounded on both sides, and I watched all of Tony and Tina's men get loaded into buses that would take them to Gettysburg.

"Well, let's go see if there are any bodies in that cabin," I said, leading Carmelita toward the ruins of the cabin. We searched for half an hour, but found no evidence that anyone had been in the structure when it was destroyed.

"No car, no tracks. Not even a hint anyone has been here in days," my partner said. "Why do you suppose Tina was so convinced he came here?"

I thought about it. "He told her. He told her that if he ever broke out, that's where he'd go. Of course, that was before she double-crossed him, but she remembered it. And I'm sure he did too."

Sudden horrified realization hit me, and I accessed my implant to check the bugs I'd placed at Tina's. My head filled with the sounds of people screaming. I took off running for my car. I had the engine running by the time Carmelita caught up and jumped in.

"Where are we going?" she asked as I found a straight, empty stretch of road and took the car airborne.

"To Tina's. Call for backup to meet us there."

By the time we reached the old Crozier mansion, two marked cop cars already sat in front of the house. We drove through the open gate and Carmelita gasped. I slowed and craned my neck to see what she was looking at. Two mummies dressed in modern clothes lay outside the guardhouse.

"Crozier's trademark," I said and drove on.

We identified ourselves to the uniformed sergeant, and he

said, "The front door was open. Inside is as bad as anything I've ever seen. I'm sorry, ma'am, but one of my men got sick, and I couldn't get him outside in time."

Carmelita and I pulled on gloves and shoe covers, then we ventured through the door. The robot butler greeted us and asked for our names. I rolled my eyes and turned it off. We walked through the house, seeing several more mummies and two people dead from gunshot wounds. Some rooms appeared untouched, while others had been ransacked.

The grand dining room was a horror show. Crozier had crucified Tina. She was spread-eagled on one wall, pinned by spikes through her wrists and ankles. Her nose was broken, her eyes blackened, and her body was a mass of bruises, cuts, and burns. Her hair was burned off. I delicately picked my way past the pool of blood to try and look behind her. Her back appeared undamaged except for burns I attributed to her hair, so all the torture had happened after he nailed her up.

None of those injuries would have been fatal, however, no matter how painful, so the final act had to have been when he impaled her with a four-foot length of steel pipe.

"What's that smell?" Carmelita asked as she fumbled in her bag and pulled out a filter mask.

"Burnt hair," I said. I didn't blame the uniformed cop for puking. I'd seen worse done by demons, but the idea of a human doing that to another human turned my stomach.

"Go check the rest of the house," I told Carmelita. "Find any more bodies, and pay special attention to the rooms that have been searched. By the time he finished, Tina didn't have any more secrets, so he would have gone through all of her hiding places as well as his. He needed money and weapons, so I'll assume he has both now. I don't know if you noticed, but those guards out at the gate had pistols when we were here before, and they don't have them now."

Carmelita left very quickly, and I understood why. I went

back outside to call Whittaker and to wait for forensics and the medical examiner. I also told the sergeant to get the license numbers of all the vehicles on the premises.

"Hi, Boss," I said when he answered. "We blew it. I blew it. Crozier wasn't at his cabin, don't know if he ever went there. While we chased that wild goose, he hit his old home and slaughtered Tina Stewart and everyone else here. He's gone, and if Susan Reed is still with him, she's gone, too."

I asked for a list of every property that Crozier or any of his companies ever owned. The man had to go to ground somewhere.

About the time forensics showed up, Carmelita came out and handed me a tablet with a list of casualties and also of areas in the house that appeared to have been searched.

I trailed her back inside, and she showed me the locations. Most looked like secret storage places in the walls or floors—often in closets. A hidden staircase in the library led to a part of the basement accessible only from that one door. The room at the bottom had shelves filled with canned food, water, and a small stove.

"This was his bolt hole. A place to hide while the house was being searched," I said. "This is where I found him when I arrested him."

"How did you find it?"

I chuckled. "Bookshelves don't need electronic fingerprint readers." I took Carmelita upstairs and showed her where several books had been taken out of the shelf next to the one that moved. A small plate, almost unnoticeable, was screwed to the back of the shelf.

"He was very surprised when I came down the stairs and shoved my gun in his face."

I looked around. It had been six years since I was last in the house before my meeting with Tina. She had redecorated, but some things stayed the same. I figured Crozier had stashed some money she never found, and he now had any money, jewelry, or other easily carried form of wealth Tina had in the house. He had a few hours head start on us, and could be anywhere in the Metroplex, or even out of the area. One car registered to Tina was missing, so I put out a bulletin on it.

We had missed the target I was hoping for, but we had also put a large crimp in the Metroplex's top criminal leadership. Not completely a lost day.

It was getting dark when I drove Carmelita back to the police station and checked my messages. I called Kirsten to check in, then called Aleks.

"I would love to go to dinner with you," I said when he answered. "Can I come over and take a shower first? Then let's go someplace close to your apartment."

CHAPTER 40

My telephone was ringing. It was still dark, and it took me a moment to figure out that I wasn't in my own bed. By the time I crawled around the room in the dark, found my pants, and fished the phone out of the pocket, the caller had hung up. I would have tossed it and gone back to bed, except the call was from my mom. She knew better than to call me at five-thirty in the morning, so I knew it was important.

I made my way to the bathroom and called her back.

"Good morning, Miss Merry Sunshine," Mom said when she answered. I must have done something terrible in a previous life to draw a mother who loved to wake up at the crack of dawn.

"What's up?"

"One of the elves up at Elk Neck sent us a report on Karolyn Moncrieff. Why don't you drive up here?"

So, I hauled my ass into the shower and was almost awake when Aleks joined me. That delayed my departure, but eventually, I got dressed and prepared to leave.

"Dani," Aleks said, reaching out and pulling me into his arms. "If you ever need any help, you only have to ask."

I loved looking at him, his finely chiseled features, the deep brown of his eyes, his incredible lips. I had known other lovers, but none who looked as fine as he did, or treated me so well. I kept waiting for the day he woke up and realized he could do so much better.

"It's my job," I said. "I don't want to pull you into all that crap."

"If it's anything to do with Akiyama and their allies, or the HLA, it's my job, also. They're my enemies, too. And I would be very, very sorry if anything happened to you, my sweet girl." He gave me a kiss that made my head swim and almost buckled my knees.

"You're a terrible man," I said when I surfaced for air. "You shouldn't get my hopes up." His eyes widened in surprise. Shock perhaps.

I pushed away from him, fumbled the door open, and ran. My face still burned when I hit the street, in spite of the cold outside. Why did I say something so stupid?

By the time I retrieved my car from Police Headquarters and headed north, the sun had risen, but traffic was still light. Deciding I didn't want to deal with the morning commuters, I took the car into the air, where I didn't have to pay as much attention to my driving. I spent the time on the way to Loch Raven replaying those last few minutes with Aleks over and over in my mind.

Surely, he was just being kind. Men, after all, would say anything to get laid. He hadn't made any promises, or said anything stupid about love. And I had practically told him all he had to do was crook his finger and I'd be his. Which was true, but it was stupid to give a man that kind of power. It had been years since I cried when a man dumped me. I was setting myself up again. Stupid, Dani. Stupid, stupid, stupid. It was just sex, just a good time, and if I wasn't careful, I'd ruin it.

I composed myself and landed on the road leading to Mom's house. I hoped the elves didn't freak out and stick a brick wall in my path. Or a tree as wide as the road, which would be more their style.

They let me in, however, and I brought the car to a stop in front of her house. The smell of peaches hit me as I walked through the door, and when I entered the kitchen, I found a plate full of peach crepes waiting for me.

"Fresh peaches?"

"No, silly," Mom said. "I canned them last summer. Tea or coffee?"

Joren came down and joined us along with a female elf named Triana. After we ate, Mom waved the dishes away, and Triana spoke.

"Your cousin Karolyn is at the compound in Elk Neck. We have managed to have one of our spies assigned as her servant-cum-jailer. They have her closely watched, and she isn't allowed to leave the house."

"What did your spy have to say about what happened the other night? About Beatrice and Karolyn being captured and brought back?" I asked.

"That is why all of Karolyn's servants have been dismissed. Our spies both at Elk Neck and at Worthington Ridge tell us that your Aunt Courtney is very unhappy. Karolyn is unharmed, however, but no one knows what Courtney plans for her." Worthington Ridge was the location of the Findlay estate. As far as I knew, only Mom called it that anymore.

"But that's not the only reason we called you out here," Mom said.

"Akiyama and its allies are planning a major offensive," Joren said. "They plan to capture the airport and the seaport and cut Baltimore off."

He conjured a map on the table and then outlined the campaign. Akiyama planned to land troop transport planes with elite warrior mages at the airport while a force of demons assaulted the troops defending the airport from the outside.

Another group of demons would flank Whittaker's mercenaries and drive toward the seaport while human mages assaulted the port's defenses from ships in the Bay.

A third offensive comprised of human mercenaries, allied mages, and demons used as shock troops would assault the Novak and Domingo estates north of Baltimore. Those troops would strike from both the Findlay estate and from the north—Elk Neck and Wilmington—along with troops landing in the Gunpowder River estuary.

"That plan requires a huge number of troops," I said.

Mom nodded. "They plan to commit more than ten thousand humans and magik users, two thousand vampires, and two thousand demons. It's a bold move, and an expensive one, but if the gamble pays off, they will control the Metroplex."

"And if they fail?" I asked.

Her grin was that of a hunting cat. "What would the Findlay Family have done to your Granduncle George if he blew several years' profit on a failure? Akiyama is flying troops in from China and the West Coast. Can't be cheap."

I thought about the magitek-enhanced plane I had disabled at Elk Neck. The cost of flying such planes was minimal. The cost of losing such planes was astronomical.

"When?" I asked.

"One week from today," Joren said. "They have started moving troops into position. The Port of Wilmington and the Elk Neck estate already look like army camps. Our spies in Wilmington tell us that one out of every three ships coming into port are troop ships."

Before I left to go back to town and talk to Whittaker, I sent a message to my grandmother, including an image of the campaign map Joren had showed me. Then I called Mary Sue.

"We need as many of those drones as you can produce in the next five days. Run people as hard as you can and promise bonuses."

Silence, then, "Is there anything I should know?"

"Take a drive around Wilmington. Just go out and see the sights. Maybe have lunch down by the harbor."

Back at Police Headquarters, I intended to make a beeline to Whittaker's office, but the desk sergeant stopped me as soon as I entered the building.

"Captain James! Someone left a message for you. Said it was important."

I grabbed the piece of paper and started off again, but the message stopped me in my tracks.

Brian Crozier is at my house. Susan

I blinked at it, then went back to the front desk.

"How did this message come in?"

"Phone call. Said she was a friend of yours and it was important you get it. I recognized Crozier's name."

"Thanks, Sarge."

I had to wait fifteen minutes to get in to see Whittaker. When I did, I handed him the note while I accessed his computer and used his projector to send Joren's map from my implant to the large screen on the wall.

"Intelligence from the elves," I said. "The launch date is one week from today."

He studied it for about fifteen minutes, then started asking questions. After studying it some more, he picked up the phone.

"Henri? I need to see you and Jorge in my office as soon as possible. Yes, this afternoon."

When he hung up, I started to rise and asked, "Do you need anything more from me?"

"Get yourself some coffee or something, but I need you here."

"What about Crozier?"

"He can wait. Tell Novak to put the house under surveillance until you get free."

He made two or three more calls, then we waited. The first person to show up was the new deputy commissioner, Howard Jefferson—my supposed boss. Two Whittaker generals showed up next, then Jorge Domingo, and finally Henri Novak with John Butler, head of the Butler Family and a granduncle of mine by marriage.

"I took the liberty of inviting John along," Henri said. "He's handling business affairs in this area for Olivia Findlay while she's out of the country."

Uncle John nodded to me, as did Novak. I had never met Jorge Domingo, Carmelita's grandfather and head of the Domingo Family in North America. Whittaker had me project the map again, and a discussion ensued that lasted the rest of the afternoon.

By the time the meeting broke up, it was past quitting time. It was getting late, but I called Kirsten and asked her to wait downtown for me. Then I grabbed a couple of detectives and a couple of uniforms and drove out to College Park.

"Anything?" I asked Novak when I got there. He and his partner were parked in the driveway of a house with a 'For Sale' sign in front.

"Nothing. We haven't seen anything to indicate anyone is there."

I ordered my men to surround the house. One of the detectives was a witch, and he confirmed that Susan's wards were still in place, and so was the police ward. Then one of the cops I'd sent around back called me.

"Captain, back here."

Brian Crozier was lying face down by the back door. The ME wouldn't have much trouble determining the cause of death. He had a bullet hole in the back of his head. A note was pinned to his shirt.

Danica, he was too psychopathic even for me. LOL! You're welcome. Susan.

An hour later, when I was finished dealing with Crozier, I drove back downtown and walked over to Enchantments. Sometime in the afternoon, Aleks had left a message. I called him and arranged to meet him later, then Kirsten and I went to dinner at The Kitchen Witch.

"It's going to hit the fan," I told her after we got our meals and she cast a spell of silence around our booth. "Can you get word out to the covens without the whole world finding out?"

"I'll talk to Mom," she said. "I think the main Coven Council should be warned, but Mom would know which ones can keep a secret. Some of the coven heads might welcome a destructive war, hoping it would weaken the Magi's hold on power."

"And people like that somehow think they'll be immune to the consequences," I said. "The amount of power being collected in this area by both sides is staggering. Wars don't stay nicely contained—take a look at the Waste. The first time Washington got nuked was over a spat in the Middle East."

The southern half of what used to be the District of Columbia, and parts of Southern Maryland and Northern

Virginia, were a radioactive wasteland, inhabited only by the poorest lower-class demons.

"Yeah," Kirsten said. "At the very least, the covens may be able to protect themselves. Have you heard anything else about your cousin?"

I smiled. "I have a plan."

CHAPTER 41

Once again, I was assigned to lead a company of magiteks gathered from Whittaker's troops and factories, as well as the Families allied against Akiyama. I did have a few days to spend training them, and I took advantage of the time to identify the strongest and most imaginative of the group. Despite their ranks—or no rank at all—in their normal organizations, I chose my own lieutenants and sergeants.

A primary concern were the Akiyama troop transports coming into the airport. If we could crash their planes when they tried to land them, it would be a major blow to their plans.

Mary Sue provided me with a truckload of magitek devices I could use for training purposes, and promised a shipment of drones and two magiteks from our factory as trainers for Whittaker's troops. Olivia had approved redirecting the drones paid for by Findlay to Whittaker, so he would have almost four hundred weaponized drones to deploy.

The third day after my meeting with the Magi security bosses, Kirsten called me. "My mom wants to set up a meeting between the Coven Council and your boss."

"Uh, this whole thing is supposed to be top secret. I haven't told anyone that I told you about it."

A moment of silence. "Oh, no problem. I'll tell Mom. Can you set up the meeting?"

What part of... I sighed. "Yeah, I'll talk to him."

I checked with his secretary to make sure he was available, then trudged up to his office.

"You know my roommate, Kirsten," I started. He nodded. "She asked if I could set up a meeting between you and the Coven Council. At six o'clock today."

His eyes narrowed. "Do you know what about?"

I shook my head. "Maybe they heard rumors of war? Or they want something? Or they want to give you an award? They didn't say you had to prepare a speech."

"There are no rumors of war."

"Whatever you say."

"Where?"

"Durban's Road House." It was a large restaurant and bar in Middle River that had private meeting rooms.

"You're coming with me."

"Sure. I'll cover your back. No telling what those sneaky witches might do."

"Get out of here, and tell your friend Kirsten to send a better liar next time."

I followed him out to Middle River in my car. He was staying in the city while they repaired the roads out to his place, and taking me home after the meeting would be out of his way.

The robot host directed us to a room past the kitchen at the back of the building. When we reached the doorway, two large men checked our credentials, then allowed us inside. There was a buffet, a make-your-own bar, and a circular arrangement of tables. The room was filled with witches.

Kirsten's mom and dad, Aileen and Blair, greeted us. Her mom was an older version of Kirsten, blonde with a peaches-

and-cream complexion, curvy, and beautiful. She wore a flowing, diaphanous lime green gown trimmed with embroidered flowers. Her dad fit the stereotype of a dark warlock—dark hair, dark eyes, swarthy skin, over six-feet tall and husky, dressed all in black. Both taught at the University of Maryland School of Magik. As far as I was concerned, they were two of the nicest people in the world.

"Commissioner," Aileen said, "how nice of you to come on such short notice. But, our next meeting would be too late, wouldn't it?"

"I'm not entirely sure why I was invited," my boss said.

"Why, to discuss preparations for the upcoming battle, of course." She winked at him. "Yes, I know, it's supposed to be a secret, but every battle has two sides, you know, and the people on the other side haven't been very discreet."

Blair spoke up. "The daughter of one of the coven leaders is sleeping with a Moncrieff guardian, and he brags a little when he's in his cups. Some more digging around unearthed some rather strange coincidences, and when we were asked about it, we spoke to Kirsten."

"Dani told me it was a secret, but I'm sure you expect your children to tell you the truth, don't you?" Kirsten said from behind her parents.

Whittaker rolled his eyes.

We were encouraged to help ourselves at the buffet and the bar. I hadn't had lunch, so I took advantage of it. Aileen showed us to seats near her and Blair. Kirsten didn't sit at the table, but on a chair next to the bar.

It seemed like a friendly dinner party, with everyone eating, drinking, chatting, and laughing with each other. It wasn't until after everyone had a chance to grab a dessert that the woman sitting next to Whittaker stood up and rang her spoon against her water glass to get everyone's attention.

"Time for the business portion of tonight's meeting," she

said. "Tonight, we have Police Commissioner Thomas Whitaker and Captain Danica James with us to discuss the coming war here in the Metroplex. Commissioner, I'm Glenda Romero, currently High Priestess of the Mid-Atlantic Coven Council. Those here tonight represent twenty-three covens from as far away as Western Pennsylvania, West Virginia, and Southern Virginia."

She went around the room introducing the thirty-five witches present, then said, "We have heard rumors of a rift, so to speak, in the Magi Council. Although we have our differences with the Magi, as I'm sure you know, we are opposed to the destruction of our homes and businesses. We also do not consider any group that allies themselves with demons and vampires as people we can trust or do business with. So, we have voted to provide any and all assistance you and the Magi Council might need in this endeavor of yours."

Whittaker asked for a projector, and when they provided one, he had me project Joren's map on the wall. I sat back and listened, as the group talked about troop movements, defensive preparations, logistics, and the establishment of places fighters could go for healing treatments. Almost all healers and magikal apothecaries were witches—other than the Fae.

Witch magik and mage magik had some similarities but were very different in most respects. But there were areas of witch magik that had advantages in battle. The casting of wards was one, as was the ability to control fire. Kirsten putting the fires out that night the demons attacked our house was an example.

It was midnight before we walked out of there, and Kirsten and I drove home.

The following day, I presented my plan to extract Karolyn from the Moncrieff compound at Elk Neck. Whittaker was underwhelmed.

"We need you at the airport. You're the only one with experience disabling those magitek-enhanced transport planes Akiyama's bringing in. Elk Neck is isolated, away from where the main fighting is going to take place."

"Our intelligence tells us that Hiroku is staying at Elk Neck," I said, "and that is where their command center is. We also know from past experience how much Moncrieff invested in magitek defenses there. Disrupting their communications and coordination should be a priority. Besides, screwing up those transports isn't hard. There are at least a dozen of the magiteks I've trained who can do that."

His stare would have done a statue proud.

"Look," I said, "the magitek devices on those planes help them fly long distances and take off from short runways. They don't have a single thing to do with them landing. Disable the devices, they won't even notice it. But the witches can crash them all."

He glowered at me. "You've been planning this all along."

"You'd rather that I go off half-assed than plan it?"

"That's your usual mode of operation."

"I'm a captain now. I've matured and I have responsibilities."

He snorted a laugh. "And now you're practicing to be a politician. God help us all."

I smiled. "See what a good mentor you've been?"

Whittaker shook his head. "I expect you'll want more troops at Elk Neck."

"Another two hundred would be nice. Include some sneaky types who can run an enemy command center."

He arched his eyebrows as the possibilities hit him. "I'll see what I can do."

I just had to finish putting together the team I wanted to go in with me. Kirsten had already agreed, and the six elves assigned to protect us wouldn't stay behind even if I ordered them to. Novak was recovering, and I figured he would want in to make up for losing Karolyn.

I went downstairs and pulled Carmelita out of the office to go get a cup of decent coffee. On the way, I pitched the idea to her, and she agreed to come along.

"I also need to borrow an armored limousine," I said. "Think you can snag one?"

She grinned. "Oh, yeah. No problem."

"I need access to it as soon as possible. I want to install some magitek enhancements on it."

"Sure. Come on out this evening. I'll call my grandfather and arrange it."

That left one more person to approach. I needed more firepower. Mychal and Carmelita would provide adequate shielding, and the elves were fierce warriors. I could supply heavy magikally enhanced weaponry to everyone. But I wanted an ace in the hole, someone with true magikal offensive firepower.

"Aleks? Are you free for dinner? I'm buying." Sure, using sex and good food to persuade someone might have been a bit underhanded, but it always worked on me. And there was a nice little Bayside crab shack right down the road from the Domingo estate.

CHAPTER 42

I picked up Aleks when he got off work and headed toward the northbound freeway.

"There's a nice little restaurant out on the Bay," I said. "I think you'll like it. Crabs are out of season, but they make a good crabcake, and the rest of the menu is pretty good."

"And it will take us how long to get there? The freeway going north is jammed this time of day."

"Yeah, for most people. You have your seatbelt fastened, don't you?" I took the onramp and drew a rune in the air in front of the dash. The matching sigil lit up in red, and I sent my magik into the converter. The sigil turned silver. The car lifted off the ground and gained altitude. I hadn't taken him flying before, and I always enjoyed the reaction from people their first time.

I didn't speak German, but I had the feeling what he said wasn't repeatable in polite company.

"Being a magitek and a cop has some advantages," I said. "This really isn't legal for most people. And by the way, before we go to dinner, I need to stop by the Domingo estate and modify one of their limousines so it will do this. Now, I've got a proposition for you. Remember when you said if I needed any help, all I had to do was ask? Well, I'm asking, and I'll throw in dinner and a little nookie to sweeten the pot."

On the way out to Domingo, I explained what I proposed to do. He didn't tell me I was crazy, or even act particularly surprised.

When I finished, he said, "You know that after university, I spent four years as a guardian. Did I ever tell you that?" He grinned. "Do I get to decide what flavor of nookie?"

"I'm yours."

His grin widened.

Carmelita and her grandfather met us when we arrived at Domingo and took us around to their garages. Aleks and Jorge knew each other, so introductions didn't take any time. One of their mechanics awaited us.

"What exactly do you want to do to the car?" the mechanic asked.

"I'm going to turn it into a flying machine," I said, indicating the boxes Aleks and I brought from my car. "I need to install a magitek converter, baffles and directional controls, along with a gyroscopic stabilizing system. I'll also install an enhancer connected to the engine that will extend its time between charges almost indefinitely. If we're going to use it for a getaway car, we don't want to have to stop at a charging station."

To say he looked skeptical would be an understatement, but he put the huge limo up on a lift so I could access the undercarriage. I had prepared the devices ahead of time and built them much larger and more powerful than what I had installed on my cop car. The limo weighed about fifteen thousand pounds, and I figured it would be a bitch to steer once I got it into the air. I planned on adding the same package to the limo we were borrowing from Novak, although only one of them would fly during the operation.

It took me about two hours to install everything and test it, then I drove it outside and took it up in the air. I discovered I was right about the steering, and I was glad I'd thought of installing the stabilizers. I hadn't done that on my Toyota, but it was a sleek pursuit vehicle, and I wanted nimble control. The limo just needed to go fast in a straight line. If anyone chased it in a jet or a helicopter, I'd take it back to the ground.

"How much for this kind of modification?" Jorge asked.

"Assuming that I get it back to you in one piece, we'll consider it payment for the rent on the vehicle."

"And to do other cars?"

I named a figure. He didn't show any surprise.

"That's with a family discount," I said. "Cost of equipment and labor plus twenty percent. Double that commercially. About two-thirds of the limo price for a smaller vehicle like mine."

I handed him one of Mary Sue's cards. "Right now, we're producing weaponized drones for Commissioner Whittaker and Osiris, but she'll schedule you in. There is one catch. You need to be a magitek to drive it."

He nodded, a slight smile on his face. "I'm acquainted with Ms. Dressler. You said 'we'?"

"We're partners. I'm the lead designer."

When we finished, I washed up and took Aleks out to dinner, then we went back to his place, and I let him have his way with me. A truly enjoyable evening, and since I didn't know if we would survive the next few days, I thought I deserved it.

☙❧

I drove out to Novak the following day. Mychal was mostly recovered from his injuries. He fed me lunch on the terrace off his suite. It was a bright sunny day but very cold. The mage shield covering the terrace made it quite pleasant, though.

His rooms were more expansive and fancier than what my grandmother provided for me at Findlay House, but he was the son of Frank Novak, the Family head.

"Has Kirsten been out here?" I asked.

He shook his head. "I don't want her to get the wrong idea. I prefer she just sees me as Mychal, a cop, not a part of the richest Family on the planet."

I chuckled. "She knows who you are. Now, if you're saying you can't marry her, that she's always going to be a mistress, then you'd better start lavishing gifts. She likes you a lot, but she won't stick around without some commitment from you."

He looked away, staring off at the immaculately cultured garden. I studied him.

"Or are you afraid she's only after your money?"

Turning back to me, he said, "I'm a nerd, socially awkward, and not that much to look at. Why else would the most beautiful, intelligent woman I ever met be interested in me? I can't figure it out."

I grinned at him. "Because you're a nerd, socially awkward, very intelligent, and actually damned good-looking. The walls in our house aren't that well insulated, so I might also postulate that you're extraordinarily good in bed." I waited a minute for him to process that. "I've known Kirsten almost twenty years, and the past few months is the only time I've ever known her to be monogamous. She almost never invites men to stay at our place. I think she's got it bad."

His expression was stunned.

"But just in case you aren't serious," I continued, "you should know that every person that's ever hurt her, in any way whatsoever, I've hurt worse." I smiled and batted my eyes at him. His stunned expression turned to one of shock.

"Anyway, let's talk business. I assume you're aware of the offensive Akiyama and its allies plan. I need you to help me spring Karolyn Moncrieff and capture or kill Akiyama Hiroku."

Mychal requisitioned one of Novak's limousines, and I installed the equipment I had brought with me. We took the car up and flew around the area to test it, then landed.

"Dani," he said as I got in my car to go back to town, "I really do love her. I want to spend my life with her."

"Then tell her before someone else makes her an offer. She's always wanted to be a fairy-tale princess. She'll say yes."

CHAPTER 43

The Akiyama offensive was set to launch at midnight. But the demons didn't get the memo, or maybe they couldn't read human. Half of the demons assigned to assault the airport began their attack at eight o'clock in the evening. Two of the five groups of demons assigned to the attack on the port facilities also launched early, but not in concert with each other.

An Akiyama convoy left Wilmington at three o'clock and met up with Moncrieff fighters at Elk Neck. The combined force moved south starting at sundown, almost clogging the freeway. Troop ships from Wilmington sailed around the Delmarva Peninsula and back up the Chesapeake, landing at the Gunpowder River estuary.

By nine o'clock, the convoy had passed the restaurant where my team waited in a suburb imaginatively named North East. I gave the signal, and two hundred of Whittaker's elite troops set out for Elk Neck via boats from the opposite shore. Another two hundred flew in on helicopters, and a hundred more followed my group in from the north.

I drove the lead car with Aleks, Carmelita, and two elves,

while Mychal drove the other car with Kirsten and the other elves. We had used illusions to disguise the limos, and the plan was to make them invisible when we reached the gates of the Moncrieff estate.

As we travelled, I received information through my implant concerning what was happening elsewhere. I already knew the demons were attacking in certain areas, and that our allies were taking advantage of the disjointed assault to flank some of the enemy forces.

Likewise, when the Moncrieff troops and Courtney's Findlay guardians set out from the Findlay estate to attack Novak, our allied forces swept down from the northwest, and using passcodes and routes I supplied, breached the defenses at Findlay House. Courtney wasn't a detail-oriented person, preferring to give orders and delegate. So, no one had changed my accesses, either to the physical properties or the computer systems. In fact, the overall system was still being administered by the mysterious Dexter.

On our journey down the road into the Elk Neck Peninsula, we didn't encounter a single vehicle traveling either way. It was sort of eerie.

I pulled to a stop at the last bend in the road before we came to the Moncrieff estate, and killed the headlights. We all got out and went over the plan again, then the elves cast their spells and rendered the cars invisible. I got back into the limo and drove it to a point less than fifty feet from the gates, praying the whole time that Mychal didn't rear-end us.

At that point, I slithered out of the car, carrying a magikally enhanced laser rifle. Leaning against the car I could no longer see, I set the rifle to full power and aimed it at the gatehouse. When I pulled the trigger, the gatehouse disappeared. Swiftly shifting my aim, I took out the brick post on the other side. What was left of the wrought-iron gate crashed to the ground.

I slipped back in the car, and we proceeded into the estate. It was quiet, and I didn't see anyone about. We knew there were troops there, but hoped most of them were guarding the perimeter walls and the great house itself.

We managed to reach the house without being detected and parked the limos at each end of the open traffic circle in front of the house.

As my group left the vehicle, I pushed a stake with a blue plastic pyramid on top in the ground in front of the car. I doubted anyone would notice it, or be concerned about it if they did. It looked like a child's block—which it was. A red cube would mark the location of the other car.

I was the only one on the whole team who could cast neither a shield nor a glamour. Siarin took my hand and cast a glamour on me, transforming me into a man in the uniform of a Moncrieff guardian. She would have to stay close to me, though, to maintain it.

We walked around the house, trying to stay in the shadows in spite of the bright floodlights. My group planned to enter the house through the kitchen entrance, while Mychal's group waited outside to cover our exit.

The two elves Joren had inserted knew we were coming. Their job was to ensure they had Karolyn ready to go, and to cover us as we took her out. Mychal's group would take her and leave the estate. If things went well, and we weren't discovered, I might also go looking for Hiroku.

Updates were coming through my implant. The demons who were supposed to flank Whittaker's troops between Annapolis and Baltimore had jumped the gun and attacked early. What they found was an ambush, including two hundred of Mary Sue's drones. By the time the rest of the demons on that front started to move, the slaughter was over, and our forces had pivoted back to meet them.

We were still two hours away from when the coordinated attack was scheduled to begin—two hours away from the transports coming into the airport.

I disabled the lock on the kitchen door, and Gildor slipped through. Siarin and I followed him, with Aleks and Carmelita behind us. I had armed each of the humans with a laser rifle like mine and convinced the elves to exchange their sidearms for fifty-caliber Raiders firing explosive incendiary rounds. I really didn't give a damn if we lit the place on fire, or who we killed, with the exception of three beings in the house. I figured the elves could take care of themselves, so that left only Karolyn for me to worry about.

The computer system had supplied me with the house's layout. We passed by the kitchen, where servants were baking for the next morning, and took the servants' stairs up to the third floor. We made it up there without encountering anyone.

"Here's where it gets dicey," I whispered. "We know there are guards on this floor, and we might encounter some of the family, also."

I pushed open the door and found a guardian standing in front of me, a puzzled look on his face. I didn't wait for him to understand that someone invisible had opened the door. The laser on one-quarter setting burned a hole through his chest, and he dropped to the floor.

Several doors down the hall, two more guardians stood, flanking a doorway. I shot them both and trotted toward them.

Gildor arrived before I did and tapped on the door. It was opened almost immediately by a human woman dressed in Moncrieff livery. Without even a blink of surprise, she reached down, grabbed one of the dead guards, and dragged him into the room. Gildor hauled the other guard inside, and we all filed into the room.

The servant morphed into the form of a female elf.

"She's in there," she said in elvish, pointing deeper into the suite of rooms.

"Let me go," I said to Siarin, and was suddenly able to see my own hand. I strode through the suite until I reached the main sitting room. Karolyn stood at the windows on the other side. I could see lightning and flashes of light in the distance.

"We've come to take you out of here," I said.

Karolyn whirled around and stared at me. "Dani?"

I walked to the window and looked over her shoulder. "I think that's our landing party, taking over the Moncrieff airport," I said. "There should be more troops coming from the north in a few minutes."

"Beatrice?"

"She's safe in Ireland."

"Thank God."

"We're going to take you downstairs, and turn you over to some more of my people."

"Dani, there's a huge attack planned for tonight. The Metroplex airport, the Baltimore seaport, as well as attacks on Novak and Domingo."

I smiled. "We know. Come on, let's get you out of here. Then I need to find Hiroku. You wouldn't happen to know where he is, do you?"

"Probably the basement. That's where all the computer and telecom stuff is located."

"Easiest and most discreet way of getting there?"

She shook her head. "I'd have to show you. You know how much of a maze these houses are."

I looked at the long dress she was wearing. "Change. Quickly."

Karolyn had never struck me as stupid, and she didn't disappoint me. Without a word or any hesitation, she hurried to her bedroom and started pulling clothes out of a bureau.

"Can you unzip me?" she asked.

I moved her hair aside, found the zipper, and pulled it down. Shrugging out of the dress, she let it pool around her feet and stepped away from it. She pulled on tights, jeans, a turtleneck shirt, and a heavy sweater, then retrieved a pair of boots from her closet.

"Ready. Did you come up the kitchen stairs?" she asked. I nodded. "We need to go back down that way to the second floor," she continued.

The elf who had been her companion led the way, and we quickly started back down the stairs. One floor down, the elf donned her servant's glamour again and opened the door from the landing to the hallway. After a brief look around, she waved us forward.

Instead of going the long way down the hall, we turned left toward a door at the end only a few feet away from us.

"It's locked," the elf said.

I cast a spell and the lock clicked. She tried it again, it opened, and she smiled.

Down two more flights of stairs to the bottom. Another locked door that I opened. Down a hallway, around a corner to the left to the end and another locked door. Through that one was another stairway down. The hallway at the bottom was larger and round, more a tunnel than a hallway. Lights in the ceiling every twenty feet provided the only illumination.

"We're not under the house anymore, are we?" I asked Karolyn.

"No, we're actually under the east lawn. You know that ugly fountain with all the cherubs? The computer system rooms are under it."

"This isn't the way most people get there, is it?"

She shook her head. "Mother would never abide all those lower-class people traipsing through her house. They take stairs down from a building next to the garages." She waved her hand in the air. "This is a maintenance tunnel. The electrical, water, and all that stuff for the house run through here. We'll take a branch off it to the computer center."

"Really? All the electrical?"

"Yeah. It runs under the garages, and the main power plant is in back of the garages."

I hung back and pulled Aleks close to me. "Do you have any magik that could break those large water pipes?"

He studied the overhead pipes. "Yes, if you don't mind drowning."

"But you could disrupt them once we're above ground?"

"Yes, I suppose."

I turned to Gildor and gave him a handful of magitek enhancers. "Could you please stick one of these on that large pipe every time there's a junction?"

He shrugged, reached up, and attached one to the overhead pipe. Nine feet off the floor, and he didn't even have to jump.

"Like that?"

"Exactly like that."

Aleks grinned. "I know how to trigger a magitek device, but how will I find them?"

"Through me. Don't worry, I can feel them from a several hundred feet away."

We followed Karolyn until she made a left turn down a smaller side tunnel. Fifty feet ahead was a bulkhead door.

"That is a back entrance to the computer and communication complex. You go through that door, and you're in a room with the power converters and a backup generator. You'll love it, lots of magitek. There's a door from there into a room where all the wiring runs, then another door to where people work. Somewhere in there is where Hiroku and Karl hold all their meetings virtually with Benjiro and other people from all over the world."

"How many people are in there?"

"Tonight? At least a couple of hundred. People have been coming in from China and Japan the past two weeks."

"Where's the closest way out of here for us?" I asked.

"Go straight the way we've been going. Another hundred feet, there's a stairway on the right that leads up to the garages."

CHAPTER 44

My original plan was to try and kidnap Hiroku, but I wasn't sure the team I had with me could take on two hundred people—most, if not all of them, mages—and make it out safely. But I also hadn't counted on being handed the keys to destroy their entire command center.

I called everyone together.

"I can disrupt all their electronics," I said. "Once we do that, Aleks can burst all those large water pipes and flood everything down here. We'll need to get up those stairs over there and be prepared for resistance when we come up into the garage."

Everyone nodded except Karolyn. "You know that both Hiroku and Karl are hydromancers, don't you?" she asked.

"Yeah, but they're going to have their hands full just to keep people from drowning," I answered. "The water is more to slow them down and short out all the electronics down here. No way they'll get anything up and running again anytime soon."

I checked the chrono in my implant. It was eleven forty-five, and the launch of the offensive—other than those demons who jumped early—was scheduled to take place at midnight.

Akiyama's transport planes were due to set down at the Metroplex airport in thirty minutes.

"Wait here."

I walked down the tunnel and disabled the keypad locking the bulkhead door. I readied my laser rifle, then turned the crank, and opened the door. Thankfully, it was well maintained and made little noise.

The room was dark except for a lot of little blinking lights. I pulled my magikally enhanced night goggles out of my bag and put them on. Karolyn had obviously been in that room before, because her description was accurate. Two major bundles of electrical cables came into the room from different directions. The magitek-enhanced backup generator sat idling on standby.

I approached the door to the wiring room and pushed it open a crack. There was a little more light in there due to a nightlight on the wall above the light switch. Wiring hubs and routers in metal racks filled the room.

Backing out, I returned to my companions.

"Everyone go to those stairs and get ready to escape into the garage when the lights go out. When I kill the electricity, there won't be any light at all in here. I'll catch up to you. Aleks, wait for me there."

I waited until I saw them turn right and then went back down the side tunnel. The first thing I did was shut down the backup generator and drain its magitek enhancer. Then I disabled the magitek converter attached to the cable bundle running in the direction of the house. That cut the electricity running through those fiber-optic cables by ninety percent. I did the same to the cables running toward the garages and other outbuildings.

Taking a deep breath, I pushed open the door to the wiring room and swept the racks there with laser fire. There was a moment of silence on the other side of the door, then people started shouting. On my way out of the power room to the tunnel, I cast a spell that shorted out every electrical device that was left. The lights in the tunnel went out.

I keyed my father's box to provide me an electrical shield. It shed enough light for me to see as I ran toward where Aleks waited for me at the stairway.

"Ready?" I asked, switching the box off.

"Yes. What do I do?"

The whoosh sound of a fireball had me diving forward onto the stairs. The darkness suddenly illuminated brighter than daylight. I looked up and saw a beam of blinding white light erupting from Aleks's hand. I waited a second but didn't hear an answering fireball.

I contacted all the magitek enhancers Gildor had planted.

"Cast the spell to destroy the pipes at me."

He recoiled, a horrified look on his face. "I can't do that!"

I chuckled and held up a converter box. "Yes, you can. I'll be acting as a conduit. You're not going to hurt me."

Taking a deep breath, he held out his left hand, and a shaft of that blinding white light shot toward me. I pulled it all into the magitek converter, then redirected it to the enhancers. The sound of high-pressure pipes exploding rang back along the tunnel.

"See? Easy as falling off a cliff. Now, if you don't mind, get a move on or get the hell out of the way. Things are going to get very wet here very quickly."

He turned and ran up the stairs with me close behind him.

It was dark in the tunnel, and almost as dark in the garage. I knew the elves could deal with it, but Karolyn, Carmelita, and Aleks would be totally blind.

"Aleks, could you please hang a little light on my back for you to follow?" I guided his hand to my back. "Not very bright, okay?"

The elves were spread out in a semi-circle in front of us, swords in hand.

"Let's go," I said, and followed them as they made their way toward the outer wall of the building.

Someone in the garage worked some magik and produced a light. I stopped, aimed, and shot him with the laser. The light went out.

The building was a huge open space. Lots of cars, as well as storage areas and places to work on the cars. We worked our way through and around cars and machines until we reached a doorway.

"Wait here," Gildor said, opening the door a little and squeezing through it. Flashes of light and the sound of thunder from outside told me that a fight was going on.

I contacted Mychal through my implant. "What's going on?"

"The mercenaries showed up and are engaged with Moncrieff and Akiyama guardians. Did you get her?"

"Yeah, and disabled their command center. Get your team out of here. Leave the fighting to the professionals."

"Don't have to tell me twice. Where are you?"

"Inside the garage. As soon as the elves tell us it's safe, we'll make a dash for the limo and fly out of here."

"Good luck."

Gildor came back a couple of minutes later.

"I think that with shields and glamours we can safely make it to the limo," he said.

He took my hand, and the elf who was guarding Karolyn took hers. Hugging the wall, we inched out the door and along the building. At the end, I looked across an open space and located the little blue pyramid sitting on the gravel beside the driveway.

In the distance, a full-fledged mage battle was going on, with Whittaker's troops fighting from the woods and their foes fighting from inside the house and the roof. About that time, lightning and fire rained down from the sky onto the roof. Mary Sue's drones. Then a large explosion blew open the front door, and the entrance portico collapsed. Karolyn's childhood home was taking a beating.

In spite of the glamours, someone spotted us. A bolt of lightning shot toward us from the house. A green-tinged bolt shot back the other way, and light flared in one of the windows. And then Karolyn really cut loose. A burst of wind turned into a whirlwind and slammed against the damaged portico. Green lightning slashed across the front of the house. Miniature suns —balls of pure energy—followed from Aleks, blowing holes in the stone walls. Bursts of elven battle magik battered the house.

We made it to the limo, and everyone piled inside. Before I got in, I switched my laser rifle to full power and destroyed the last large magitek lightning generator on the roof of the house.

Without any delay, I jumped into the car and started the engine, then threw the car into reverse, and stomped on the accelerator. Fifty feet back down the driveway, I spun the wheel, put the car in a forward gear, and roared off. Halfway to the road leading out of the estate, I sketched the rune and took to the air. I didn't really feel safe, though, until we were out over Chesapeake Bay, making a very long, wide turn that would take us to Loch Raven.

As I settled into a cruising speed, Whittaker contacted me through my implant.

"How's it going?"

"We have Karolyn Moncrieff, and we've destroyed the command center where Hiroku was directing their operations. Last I saw, your forces were taking command at Elk Neck. How about the rest of the world?"

"Akiyama just tried to land their planes at the airport. Your plan worked just like you said it would. Thought you'd like to know. Where are you now?"

"Headed to Loch Raven. We'll probably spend the night there."

"Party pooper. Things are just getting interesting around here."

"We've already done interesting, and no casualties. I'll take that as a win."

"Have a good night, Dani. Call me in the morning."

I had told Whittaker and the others that they didn't need magiteks to deal with Akiyama's troop planes. All they had to do was erect poles on either side of the runways. A circle of witches could cast a ward using the poles as anchors. When a plane going two hundred miles an hour hit the ward, the plane would lose. The witches had agreed with me. Another circle of witches cast an illusion so that the planes following the first one would see a clear, unimpeded runway. I was looking forward to seeing the video.

CHAPTER 45

The sun on my face woke me up. That seemed a little strange—since my room didn't face east—until I remembered that I had brought a lot of people home with me. The house didn't have a problem reconfiguring itself, but it still had to deal with some of the laws of physics, and adding multiple rooms had evidently twisted my room into a different orientation.

The man sleeping beside me was familiar, though. I studied his face relaxed in sleep. I never got tired of looking at him. Purposefully, I avoided accessing my implant. If the world was falling apart, or someone needed saving, I didn't want to know about it yet.

Kirsten and Mychal were in another room, while Karolyn and Carmelita had rooms of their own. The elves had their own beds someplace, and I was sure the woman who had guarded over Karolyn was glad to be in hers. The other limo—land bound—arrived two hours after we landed at Loch Raven.

After a while, I did send a message to Olivia, telling her that Karolyn was safe and we would send her along as soon as we could. I figured Beatrice would welcome that news.

The sheer savagery of Karolyn's outburst the previous evening erased any doubts I might have had about her sincerity. I was also glad I had never pissed her off enough to attack me. The reports I received from Whittaker's men after we left said they had little resistance after that.

They hadn't found Hiroku or any of the Akiyama generals Karolyn said were at the estate. Karl Rudolf was also missing.

My inherited sense of smell—a blessing or a curse depending on the scent—told me that my mother was in the kitchen. That was an event not to be missed. I prodded Aleks awake.

"My mother is fixing breakfast," I said.

He cracked an eye. "I don't care."

"Suit yourself." I crawled out of bed and hit the shower. I was barely wet when he joined me.

We made our way down to the kitchen and found a table set with crepes, egg bread, eclairs with a divine custard filling, and a selection of fresh fruit. The smell of espresso laid a soft blanket over everything. It was December, and fresh berries and peaches would have been difficult to find on Olivia's table that time of year.

"I was feeling French this morning," Mom said. Her mother was French, but Mom never talked about her.

Far be it from me to object if she wanted to stuff me full of sweets instead of feeding me healthy—although everything was whole grains, honey, and other natural ingredients.

Kirsten and Mychal were already there, of course. Among the more obnoxious things they had in common was a tendency to rise with the sun. Carmelita showed up about when Aleks and I did, but Karolyn was a no-show.

"She's all right," Mom said when she caught me glancing at the stairway. "I don't know what went on last night, but her energy levels were severely depleted when she showed up here. The sleep will do her good."

"She threw a tantrum," Aleks said, reaching for another helping of egg bread. "I hope she never gets that angry at me. Damned near blew the front off the house."

Mom's eyebrows shot up. "Moncrief House?"

I nodded. "Yeah. She may not be a full-powered storm mage, but she's still impressive. Whipped up a mini-tornado out of a clear sky. I think she was a little miffed at the way her mother and her lover have been treating her."

"He's not my lover. Not anymore, the sorry bastard," Karolyn's voice came from behind me. "Are those eclairs?"

She took a seat at the table and poured herself a cup of coffee to go with three eclairs. "A girl has a right to throw a tantrum occasionally," she said between bites. "Besides, it's my house, and if I want to do a little redecorating, that's my prerogative." She glanced up. "My father built that estate, and my mother has forfeited all rights to it."

"Where is William?" I asked about Karolyn's illegitimate son with Karl Rudolf.

"Mom is holding him at Findlay in exchange for my good behavior. She won't hurt him, though. He's her great hope for merging the Moncrieff and Findlay Families and ruling the world."

※

After breakfast, stuffed to the gills and feeling like a beached whale, I lay back in the sunroom and accessed my implant. In the twelve hours since Akiyama launched their assault, a lot had happened.

Fierce fighting had raged all night. The vampires had gone to bed with sunrise, the demon assaults wound down, and the humans on both sides had stopped to lick their wounds and take stock.

The Moncrieff estate at Elk Neck was in the hands of the

Council. The assaults on the Novak and Domingo estates had been repulsed. The force Courtney had sent out from Findlay to join in the assault at Novak had been ambushed and decimated when it passed Loch Raven. Whittaker's assault on Findlay House had failed, but the estate was surrounded. As a result, the Council controlled the north and had cut off reinforcements from the Akiyama base in Wilmington except by sea or air.

One of the major concerns was the demon horde that had been encamped west of Annapolis all fall. Akiyama's plan was for them to break out of their containment, join with a force of demons from the Waste, and move on the airport from the south.

In the week before the attack, Whittaker had drawn more than half of his troops from the containment line and positioned them to attack the demons from their flanks once they broke through. That battle stalled without either side holding the upper hand.

Akiyama's air support—primarily helicopter gunships and troop transports—was ambushed by Whittaker fighter planes on its way south and never joined the battle.

On the other side of the Atlantic, in a series of blitzkrieg attacks, Findlay and its Kennedy and Flanagan allies had overrun the Moncrieff estate in Scotland and taken control of the ports of Glasgow and Leith at Edinburgh. Forces of Butler and Dressler had seized the Moncrieff holdings in England and Wales. Alan Moncrieff had not prepared for an attack, evidently considering the spat between Akiyama and the Council as being a North American problem. For all practical purposes, Family Moncrieff had ceased to exist as a major player on the world stage.

"Have you seen the news?" Kirsten asked as she plopped down in the chair beside me.

"Nope."

She turned the screen of her laptop so I could see it. The news announcer was warning everyone of a general lockdown across the Metroplex. All businesses were closed, and everyone was warned to stay in their homes. There was a number to call if someone needed medicine, a hospital, or food help.

There were snatches of video showing fighting near the airport, and also of looting in various commercial areas of the Metroplex.

Deciding I should get off my butt and do something, I called Whittaker.

"I hope you enjoyed your beauty sleep," he said when he answered the phone.

"Hey, I was up working all night, putting my ass on the line. What were you doing? Strutting around and issuing orders and drinking coffee."

He chuckled. "What do you plan to do with Karolyn Moncrieff?"

"Keep her here at Loch Raven until it's safe to fly her to Ireland. How long until you clear the runways?"

"We still have two operational, but we're using those for our warplanes. They aren't really long enough for long-haul aircraft. But you're right, the skies aren't safe right now." He shifted gears. "I could use your team in the city. In addition to our normal law and order problems, we seem to have saboteurs infiltrating and causing mischief."

"Okay. We can be down there in about an hour."

I rounded up Mychal and Carmelita. Kirsten was fretting about her shop and also wanted to go back to town, and Aleks tagged along, so I had a full car. Our elven bodyguards took their own vehicles, of course, and followed us. Because of that, and being mindful of Whittaker's warning, I kept the car on the ground.

Our route took us through the area where the elves had ambushed Courtney's forces earlier that morning. There were a lot of destroyed vehicles, and the authorities were still dealing with bodies. Only my police credentials got us through, and we discovered that going around wouldn't have been an option either. I was told that southbound traffic was being diverted through West Virginia.

The general lockdown meant there was no traffic south of the beltway, so I made good time. The wards on Kirsten's shop were holding, but there was a lot of damage downtown. Since that was well within the areas where the fighting had occurred, I understood why Whittaker had cancelled all leave and days off, and ordered all cops to report for duty.

I had officially deputized Kirsten and Aleks for the operation the night before, so I used their temporary credentials to get them inside Police Headquarters.

After a meeting of all personnel under my command, I made assignments, ordered a third of the people to bed in the basement dorms, and headed out with Carmelita to patrol a section of the Inner Harbor area. The elves followed us when we left the building.

CHAPTER 46

We dropped Kirsten and Aleks off at his apartment. She wanted to stay close to her shop, and with her elven bodyguards, I couldn't imagine anywhere she'd be safer. I tried to tell my bodyguards not to follow me, but they pretended to be deaf, and when Carmelita and I pulled away from the curb, an armored car disguised as a sports car fell in behind us.

Most business owners downtown had taken the hint after the Rifter riots earlier in the fall and paid witches to cast wards protecting their stores. It was readily apparent who had not. We drove by a place that sold cute dresses to younger women. Its windows were broken, the front door was missing, and the inside looked like a tornado had hit it.

The jewelry store next door was untouched.

One thing that we immediately discovered was the lack of any places to get any food or even a cup of coffee.

"We should have got coffee at the station," Carmelita whined.

"Oh, no. You're not going to take the easy way out. Sick leave is not an option today." I fished a bottle out of my jacket pocket and passed one of Kirsten's potions to her. "Drink this and shut up."

"I'm going to tell my daddy you're mean to me." She drank the potion and shuddered.

"He'll thank me when he sees how my elegant example is influencing your growth into womanhood."

She cracked up.

A couple of blocks farther along, I heard some unusual sounds. Of course, since we were the only people out on the dead-silent streets, any sound was unusual.

I turned down the next street, then stopped at the end of an alley. A bunch of purple monsters were raiding the dumpsters. Not demons, but some of the creatures that lived along the shores of the Chesapeake Bay. The Rift ensnared a wide collection of beings, not all of them intelligent, and most of them not what humans would call civilized. I had once run into such a being after he killed two drug addicts he thought were trying to steal his food.

"What the hell are those?" Carmelita asked.

"I don't really know. Nasty and smelly, savage but intelligent. If our city fathers had any brains, they'd contract all the garbage collection in the Metroplex to them."

"Are we going to do anything about them?"

"Nope. Considering the state of things around here, normal trash collection probably won't happen anytime soon. Those purple guys will help keep the smell down."

I drove on.

The next group of Rifters we encountered was not so benign. Three demons were using their magik to break into an apartment building. Demons preferred their food alive, or at least very recently dead. I screeched to a stop, and we both jumped out with our pistols drawn.

"Stop right there! On the ground!" I shouted.

Two of them didn't pay any attention. The other one

whirled around and cast an ice spell at me. I activated my father's electrical box even as I dove and rolled. I heard Carmelita's gun fire three times, and when I came to my knees, I saw the demon on the ground. He still had his head, so I aimed a shot at his head, then fired at one of the demons still battering the ward on the front entrance of the building.

I hit one, and Carmelita hit the other, drawing attention of both of them. They left off what they were doing and charged us. A moment later, three headless demons lay on the street.

We ran into similar situations twice more that day. Mostly the elves just watched, but they stepped in a couple of times when the numbers weren't in our favor.

Late in the afternoon, we came across a gang of about ten human teenagers breaking into a shop that sold food, tobacco, and liquor. Carmelita and I managed to bag two of them, and the elves brought us two more, but I doubted any of the ones we caught were the leaders. Just the youngest and the slowest. It did give us an excuse to go back to headquarters and book them in.

"Can we get something to eat now?" Carmelita asked.

I figured it would be a long night. "Sure. Let me make a phone call."

I called Kirsten. "How is Aleks's food supply?"

"He's a bachelor," she replied. "Junk food and beer."

"If I bring supplies, will you cook them up?"

"And marry you."

We hit one of the grocery stores that had been looted, and collected a substantial portion of what the original looters missed. I figured it would all spoil before the owners were allowed back, and it would get thrown away.

We drove over to Aleks's place, and the elves cast a ward on my car. Aleks came down to let us into the building and help us cart the food upstairs. Kirsten shook her head at what we'd brought, then set to work.

After we polished off one of the most creative dinners I'd ever seen her cook, Aleks asked, "What's going on tonight?"

"Probably more of the same," I said. "From what I could tell driving around today, more than half of the properties down by the harbor are undamaged, and things are better up here. The vandals still have a lot of work to do."

"Mainly we're concerned about protecting residences," Carmelita said. "It looks like the demons are trying to draw troops away from the front lines."

I nodded. "Sometimes it's a choice between property damage and people getting eaten. One of the things my boss is worried about are air strikes against Police Headquarters. We expect another assault on the seaport as well."

"Do you need help?" Aleks asked.

I got up and walked to the window. His apartment was on the ninth floor, with a view of the harbor and south. The sun was setting, but there weren't a lot of lights coming on in the city.

"We could use some more eyes," I said. "Look out for any incursions. Our front is fairly porous—just not enough men. If I was one of the Akiyama commanders, I'd be trying to infiltrate fighters into the city."

As I watched, fireworks started in the distance. There were two major fronts to the south—the airport and the seaport. It looked as though the battles were resuming in both places.

"Why don't they give it up?" Kirsten asked. "They suffered a major defeat last night. Why don't they just quit and go home?"

"Too much sunk cost," Aleks replied before I could say anything. "Both money and prestige. Akiyama has tossed the dice, and they have too much at stake to pull out now. The incremental cost of staying and losing isn't much more than what they've already lost."

"Hiroku got away last night," I said. "I assume they've set up a new command center in Wilmington by now, so their efforts should be more coordinated tonight."

"Assuming he got off the Elk Neck Peninsula," Aleks said.

Carmelita shook her head. "He's a hydromancer. He got out."

Half an hour later, she and I headed out with Llerywin and Elbereth, who had evidently drawn the short straws that night. We drove around, looking for any signs of trouble, and when the buildings didn't block our sight to the south, we could see the flashes of battle on the horizon.

It was about nine o'clock when the first reports of infiltrators came in. A uniformed cop reported armed men coming ashore in the Canton area. It had once been a fashionable neighborhood, but the rise in sea levels had inundated the lower areas, and by the time I graduated from college, the water lapped against the foot of the hills rising to the north of the harbor.

We drove in that direction but ran into more armed men before we got there.

"Enemy in Fells Point," Carmelita radioed the dispatcher. "We have multiple infiltration points along the Inner Harbor."

"Tell them not to pull men from Federal Hill," I said. "We need to be careful, or we'll end up playing whack-a-mole." Federal Hill was south of the Inner Harbor and bordered by the Patapsco River on the other side. If the enemy captured that high ground, they would control the harbor and downtown.

She passed the word along while I found an alley to park the car.

"Carmelita, can you lift us onto the buildings? I think we have a better chance from the rooftops." All four of us were armed with magikally enhanced laser rifles and Raiders, and the elves had their bows. We all had magik of one sort or another.

Llerywin laughed. "We can climb without help. Where do you want us?"

I directed them to a couple of buildings, then my partner lifted us to a roof on the next street over. We were able to cover four streets that way, so the men sneaking toward us would have to change their course to get past us. We waited.

From my perch, I spied the first soldiers coming up the street in our direction. I aimed at the man farthest away from me, and shot him. He didn't even flinch. Obviously shielded. I picked out another man and shot at him. He was also shielded. The good thing about the laser, though, was that neither man seemed to notice.

I accessed my little electrical box, paired an enhancer with it, and switched it to the highest level. When I triggered it, a massive bolt of lightning crashed down on the men below me. When my vision cleared, the street was empty of men standing upright. Shielded or not, the concussion had knocked them all off their feet. I hoped it had also rattled their brains. I aimed the laser again and fired at a man crawling. He collapsed. I looked for anyone else moving, but I could tell that my companions were also shooting at the wounded.

It was another minute or so, but a fireball arced up from two streets over toward my position. I kicked the laser up to full power and fired at it. The fireball disappeared, and I felt inordinately pleased with myself. Then a bullet or some other sort of projectile hit the edge of the roof next to me, and I ducked back.

We exchanged fire with the men on the street for about five minutes, and then I got a call on my radio.

"Captain James," I said.

"Captain, this is Staff Sergeant Lewis with Whittaker's Second Arcane Battalion. We're moving up on your position from the north."

I directed them to flank our adversaries and try to come on them from the rear. Another ten minutes, and a fusillade of fire erupted below us. Several of the Akiyama men tried to run out of the streets where they had been hiding, and I loosed another lightning strike on the street. Things got a lot quieter after that.

I checked, and our people had engaged the insurgents coming ashore in Canton. But there were also reports of gunfire and magik in Federal Hill. I resigned myself to not getting any sleep.

CHAPTER 47

The fighting continued for another week, then mysteriously, all the demons melted back into the Waste. The following night the vampires didn't reappear. No one knew why.

A counterattack by Whittaker's forces, including the drones that Mary Sue had provided, smashed the Akiyama forces surrounding the airport. That was followed by a frantic sea evacuation of their forces at the seaport. Most of their ships managed to make it back to Wilmington, but they sailed under constant harassment from fighter planes, helicopter gunships, and more drones.

The silence from the Akiyama Family was deafening. No announcements, no messages, no attempts at communication whatsoever—either from their headquarters in Nanking or from Hiroku in Wilmington.

Courtney Findlay-Moncrieff did send a letter of protest to the Magi Council, complaining about Whittaker's troops surrounding Findlay House. She said they were preventing her from going into town to do her shopping and get her hair done, and they were preventing grocery deliveries. Not a word about the damage to the Moncrieff estate or its occupation by Council forces.

It was like they were pretending the whole thing never happened. I wondered what they told the widows and children of their fighters who would never come home.

The areas of the heaviest fighting—around the airport, the seaport, and Baltimore's downtown—had sustained heavy damage. Kirsten knew a couple of people who worked in the construction industry, and they told her they expected to get rich over the next couple of years.

The Domingo and Novak Families—whose interests included insurance—were not pleased. They filed claims for massive compensation from Akiyama, Moncrieff, Rudolf, Johansson, and any other Family they could remotely connect to the war. Considering the current makeup of the Council, I thought they would probably win but have trouble collecting.

That would finish the Moncrieff dynasty for good. Alan Moncrieff was a prisoner in his own house in Scotland, and his heir had died in the fighting. Olivia sent for Karolyn, intending to install her as Moncrieff Family head—under her thumb, of course. I drove out to Loch Raven to talk with my cousin.

"Want to see a sick joke?" Karolyn asked when we sat down at my mom's table. She shoved a small stack of papers toward me. "Novak and Domingo and Whittaker, and half a dozen other Families, want me to pay them two billion dollars for the damages Moncrieff and *my* allies caused." She laughed, but it wasn't a happy sound. "Why didn't they send this to my darling mother?"

"Because the Council doesn't recognize your mother as having a legitimate claim to diddly-squat," I answered. "That's part of what I came to talk to you about. Olivia's filed a petition to have you named head of the Moncrieff Family. She's also proposed giving Novak the Elk Neck estate as part of a settlement, plus she'll pay off the rest of Novak's and Domingo's claims against Moncrieff." I didn't mention that Olivia essentially owned Moncrieff and would use their assets to pay the debts. But she wanted Moncrieff's Glasgow shipyard very badly, and two billion was far less than it was worth.

Karolyn stared at me with her mouth open. She sputtered a couple of times, shook her head, looked off into the distance, then returned her gaze to me.

"In return," I said, "you must go to Scotland and stay there. Moncrieff will become a subsidiary of Findlay. You don't have to be involved in the business. In fact, I think they'll rather discourage it. But they want someone in the bloodline to help stabilize things."

"A prisoner?"

I shook my head. "No, a figurehead. You can travel as you wish, and you'll be handsomely paid, but your domicile for at least the next ten years must be in Stirling. The estate, the castle, is yours. The kicker is, she wants the same thing Courtney does. Your son William must be declared your heir and educated as Olivia directs."

"Oh, shit. We're back to trying to get him away from Mom."

"Looks like."

Karolyn rolled her eyes. "I hope you have another plan."

Joren still had spies inside Findlay House. When we told him what we needed—young Mr. William Moncrieff—he shook his head.

"Getting in or out of that place right now is going to be difficult. As you might imagine, it's a little tense there at the moment."

"Do you have any information on Bill Moncrieff?" I asked.

Joren shrugged. "A little. He seems to be able to move around inside the compound, but he doesn't go out, and no one comes to visit him. My sources list him as one of the people who always attend evening dinner with your aunt. I'll have to ask for more information."

"Who else always, or mostly, attends those dinners?" I asked.

"Karl Rudolf and Akiyama Hiroku when they're on the premises," Joren said. "At the moment, access is by helicopter only. Joseph Johansson, his wife Ivanka, Miriam Oliver, and Adam Veatch are the regulars. They were all staying at the estate before the battle, and haven't been able to get out since."

Karolyn nodded. "Mother's closest friends. I suspect they're all bedmates of hers."

"Anyone from outside that she might be missing? A friend she'd like to see, but who is now cut off?" I asked.

She looked thoughtful. "Hmm. No one you'd know. There's a guy she meets at a hotel in town every week." She shrugged. "Dad had his own flings. Ever since I was old enough to understand what was going on, they both slept around."

"How long has the guy in the hotel been going on?"

"Oh, God. Years. He's her hairdresser." Karolyn snorted. "He lifts weights, built like Adonis. I overheard her and Ivanka discussing him one time. She's also a fan."

"Is he talented?" I asked.

Karolyn snorted. "Evidently he is in the bedroom, but magikally? No. No magik."

I had the seed of an idea, but I didn't like it. Coercion was one of the major crimes the Magi forbade. An illusionist wouldn't be able to pass a bedroom test, or at least I didn't think so. And how many illusionists could style hair?

When I got back to the city, I reported to Olivia through my implant that Karolyn was amenable to her proposal, but that we didn't have access to her son at the moment.

Then I asked Kirsten, Carmelita, and Aleks out for dinner

at the Kitchen Witch. I needed devious people to brainstorm with.

I laid out the situation and some of my vague thoughts and waited for a response. It wasn't what I expected.

"Dani, I'm very disappointed in you," Aleks said. "Coercion? How gauche. There's a far easier way to get the hairdresser to do what you want."

"What?"

"Bribery," Carmelita and Kirsten said in unison.

"Good Goddess," Kirsten said, "how dense can you be? The guy's a gigolo. Just pay him."

I felt like a dunce. "I guess I never think of that because I don't have a lot of money."

"Olivia does," Aleks said. "Now, once we have the hairdresser in our pocket, what are you going to do with him?"

CHAPTER 48

"Mr. Rump? Mr. Richard Rump?" I asked the dark-haired beauty who answered the door of the penthouse apartment in a twenty-seven-story building overlooking the harbor.

"Yes? And you are?"

"Danica Findlay. I called for an appointment."

"Oh, yes, please come in. You were recommended by Courtney Moncrieff, I believe?"

"By her daughter, actually."

Her brow furrowed slightly. "May I get you anything to drink?" she asked. "Champagne? A cocktail? Coffee or tea?"

"Tea would be nice."

She showed me into an expensively decorated ultra-modern sitting room with a wall of glass providing an incredible view of the harbor and south all the way to Annapolis, probably. I was sure the fireworks the previous week must have been spectacular from there. I wondered what the riots looked like from up there, the fires and the smoke and the looting.

"Miss Findlay?" A man's voice sounded behind me, almost as deep and melodious as Aleks's.

I turned to face him. "And you're Mr. Rump?" He was handsome, with styled black hair, perfect teeth, and shoulders as wide as a door. His arms and chest strained his tailored shirt, and his slacks hugged an ass—or maybe that was a rump?—that I'd follow anywhere.

"Yes. Welcome to my salon," he said, handing me a burgundy-colored business card with white lettering.

Richard Rump
Coiffeur and Cosmetologist

The right side of the card had a white stallion rampant—and very obviously erect. *Not exactly shy, is he?* I thought.

He moved closer, taking my hair in his hand. His scent was so masculine—so intensely masculine—that it caused sensations between my legs. I realized his assistant must be a client of Kirsten's. I recognized that pheromone-laden cologne. I made a note to ask Aleks when his birthday was so I could get me—him—a bottle.

"Wonderful hair, fantastic raw material," Rump said. "But damaged. It will require a lot of work." He reached for my hand and frowned at my nails. "Oh, these are terrible. It's going to take time and effort. For now, we'll have to do appliqué." His hand rose, and his fingertips brushed my cheek. "But other than needing a moisturizer and light makeup, your skin is wonderful, so smooth and soft."

We were the same height, so he was looking me directly in the eyes. "Yes, Miss Findlay, I believe I can help you display your full potential. Your ravishing beauty simply needs to find its proper expression." He smiled. "Your cousin did explain my charges, and my full range of services, did she not?"

I found myself almost breathless. "Yes. Yes, she did."

"Good. Just give my assistant your card, and she can take care of our first session while we get to know each other."

The assistant was suddenly there, as if by magik, with her

hand out. I glanced around. A cosmetic chair and all the tools for washing and cutting hair were in a room to my right. To my left, where Rump was starting to steer me, was a room with a huge round bed.

I reached in my pocket and pulled out a payment voucher, electronically signed by Olivia Findlay. The payee line was blank, but the amount was a quarter of a million dollars. I held it up so he could see it, and his eyes widened.

"I'm seeking some very special services," I said. "Something a bit unusual. Why don't we sit down and talk?" I glanced over my shoulder at his assistant. "We won't be needing you. Why don't you go file your nails or something—and don't eavesdrop. I'll know, and it will take forever to grow that hair out again." I smiled and let electricity play across my fingertips.

She got the hint and left the room, closing the door behind her. I immediately cast a spell to disable all the electronics in the apartment. Taking his hand, I led him to a loveseat and pulled him down beside me.

"This is all yours," I said, "if you play your cards right. And if you don't," I pulled my badge out of my other pocket, "you'll be old and gray before you dress any more hair."

"I haven't done anything wrong!"

"I didn't say you have. But Courtney Findlay-Moncrieff has, and if you don't do exactly what I tell you, you'll not only miss out on all this money, I'll charge you with accessory to murder. Because Courtney is a murderer. Do we understand each other?"

※

It took some effort to convince Olivia to go along, and then for her to convince the Council. But instead of dropping a magitek bomb on Courtney's head, the Council answered her complaint in a more civil way.

If Courtney was caught anywhere outside her compound, she would be arrested and hauled before a magisterial tribunal. But the Council wasn't cruel. They would allow groceries to be delivered, and her hairdresser would be allowed to visit her weekly.

Of course, Rump's assistant would have to accompany him. He didn't do all that hair washing and nail filing himself, although he did do the hair cutting and styling.

Unfortunately, Carmelita had no clue about pampering rich women. She just knew how to sit in the chair and be pampered. The elven women had even less understanding of human cosmetology. Elves didn't need makeup, and the way they styled their hair when they did made any human hairdresser look like an amateur.

Witch magik operated much differently than mage magik. Kirsten couldn't just think her hair black, or change her features with a wave of her hand. But with adequate preparation, proper materials, and time, her change into a perfect copy of Rump's assistant was more solid and less ephemeral than a mage's illusion or an elf's glamour. I could touch her and not be able to tell the difference. It would also take the same preparation and magik casting to dissolve the spell.

And Kirsten knew more about hair and cosmetics—and how to enhance them with magik—than Rump and his assistant could ever learn.

Kirsten and Rump arrived at Findlay house in his car, showed their identification, were scanned, and their images sent up to the house. Then they were told to drive to the front door.

Aleks, Carmelita, and I, along with two glamoured elves—Siarin and I invisible—drove up in a grocery delivery truck. The guards waved us through without a second glance after telling us to drive around to the side kitchen door. Which was fine by me—that was the entrance I was most familiar with.

Aleks pulled the truck up to the loading dock, and we opened the back. Carmelita knocked on the kitchen door, and soon someone opened the large door on the dock.

One of the elves and Aleks started unloading food while Carmelita stood by with a clipboard checking things off and flirting with the cooks supervising the operation. Siarin and I slipped invisibly through the dock and into the kitchen.

I led her to the servants' stairs, and we climbed to the second floor. I could have found young Moncrieff's room with my eyes closed. An elf spy informed Joren that Courtney had personally emptied my closets and stood on my balcony watching her servants burn my clothes. Then she had put her only grandson in my suite.

The one major thing that had changed were the two guardians standing outside the hallway door. Even in her craziest moments, Olivia had never been stupid enough to try and lock me in.

I pulled Siarin back into the stairwell and eased the door closed.

In a whisper so low that only an elf could possibly hear it, I said, "Do you have any magik to put them to sleep?"

While we couldn't see each other, I could tell she hesitated. Silence for a moment, then, "No, not really. You don't want to kill them?"

Anyone who had illusions of elves as pacifists should have been there.

"Too much trouble, too much noise. I want to grab him and get out before anyone knows he's gone. And if we kill the guardians, they'll be looking for more than him."

"So?"

I pulled out two small bottles containing potions Kirsten had prepared. Pushing one into her hand, I said, "We sneak up on them. When we're close enough, hold your breath, pull out the stopper, and roll the bottle toward them. Then we head back here as fast as we can."

"Got it."

We snuck up within five or six feet of the closest guardian. I stopped, felt around for Siarin's foot, and stepped on it. Pulling the stopper out of the vial, I rolled it on the floor toward the guardians, then started backing up. Fast. Siarin was a little slow on the start, but her legs were longer than mine, and she kept up. Reaching the stairwell, I opened the door and slipped through with Siarin hot on my heels. My last glimpse of the guardians showed them staring at the little vials on the floor, then they started to slump.

I let go my breath in a whoosh.

"How long before it's safe?" Siarin asked.

"Five minutes. Know any quick games to pass the time?"

She chuckled. "I might if you were male. What do we do if someone comes along?"

I pulled two more vials out of my pocket and handed her one.

"And if it takes too long and Fasparin and the others have to leave?"

"I have the key to the trunk of Rump's car. We drug the boy, stuff him in there, and then you and I go out the secret way. If we can't get to the car, we take him with us."

"Secret way?"

I winked at her. "The way I used to sneak out at night when I was a teenager. I know they never found it, because it has a magitek lock on it that's keyed to my DNA."

She chuckled. "How long will they be out?"

"At least a couple of hours."

We waited while I worried about everything that could go wrong. Rump had told me that Karolyn was correct about Courtney's friends. And when Rump called her to work out the details for his visit, they had discussed a little orgy. That wasn't what I expected. I just wanted him to distract Courtney while we kidnapped William.

When I told Kirsten about their plans, she laughed. "Don't worry. As soon as everyone starts to get frisky, I have some incense that will take care of them."

"What about you?"

"Filter plugs in the nostrils. The incense won't knock them out, but it will cause some wild erotic hallucinations. They'll still get their jollies, but I'll just watch. Hell, if I get skittish, I'll just steal his car and tell the guards he decided to stay the night."

"Are you sure?"

With a chuckle, she said, "Hon, I've escaped wilder fraternity parties than this promises to be."

CHAPTER 49

After the five-minute countdown, I cautiously peeked into the hall, then motioned for Siarin to follow me. I wasn't worried about the guardians, who were slumped on the floor, but I also had Siarin's worry about the time. We reached the door, and no one had entered the hallway.

I unlocked the door, grabbed one of the guardians, and hauled him with me into the suite. Siarin followed with the other guardian.

"Stuff them into this coat closet," I said, and tiptoed on into the suite.

It was early afternoon, so I didn't expect anyone but William to be there, though I couldn't be sure. I found him in the sitting room on the couch, using the screen to play a game. He had earplugs in, and I walked right up behind him without him hearing me.

I clamped down on both his shoulders, holding him in place. He startled and turned his face up to mine. He tried to twist away from me, but I was too strong. Ripping the earplug out of one ear, he asked, "What do you want? What are you doing here?"

"Your mother would like to see you. Would you rather stay a prisoner here, or join her in Scotland as a free man?"

I gave him a minute to process things, then said, "Boyo, you're going, whether willingly or unconsciously. You can always make the choice to come back here, but I don't think you're going to get any better opportunities to leave."

"Okay. Just let me get a few things."

"Are they things money can buy?"

He gave me a strange look. "Yeah."

"Then they can be bought again. Your life can't."

"How do I know I can trust you?"

I slid the Raider out of its holster, showed it to him, then put it away. "Because if I wanted you dead, you'd already be dead."

With a short jerking nod of his head, he said, "Yeah. Mom's in Scotland?"

"Not yet. Beatrice is, and there's a plane waiting to take you and your mother there tonight."

Siarin waiting in the foyer startled him again, but he grabbed his coat. "You know how to get out of here?" he asked me.

"This used to be my room."

I checked my chrono on the way down the stairs. Twelve minutes had passed from the time we left Aleks and the others. We should be in time to hitch a ride out in the grocery truck.

The back stairs branched at each floor's landing. The servants used them to service different parts of the mansion. We hit the first floor, and Siarin started to open the door.

"No," I said, stopping her.

"I thought we were on the second floor."

"We were. The kitchen is on the ground floor. The house is one story taller in the back than in the front."

Descending another floor, she peeked out, then withdrew,

leaving the door open a crack. I put my eye to the gap and saw Carmelita in disguise arguing with a cook.

"I don't know what you ordered, I just know what's on the invoice, and we delivered everything. You want black truffles? I don't have them. You'll have to wait until next week."

Where they were standing left a clear path across the loading dock and into the back of the truck. The cook's back was toward us. I pulled back and nodded to Siarin. She grabbed both our hands and cast her glamour over all three of us, then led us across the dock and into the truck. I sat down and pulled Bill and Siarin down with me, then pulled out the Raider and rested it in my lap.

As we passed Carmelita, she was nodding. "Hey, I hear you. I'll tell them. If there's any way I can get them out to you, I will. Okay?"

The cook grumbled, but agreed. Carmelita turned away, pulled down the back door of the truck, and I heard it lock. The truck doors slammed, and the engine started. The truck started moving.

"Are we safe?" William whispered.

"Shhh."

He subsided.

I heard when we stopped by the gate, then as Aleks started to pull away, I heard a helicopter, and he slammed on the brakes.

"What the hell is going on here?" Karl Rudolf shouted. I looked at William, who looked at me. His fear was obvious.

"Don't worry," I said. "Siarin, take care of him."

I pounded on the front wall of the van, shouting as loud as I could. "Drive on! Drive on!"

Aleks must have heard me, because the van lurched forward, gained speed, and then there was a horrendous crashing sound that continued for what seemed a long time. Gunfire erupted all around us, and I cringed, but no bullets penetrated the flimsy metal walls of the box we huddled in. After what seemed an eternity, we gained speed, and the ride smoothed out.

I called Carmelita. "What the hell?"

"A helicopter landed in front of us. Some guy jumped out and started yelling. When you told us to keep going, we threw up a shield and just rammed the helicopter. It took a while before Aleks could push it out of the way."

"What about the gunfire?"

"They shot at us but didn't penetrate the shield."

"Well, keep those shields up until we're safe."

Carmelita chuckled. "We plan to. We're sure not going to outrun anyone in this old truck."

It was fourteen miles from Findlay House to my mom's by the fastest route. I could tell when we merged onto the freeway and Aleks sped up. A couple of minutes later, we heard the distinctive sound of a helicopter overhead, and then an explosion. The truck swerved wildly, and then there was a second, larger explosion farther away and above us.

"What's going on?" I asked Carmelita when she answered her phone. Not being able to see anything was driving me nuts.

"Helicopter fired a rocket at the road. I guess they were trying to make us wreck or stop or something."

"And?"

"Aleks blew it up."

"With what?" I practically yelled.

"Magik." She sounded puzzled that I couldn't figure that out for myself.

The three of us in the back of the truck were nervous wrecks by the time the truck stopped, although Siarin would have never admitted it.

Karolyn and my mom came out to greet us, and Karolyn enveloped her son in a hug.

"Are you all right?" she asked William.

"Yeah. A little too much excitement getting here, but I'm fine."

She looked at me.

"We got him away cleanly," I said, "but somehow Rudolf got wind of things and tried to stop us."

Just then, Rump's sports car careened down the lane and skidded to a stop. His assistant got out and said, "It's me! Kirsten. Dani, I think you have a leak at the police station. That Rudolf guy came charging in, madder than hell."

"Yeah, he tried to stop us," I said. "Where's Butt-boy?"

"Probably still in bed with your aunt. I figured I should duck out while everyone was running around shouting at each other."

"Karolyn," I said, turning to her, "are you ready to go?"

"As ready as ever. How are we going?"

I ushered her and her son into my car. Then I turned to Aleks. "Want to go for a ride?"

He grinned. "Sure. Haven't had so much fun in years."

He opened the shotgun-side door, and Kirsten squeezed past him into the back seat with Karolyn and William. Aleks looked to me, and I shrugged.

As soon as we were past the narrow lane leading from the road to mom's house, I took the car into the air.

"Are you planning on playing fighter pilot with Rudolf's helicopters?" Aleks asked.

"I have a lot more room to maneuver up here, and they can't blow holes in the road in front of me," I answered. Raising my voice, I said, "Anyone who can cast a shield around this car, there's no better time than the present."

My car was smaller, quieter, and more difficult to see than a helicopter, so we made it most of the way across the city before we ran into any trouble. I was flying as low as I dared, but a helicopter spotted us. It was faster than my modified car and swooped in, firing a rocket at us.

The rocket exploded against our shield, the shock sending us tumbling. I managed to get the car under control and steered us higher for more safety.

Looking around frantically, I asked, "Where is he?"

"Behind us," William's said.

I glanced in the rearview mirror and saw the helicopter lining us up.

"Hold onto your breakfast," I said, pulling the car up into a climb. I kept pulling the car into a loop. When I leveled off, we were behind the helicopter.

"Slow down!" Aleks said, and held out his hand in front of him. A shaft of white light bored a hole through my windshield and struck the helicopter, which exploded in a spectacular fashion. I hit the brakes and pulled the nose of the car up and to the side. Perhaps some debris hit our shield, but I managed to fly over most of it.

A detachment of Whittaker's mage-soldiers was waiting for us when we reached the airport. I took the car down, landed on the tarmac, and drove over to the hanger where I had put Beatrice on the plane.

We hustled Karolyn and her son out of the car and rushed them into the hanger. William charged up the stairs into the plane like his tail was on fire, but as Karolyn started to climb the stairs, she stopped.

Before I could react, she was on top of me, pulling me into a hug. "You come visit us, you hear? I'll feed you haggis, show you the sights, and I promise to try and not be too big a bitch."

She had tears in her eyes, and suddenly I did, too.

"Only if I can skip the haggis," I said. "Take care. Give my love to my grandmother."

"Will do." She climbed the stairs into the plane. As soon as the door closed, the engines revved up, and the plane began to move.

We stuck around until it became airborne, then walked back to my car.

"Do you do windshield repair?" I asked.

"Nope," Aleks answered. "I just break things."

"I'm hungry," Kirsten said. "I assume the Riverside Inn is out of the question."

I shook my head. "Yeah, too many demons. The neighborhood has gone to hell from what I hear."

"There's a great place in Ellicott City," Aleks suggested. Old Ellicott City was a neighborhood about ten miles west of the airport. "Eastern European cuisine and great beer."

"You're on," I said.

Perhaps I should have taken to the air again, but I didn't. We were on the onramp from the airport to the freeway going west when the bomb went off, sending the car cartwheeling end over end. I barely had time to realize that Aleks had shielded us when we began bouncing off the roadway and down an embankment to a stop.

"Everyone all right?" Aleks asked.

"I think so," I said.

"Yeah," Kirsten said from the back seat.

My door was hanging open, in a crumpled sort of way, and I was hanging in the restraining harness. I drew my Raider as I released the harness and tumbled out of the car into the ditch.

"Don't move!" The order came from above me. Standing on the side of the road were several soldiers in Akiyama uniforms and Karl Rudolf.

"You have caused us far more trouble than you're worth," Rudolf said.

Without warning, the soldiers fired their automatic weapons, spraying bullets at us. Thankfully, Aleks continued to maintain the shield that covered us all.

Rudolf shook his head. "That won't save you."

Out of the corner of my eye, I saw Kirsten sketch a rune and start to chant. I started to feel a little weak and broke out in a sweat. I glanced at Aleks and saw he was also sweating. The temperature was barely above freezing.

Kirsten sketched another rune and chanted another spell. The weakness I was feeling spread, and my head began to spin. Rudolf stood above us, not moving, not making a sound, just staring at us.

Kirsten sketched a third rune and said a Word. I stumbled and fell on my butt. Aleks was leaning against the car, and he didn't look too good.

Whatever was happening, it didn't get worse. All I could do was stare up at Rudolf. Hydromancer. Somewhere in my fuzzy brain, I realized he was pulling all the water out of my body. He was going to turn me into one of those mummies I'd seen at Tina Stewart's house. And if Aleks dropped his shield so I could shoot the bastard, the soldiers would shoot us.

"No," Rudolf whispered. Then louder, "No. No! NO!" he stumbled backwards sweat pouring off him. He fell, writhing to the ground. The Akiyama soldiers stared at him.

And as soon as they took their eyes off us, a blazing scythe of energy poured from Alek's hand, cutting the three soldiers down.

"Here, drink this," Kirsten said, kneeling down beside me. It wasn't a potion, but a bottle of water. Nothing ever tasted so good. I chugged the whole thing.

She rose and went to Aleks, handing him a bottle as well.

"What happened?" Aleks asked.

Kirsten shrugged. "I guess you can't shield from his magik, or at least from that spell. I cast a reverse-magik spell. It turned his own magik back on him."

I managed to climb out of the ditch. The three soldiers hadn't bled, even though each of them had been cut completely in half. A desiccated mummy wearing Karl Rudolf's clothes lay with them.

"Now I'm really hungry," Kirsten said. "Do we have to wait around for the cops and a wrecker, or can we just call a taxi?"

CHAPTER 50

The week after I packed Karolyn Moncrieff and her son off to Scotland, intelligence filtered out of the Waste that a new demon lord had come across the Rift and taken control of the Metroplex. That, the rumor went, was why the demons had stopped fighting. The alliance Akiyama had with Ashvial was finished. The new lord was more interested in consolidating his rule than in sacrificing his minions to human mages.

I had no idea if the rumors were true. I heard three different versions of the story from three different vampires.

What I did know was that no new fighting had occurred. Life, to a certain extent, was getting back to normal. Construction crews—many of them with mages—were starting to clean up the debris and wreckage. Stores and restaurants that hadn't been destroyed were reopening. Trucks delivered food to restaurants and grocery stores. Kids went back to school.

Courtney was still surrounded and isolated at Findlay House. Her children and grandchild were in her archenemy's care, and she was afraid even to leave the Findlay estate. Akiyama still held the Port of Wilmington. They had taken huge casualties at a massive cost. Humans hated the Magi more than ever, and the Coven Council was calling for representation on the Magi Council. Or at least a sharing of power.

Kirsten reopened her shop, and Aleks asked me to think about moving in with him. Considering that Mychal Novak was practically living at my house with Kirsten, she probably wouldn't notice if I did.

I was on my way over to her shop after work when a demon stepped out of a doorway and confronted me. Tall, even taller than my grandfather, he had a face that was dominated by horns that grew out of his forehead and swept to the side and back, curling like a mountain sheep's. His skin was red, which often indicated a fire demon, but not always. He was dressed in a tailored purple suit, and his grin showed teeth that could easily tear the flesh from my bones.

"Danica James," he said, his voice a rumbling growl. "I am Besevial. You have something that belongs to me."

"I don't think so, but what is it?" I placed my hand on my Raider, prepared to draw.

"An avatar of Akashrian."

"I don't know who or what that is."

His eyes narrowed and he leaned closer. "Take care, daughter of Lucas James. You play with the fires of hell."

And then he was gone. Besevial. That was the name of the rumored new demon lord. And I had a very bad feeling I knew who Akashrian was as well.

If you enjoyed **War Song**, I hope you will take a few moments to leave a brief review on the site where you purchased your copy. It helps to share your experience with other readers. Potential readers depend on comments from people like you to help guide their purchasing decisions. Thank you for your time!

Get updates on new book releases, promotions, contests and giveaways! Sign up for my newsletter.

BOOKS BY BR KINGSOLVER

Get updates on new book releases, promotions, contests and giveaways! Sign up for my newsletter.

The Rift Chronicles

Magitek

War Song

Rosie O'Grady's Paranormal Bar and Grill

Shadow Hunter

Night Stalker

Dark Dancer

Well of Magic

Knights Magica

The Dark Streets Series

Gods and Demons

Dragon's Egg

Witches' Brew

The Chameleon Assassin Series

Chameleon Assassin

Chameleon Uncovered

Chameleon's Challenge

Chameleon's Death Dance

Diamonds and Blood

The Telepathic Clans Saga

The Succubus Gift
Succubus Unleashed
Broken Dolls
Succubus Rising
Succubus Ascendant

Other books
I'll Sing for my Dinner
Trust

Short Stories in Anthologies
Here, Kitty Kitty
Bellator

Printed in Great Britain
by Amazon